THE HOUSE OF MOSES ALL-STARS

Also by Charley Rosen:

FICTION

Have Jump Shot Will Travel (1975)

A Mile Above the Rim (1977)

The Cockroach Basketball League (1992)

NON-FICTION

Maverick WITH PHIL JACKSON (1976)

Scandals of '51: How the Gamblers Almost Killed College Basketball (1978)

God, Man and Basketball Jones (1979)

Players and Pretenders (1981)

THE HOUSE OF MOSES ALL-STARS

a novel by

CHARLEY ROSEN

SEVEN STORIES PRESS
New York

A Seven Stories Press First Edition

Library of Congress Cataloging-in-Publication Data

Rosen, Charley
The House of Moses All-Stars : a novel / by Charley Rosen.
p. cm.
ISBN: 1-888363-33-9
1. Jews—United States—Fiction. 2. Basketball players—
United States—Fiction. I. Title.
PS3568/076473H68 1996
813'.54—dc20
96-30235
CIP

Book design by Adam Simon

Seven Stories Press
New York

Printed in the U.S.A.

10 9 8 7 6 5 4 3 2

For Eddie Mast:
Thanks for the run, the wins and losses,
the love from tip to buzzer.

For Daia, and the courageous vision of her heart.

Look at them, the lucky bastards. Barely thirty minutes since our five A.M. departure from the Henry Street Community Center and they're asleep. My teammates, safely asleep. I can almost see their dim reflections in the rearview mirror, their familiar forms and features illumined only by the dull yellow shadows dropped by the streetlamps that I drive past and the green gleamings of traffic lights somewhere in the Bronx.

What's that sign say? SIMPSON STREET. FULTON AVENUE. Where are the numbered streets? Where's the bridge? Where the fuck are we?

There's Saul, Ron, and Brooks squeezed together side-by-side-by-side on the two mattresses in the long, narrow rear section where the coffins used to ride. But their sleep is restless, listing whenever we corner left or right, snorting and sighing when we stop for a red light. Ron, in the middle, has staked the largest space, his elbows and forearms twitching in some secret, violent dream. Saul sleeps on the portside with his hands folded demurely across his virginal *putz ah Yid.* Brooks always sleeps with his face clenched like a fist. And there's Leo and Mitchell sprawled across the backseat—Mitchell with his mouth hanging open, a dead man's flytrap, while Leo is turned away from the meager light, his face hidden in its own shadow. Beside me, Kevin sits erect, sleeping in spite of himself, waking only when his red-bearded chin bounces off his chest.

That makes seven of us. Lucky seven. Symbolic of perfect order, the union of the ternary and the quaternary. The seven days of the week. The seven seas. The seven deadly sins. The seven virtues. The seven wonders of the world. The seven against Thebes. Five starters plus two substitutes equals the House of Moses All-Stars.

And I've gotten us lost already. BARKER AVENUE. MOSHOLU PARKWAY. The river has to be downhill, right?

The sudden downward pitch of Sedgewick Avenue snaps Kevin awake long enough for him to mumble, "I'm awake," before he dozes off again. What an outfit! On the road for less than thirty minutes and not only are we lost, but one of the most basic tenets of "The Official Rules and Regulations of the House of Moses All-Star Team and Tour" has already been violated.

Yes, we each have our own neatly typed copy, ten pages long, a comprehensive document that was finally ratified after lengthy deliberations by a vote of 5–1 (with only Leo saying nay and with Kevin forced to abstain by an identical vote of 5–1). See Section B, paragraph 3a:

Whoever rides shotgun must stay awake to navigate and to make sure the driver stays awake. The penalty for sleeping on duty is forfeiture of a full three days rotation on the mattresses.

But I'll let Kevin slumber undisturbed. Because I'm such a mensch, so compassionate and forgiving. Because I don't want Kevin to discover my blunder.

JEROME AVENUE. BRONX PARK EAST. What the fuck?

We gently rumble over cobblestoned streets. "Amma," says Kevin in his sleep. "Amma."

Our vehicle, our portable utopia, is a four-year-old 1932 Chevrolet Confederate Series BA DeLuxe four-door Special sedan that was modified at the factory to serve as a hearse. A death wagon. And if ships are feminine, so, too, are automobiles—with their fuel-sucking holes leading to delicate and mysterious interior mechanisms. With their elastic flaps and lubricated chambers. Their orgasms of fire and air. So, without consulting my teammates, I've dubbed her the Queen of Spades, or the Black Lady for short.

A gleaming beauty, she features four chrome-plated vent doors on each side of the hood, also a flashy chrome-plated set of torpedo-shaped headlamps. The spare tire is mounted on the driver's side, securely chained into the fender-well, and there's more chrome flashing at every joint and juncture. Brand-new, she cost $725, and like every femme fatale she has a shady past.

Until the Volstead Act was repealed in 1933, she led a secret life, hauling stiffs but also smuggling still-fired hootch from the wilds of northern New Jersey into Manhattan's Lower East Side. Since then she'd been used after-hours to transport fugitive members of the Black Hand from hot hideouts throughout the city to cool sanctuaries in upstate Saugerties. Then three weeks ago, just before Christmas, the mortician's foolish son took his favorite floozy and a fifth of rotgut for a midnight joyride. No surprise when the car and her passengers wound up maimed and battered in a ditch somewhere in the flatlands of Brooklyn. That's why my brother, Max, was able to purchase the Black Lady for only $150 cash. "But it's cursed," I protested when Max first handed me the ignition key. "Only for the goyim," said Max.

Max also shelled out $2.00 for towing, $25.00 for a new rear axle (installed), and $18.54 to hammer out the dents and replace all the broken glass. The rear door has been fixed so that it locks but unfortunately no longer seals out the weather. So far, counting the $50.00 Max "advanced" us for supplies and another $150.00 for booking fees and appearance guarantees, his total expenditure has been $395.84. A fortune in this day and age, even for a bachelor.

But Max has a steady job. He's a tenured full professor in the philosophy department at City College. Come boom or depression, Max still earns a fat $3,650 per annum. "I can afford it," Max said when he gave me the car. "What I can't afford is having my baby brother end up in a rubber room at Bellevue."

Thanks, Max.

The Queen of Spades' interior is spacious for normal-sized people. ("Midgets," Leo calls them, only five foot seven himself. Saul is six-ten, our reluctant Goliath, who always refers to nonplayers as "civilians.") All her inside surfaces, including the plump seats, are upholstered in some kind of soft brown leather. And Mitchell has assured us that every interior nook, every niche, has been fully utilized. Of course it was the always fastidious Mitchell who took the trouble to record all the inside measurements, then to painstakingly assemble and stow our cargo. To whit: seven (live) ballplayers, fourteen army-surplus blankets, seven cardboard suitcases (each one four feet by three feet by one foot deep), three basketballs, one air pump and needle, three gallon cans of gasoline, three gallon cans of water, three baseball bats (Ron's suggestion—Hank Greenberg models for weight and balance in possible defense of our lives), a dozen cans each of beans, peaches, and evaporated milk. These, plus innumerable other items, are intended to sustain us safely through seventeen days, at least two dozen ball games, and approximately four thousand miles of our barnstorming basketball excursion to Los Angeles, Los Diablos, or wherever we wind up.

Because of the heavy load, the Black Queen's V-8 engine still struggles out of the chute and up hills. Also, the damage to the rear end causes the newfangled synchromesh to grind and clash like a tractor. The steering wheel is unusually stiff, but I don't mind the struggle, the therapeutic pain. Maybe by the time we reach the West Coast, my hands will be stronger and I'll have some extra range on my hook shot.

GRAND CONCOURSE. EAST 164TH STREET.

GEO. WASH. BRIDGE ➡

Baruch ataw adonoi. All who are lost shall be found.

Still too early on a Sunday morning, there's no traffic on the streets and the night lamps are still burning. As we finally approach the bridge, cresting over the top of the steep hill at West 179th Street and Dyckman Avenue, the tires get grooved into the trolley tracks and for a thrilling instant the car slides downhill out of control . . . Here's my chance! Suicide by minority vote, 1–0, with six abstentions, a mass mercy killing . . . But no, death's inevitable answers will find me all too soon, all too easily. No, I'm after something more impossible, more godlike, than the puny power to end my own puny life. I seek a rebirth into innocence, and guiltlessness, not hope, not love, merely the dumb absence of pain . . . Then Kevin snorts as his head snaps forward and I squeeze my foot to the brake.

Just because my brother, Max, is the Daddy Warbucks for this entire harebrained scheme doesn't mean that any of it was my idea. No siree. The House of Moses All-Stars was originally the brainstorm of Leo Gilbert (that's him, his face still hidden, snoozing right behind me in the backseat), who was still wearing knickers when I was the starting center for the powerhouse Metropolitan University basketball team in the fatback 1920s.

In those days, I lived on Orchard Street and Leo lived two blocks away on Bayard Street. He was a little pip-squeak with a big mouth and no respect for anybody. Leo reached his full growth in the ninth grade (five foot seven inches, a chunky 175 pounds) and was so talented that we'd let him play with us in the Men's League at the Henry Street Community Center. Like me, Leo went on to play basketball at Seward Park High School. (Those days of innocent and frivolous joys!) By the time Leo became a famous play-making guard for the College of St. Bridget's Fabulous Five, I was making fifteen legal dollars per game with the Trenton Tigers in the American League of Professional Basketball.

I was always a superior rebounder, a modest scorer, and, at six-three-and-a-half, a powerful leaper. Sure, when the center-jump after each made basket was abolished in 1931, my influence on a ball game was drastically diminished, but even now, at age thirty-two, I can still rebound, play stubborn defense, and hook both ways. I'm a Warrior of the Sacred Hoop, making plays that only other players notice—a pick, a box-out, an elbow to the sternum. As long as I'm physically able, I'll continue my exploration of this exhilarating, constantly evolving sport, to see how close it can lead me toward my own lost soul.

Whatever my offcourt failures and countless civilian fuckups, I'm focused enough on the hardwood so that every team I've ever played for has been successful. During my four-year stint at Metro, we were 91–16. I'm a winner all right, within the white lines.

Anyway, Leo was always a wiseguy and I never really liked him or even liked playing with him. Me, I still avoid booze, fatty meats, and fried foods, but Leo never trained right. A foulsome cigar clamped in his teeth, a drink in his hand, a bimbo on his arm, staying up to blow out all the lights on Broadway. That was always his style, even the day before a ball game.

During a game, Leo's just as flamboyant—with his showboating behind-the-back dribble, manipulating the ball like a two-bit carny flashing a gold coin. After he scores, he'll trot downcourt like Babe Ruth cruising the bases after parking one in the bleachers. Should Leo hit two in succession, he's liable to laugh out loud, saying, "Can't anybody here guard me?"

Sure, Leo's got reasons enough to be arrogant: His set shot is accurate even at thirty feet and the Fabulous Five was the first college team to win thirty games in a single season (1930–31). *The Saturday Evening Post*, *Life*, and *Collier's* all did feature stories on "St. Bee's crafty cagers." It surely was a bizarre situation at St. Bridget's—the Five were composed of four Jews and one apostatic Yugoslavian. They played for a mick school, received stacks of greenbacks under the table, and occasionally shaved points on the side.

Certainly, even at Metro we all found a sawbuck or two tucked in our lockers after defeating an intracity rival like St. John's, City College, Fordham, LIU, Manhattan, or St. Bridget's. And sure, we all did business from time to time. What the hell? To this day, gambling and basketball are a traditional parlay in New York City. There's even side bets on the Men's League games at Henry Street.

Furthermore, during the summers we'd all work as bellhops or waiters at various hotels in the Catskills, and on Sunday afternoons the hotel staffs would play against one another strictly for the "entertainment" of the guests. We'd never think of consorting with gamblers to rig the outcome of those lighthearted summertime frolics, so the high-flying bettors contented themselves with trying to predict the total number of points scored by both teams. What we'd do was find out what number one of the hotel chefs bet on, make whatever minor adjustments were necessary, then feast like kings until the next game.

But Leo always carried a good thing too far. Even in the summer he'd shoot ridiculous rimless and boardless shots to control the score, then, to make sure everybody knew what he was doing, he'd stare incredulously at his traitorous hand and laugh. Strictly bush league. Until last summer, the only words I ever spoke to Leo were "Hello," "Goodbye," and "Pick on your right."

I mean, let Leo be an asshole. Who cares? Right?

Right, left, up, down, and sideways, eventually Leo came and found me where I lived.

Money was tight after the stock market crashed. The American League of Professional Basketball persevered until the spring of 1932 before going belly-up. "Even basketball," said Brooks the Bolshie, "is a casualty of capitalism." But I was always a quick healer and I soon eased into a cushy job teaching English at Seward Park High School (Max knew a guy who knew a guy). All the other neighborhood hoopsters had to scramble—Brooks peddled fruit and vegetables from a pushcart, Mitchell worked for pennies in a junkyard. We all continued playing in the Men's League and in periodic pickup games at the 92nd Street YMHA—but Leo was the only one who stayed in basketball full-time. That's because the Fabulous Five still had a following hereabouts.

So, playing as the Brooklyn Gems, Leo and his mates competed in a rinky-dink Pennsylvania pro league (at five dollars per game) and also played in money tournaments in places like Kingston, Haverstraw, and Albany. Then, one hot night last July, out of nowhere, Leo came knocking at my door.

My wife, Judy, and I were living in a ground-floor two-bedroom apartment on Gramercy Park (twelve dollars a month plus utilities). We'd been more or less happily married for eighteen months, Judy was gloriously pregnant and due in early October. Everything seemed so much simpler in those days. For sure, I had been in league with gamblers and I was just another selfish kid, trivializing the breadlines and the soup kitchens. "Sawdust bread and cockroach soup." But I was convinced that I was one of the good guys. Even freer and braver than thou. After all, I had "meaningful" employment and Judy's parents were well off. Like characters in some corny movie, Judy and I would live fortuitously ever after.

I'd first met Judy Goldfarb on a blind date (Max knew a guy who had a sister). We went to Coney Island, where we started grabbing each other on the Ferris wheel. I got to second base on the Caterpillar and gratefully received a shrieking hand job while in free fall on the Parachute Jump. She claimed she was a virgin (she was), and she was hot enough and pretty enough to marry. I loved the whole idea of being in love.

It no longer mattered so much that I never knew my mother, nor that Max was more of a father to me than Dad had ever been. So what if my in-laws would be mildly annoying, so were Fibber McGee's. No big deal.

Judy's father was called Cy in lieu of Seymour, a successful lawyer who got the Big Tip two weeks before Black Monday and converted all his stockholdings into cash. He was an overbearing Yalie, a five-foot-six-inch, 150-pound football fan, who would contemptuously refer to basketball as roundball, a game played by "oversized goons." What a twerp. During my brief engagement to his daughter (we couldn't wait any longer than six weeks to start hitting homers), Cy and I'd developed a poisonous relationship. He didn't even have the decency to mask his glee when he discovered that both my parents were deceased (my mother, two days after birthing me; Dad, fours years ago from influenza). To Cy, my being an orphan only meant that he'd have total control of the wedding arrangements (right down to the chopped-liver dinosaurs and the cherries *flambé* tar pits).

Judy's mother, Sylvia, had tuberculosis. Three years at a ritzy sanitarium in Arizona failed to effect a cure, so in the spring of 1934, Sylvia had her right lung surgically excised. That's why she's so grossly misshapen, her torso so lopsided. I still have nightmares about Judy's long-suffering invalid mother, barely alive, gasping her life away through clenched teeth.

What's remarkable is that Judy was so happy and well adjusted. From the start, we had plenty "in common." Both of us were avid readers, the difference being that she preferred Sherlock Holmes and Agatha Christie mysteries, while I took the high road, priding myself on having read the likes of *Crime and Punishment* four times and *War and Peace* thrice. We both savored Chinese food, moonlit rides on the Staten Island ferry, Coney Island at high tide, and (most importantly) setting our alarm clock every weekday at precisely 6:15 A.M. to make joyful, violent love. True, Judy inherited her father's prejudice against basketball and wouldn't even walk the three blocks to Henry Street to watch me play. But she was kind, intelligent (if somewhat frothy), possessed of a pleasing sense of humor (she liked Jack Benny, I sided with Fred Allen), and she washed our apartment windows twice every week. Only sometimes did she exhibit a darker side, a kind of cloying martyr's complex, obviously influenced by Sylvia.

So it was, acting upon the misbegotten advice of her obstetrician, that Judy forswore sexual congress during the last four months—count 'em—of her pregnancy. She'd proudly display her swollen teats, permitting me to stroke and slurp them to my heart's content, but any activity "downstairs" was strictly verboten. "It's the greater privation for me," she'd say sweetly, "because a woman's orgasm is so much more intense and longer lasting than a man's. And I do love you, Aaron. I really do. Here, let me prove it." But I stoutly refused her offers to give me succor. We'd suffer together. She'd weep softly and say that no sacrifice was too great to make certain "we" had a healthy baby.

All told, my life was good enough to suit me. Certainly good enough for me to scoff at Leo's madcap proposal.

"Aaron," he began, his beady blue eyes stretched open in blind supplication. "I'm in trouble. Real deep shit this time. It happened last week when the Gems played in that hot-shot tournament in Union City. At the Sacred Heart Church? Remember? You played there three years ago with Mitchell and Brooks? Anyways, it's even a bigger deal nowadays. We made it into the finals against a team sponsored by some beer distributor out of New Britain, Connecticut. They had Nat Holman and Joe Lapchick from Kate Smith's Celtics. Plus some guys who used to play for Eddie Gottlieb in Philly. Anyways, the pot was five thousand smackers, winner take all, and there was all kinds of action in the stands. Big-time Broadway heelers. Guys from Atlantic City, Boston, even Black Jack McCue was in from Chicago. Anyways, one thing led to another and I was investigating my options. You know how it is, Aaron, a guy's got to look out for himself. So I made a side deal with McCue, taking New Britain and giving him four points. Then I cut another deal with a wop from Jersey City name of Carmine something, giving four points and betting on New Britain. Right? All's we got to do is win by three or less and I collect from the mick, the wop, and also get a piece of the pot. I'm on Easy Street, right? Plus, there's that little edge that I like, just to keep me interested, you know? Anyways, I'm working my ass off, making shots, missing shots, walking a fine line. I'm working the game like a fucking genius and we're up three and I'm dribbling the clock away. Jeez. They can't even catch me to foul me. And I figure that so many players are probably doing business with sharpsters that nobody quite knows what the fuck to do anyway. Excepting me. Anyways, I'm still in the backcourt, maybe fifty feet out, and the clock's ticking down . . . Three, two, one . . . And just for a laugh, I heave the fucking ball at the fucking basket. Maybe forty-five, fifty feet in the air. Then, whammo! Off the fucking backboard and in like a homing pigeon. Which is what I turned out to be, a fucking pigeon. I owe McCue two G's and the wop another two."

"Leo," I said, showing my empty palms. "I don't have near that kind of money."

"No, no," he said quickly. "I ain't asking for a loan or nothing like that. What I'm needing is this: I can stall both of them guys for a couple months. Till Christmas maybe. Goys are saps about Christmas. Then I got three options—get the dough, get gone, or get dead."

It was Leo's fervent hope to get gone on a "long-term and distant" barnstorming tour. He even had a gimmick. "We could call ourselves the Wandering Jews or something. Wear long beards, *payess*, yarmulkes, the works. Have jerseys that say 'Fuck You' in Hebrew. Whatever. There's plenty of people in the boondocks ain't never seen a Jew in their whole life. We could—"

"Who's 'we'?"

It seemed that Leo had already recruited Mitchell Sloan and Brooks Moser—both from the neighborhood, both outstanding collegiate players in their day, both with professional experience, and, with me in the pivot, eighty percent of a damn good team.

"When is this supposed to happen?"

Leo swore that October-November-December tours invariably went bust because the goyim hoard their "extra money" to buy one another Christmas presents. Springs tours are flops because the baseball season is too tough to buck. The way Leo had it figured, "The sooner we leave after New Year's, the better."

Not a chance, bud. How could I leave a solid job paying $2,250 per year (especially with a baby due) to go galavanting off (especially with an asshole like Leo Gilbert) on some junket into the boondocks? I should have booted Leo into the street then and there, but for some reason (just to be polite?), I kept on asking questions. "Where?"

Leo also had a fix on that. "California," he said, "the land of milk and money." Basketball was "the latest thing" out there, especially in Los Angeles. (Only yesterday, Brooks reported that Leo had an ulterior motive for aiming the tour at L.A. "He's job hunting." Apparently, an old "out-of-town" basketball buddy of Leo's is the new athletic director at Orange County University, and the holdover basketball coach is scheduled to retire at the end of the current 1935–36 season. Imagine Leo as a college coach!) "There are plenty of good roads cross-country," Leo told me. "But we should stay on a northern route until we cross the Mississippi 'cause Jews traveling in the South are just as likely to get lynched as niggers."

"Who's there for us to play?"

His dark face brightened and he flexed his crooked yellow smile, excited because I said "us." Leo knew of "a grillion" semipro teams from here to there, also city-league ball clubs, YMCA all-stars, AAU outfits. Not to mention possible bookings at county fairs, military bases, even penitentiaries and Indian reservations. "All of them anxious to play against a Jew team," Leo insisted. "Most of them curious to see for themselves if Jews really have horns."

"What kind of money are you talking about? How much can we make?"

A fortune! Over four thousand dollars for each of "us."

"What do you need me for?"

My experience, my talent, my attitude, etc.

"And?"

"We'll need to hire a booking agent," Leo said, "We'll need to lay out for forfeit insurance, for a car, for expenses. Maybe your brother could help get us started."

What made Leo think Max had that big a bankroll?

"Don't kid a kidder," Leo said, almost indignant. Leo swore that Max had won a "wad" last June betting James Braddock over Max Baer for the heavyweight title. Less than two weeks later, Max won "another bundle" when Joe Louis KO'd Primo Carnera. "Believe me," Leo said (and I did), "your brother's got dollar bills coming out of his ass."

"Sounds great, Leo, but . . ."

Over the next few weeks I'd see Leo scurrying around and about, at Nathan's candy store, the A & P, the dairy restaurant over on Hester Street, and, rarely, on the basketball court at the Community Center. "Speak to your brother yet?" he'd ask, and I'd say, "Not yet."

Meanwhile Brooks and Mitchell were also working on me. According to Brooks, I was the only available big man who was accepted by a unanimous vote. "We want to do this right," Brooks went on. "Dot every *i* and cross every *t*. More than a barnstorming tour, we want to create a perfect social entity. Sort of a commune on wheels . . . Aaron, for Christ's sake, I'm peddling produce from a pushcart." Mitchell never mentioned his labors in the junkyard, saying only, "Aaron, I can certainly understand your situation. You're a married man, not like the rest of us, and a man's got to take care of his family."

Maybe everybody else had a good reason to go (or no reason to stay), but for me the proposed tour of the boondocks seemed a pipe dream, fun to do (I loved playing with Brooks and Mitchell) but blatantly irresponsible. Then school started up again after Labor Day, and suddenly the corny movie of my life went haywire.

Flap-flap-flap-flap-flap ...

Debra Goodman was a senior in my creative writing class and, through her smiles, her conversation, her poems and short stories, she pronounced herself "a modern woman." Whereas Judy had been waddling around for months with her "downstairs" off-limits, Debra wiggled into my classroom with her tail up like a mink in heat. Whereas Judy squeezed her thighs shut even when she peed, Debra sat in the first row flashing her panties. Yes, I was horny. Yes, by the second week of classes Debra and I were meeting after school at her apartment (both her parents worked), where we fucked and howled like monkeys.

When Judy asked why I was home so late, I told her I had detention duty. Yes, I felt guilty. But not guilty enough to stop.

Then, on October 29th, after a brutal sixteen-hour labor, Judy gave birth to Sarah (after her mother) Pearl (after mine) Steiner, twenty-one inches long, weighing seven pounds five ounces, *kunn a hurra*. Born also with a cleft lip, a cleft palate, and water on the brain.

Halfway across the bridge, I reach over and prod Kevin's shoulder.

"I'm awake!" Kevin says too loudly. "I'm not asleep!"

"It's okay, Kevin."

"Dang it. I was up all night talking with my father," he says, his green eyes twitching. With his ten-week-old dark red beard Kevin looks like a little boy whose face has been thickly smeared with strawberry jam. "I'll take whatever punishment I've got coming. There's no excuse. Mitchell told me to read the bylaws and I did. Some of them're kind of confusing, but I know I'm not supposed to fall asleep when I sit here. What happens now? Something about rotating the mattresses?"

"It's okay," I repeat. "Don't worry about the mattresses."

Not even Mitchell's mania for perfect justice enabled him to find a precise solution to the mattress rotation. Sure, the backseat is roomy enough for any two of the backcourtsmen (Mitchell, Leo, and Ron) to curl up in relative comfort. But in "the crypt" the outside mattress positions are much more comfortable than having to lie sandwiched in the middle on a seam. Mitchell ultimately proposed that the driver gets to stretch out on a side mattress the night (or day) before driving and the night after. The middle-mattress slot is reserved for the shotgun rider after his stint. (See Section D, paragraphs 2c–d.) Mitchell was upset when he couldn't chart a complete "position rotation" for the entire trip. Second best is keeping track of who sleeps where and assigning positions daily.

"Not even across the bridge," Kevin moans, "and already I messed up. Nuts! I wanted this trip to work out so bad. . ."

The kid's about to weep, so I say, "Don't worry. Nobody has to know. Actually, it's partially my fault. I should have turned on the radio to help keep you awake." (According to the bylaws, whoever's driving has total control of the radio—on, off, station, volume. By majority vote those in the backseat and the crypt can decide whether the sliding-glass chauffeur's window is to be open or closed.)

"Thanks," Kevin says heartily. "It'll never happen again. I swear by the Holy Mother."

Kevin McCray is the only gentile among us and at age eighteen he's also the youngest. A bruising six-foot-two forward/center, Kevin played for Morningside High School uptown in West Harlem, terrorizing his peers with his strength, toughness, and quickness. But Kevin loathed going to school, citing his classroom chores as "boring, useless, and too hard." Accordingly, Kevin played hooky whenever the sun shone brightly, and he failed to graduate with his class last June.

Brooks found Kevin last summer in a lunchtime pickup game at the West Side YMCA and brought him down to Henry Street for our approval. The kid's got a smooth hook shot (better right than left), although he toys too much with a West Coast one-hander. The kid also has great instincts and is eager to learn. "A sponge," Brooks calls him. Kevin's easy to play with and, shit, he left enough lumps and bruises on my body in our rebounding battles to get my vote.

Kevin's father is a cop working out of the 34th Precinct at Amsterdam Avenue and 112th Street. Kevin swears that except for two trips to the Bronx and one to Brooklyn, his old man's never stepped a flat foot out of Manhattan. Kevin "sort of" wants to be a cop, but there's no openings on the force these days. And Kevin refused his father's request that he join the army instead. "I don't want to shoot nobody," Kevin says. (No, he'd rather beat someone to death with his elbows.)

So Kevin's come with us "to see the world." And he brings us young legs, a rookie's enthusiasm, and two valuable bon voyage gifts from his father—a .24 caliber automatic pistol and a gold badge. Also, Brooks claims that Kevin's presence ensures that we won't get "too insulated," a dubious assumption since the kid rarely speaks and only gets to vote on peripheral issues. Still, I like Kevin and I'm determined to treat him like a fully endowed member of our troupe.

Our first game is scheduled for three o'clock this afternoon at the Calvary Baptist Church in upstate Glens Falls, which Mitchell calculates is "239 miles as the crow flies" from Henry Street. We left so early "just in case" (one of Mitchell's favorite *causa causans*). From Glens Falls we're off to Buffalo tomorrow and Cleveland on Tuesday. Even though Mitchell's also provided a typewritten schedule, two or three days is as far into the future as I care to peek. And I've told Mitchell that I want to drive as much as possible, so that my eyes, my hands, my feet, and (hopefully) my mind will stay busy.

So, as we traverse the bridge, I look hard at a shelf of ice along the Jersey shore, then at an aimless squadron of raucous seagulls. (Remembering nonetheless my baby girl's grotesquely swollen skull.) The steel-colored river, with each uncrested wave glinting sharply like a razor. (Her flanged upper lip.) The feeble winter sunrise bronzing the long, swooping steel cables. (Somehow reminding me of her tight red eyes.)

I want to drive faster, but I must slow down for the tollbooth at the New Jersey end of the bridge. On the dashboard there's a small cloth bag that once held Mitchell's mother's clothespins and is now suspended by its drawstring from the radio's tuning knob. A tiny spiral-bound notebook and a blunt pencil are likewise rigged to dangle from the On-Off-Volume knob. Tending to the log is another of the shotgun's assigned duties, but Kevin is still fretting over his venal sins—so I pinch a nickel from the bag, check my wristwatch, and record the first official entry of our trip:

1/5/36 ....6:19 A.M. ....5¢ toll.........G.W. Bridge

The toll taker is a small Italian-looking man peeping out of the booth showing a black watch cap and a heavy rib-knit gray sweater. Curiosity is part of his job, so he bends forward and brazenly peers into my window inspecting the bodies, noting the beards. "What's this all about?" he asks with annoyance.

"We're anarchists," I say. "The Sacco and Vanzetti Fan Club." But I also jab my thumb at the side of the car where

THE H✡USE ✡F M✡SES ALL-STARS

has been painted in twelve-inch-high white block letters.

It was Mitchell who proposed using Jewish stars in place of the *O*s. "Stars and All-Stars," he said. "A light shining in the darkness. We should also have the booking agent's telephone number painted on there. It's free advertising." Naturally, an argument ensued. Leo was willing to wager that by the time we reached Cleveland, there'd be bullet holes punctuating the center of each vowel. Mitchell said that we should be proud to be Jews, while Leo's platform was just as concise: "Stay out of trouble." The telephone number was voted down 5–1 (with Kevin forced to abstain), but the Stars of David passed by 4–2.

The sideview mirror is mounted on the top edge of the spare tire, and I can see the toll-troll shaking his head and shouting something after us as I grind up the gears and crank the window shut. The gulp of quick cold air awakens Mitchell. "Where are we?" he asks.

"On the outskirts of Jerusalem," I say, and Kevin laughs softly without understanding.

Mitchell Sloan is a six-foot-one-inch, 175-pound, high-scoring guard from New York University who shoots radical one-handers. Far as I know, Mitchell is the only one of the neighborhood ballplayers who never conspired with gamblers. With his sharp nose, his prominent cheekbones showing above a long, curly black beard, his blue eyes sharp and sere, Mitchell exudes passion, and in fact is a devout Zionist. Whenever he mentions "the Holy Land," he nods and bows like a Hasid blessing the unnameable name of God. Mitchell is a Maccabean warrior who both lives and plays with the same messianic fervor.

Playing with the Newark Knights in the defunct American League of Professional Basketball, Mitchell led all scorers in 1929–30 (averaging 12.7 points per game), and again in 1931–32 (14.6, a league record). Thankful to be rescued from the junkyard, he entertains only vague hopes of earning enough money to book passage on a ship bound for Palestine. Sure, Mitchell's a nitpicker and a constant annoyance (he voted against including Kevin because it would "introduce an X factor into our experiment"), but his zeal is infectious. Even when we were kids, Mitchell would do almost anything to win.

I can remember how we loved to play punchball on Division Street, a one-way venue just off the Bowery. We were all right-handed and the ground rules were explicit: Any ball punched onto the right-field sidewalk was out. Balls hit past the third-base lamppost and up against the left-field line of buildings were in play. Any fly ball caught off a building or a car was out, but each fire escape was a target for ground-rule doubles. And the most important ground rule stipulated that should the ball beat the runner home, the runner must return to third base.

We played with a first and third baseman who could practically shake hands across the narrow infield and were responsible for calling, "Time-out! Car!" The second sacker straddled a manhole cover, and the lone outfielder usually roamed the sidewalk. Most of the time, Mitchell was a brave-handed first baseman, and his offensive game plan was to shrewdly angle hot grounders through the infield and under parked cars for extra bases. Brooks, on the other hand, loved to gamble on the ground rules.

"There it goes!" Brooks used to yelp as he expertly tapped the Spaldeen on a soft line into Dr. Klorman's second-story fire escape. "I can hit the ball anywhere," Brooks would boast as he eased into second base. "Just like Rogers Hornsby! I'm the king! The king!"

According to the rules, the ground-rule doubler was responsible for retrieving the ball, but Dr. Klorman was usually too quick for any of us. More often than not, the window opened and a fat arm reached out and snatched the precious Spaldeen. "Go play someplace else!" Klorman would scream. "Look what I'm doing!" With a scalpel he'd slice the ball along the seam, then he'd toss the useless halves back into the street. "I'll call the police! I'll throw hot water on you!"

"Go back to sleep!" was Brooks's usual rejoinder, and we'd caucus to raise two cents for a new ball.

I can remember one game in particular—bottom of the ninth, the last game before supper. Brooks was up and Mitchell was the potential winning run on second base. Slowly, Brooks bounced the ball on the midstreet manhole cover that served as home plate, approaching his rhythm, studying the defense. I always played a shallow outfield, daring Brooks to hit one deep off the buildings. Brooks finally rocked back and tossed the Spaldeen shoulder high, then a sidewinding fist socked the ball on a line off the bottom edge of Klorman's fire escape. The ball ricocheted sharply off an old Ford, then bounced high over the third baseman's head for a hit. But I recovered quickly, and as Mitchell rounded third base, a green Studebaker sedan zoomed off the Bowery and turned too swiftly onto Division Street. My throw, the winning run, and the Studebaker rapidly converged on home plate.

For an instant the driver saw Mitchell, but was too astounded to hit the brake. With the ball gaining on him, Mitchell dove for home, hoping to roll onto his right shoulder and so avoid the car. Then, whammo!

When all the movement stopped, Mitchell was bleeding from the head, his left arm was clearly broken, and we didn't know what to do. Except listen to the invisible sound of the sun shining, of flowers growing. Until I started shouting, "The ball beat him home! He goes back to third!"

And Mitchell moaned, "I'm safe, Aaron! You asshole!"

"What time is it?" Mitchell asks. "How's the gas level? What's the mileage? Did you record the toll? Did I lose an hour somewhere? I got to pee."

I tell him of the Con Ed crew tearing up the street to make emergency repairs on upper Broadway, of the unfamiliar detour over the Willis Avenue Bridge, and of my aimless wanderings through the Bronx. Mitchell sympathizes with earnest noddings of his head before recapitulating in tedious detail exactly what alternate route I should have followed. Then he says, "I thought you knew your way around," annoyed more with himself for his first careless presumption having cost us time and money.

Then Mitchell leans forward, careful not to wake Leo, poking his head over the seatback just behind and between me and Kevin.

"We play at three," Mitchell says, just loudly enough to be heard above the rattle of the Black Lady's bones, above the high-whining vibrations of her racing heart. "That means we have to be on the court at two-thirty. Getting loose is important. We can't afford any injuries. We should also eat our big meal by ten-thirty the latest. We're already behind schedule. Let's say nine-thirty just in case, so we don't have to eat in a rush. Good nutrition and good digestion are also important. We can't afford someone getting sick either. But the big question is this: Can I hold it in till then?" He pauses to silently flex his bladder. "It's close," he decides, "but if we stop, then everybody'll wake up."

"Screw them," I say, and Kevin smiles because I do.

"It's not very utilitarian," Mitchell says, "to sacrifice the comfort and rest of the four sleepers just because I stupidly forgot to piss before we left. No. I'll manage. Right, Kevin? Reap what you sow?"

Kevin re-smiles and says, "I agree with you a hunnert percent."

Then Mitchell taps my shoulder and whispers in my ear, "How're you doing, Aaron? How's the kid doing? Is he staying awake?"

"Everything's shipshape, Mitchell. Go back to sleep. Just don't dream about a waterfall."

Picking up 9W North, winding through Fort Lee, Tenafly, crossing back into New York near Tappan, then breaking out of the metropolitan knot near Nyack, a colony of rich Hasidic Jews. I'm caught at a long red light in the middle of the village, the Sabbath over, the streets swarming with men in black greatcoats and curly black-haired hats. Children point at us. An ancient crone wearing a black babushka over a wig stares in dumb bewilderment. Then an old man with a long gray beard hobbles over and taps on the side window with his cane. As I roll the window down, he says something that I can't quite hear.

"What's he saying?" Kevin asks.

"I don't know. Just nod like we're agreeing with him."

The old man rudely pokes his face in through the open window and speaks again. He spits when he talks and his rancid herring-breath makes me wince. *"Ba ha. Ba ha,"* I think he says. *"Ba ha Shabbes ba Nacht?"*

"Yeah," I say. "Sure. Of course."

Then he starts screaming. *"Ba ha! Ba ha!"* And he slams his cane hard against the roof of the car.

"Hey!" I shout. Then bust through the red light, and *zoom,* we're gone.

"What the fuck was that all about?" Mitchell asks from behind me.

"God only knows."

Crazy old-world Jews. My *landsmen*? They might as well be Eskimos. Eskimoses.

Heading toward Ossining, the river to my right, trees whooshing by, houses fronting the road, dairy farms, cows bunched before a red barn. Kevin is sleeping, so is Mitchell. So are my parents and my child.

The vigil has fallen to me. And my eyes are wide open, searching the road, searching my heart, even as I bear the burden of my life like a hunchback bears his hump.

My brother, Max, likes to remind me that Momma kept a kosher home, that she was a *bollabusta*. And I should always remember "until my dying day" how hard Dad tried to keep things together.

Sure, Dad tried, and I loved him for it. Working ten hours daily behind a sewing machine in a loft on West 19th Street, then walking home to save the bus fare and donning an apron to cook chicken soup or chicken fricassee. Sure, Max and I tried to help, cleaning the dishes, sweeping the floors. But the old man wore out in a hurry. He cried himself to sleep most nights. He started shopping at the A & P instead of at the "appetizing" store. And by the time I started going to school, all that Dad ever cooked was hamburgers or spaghetti.

I can't see the penitentiary from across the river, but I can imagine what it looks like. Sing Sing, with tall bullet-pocked walls, guards in towers smoking cigarettes, eager to shoot someone, anyone. We're due back here sometime near the end of the week for a game against the inmates. Strangely enough, it's one of the few dates I'm looking forward to.

Passing through Haverstraw, where the annual Easter Tournament draws the finest players from the city. A factory town, so even on Sunday morning the smokestacks are still firing. The river bluer now, the waves softer. Farther up, the heights of West Point as we drive within range of their cannons. (Sarah Pearl's bloated brain, the idiot's drool draining from her broken mouth.) As we approach Newburgh, everybody stirs at once.

"Time to eat," Mitchell says in my ear. "Time to pee."

Ceremoniously I announce that we're in Newburgh, New York, 127 miles from Henry Street. Then I say, "At the tone the correct time is nine-twenty-seven A.M. eastern standard time. Boing." There follows a lively debate about where we should eat.

Ron suggests that we drive around town until we find a dairy restaurant. "I'm in the mood for lox, onions, and eggs," he says. Brooks wants us to search out a deli: "It's never too early in the day for a pastrami sandwich."

"Anywhere," says Mitchell. "Long as they have a bathroom."

A quick reconnoiter of "Broadway" discovers no deli, no dairy restaurant, only a pair of diners. I ease the Queen into the parking lot of Ernie's Eatery, a shabby-shingled Cape Codder that once was somebody's dream house. There's a big red-lettered sign tacked to the front door: BREAKFAST OUR SPECIALTY. Another smaller sign is posted beneath it, NO NIGGERS ALLOWED.

"It's chow time," Leo says as he unfolds his legs and prepares to climb out of the car.

"We can't go in there," Brooks says.

"Why not?" Leo protests. "We ain't niggers. At least I know *I* ain't."

"Brooks is right," Mitchell says. "Let's try the other place."

This necessitates a complicated broken U-turn on a side street (Maple Lane), then retracing our route back down Broadway before parking in a crowded gravel lot behind The Red Rose Diner, a gigantic torpedo-shaped building, all silver-bright and shining. Still inside the car, we can see that the joint is thronged with customers dressed in their Sunday finery, fresh from church and presumably still in a state of grace.

Mitchell turns in his seat so that we can all hear him.

"This is the first time we'll be appearing as a group in a public place," he says, "so let me go over the rules and the proper decorum." A gold Star of David and two sturdy brass keys are suspended from a leather thong that loosely encircles his neck. The larger key unlocks our steel money box. The smaller key unlocks and unlinks a small iron chain that curls through a set of special rings on the money box, and is wrapped around a steel post where the frame of the driver's seat is welded to the floor.

"We're each allowed thirty-five cents for breakfast," Mitchell says as he loosens the chain and opens the box. "That's including a tip for the waitress. If you go over your limit, the difference comes out of your own pocket. Also. Let's be polite to everybody. They live here, we don't. That's our motto for the whole trip. And let's each of us wear a hat, a yarmulke or something. Never forget what and who we represent."

"What?" says Leo, feigning total confusion. "Who?"

Saul always wears a black leather yarmulke stuck to his skull like a scab. Kevin sports a porkpie cap of a red-plaid design. Brooks, Mitchell, and I have identical black berets tilted at the same rakish angle. Ron wears a crisp black derby, Leo, a brown leather aviator's hat (sans goggles) with the two earflaps left to dangle and flop. Otherwise we're dressed in a variety of dull-colored cotton pants and threadbare dungarees with home-knit sweaters or faded gray sweatshirts. Saul's sacramental fringes (*tzitzit*) show beneath a neat brown cardigan. And Max has provided us all with U.S. Navy surplus pea coats. Standing in the parking lot, we most resemble:

(a) Deserters from the Russian submarine corps
(b) A rabbinical choir
(c) A tumbling act, the Flying Kazatzkis
(d) The Elders of Zion

Once inside the diner, we ignore the rude stares, the heads turned, the jaws agape. In similar circumstances we will always use the bathroom one at a time while the others wait patiently in line for a table. This procedure is necessary, says Mitchell, "to avoid panicking the civilian population." The long counter is chrome-trimmed, the booths offer red leather seats, and every eating surface is composed of heavily shellacked planks of red wood. ("Nice decor," I whisper to Brooks. "Chippendale meets Flash Gordon.") The cooking is done on a huge rectangular grill that parallels the counter and is manned by three white-suited good guys wearing puffy chef's hats.

When it's my turn to use the bathroom, an elderly man in the adjoining urinal tries to sneak a peek at my unhooded *shmeckle*. "Hey," I bark. "You the pecker checker around here?" He leaves in a huff without washing his hands.

We're still in line when a blond waitress passes close by, carrying a tray loaded with food. Ron catches her eye, winks broadly, and pantomimes a smooching kiss. The waitress says, "Eek," juggles her tray and makes a job-saving shoestring catch.

Another waitress appears, mousy-brown hair, pinched face and flat-chested, to lead us to our table. "I got bigger tits than her," Leo sneers under his breath. When we're all seated, the waitress asks, "What're you guys—Jews or something?"

"Or something," Brooks says.

According to the breakfast portion of the menu, our thirty-five cents will go a long way:

Orange or grapefruit juice .... 5¢
Boiled oatmeal .... 10¢
French Toast .... 10¢
Pancakes ....10¢
Ham or bacon and eggs .... 15¢
C.B. hash with 1 egg .... 20¢
Spinach and eggs .... 20¢

The most expensive item on the entire menu is "Pig's knuckles with red cabbage" at thirty cents. Everything comes with a choice of coffee, tea, or buttermilk. I order the oatmeal plus the spinach and eggs. Kevin wants a double order of bacon and sunnyside-up eggs. Ron will have one order of ham and eggs, one with bacon. Leo likes hash. Brooks orders "orange Jews" and two stacks of "Frog toast."

"I think I'll go for the oxtail stew," Mitchell jokes at large.

"It's real good," Kevin enthuses. "My mom makes it on Sundays." Then he reddens when he realizes the joke's on him. Saul opts for oatmeal, pancakes, and "a glass of tea."

While waiting for our food, Mitchell explains "what the deal is" for the upcoming game in Glens Falls. "Win or lose," he says, "our total take is seventy-five bucks. I know, I know, it's a small payoff, but we should look at it as a kind of dry run. Another thing, there's a dance afterward and if we want to stay to help them clean up and move the chairs, they'll feed us and let us sleep overnight in the church. Believe me, we're going to get sick of sleeping in the car soon enough. Buffalo's only two hundred and ten miles from Glens Falls, and tomorrow's game isn't until seven at night. So I think getting a free meal and a night's lodging is a good deal for us."

We all mumble our support, and Mitchell leans back in his chair showing a smug grin. He loves being so reasonable, so incontrovertible.

"You know," Leo says snidely, "I can't tell if this is breakfast or a meeting of the fucking board of directors."

Mitchell shrugs. "Business is business."

"Speaking of which," says Brooks, "now's as good a time as any to talk about the ball game." Then he clears a space in the center of the table and collects one pepper and four salt shakers, an ashtray, and a crumpled paper napkin.

"Oh, no," Leo gripes. "It's a fucking skull session."

As a group we've only been together for two practices, but Mitchell, Brooks, and I are totally familiar with one another's style of play. Leo's game (and personality) will be a problem, yet even Leo understands that Brooks is our theorist, our lost professor of *X*s and *O*s. No official vote has been requested because we've all assumed from the start that Brooks will be our coach. It's a headache nobody else wants.

"First off," Brooks says as he arranges his pieces, "we've got to realize that there's a lot of games and a lot of miles ahead of us, and this realization has to influence the way we play. Basically, we want to play with patience, with intelligence. We want to get easy shots without having to bust our balls. Right? Against a man-to-man defense? We've got our four-man weave."

The pepper shaker is positioned near the ashtray while Brooks moves the salt shakers in graceful parabolas, cleverly sliding the crumpled napkin from shaker to shaker.

"The pivot man," Brooks says, lifting the pepper shaker, "always moves from weak side to strong side. If he is open, bang, he gets the ball inside for a layup or easy hook. Right? Aaron? Saul? If there's no shot, it's an automatic give-and-go. Still nothing doing? Everybody cuts and screens away, like so . . . If we still can't find an easy shot, the big man passes to a guard and we're back to the weave. Sharp cuts, crisp passes. If your defender turns his head, bingo! You're gone. Backdoor for a layup. Easy as pie . . . . Against a zone we play our wheel. Like so . . . Same principles. Always moving, cutting, passing. All right? We want to play a half-court game as much as possible, a deliberate tempo. If we do get tired, we'll give the ball to Leo and let him dribble around for a while. All right? The idea is to save our legs. We'll have plenty of running to do once we get out West . . . . On defense? Easy. Push your man to his off hand. Don't turn your head. Don't go for fakes. And box out. Above all? Help each other. Be unselfish. Right?"

"Jeez," says Leo. "You got me all pumped up, Knute. I want to play right now. Fuck later."

"One more thing," Mitchell adds. "If they hate us? If they're abusive? Then we'll kick their fucking asses and make them say 'uncle,'"

We're all laughing when our food is served.

Saul is seated between Kevin and Ron, visibly disgusted by the bacon to the right of him, ham to the left of him, but he leads us in the blessing: *"Baruch ataw adonoi eloheinu melech ha'olam ha'motzi lechem min ha'awretz."*

Saul Jacobson is a six-foot-ten, 240-pound giant. "He's the future," Brooks says. Two years ago, Saul played for the Metro. U. frosh team, scoring an unprecedented 19.4 points per game and clearing rebounds at the record rate of 9.6 per game. "Someday," Brooks promises, "Saul or somebody like him will revolutionize the game."

For the time being, Saul is a quick jumper, fairly athletic, active with both hands, admirably unselfish, and is the only player I've ever seen who constantly plays above the rim. Besides his youth and the time he'll need to grow into his body, Saul's problem is that he's too much the scholar. Not at all mean-spirited, Saul lacks the big-time big man's basic instinct to knock somebody ass over teakettle. However, he's another nice kid and there's a steadfastness about him that's appealing, an offbeat kind of near wisdom rarely found in a twenty-year-old.

According to what I've heard, Saul's father was a highly respected Hasidic rabbi, renowned for his devotion and the purity of his deeds. Compassion was the touchstone of the old man's religion, and he stout-heartedly permitted his outsized son to play basketball (excepting, of course, on the Sabbath). "It's a new world," the old man used to say "and a new generation." Saul's mother was a typical *rebbe*'s wife from the old country—quiet and efficient, she washed the dishes and waxed the floors while her husband pleaded with God. That's why Saul is so deeply steeped in the Judaic tradition and is the only one among us who's brought his *tallis* and *tefillin*, the only All-Star who greets each new day saying, "Hear, O Israel! The Lord thy God is One!"

Tragically, one sunny *Shabbes* morning shortly after Saul's spectacular freshman season, his father dropped dead in the street, the victim of a sudden heart seizure. His mother grieved for twelve months, then, adhering to the dictates of the Torah, she married her husband's older brother, Shloimie the *Shtunk*. Ostensibly a housepainter by trade, Shloimie would rather drink than work, a predilection that made finding employment difficult even in plush times. By and by, Saul's stepfather contented himself with sleeping all day, carousing every evening, and making sure he met the mailman every Tuesday morning to receive the stipend of $10.96 from Home Relief.

Of this sum, Shloimie apportioned three dollars to his wife (formerly sister-in-law) to "run the house." Shloimie was lazy, but never stupid—he was terrified of Saul and, although he mercilessly scolded his new wife, he never raised a hand to her, not even when deep in his cups.

Was there money for Saul's tuition? For his books? His notebooks? Pencils? Carfare? "Feh," said Shloimie, so Saul left school and tried to earn a livelihood playing basketball.

The ball is always round, the court is always smooth, but alas, Saul was proved a novice in his competitions with experienced pros. His postpubescent awkwardness, his ignorance of the game's subtleties, and his lack of focused aggression made Saul more of a sideshow freak than a bona fide player in the tough play-for-pay tournaments around town. Even so, if Brooks believes that Saul can develop into a real player, who am I to vote against him? Maybe Saul can say a few prayers for me while he's at it.

"Blessed art Thou
O Lord our God
Who bringeth forth
Bread from the earth."

While Saul gags on the unfamiliar smells, the rest of us attack our food like starving Armenians. But Saul has another problem. "Waitress?" he says. "I distinctly remember ordering a glass of tea, not a cup of tea."

Obviously intimidated, thinking she's violated some exotic religious rite and her life might be at risk, the waitress quickly makes the exchange.

"A glass," says Leo, "a cup. What's the fucking difference?"

Saul clears his throat and says, "When you drink tea from a cup, who can see what's in it? A broken piece of glass maybe. Or a dead cockroach lying drowned on the bottom. A glass of tea hides nothing. Also, consider this: How do you hold a cup of tea? Answer: By the handle with just your fingers. Question: How do you hold a glass of tea? Answer: With your whole hand. A glass of tea warms you from the inside and from the outside. A glass of tea is more practical and also more aesthetically pleasing."

"Whoa!" says Mitchell. "What about Psalm Seventy-five? '. . . in the hand of the Lord there is a cup . . .'?"

"From the Psalms you quote me, you goy?" says Saul. "Besides, that's a cup of *wine*. God doesn't drink tea . . . Let me boil the entire matter down to the most fundamental tenet of Judaic law: For the same price, you get more tea in a glass than in a cup."

"Jeez!" says Leo in amazement. "I ask him for the time and he tells me how to make a watch!"

Back in the car, Brooks trades places with Kevin. Mitchell grumbles, but makes the appropriate notations in his log book. I turn the ignition key, lightly step my left foot on the large starter button, and presto! The Queen is purring, raring to go! Another miracle of modern science.

"It's going to work," Brooks says as we ease back into the meager traffic on 9W. "We're the microcosm, Aaron. And I know in my heart that the revolution will come before the Messiah comes."

Brooks Moser is a half-inch taller than I am and a better player by ten yards. We grew up together and he's my dearest friend in the entire known universe, but Brooks has always been crazy. Before he was Brooks the Bolshie, he was known as Bellevue Brooks, the scourge of the neighborhood.

Nobody knows the whys or wherefores, but by the time he was ten, Brooks had developed a fondness for ruthlessly torturing cats. He'd prowl the basements, luring them into a canvas sack with sardines. His favorite stunt was tossing live cats from the roof of his apartment building. Sometimes he'd tie two together by their tails and fling them to their caterwauling deaths. Another of his amusements was dousing a cat's back with cigarette lighter fluid, then igniting the poor creature and laughing as it screeched and careened through the neighborhood after dark. His most humane antic was to ring somebody's doorbell (usually mine), then throw a desperately clawing alley cat into the chest of whoever opened the door.

All of the kids in the neighborhood were cautioned not to play with that meshuggener, and a career with Murder, Incorporated, was the best anybody ever predicted for him. But Brooks was the finest athlete on the entire Lower East Side, so how could we not choose him into all of our games? From kick-the-can to Johnny-on-the-pony. From four-box baseball to fire-escape basketball. And with his utter disregard for the opinions of grown-ups, he was bound to be our hero.

Brooks's father, a retired butcher, tried to ignore him. His mother went from stoop to stoop, crying, "*Gevalt! Gevalt!* What can I do? He was born meshuga!"

Brooks and I were teammates at Seward Park High School (although he didn't play basketball there until his senior year), and we went on to play four more seasons together at Metro U. At six-seven and a tensile 210 pounds, Brooks is still quick as a wish. He handles like a guard, can hook in the pivot, and bombs set shots from beyond the pale. When he wants to play, he's as good as anybody I've ever seen.

For his three-year varsity career at Metro U. Brooks averaged 11.2 and 8.7 rebounds per game (the latter a varsity record), shot 43.2 percent from the floor (another record), and in our senior year (1926–27) he led the nation in free-throw shooting with 87.9 percent.

Always a ringleader, it was Brooks who perpetuated the school's time-honored tradition of shaving points. When the old guard graduated after our sophomore season, it was Brooks who took over the business—arranging the dates and the payoffs, deciding who was in and who was out. "You hate Coach Halperin as much as I do," Brooks told me. "He treats us like dogs. Whenever we win, he takes the full credit. When we lose, it's strictly our fault. Shaving points is a way to get even with him. Make the bastard squirm a little. Come on, Aaron. I know you can use the money. Look at that raggedy shirt you're wearing. Nobody gets hurt, Aaron. And everybody's doing it."

During his senior year, Brooks fell in love. Her name was Greta and she was president of the on-campus Social Awareness Club, a Communist-party coterie that welcomed Brooks with open arms and legs. So instead of atrocitizing cats, Brooks now stood in the rain at bus stops and subway stations foisting party pamphlets on passersby. Even when Greta ran off with a Wall Street lawyer, Brooks kept the red flag flying.

Through it all, he also continued hooping and, for some reason, his game got sharper, more intense. We were teammates again with the Trenton Tigers in the late, lamented American League, and Brooks was devastated when the league folded. Pushing his produce cart around the neighborhood was humiliating, but his parents were ailing (his father died last November), so Brooks took the bit and he endured.

Brooks was always proud of being so "independent," but it seems to me that ever since his father died, he's become more cynical, more morose. I fear for him, that his divine spark of madness might be extinguished forever. Brooks still retains some sort of party connections, and his latest dream is to become a union organizer among the migrant fruit pickers in southern California. It is Brooks who shall be, must be, proof that dreams can save us, that our dreams of bliss and justice are not just the illusions of powerless men.

We're buddies through thick and thin, and I'm glad that we can still suffer for each other's pain.

We ride quietly for a while, lulled by the Queen in her labors, hearing Mitchell and Leo chattering like magpies in the seat behind us. Passing through Middle Hope, Marlboro, Milton, all one-horse towns. The rugged roads give us an occasional jolt, drawing moans from the crypt. Bending west now, near Hyde Park across the river, ancestral home of the Roosevelts. Maybe FDR is the Messiah. Passing through Port Ewen. Lincoln Park. Brooks is unusually somber. He likes to talk about "revolution." Excuse me, "*The* Revolution." Me, I want a revolution in time and space. Maybe Einstein is the Messiah. I wonder—walking backward through my life—at what point would I revolve and start it up again? A police car trails us the fifteen miles from Saugerties to Catskill, before turning off and vanishing.

"Brooks," I say, breaking into our long silence, an inertia of our souls. "All told, how many games did we play for Benedetto?"

"On our own?"

"Yes."

"Let's see. As juniors, we did Holy Cross, Columbia, ummm, Saint Anthony's, and NYU. As seniors, all those plus Fordham, Saint John's, and Canisius. Is that right? That makes . . . eleven? Yes, eleven. Oh, yeah, we also did one game for that jerkoff bookie from Chelsea, what's his name? Malloy? McCoy? That was the Saint Bonaventure game in our senior year. So that's twelve all together. How many of those games did we actually lose? Can you remember?"

"I never forget a ball game," Brooks says stiffly. "Let's see. We lost the first Holy Cross game because we were too nervous. Remember that one?"

"Of course. We were minus four and we led by four in the last minute. We were so afraid of a push and losing our very first payday that we went nutso. You missed those foul shots down the stretch."

Here comes Athens (a gas station, a church, a bar, and a stop sign). Next is Coxsackie (Coxsuckie?). Roadside antiques. Curios. The Dew Drop Inn, just south of Ravena. Getting low on gas.

Brooks sighs and finally says, "Remember the Fordham game up in the Bronx? When we saw a couple of Benedetto's tough guys on the sideline with big bulges in their jackets? Remember? We were up by one with twenty-something seconds to go, the spread was minus two and it was our ball?"

How could I forget? "Tannenbaum wanted to fuck us and he wouldn't give up the ball. If he scored at the buzzer, we were dead men. Tanny was pissed because you wouldn't cut him in. So I set a pick for him and kind of leaned over and knocked him off stride. Thank God the ref called the discontinued dribble."

"I think there was another game somewhere," Brooks says. "Against NYU when we were seniors. Damn! Coach Halperin was roaring when we kicked that one away."

“Brooks? I know every school had two, three guys who were fucking with the spread. I know that Coach Halperin was an arrogant, unbearable asshole. And I know we surely did need the money. But. Looking back at it, we were wrong to get involved with Benedetto, weren’t we?”

“Hey, Aaron. In 1925 we were nineteen-and-six instead of twenty-and-five. A year later we won twenty instead of twenty-two. So who cares? Eight hundred million people in China never heard of Metropolitan University. Never heard of basketball. Hey, there are no Bowl games for basketball teams. Some guys made some money, some guys lost some money, and Coach Halperin spent a couple of sleepless nights. It’s ten years ago. What’s the fucking difference?”

“If you’re Leo, there’s no difference. But neither one of us is Leo.”

“Ah,” Brooks says, “fuck Leo. He doesn’t know shit from Shine-Ola. Hey, Leo was doing business in the American League. Don’t talk to me about Leo.”

“Brooks. We were wrong, weren’t we?”

“Yes,” he shouts. “Yes, we were wrong! Shut the fuck up, will you?”

Leo sticks his face through the chauffeur’s window. “What’s the matter, fellas? Having a little lovers’ spat?”

Brooks rudely pushes the window shut, nearly clipping Leo’s nose.

We stop for gas just before entering Albany, another one-horse town. A yokel in overalls is astounded to see three live bodies emerge from the crypt, and he pumps his pump with his eyes wide open and his mouth snapped shut. Everybody scatters to pee in the bushes while Mitchell handles the finances.

“Ten-point-four gallons at sixteen cents a gallon,” he says. “Equals . . . a dollar-sixty-six. Now we have a hundred and seventy-eight point nine miles on the trip odometer, divided by ten point four gallons, equals . . ." He scrabbles on the back of his log book, licking the tip of his pencil before making a mark. "Equals seventeen and a half miles per gallon. Not bad considering the load we're pulling. You okay, Aaron? Need some rest? I'll have one of the kids take over."

"Let me finish up. It's only what? Another sixty miles?"

Near Round Lake, Brooks says softly, "Watch your speed. The limit's twenty." Then I flick on the radio. An announcer with a resonant English accent is reading the news:

"In a fiery speech before eighteen thousand Nazis, German minister of propaganda Dr. Joseph Goebbels declared that Germany must soon have colonies. 'The German people,' he said, 'are a truly poor nation. We have no colonies and no raw materials.' Referring to the army's increasing need of copper, wool, and other products either not or insufficiently produced in Germany to equip the new military establishment, Dr. Goebbels said, 'We can get along without butter, but never without cannon.' Meanwhile, in the wake of the recent Nuremberg laws denying citizenship to German Jews, agents of good faith have relayed to Jewish citizens prominent in Great Britain a Nazi plan calling for the mass deportation of German Jews to Palestine, or British territories, if British and American Jews will reimburse Germany for the subsequent removal of Jewish capital. Since such compensation may be made only in the form of German goods, the plan would really subsidize German industries and exports. The alternative would be a further tightening of the screws of Jewish persecution, Dr. Goebbels said. He added . . ."

The First Calvary Baptist Church is on the near side of town, right smack on 9W (called Front Street as it winds through Glens Falls), easy to find as a wart on your nose. We're 237 miles into our journey and I berth the Queen in a crowded parking lot at precisely 2:11 P.M.

"Nice job," Mitchell says.

There's a welcoming committee waiting for us on the front steps, a bevy of elderly matrons and a preacher who looks like Ichabod Crane. The black-suited preacher introduces himself as Reverend Boswell and says, "I'm so glad you've arrived safely. We were beginning to get worried. The congregation's been looking forward to seeing you, to meeting you, for weeks, and we've got quite a bang-up crowd inside." He gestures with his long, bony face over his shoulder toward the church, a stately wooden edifice, freshly painted, neatly trimmed, and topped with a modest bell tower.

The ladies are variously clad in gray tailored suits, cutesy nautical outfits, or unadorned white blouses and skirts. They cluck their agreement with each of the preacher's words and sentiments. One of the women steps forward and addresses herself to the player closest to her eye level, Leo. "Are you planning . . . ?" she flutters. "That is, will you be staying here with us? Overnight, I mean."

On his best behavior, Leo says, "Yeah, lady. What's for supper?"

"Well," she says, totally flustered. "I mean . . ."

The preacher bails her out. "It's a potluck dinner," he says brightly. "The women's auxiliary has arranged a variety of covered dishes. I'm sure you'll find something you like."

"Reverend Boswell!" the woman gasps, wringing her hands in sudden distress. "I've just thought of something! None of the food is kosher!"

"Goodness gracious!" says the preacher. "That's a consideration we've completely overlooked. What shall we do?"

"Nah," says Leo. "It's okay. You got any corned beef hash?"

Then Mitchell intercedes: "We'll be fine, sir. There's sure to be something that won't compromise our dietary laws. If not, the rabbi here can say a special blessing."

Brooks bows deeply, touching his right fingertips to his navel, to his heart, then to his forehead as he straightens up. *"Shalom,"* he says. *"Gai kockin offen yam."*

"A basketball-playing rabbi!" the preacher exclaims. "What an unexpected delight. We must have a chat once the festivities are over."

"Gupple leffle bupkes," says Brooks. *"Zaydes kishkehs."*

"He doesn't speak English," Mitchell says.

"Oh." The preacher is crestfallen. "Well, why don't I show you where you can change?"

We follow the preacher through the front doors, then along a dark corridor to the right, down a flight of musty stairs, through another door, and into the furnace room. Aside from the glowing furnace, a coal bin, and a series of low-hanging sooty pipes, the main room also features a sink, a plastic-curtained shower, and a shitter. Tucked behind an L-shaped corner are a rusty brass bed, a lumpy easy chair, and a paint-splattered armoire. In the living area, the pebbled cement floor is partially concealed by a ratty brown rug. "This is where the custodian resides," the preacher says. "You can leave your valuables here if you wish. You needn't fear. Nobody will violate your privacy. Please take as long as you need to get ready. We can't very well start the game without you, eh? There are towels and soap over near the shower, but if you require anything else, just ask." Then he leaves.

"Looks like a nice guy," says Saul.

"Looks like he needs to get laid," says Leo.

"He's a Baptist," I suggest. "He's probably married. It's Catholic priests who take a vow of celibacy."

Kevin nods his agreement, but he's been reluctant to catch my eye ever since he went back to sleep after we crossed the bridge. The kid owes me one, make that two. I'll bet he's afraid that the Holy

Mother is also out to kick his ass.

Kevin does approach Brooks, however, asking in good faith for a translation of what he told the preacher. "Well," says Brooks. "I was mostly faking it 'cause I don't know much Yiddish. First I said, 'Howdy.' Then I said, 'Go . . . visit the ocean.' Then I said, 'Spoon, fork, potatoes.' Then, 'Grandfather's intestines.' That's about all the Yiddish I can muster. I really wasn't trying to pull the man's chain. I just wanted to avoid discussing theology with him. I didn't mean any disrespect."

"Oh," Kevin says. "Neither did I."

Each of us carries a small laundry bag stuffed with bottles of our favorite shampoo, with towels, rolled-up socks, jocks, gym shoes, and uniforms. When full, the bags double as pillows *en transit*. We'll use Mitchell's empty bag to hold our wallets, watches, rings, and the keys to the car. "On the road, a team should always take the valuables bag with them to the bench," Mitchell constantly reminds us. "If for some reason only five guys show up, then the youngest plays the game with the valuables bag tied around his waist."

Our gray woolen socks (also army surplus) reach up to the middle of my shins (Leo's extend nearly to his knees). The theory being—the higher the socks, the less chance of suffering a painful floor burn should we take a tumble. Our gym shoes are fashioned of thick black leather with as many lace holes as ice skates. The soles are unpolished slabs of an even thicker leather. On a dusty, unkempt floor, the shoes tend to slide during any abrupt changes of direction, but an experienced player will score the soles with the point of a nail to increase the traction. The shoes are durable and, with the laces caught and tightened with a crochet hook, sufficiently formfitting to sometimes prevent sprained ankles.

Our snazzy short-sleeved jerseys are a silky royal blue trimmed in white. There's a small digit sewn high on the backs of the shirts (to avoid unnecessary conflicts we are numbered according to height—so Leo is #1, Saul is #7, and I wear #5). Hebrew letters are embroidered on the front—שלח את עמי—"Let my people go." (Mitchell's idea, accepted 5–1 with Kevin voteless and Leo holding out for "Fuck you.") The matching shorts feature the moderate protection of plump cotton hip pads. Thanks once again to Max.

We also wear kneepads, a halfmoon of black leather strapped at the bottom and buckled just below our kneecaps. Our yarmulkes are a dark blue denim and secured with bobby pins. As a gesture of forgiveness, I help Kevin adjust his yarmulke. We're just about ready to go when Mitchell notices that Ron is nowhere in sight.

"He'll be right back," says Brooks. "Ron can't help it. He's casing the joint."

Ron Rubin's father was a wealthy fur merchant in Prague and his mother was the only daughter of the city's most highly esteemed rabbi. No Matter. Both were slaughtered in a brutal pogrom when Ron was barely three years old. Ron was hidden by a sympathetic Christian family, with whom he masqueraded as a "cousin" for the next five years, when contact was finally established with Ron's father's brother, Stefan, also a furrier, and now living in New York. The appropriate officials were bribed, papers were forged, and, at age eight, Ron was put on a cargo ship bound for Ellis Island. Upon his arrival, a few more efficacious bribes were dispensed before Ron went home with his uncle, a bachelor living in a ritzy apartment in a fashionable section of Greenwich Village. Ron was twelve when the stock market collapsed, and the morning after Black Monday, Uncle Stefan went to the warehouse and was never heard from again. Did Stefan abscond with someone else's funds? Did he tap dance off the edge of a roof? No one knew. Ron was evicted from the apartment at the end of the month, and he's been on his own ever since.

For a while, Ron cast his fortunes with a gang of hoodlums in Hell's Kitchen, terrorizing bakeries, small groceries, and candy stores, snatching purses, begging in front of fancy restaurants, and rolling drunks. At night, they slept in flophouses, or else inside of unlocked cars and hallways. When he was fourteen, Ron became a mule for the Beagle Boys (a notorious stickup gang), carrying their gats to and from a job. Ron's been arrested a dozen times for various petty crimes and has served a total of four months in the juvenile hall on Chambers Street. The only legit job he's ever had was last summer's stint as a singing waiter in a suds palace on the Bowery.

Just about a year ago Brooks discovered Ron playing one-on-one against all comers for five cents a game in a playground over on West Houston Street. Ron is six-one-and-a-half, a stringy 155 pounds, and Brooks won a nickel trouncing him by a score of 11–5. After the game, Brooks pronounced Ron a natural, took him to dinner, arranged for him to sleep on a folding bed in the nursery room at the Henry Street Center and enrolled him in the Men's League. Imagine my surprise when Ron proved to be a dynamic defensive player against guards, forwards, and even centers. He played with a furious tenacity, never retreating from any challenge.

Ron actually played with Brooks and me in several hot-shot tournaments, his defensive ferocity scaring the bejesus out of the occasional pro, who was more concerned with an injury-free payday than with winning a ball game. But after a few games, Ron would disappear into the streets again. Brooks would relentlessly search him out, Ron would bunk down in the nursery and play with us for a week or so, then poof! He was gone again. That's why Ron was never a charter member of the All-Stars.

Then just a few days ago, we discovered that Allie Schulman had eloped with a shiksa and Maury Goldberg had joined the army, so we were hard-pressed to find an acceptable forward. "Six is not enough players," Brooks insisted. "We need at least seven." But no dice. Everybody else we wanted had other plans. Tannenbaum begged us, but we'd never stoop that low. Then last Friday, Ron chanced to turn up at the gym. Seems he'd heard some rumors and he was bold enough to find us and ask to be included in our plans. That was fine with me. Ron was capable of playing three positions and was happy to come off the bench. Besides, he'd just bungled a gas-station heist on Thursday and needed to get out of town pronto.

"Give the kid a break," Brooks pleaded just before we voted. "He plays smart enough to start and he's got fire. As for his off-the-court carryings-on, I say we should think of him as a valuable resource."

"What he is," said Mitchell, "is a fucking criminal."

"By necessity," Brooks countered. "Not by choice. He's just another victim of the system. Don't worry. I'll be personally responsible for him. Besides, we need a stopper on defense."

Mitchell didn't "trust" Ron so the vote was 4–1. "Shit," Leo said afterward, "I don't even know if I trust myself."

Ron enters the furnace room with a complete scouting report: "They're charging two dollars' admission and there's about three hundred people in the hall. There's one old guy in charge of the money box, a pushover. No cops, no other security personnel. There's a side exit upstairs and another exit out the basement. The playing court is laid out on the floor of the church with the lines marked off in black electrician's tape. All the pews have been stacked in a side room. The floor is made of tile, it's hard and slippery. The baskets are portable, set up right on the baseline, on rubber wheels with no backboards. The team is a bunch of bushers. There's a middle-aged gray-haired guy who can hit a set shot, and a big, strong kid maybe six-five. That's about it. An easy game. Start the car with two minutes left, I'll grab the cashbox, and we're out of here."

Leo loves the idea. "Let's vote," he says, but Mitchell ignores the proposal.

Inside the main hall, Ron's report checks out to the last detail: About three hundred well-dressed, well-fed spectators greeting us with shouts of joy; the boardless cylindrical porto-hoops; the tile floor; and the amateurish nature of the home team (apparent even as they warm up). There are catch-lock mechanisms on the floor (the attachments for the pews), which can cause a misstep or a bad bounce. The score will be kept on a blackboard propped on a chair at midcourt, and the Reverend Boswell is the one and only referee.

A huge ten-foot cross overlooks the far basket—Jesus mounted with his legs crossed at the ankles, with his arms outstretched, poised to do a clumsy, painful pirouette. The Son of Man is at least an eight-footer, an almighty rebounder.

The hometowners wear glitzy yellow uniforms with "The Crusaders" scripted on the front of their jerseys in black. Smiling, they come over to our bench en masse to shake hands. The gray-haired set-shooter (wearing #1) looks like he used to be a player. The six-foot-five farm boy has big feet and big hands, more a Saint Bernard than a serious hooper. The others are either too fat, too thin, or too washed out. "Welcome, fellas," says #1. "Don't beat us too badly, eh?"

The Reverend Mister Ref approaches our bench armed with a megaphone. He thanks the spectators for showing up and thereby contributing to the building fund. He announces that the game will consist of four ten-minute "periods." Then he asks each of us in a whisper for our names before grandly introducing us to enthusiastic applause. Leo gives his name as Leo D. Lyon.

The Crusaders are introduced— #1 is the high school basketball coach, the big guy is his son, someone else is the mayor, there's an alderman, a potbellied sheriff and several other local celebrities.

I easily capture the opening center-jump, and we begin the game by unwinding our wheel against their standard 2-1-2 zone defense. In a flash, Leo backdoors #1, but misses a little flipper from five feet. "Who ever heard of a basket without a fucking backboard?" he gripes while racing downcourt.

We always play man-to-man defense unless someone is in foul trouble—and we sag into the middle, expecting the Crusaders to have as much trouble as we have shooting at the naked hoop. But #1 hits a couple of quick step-back set shots, and they jump out to a 4–0 lead.

The big kid has a tricky step-through move and the first time he shows it, I bite at his fake. He scores the bucket and draws the foul. Now we're down 7–0 and Brooks calls a time-out.

First off, he wants Ron to switch onto #1. Leo will now guard the sheriff. Next, Brooks calls for me to get busy in the pivot. And he wants everybody but Leo to storm the basket after each shot. Following Brooks's orders, we begin to overpower the Crusaders, and at the conclusion of the first quarter, we're ahead by 11–9.

We are ragged throughout the ball game and we never really shoot well, but we settle their hash midway through the second quarter: Brooks roams the baseline in our wheel offense, jumping to the moon and catching lob passes over the back of their zone. Mitchell keeps the ball in motion and, after missing his first three, finally hits a ceiling-scraping bomb from thirty feet. As the Crusaders wear out, Leo can now beat their zone off his dribble, going one-on-five for a left-handed layup. The next time Leo attempts the same maneuver, the ref whistles him for a palming violation. Leo gasps and spits, but says nothing.

Our lead stretches to 24–16 at the half-time intermission, and there are quartered oranges waiting for us on a tray in the custodian's room. "This is a piece of cake," Leo says. "What a great idea this trip is. Whose idea was it anyway? Oh, yeah. Mine."

Saul is puzzled. "Why are they so nice to us?" he asks Mitchell.

"Because the Bible says that the Jews are the Chosen People," Mitchell says, "and they'd like nothing better than to convert us. They're nice to us because Jesus was a Jew. Because they respect our covenant with the Lord of the Old Testament. But don't get used to it, kiddo. We'll be spit on plenty before this whole trip is over."

We come out like gangbusters to start the third quarter. Ron rips the ball from #1 twice running, and dashes wall-to-wall for layups. He's snarling on defense, and #1 calls for the sheriff to take over the ballhandling chores. By now I've learned the big boy's pet move and I put his game on ice. Leo stuns the crowd when he dribbles behind his back, but I hear #1 muttering, "What a hot dog."

Kevin is nervous when he enters the game. His yarmulke falls to the floor just as his man catches a pass. Confused, Kevin bends to retrieve the yarmulke and his man dribbles to the hoop for an unmolested score. The crowd laughs good-naturedly and Kevin responds by rebounding like a fiend. Then he draws a rousing cheer when he drills home one of his radical one-handers from the top of the key.

After three quarters, our lead is 35–20.

The fans get a kick out of Saul, calling him "Goliath." They roar when he converts a sweeping hook from the baseline. As the game winds down, Saul captures an offensive rebound, leaps again, then reaches over and above the rim to gently drop the ball through the goal. He calls it his drop shot, and three old ladies faint.

Just before the game ends, Rev. Ref calls a hacking foul against Ron, who says too loudly, "That's a fucked-up call and you're a fucked-up ref!" Mothers place their hands over their children's ears. When an old man behind the scoreboard shouts, "Time!" the final score is 49–28.

The rest of us rush for the shower before the hot water is used up, but Leo always storms the table demanding to see the scorebook: Brooks has 12 points, Leo, 11, I have 9, Mitchell, 6, Ron, 5, Saul, 4, and Kevin has 2.

We take quick showers and the hot water lasts until Saul is in full-lather. "Anybody hurting?" Mitchell wants to know. Nope. Then he cautions us to "behave" once we go back upstairs: "Ron and Leo? This means you."

By the time we reenter the main hall, long tables have already been assembled to hold the food, and several smaller tables and chairs have been set up on the court for the comfort of the diners. Everybody seems to be waiting for us, and indeed the preacher motions us to the head of the line.

What a feast! Huge platters of chicken (fried, broiled, and baked—do only Jews eat boiled chicken?), several large hams, roast turkeys and roast beefs, racks of pork ribs, legs of lamb. There are overflowing bowls of mashed potatoes, candied yams, coleslaw, macaroni salad, various stuffings, gravies, and salads. Also, pitchers of ice water, milk, and buttermilk. Homemade rolls and hot cross buns. A crock of freshly churned butter. Shivering mounds of Jell-O. Dozens of cakes and pies.

Leo has wormed his way to the front and is reaching for a fried chicken breast when the preacher says loudly, "Thank you, Lord, for this bounty set before us. For this fellowship. And for this opportunity, dear Lord, to welcome these our special guests and remind ourselves of your divine plan. For all these things and more, we thank You. Amen." (Kevin has instinctively removed his porkpie hat. And later, I give him an insistent "pssst!" when he reaches for a slice of ham.)

"Amen!" Leo says a beat behind everyone else. "Let's dig in! The best kind of food is free food."

The seven of us find a large table in the rear corner of the hall. From time to time, a young boy, a starched matron, or an old man stops by to congratulate us on our "performance." The rest stare at us from a discreet distance. We're too busy eating to bother talking to one another.

When all the food is gone (only Leo has the gumption to line up for a second helping), it's our task to help clear the chairs and tables for the dance to follow. Leo fetches one chair at a time, moving with a dainty precision. Kevin carries four chairs as well as a table. We labor alongside several smiling teenagers and the whole business takes only twenty minutes.

It's a square dance with an ancient fiddler and another teenaged towhead playing banjo. The caller is a turkey-necked old-timer with the hint of a southern accent. The first tune is "Turkey in the Straw," followed by "Virginia Reel." The dancers whirl and whoop, skirts flying, boots thumping. The preacher cordially invites us to "join the fun," but we decline.

Ron, Leo, and I chance to be standing near the fruit punch when gray-haired #1 approaches. He wears neatly pressed gray pants, a natty blue blazer, a starched white shirt replete with celluloid collar, and a bright red bow tie. Patting his jacket above his heart he says, "You gentlemen inclined to join me for a little snort behind the wood shed?"

Sure.

We follow him out the front door and into the parking lot. As we leave the building, Mitchell catches my attention, raising his eyebrows to ask what we're up to. I just shake my head. None of his fucking business.

In the fragile shadow of the bell tower, #1 produces a silver flask and passes it around. "Here's mud in your eye," he says merrily as he takes a slug.

"L'chayim," I say. "To your health."

"We really appreciate you guys coming here and helping us out," he says, wiping his lips with his sleeve. "I know you're not getting all that much money, but this little shindig here will go a long ways to help restore our church. Yessir. This ol' place was built in nineteen-aught-one, so the plumbing needs fixing and the electrical circuits have to be rewired. Anyways . . . It's good to have some genuine excitement around here. We're mostly dairy farmers and corn growers in these parts, so we can still mostly feed ourselves even in bad times . . . Here's looking at you."

Ron takes too long a draught and starts coughing.

"We're all clean-living Republicans up here," #1 continues. "We vote for FDR only because he's from downstate, but we don't like him much. No sir. Used to have a Jew in town, we did. Had a little watch and clock repair shop over to Applewood Drive. Quiet fellow, always got along pretty good. Him and his wife. Weren't enough business to keep him here, though. Left after a year or so . . . Down the hatch! Yessir. Won a county championship five years back when my boy played. Yessir."

"He's a tough kid," I say.

"Maybe yes. Maybe no. But you sure did lock him up and throw away the key. You fellows are good. Smart. Big. Quick. It's a pleasure to be in the same game with you. Yessir. Where's your next stopover?"

"Buffalo," I say. "Tomorrow night."

"Zatso? Who you playing?"

"Don't really know." I shrug. "Another church, I think."

"Be careful," he says, his words beginning to bump into each other. "Lotta Polish folks over that way. Don't take kindly to no Jews, no how, no way . . . What say? One last one for the road?"

Back inside, Ron is itching to dance, and the preacher eggs him on. When Mitchell nixes the idea, Ron is visibly upset. Pulling Mitchell into a secluded corner, he lashes out. "Who the fuck do you think you are?" Ron says. "You ain't my father!"

Mitchell is also agitated. He smells the booze on Ron's breath and reads him the riot act: If Ron fucks up one more time, we'll abandon him here, there, anywhere. We can play with six if we have to, and we'll each get a bigger share without him. Mitchell didn't approve of Ron in the first place.

The dance breaks up at nine o'clock sharp and we pitch in to clean up. Mostly we carry the pews back into the main hall and reattach them to the floor, a backbreaking job that forces us to crawl about on our hands and knees. Meanwhile, Leo casually pushes a broom and Ron grumbles into his beard as he picks up the trash. By ten-fifteen the joint is spotless and the preacher sidles up to Mitchell, expresses his thanks, and palms Mitchell five twenty dollar bills. "Something extra," the preacher says, because we gave such a "sterling performance."

One of the ubiquitous yellow-haired teens has set up seven cots, several blankets, and real feather pillows off a side aisle right near a furnace vent. The custodian will be knocking around downstairs at six o'clock to rekindle the fire, and services commence at seven-thirty. We're certainly welcome to stay. The preacher shakes our hands and wishes us "Godspeed."

We're much too tired to fuss with one another, and Ron is the first to start snoring. But I can't fall asleep so easily. It's too hot and stuffy so close to the vent. The red lights over the front and side exits, the rose-colored moonlight seeping through the stained-glass windows, all seem to converge on the cross and its burden. Looming over us, his bloody hands reaching out, Jesus and his ransom of blood.

Was he the Messiah? Could the goyim possibly be right? Has nearly two thousand years of our suffering been for naught? How happy these people appear to be here in Glens Falls with their eternally forgiving God-on-a-stick. How simple and uncomplicated their lives are. I'd much rather live here than with the Hasids in Nyack.

And I find myself weeping. If Jesus can forgive me, I'll stay here in this church and offer my soul to him.

But what's that yellow circle around his head? His brain on fire? Is there something dripping from the cross into the baptismal fount? Water. Holy water. Does Jesus have a cleft lip too?

No, I am beyond forgiveness. Beyond redemption.

From Mitchell's Log:
Day One — January 6, 1936 — Sunday

	Today	Total
Mileage	237	237
Expenses	$4.16	$4.16
Income	$100.00	$100.00

Net Income - $95.84
Average Share - $13.69

Won - 1
Lost - 0

DAY 2

It's still dark when I awaken from a vague but menacing dream: I'm lost at sea on a flimsy wooden raft, imperiled by circling sharks. The stars above me are small explosions of pain in God's vast black hands. When suddenly a huge, towering boat looms out of the night, the swan-diving Jesus at the masthead, the prow parting the wind and the water . . . As the dream fades, I can hear a loud metallic scraping from a tunnel leading to the roaring furnace at the center of the earth . . . For a long moment I am dislocated in time and space.

Until, pivoting on my tailbone, I sit erect on the cot with my feet firmly on the floor. Above me, the cross seems unbalanced, about to topple. Below me, the custodian shovels coal. Through the glimmering darkness, I can see Saul two cots over, his phylacteries entwined like a thin serpent around his left arm and his forehead as he prays silently, nodding every time he says *"Adonoi"* as though he were ducking a cosmic knockout punch.

Despite the gusts of warm, dusty air from the vent, my breath turns to icy smoke. 6:32 A.M. Time to wake everybody else. We've all slept in our clothes, and the bathroom's off the corridor leading to the basement. Then we fold the cots, stacking them along with the blankets and pillows in the storage room where the pews were stashed.

"Nice people," I say in passing to Brooks. "They really took care of us."

"Fucking imbeciles," he snaps.

And we're on the road by seven, headed for Buffalo.

Ron drives, Leo navigates, Kevin and Saul share the backseat while Brooks, Mitchell, and I occupy the crypt. Flexing his long, bony nose, Brooks indicates the seat in front of us. "Look at the two kids getting along," he says. Then he raises his voice in a grand gesture: "Kevin. Saul. What're you two gabbing about?"

"Exes," says Saul.

"And ohs," Kevin adds, almost giggling with delight.

Brooks approves. "That's right, rookies. Study the plays. The more you know, the more you play."

"Rookies!" Leo chirps from the front seat. "Hey, Mitchell! Don't rookies have to do stuff like carry the veterans' bags?"

However reluctant he is to agree with Leo, Mitchell remains mindful of road-trip protocol and the traditional razzing of hooplings. "Yeah," Mitchell says, looking to me and Brooks for confirmation. "You're right, Leo."

"Right as rain," Brooks says. "Bags, balls, groceries, whatever .... Sweep out the fireplace. Tote that bale. That's why God made rookies."

I can only laugh. "Rookies of the worlds unite," I announce. "You have nothing to lose but your playing time."

Leo always laughs loudest. Then we begin chattering about the ball game:

"That was a great shot you made at the start of the fourth quarter, Leo. That away to use the whole rim."

"Shooter's touch, buddy. Comes from clean living."

"Hey, keep your eyes on the fucking road."

"Mitchell," Saul asks. "How come Ron isn't a rookie?"

"Mind your own beeswax, Frankenstein. Jailbirds ain't no kind of rookies."

"Frankenstein," Leo says. "I love it."

"Say, what kind of leather is on these seats, anyway? Pigskin?"

"You mean the car ain't kosher? Let me out."

"Horseskin."

"Foreskin."

"How come this armrest has freckles and a wart?"

"Look at those two kids still yakking away. Pretty soon they'll want to travel in cahoots. Stay in the same seats, share the same rotations. Just another logistical nightmare."

Most of us fade out and snooze lightly for an hour or so, then wake up demanding breakfast. In the meantime we've returned to the outskirts of Albany, heading south before picking up Route 20 West, when another of yesterday's themes is repeated: Saul wants breakfast at a dairy restaurant, Brooks favors a deli, et cetera. Each of us still afraid to swim in unknown and perilous waters, still clinging to the familiar wreckage of our imaginary lives.

Everybody has an opinion except Kevin as Ron steers us swiftly through the sleepy streets of the state capital. We notice a profusion of lawyers' shingles and corner taverns, fancy chophouses and repulsive greasy spoons, but no prospect of breakfast that satisfies one and all. When Ron pauses at a stop light, Mitchell offers a compromise: "Let's eat at the very next breakfast-type place we see, no matter what kind of joint it is. Let's place the fate of our taste buds, our stomachs, and our bowels in the hands of God, chance, necessity, Allah, whatever. Agreed?"

Sure.

So, all the cultural, political, economic, and spiritual vectors in the history of Western civilization thereby converge on Aunt Phoebe's Food Emporium on the corner of Farrow Street and Jefferson Avenue. "We can't eat here," Brooks says, pointing at two other signs prominently displayed on the porch of the weatherworn and otherwise peaceable cedar-shingled house—BREAKFAST SERVED 6:00 TO CLOSING and WHITE TRADE ONLY.

"A deal is a deal," I say to Brooks. "It's dangerous to tempt God."

"Not to mention Allah, chance,and necessity," Leo says.

Brooks says he'll wait in the car. "No," I insist. "There's no provision in the bylaws for secession."

Leo is hungry "right now" and doesn't want to drive around "this hick town all day."

Brooks calls for a vote, and another argument ensues over the original disenfranchising of Kevin. "It's his stomach too," I argue.

Brooks yields with annoyance. "All right. All right. You guys are showing your true colors."

"Yeah," says Leo. "White."

We vote to breakfast in Phoebe's by 5–2, with Mitchell unexpectedly siding with Brooks. Muttering that we're "fascists and Nazis," Brooks will enter the restaurant but will not eat. "A hunger strike," he says, "against bigotry."

"If you're not eating," Leo says quickly, "does that mean the rest of us can spend forty cents each?"

"Absolutely not."

Leo clamors for another vote, but we've pushed Brooks far enough.

A thin sour-pussed waitress gives us the once-over while we're waiting to be seated. She wears a large pin on her right breast that says "HI," and her white uniform is immaculate. "You people white?" she asks Leo.

Leo leans forward and pretends to unbuckle his belt. "Honey," he whispers, "my ass is whiter than yours and I'm ready to prove it."

She nods, beyond insulting, then she leads us to a large table around a corner, behind a post and adjacent to the kitchen. Silently, we scour the menus while she waits pencil in hand. I'll have the oatmeal, Leo the corned beef, et cetera. Brooks passes, saying, "I'm on a very strict diet."

After the waitress leaves, Leo has a question for me: "How come you always order oatmeal?"

"How come you always order corned beef hash?"

"Because it tastes good. It's delicious. You can't say the same about oatmeal, can you?"

"You're right, Leo. Oatmeal isn't what I'd call delicious. But there's another, more important reason why I always have it for breakfast. On the road, Leo, there's one consideration that takes precedence over everything else. Over winning, over playing well, even over getting paid, laid, sucked, fucked, and Donald Ducked. And that primary consideration is this, Leo: taking a good shit."

"What?"

"You'll see the light soon enough, with your hash, your pancakes, and your bacon. See how you feel trying to unload a healthy, cleansing shit off in the bushes somewhere, in a patch of poison ivy. Or trying to shit on a cold toilet seat in a bathroom in the Church of the Most Sacred Pancreas with the Cossacks pounding on the door. On the other hand, a humble bowl of oatmeal moves like a gentle broom through your digestive system, inducing quick, reliable, and extremely satisfying dumps. To say nothing of totally efficient wipes."

When our grub comes, the eggs are runny, my oatmeal is watery, and Leo's hash is chunked with pieces of gristle. We fill up on toast and leave no tip.

As we approach the car, Mitchell pulls frantically on my sleeve. "Look at that!" he says. "Look at the driver's seat, quick before Ron gets in. That fucking *ganef* stole a pillow!"

Inside the crypt, the three of us sit upright, propped against either side of the car, Brooks and I opposite Mitchell. "He's going to get us all in trouble," Mitchell fumes, nodding toward Ron. "Sooner or later! A thief! A fucking thief!" Mitchell is choking on his righteousness. "Are we even sure he's Jewish?"

"Why?" I ask. "Jews don't steal?"

"Talk to him, Aaron," Mitchell pleads. "He'll listen to you."

"Sure . . . Hey, Ron!"

"What?"

"Don't steal any more fucking pillows, okay?"

"Okay."

"Two fucking assholes," Mitchell grumbles.

We re-cross the Hudson River at a small, nameless bridge, then drive west on 20. Dairy farms at every crossroads. The wild, unplowed fields strewn with sharp-edged slate and rounded fieldstones, the hillsides choked with oaks, the lowlands with stark white birches. We pause at a red light in a small town whose name I miss. A quaint village green with its white-gabled church. A scattering of Model Ts. And a huge dappled bay pulling a creaking wagon. Mitchell appears to be asleep.

"Brooks," I say. "Tell me something, Brooks. We've known each other for a long time and we've always been on the up-and-up with each other. We've played ball together, we've gotten drunk, we even fucked the same girl once."

"Melissa the Machine from Madison Avenue. Yeah, so?"

"We're both hurting right now, suffering. But we've always hung together. Right? Even when you were a nutso kid. Even when you were a crazed Commie."

"Yeah, so? What is this, true confessions?"

"I want to ask you something about the people we saw at the church in Glens Falls . . . To me, they look like decent folks. Not harming anybody, just living their lives trying to stay on a righteous path. So, tell me, how can you be so negative about them? What's your complaint with Glens Falls?"

"I object to their mindless adherence to the system," he says, but his tone is so smooth that I don't know whether to believe him. "They don't care, or don't know, about the plight of the poor, the colored, all those who are downtrodden by capitalism. When the system crumbles, so will the good folks in Glens Falls. Their seemingly idyllic life is built upon the blood and sweat of others."

"Do me a favor, Brooks. Save the polemics for the street corners and talk about them as people. Are they so evil? Exactly whom do they exploit? Whose sweat, whose blood but their own?"

"Don't be so naive, Aaron. That's always been your problem."

"How come every time I disagree with you, I'm being naive? Can't we just have a simple difference of opinion?"

"There's nothing simple about it," Brooks says, a flare of passion finally brightening his voice. "Lookit. What are the working and living conditions of the factory workers who built the plows, the tractors, the shoes, the clothing, everything that the farmers in Glens Falls need to conduct their own businesses? Hey, farmers are exploited too. They're also at the mercy of the Wall Street jugglers. I repeat, when the whole system collapses, so will the righteous, God-fearing folks in Glens Falls . . . Shit. The whole shebang is falling apart already. Have a good look around you, Aaron. Read the newspapers. Capitalism doesn't work. Unless . . . unless you belong to the two percent of the population that owns ninety percent of the country's wealth. If you're a member of the privileged class, then the whole damn thing works like a clock. But it's really a house of cards, Aaron. Any economic system built on oppression is doomed to fall."

Mitchell has been awake all this time, snapping his eyes open and saying, "That's bullshit, Brooks. You're the one who's naive." (There's always been an antagonistic edge to their friendship. If Brooks tossed a frantic alley cat at my chest, he'd throw one into Mitchell's face. To Mitchell, Brooks remains the neighborhood loony. To Brooks, Mitchell is a pedantic *putz*. The wonder is how well they're attuned on the basketball court.) "You call it 'the system,'" Mitchell continues, "but all 'it' is, is people trying to earn a living and some people doing it better than others."

"That's too simplistic," Brooks counters, waving his hand to erase Mitchell's argument.

Mitchell laughs. "You say *potayto*, I say *potahto*. Face it, Brooks, the system will never collapse because whenever things get too shaky, the people who make the rules will just increase the handouts. Home Relief. Social Security. The WPC. The CCC. The people with the whips will do whatever they have to do to keep their whips in hand."

"I disagree," Brooks says stoutly. "It's a fact that more people than ever are voting on the Socialist-party line. Communist-party membership is skyrocketing. Look around. Listen to the radio. America's new national anthem is 'Brother Can You Spare a Dime?' Meanwhile, the lines at the soup kitchens are winding around the block. Evictions and foreclosures happen every day. People getting thrown out of their homes. Furniture piled on the sidewalk. You've seen it yourself."

"No question,' Mitchell says, "but there's one vital factor that you're not seeing. There's one across-the-board remedy for every woe, for every injustice, for every fly in your ointment."

"This I've got to hear," Brooks smirks.

"War."

"Against whom?" I ask. "Mexico?"

"War against Germany."

"That's ridiculous," Brooks says, his hands working again. "Hitler is a fool, a clown, a housepainter."

"Wrong," Mitchell insists. "Hitler's building an army, an air force, a navy. And we're told by our people over there that there are now in Germany, and will continue to be, pogroms like the world has never seen."

"But Mitchell," I say, laughing in spite of myself, "who cares about Jews being killed? No one ever has before."

"Wait and see."

Brooks resolutely maintains that Germany is no threat to America. "It was the big American industries that privately financed Hitler, that built up Germany's economy and military so that Germany would be capable of destroying the Soviet Union. In the capitalists' eyes, the enemy is communism, not fascism. That's because communists are ungodly, unyielding, unpredictable. And any rich, pious practitioner of capitalism can always cut some kind of sweetheart deal with a dictator.

"Mark my words," Mitchell says ominously, "Hitler will swallow all the small nonallied countries in Eastern Europe. Then he'll turn on England and France, and that'll pull us into the fire. That's the real reason why America is subsidizing Hitler. War is the ultimate spur to industry. What other situation can you imagine that creates and consumes goods like war does? A good healthy war also kills off large portions of the available workforce, so unemployment disappears. War is the savior of capitalism. And they'll sell it like they sell soap. Hurrah for the red-white-and-blue. A nice righteous war also gives the government an excuse to crack down on so-called 'subversive' organizations. Forget about America, Brooks. I don't care what Uncle Joe says, there'll never be a revolution here. We've already had ours. The only thing to do is say 'Fuck it', then start all over and build an ideal state in Palestine."

"You don't solve a problem by running away," says Brooks.

"And you don't solve a problem by sticking your head up your ass and hollering, 'Revolution!'"

"That's what you say."

"Fuck you too."

We gas-up in Geneva just past the northernmost tip of Lake Seneca, and find an appealing family-owned Italian restaurant (Luigi's) just two miles west of there. It's a cozy, wood-burnished place, and our luncheon allowance is fifty cents each. Since it's game day, we all have minestrone soup, salad, and steak. The waitresses are plump and polite, and the other patrons ignore us.

While we're waiting for our food, I call Max's office collect from a pay phone in the vestibule. "Did you win?" is his first concern and he insists that I recap the entire ball game. Only then does he start nagging at me: "Aaron, Aaron. You want to desert your wife? That's your own personal business. But you can't just walk away from such a good, steady job. Look around you, Aaron. People would kill for a job like that. Before you left, I thought you were going to talk to the principal, what's his name, Silverman? You promised me you'd talk to him."

"Yeah, Max, I know I promised. But I thought it over and decided that I really don't care about teaching anymore."

"Ach. You say that now. But later, when you need a job, you'll sing a different tune."

"Max."

"Ach, Aaron. You're such a *shmendrick*. What am I going to do with you?"

"Max, please."

"All right already. Listen, *boychik*. I did some fancy stepping to cover your *tochis*. When you come back to New York, we'll get some *fakockta* doctor to sign a paper and you'll be all right. Aaron, you've got to think about what you're doing. You can't go off half-cocked . . . Listen. The secretary says there's a telephone call I've got to take. At least one of us has to earn a living. Call me tomorrow. *Shalom*, Aaron. Don't do anything stupid."

Heading back to the table, I realize that I never asked Max (nor did he volunteer to tell me) how Judy was doing.

While we eat, everybody complains that the tile floor in Glens Falls has left them with aching feet. "Wear an extra pair of socks tonight," Mitchell suggests. "Make sure to put the dry ones on first, next to your skin." Then he previews tonight's game: We're to play another fund-raiser, this one at St. Jude's High School against a team sponsored by the church. Our payoff is two hundred dollars with a fat one-hundred-dollar bonus should we win. No meals. No lodging. From here, we're due in Cleveland tomorrow night to play against the Redheads, an all-girl touring team out of Dallas. Then we'll travel all day Wednesday back to Ossining for a game in Sing Sing on Thursday night. Friday, Saturday and Sunday we're scheduled to play at various stops in Illinois and Indiana. Any questions? "It's all there," Mitchell says, "in your itineraries."

We all look at Leo, expecting him to say something about boxing out the Redheads or penetrating their defense and taking them to the hole. Instead, he asks for the whereabouts of the bathroom. "If I don't shit," he groans, "I'm going to explode."

Mitchell has capitulated and put us on the honor system. Kevin wants to drive and Mitchell will read the map. Saul, Leo, and Ron are in the crypt, leaving me and Brooks in the backseat. By removing our shoes, Brooks and I can find an extra few inches to stretch our long legs. The trade-off is that our feet get cold.

We're just under way when Brooks nudges up against me. "You know?" he says, "it wasn't your fault, Aaron. You're torturing yourself for no good reason. God doesn't know about the baby, and if he did, he wouldn't care. Let it go, Aaron."

"I don't want to talk about it."

So we drive in silence, belching, farting, and trying hard to fall asleep. Near Rochester, the sky turns gray and thick pieces of snow begin to fall. Kevin gears down to a steady twenty-five miles per hour. "Not to worry," Mitchell announces, "we've got chains for the drive wheels just in case." Beside me, Brooks falls asleep with his face clenched in a private fury.

The baby couldn't nurse, so the doctors decided to nourish her through her umbilical cord, and her tiny body was strapped down so that she wouldn't shake loose of the needle. The palate would eventually heal on its own, they said (if she lived long enough), and even though they worried about "growth planes," they crudely stitched her lip. One kindly doctor told me, "Her brain is irreparably damaged from the pressure of the fluid. She'll undoubtedly be retarded, but we don't know to what degree. Personally, I think the best thing might be if the child failed to survive. It would certainly save everybody a lot of heartache."

So they left her there in an oxygen tent, wailing and suffering. In another time, she would have been taken to the woods and abandoned to the wolves. After three days, she developed a systemic infection and was dead within another twenty-four hours.

Meanwhile, Judy lay drugged and oblivious in her hospital bed. Her mother stayed away ("I detest hospitals," she said), but Cy sat patiently at his daughter's bedside throughout all the long visiting hours. From time to time we exchanged formal declarations of remorse. Even so, his rigid, unforgiving stare insisted that my genes were the faulty ones.

On my own, I decided to have the body cremated. (Max made some sort of discount bargain with the mortician, from whom he later bought the Queen of Spades.) Cremation. My intention was to free little Sarah Pearl's soul forever from her mutilated body. Then, with her ashes stuffed into a small, clay-colored urn, I took the subway to Coney Island.

Without knowing exactly why, I found myself on Surf Avenue, standing in front of a freak show. There was a large billboard above the entrance showing several stylized drawings of the featured "exhibits." A gorgeous young woman wearing a scanty bra and panties—her skin was covered with some kind of brown spots and she had long fingernails and two fanglike teeth. The sign identified her as "Sheema, the Leopard girl." Other attractions were "The World's Tallest Man," "The Tattooed Lady," and "Komar the Great," an armless man who did "astounding" things with his feet. The billboard also promised a "startling and terrifying surprise."

I paid my dime and entered a semi-illuminated room with a small stage at one end faced by several rows of institutional folding chairs. There were about ten people already seated and the "show" was in progress. A neatly lettered sign propped up on an easel told me that the forlorn individual seated on the stage was the resident giant. After I folded myself into a chair, the giant's stare met my own. He tried to smile (out of kinship perhaps), but the humiliation of where he was quickly crushed his face back into a frozen mask of lump-jawed tragedy. Through a tiny speaker, a metallic voice spouted all the relevant details: He was seven foot one, weighed 427 pounds, and was thirty-five years of age. His name was never mentioned. When the voice ceased, the giant arose, picked up a huge cane, and limped off the stage. I could see the outline of a pair of steel braces running from his knees to his shoes.

(All the while I cradled the urn in my lap. What a good baby. Daddy's sweet little girl.)

A teenager with badly pitted skin came out onto the stage and put another sign on the easel. As Komar the Great came striding forth, a young couple sitting nearby gasped loudly and then started giggling to each other. Komar was a toothless old man who squirmed out of his unbuttoned short-sleeved shirt and automatically displayed his stumps. The speaker voice started up again, cueing Komar as he manipulated a knife and fork with his feet, drank a glass of water, wrote his name with a long pencil, and finished up with a flourish by picking his nose with his toes. The young couple laughed.

After Komar exited stage left, the kid came out again to

announce for an extra five cents we could all get to see the show's mysterious featured performer—the Human Platypus. The only spectators who sprang for it were the laughing young couple.

But I had seen enough. (Did you like the show, Sarah? Maybe if you're good, Daddy will buy you some cotton candy. Maybe when you grow up, you can be in a freak show too.) I wandered around for a while, showing Sarah the Ferris wheel, the roller coaster, even the parachute jump where it all started. As I passed Nathan's Famous, I saw the same pair of giggling sightseers, balancing two hamburgers, some french fries, and two orange drinks.

"Hey," I called to them. "Weren't you just in the freak show?"

"Yeah," the guy said. "You were there too."

"Right. But I was wondering . . . I saw you go inside to see the Human Platypus. What was it? I mean, what did it look like?"

He shrugged. "I don't know. It was dark in there and something was wriggling around on the floor. It was too dark to see."

Later, I walked out to the end of a stone-piled jetty, cupped the urn in my hands, and watched the tide recede. I must have sat there for hours, searching the waters, watching the waves retreat, seeking some kind of image in the foam. I stared transfixed until the tide finally pulled the ocean away. The tideshelf was strewn with broken shells, seaweed, and green garbage. Finally, I climbed to my feet. Then I poured the ashes into my right hand and gently sprinkled them into the retreating waves. (Goodbye, sweetie pie. Daddy loves you.) As I hurled the urn as far out to sea as I could, I howled my misery. A passing seagull shrieked in sympathy.

The snowfall thickens, covering the fields, the towns, the road, in a virgin's robe. The single windshield wiper works from the top down, streaky and erratic, the rubber blade frayed, a detail Mitchell has overlooked.

"Brooksie? You awake?"

He sighs. "No, I'm talking in my sleep."

"I've got to ask you something, Brooks. Seriously."

"So ask."

"What the fuck happened to us, Brooks? We had the world by the short hairs, remember? Big men on campus. Money. Laughs. The ol' boop-boop-a-doop. It was ours. The whole fucking jackpot. Now look at us. If we didn't have basketball, we'd have nothing."

"It's not us," Brooks says. "The whole country's falling apart and we're just innocent bystanders."

"Bullshit! There's nothing innocent about either of us. I'm so loaded with guilt that I can't stand being alone. And you? You're a total bedbug. Who else but the Communist party would have you?"

"Lay off, Aaron. You asshole. Why are you being so nasty? Don't take your problems out on me."

The snow falls, offering to forgive all our sins.

After a while, Brooks says softly, hopefully, "Maybe this trip will save us. Maybe somewhere, somehow, we'll both find . . . something."

"You know something, Brooks? Maybe Mitchell's got the right idea . . . about Palestine. About forging a new country. About starting all over."

"I can't imagine living in a desert, Aaron. Whenever I go to the beach, I break out in hives."

The snow persists and darkness falls as ruthlessly as a guillotine. Caught in the beams of the headlights, a roadside sign says:

BUFFALO — 24 miles

NIAGARA FALLS — 36 miles

Even though the traffic is scarce, the snowfall makes Kevin uncertain behind the wheel, accelerating, braking, driving with an abrupt, spastic rhythm. "There's no rush," Mitchell says to soothe him. "We've got plenty of time." Kevin nods, and settles into a groove at twenty-five miles per hour, the circular speedometer barely spinning behind its small, fragile window.

Everybody is awake and alert because of the weather. "Hey, guys," I say brightly. "When I was a kid my father used to tell me that the rain was really God's tears falling. If that's so, then what's snow?"

"God's dandruff," Saul says in a deep tone from the crypt.

"And a hurricane," Leo chirps, "is a divine fart."

We all jump into the game: Mitchell supposes that volcanoes are pimples and boils. Fog is bad breath. Hail is spit. Earthquakes are heavenly hiccups. Meteorites are purged kidney stones. And floods? "Hallelujah," says Saul, "for the Lord cometh." What about lightning? Brooks suggests a flash of pain from a bad tooth. A fire in a coal mine is a hemorrhoid. A tornado is a bad cough. "What about shit?" Leo wants to know. But before we can exhaust our scatological theology, Kevin hits the brakes.

There are nasty skid marks on the road ahead of us and an old-fashioned Model T is angled into a ditch. The wayward car's headlamps are still burning and a cloud of hot smoke bellows up through the hood vents. An elderly woman sits behind the wheel, furiously, uselessly, gunning the engine. We pull up behind and Mitchell assigns Saul to stand on the road and wave a towel to caution any other passing traffic. Leo spreads out luxuriously across both mattresses while the rest of us advance on the Model T.

When she sees us, the old woman scrambles out of her car, babbling in some hysterical language incomprehensible to any of us. Her eyes beg for mercy and her arms press her purse tightly against her heart. "It's okay," says Mitchell. "We're here to help you." He makes reassuring gestures, pointing at her car, at the Black Lady, even at his own heart and head, forming salutary circles with his thumbs and fingers, miming "O.K." But the old woman remains convinced of our evil intent.

Kevin is our designated mechanic, so he reaches inside the Model T's opened door and turns the key to still the engine. Then he moves to the front of the car and lifts the hood vents to inspect the wires and plugs. Next, Kevin pulls a handkerchief from his pants pockets and slowly unscrews the radiator cap that's perched atop the hood, releasing a small sighing sound that slides into silence. "Looks good," he says before resealing the hood.

Kevin then ambles to the rear of the car, crouches, and quickly announces that the left rear wheel is stuck in frozen mud at the bottom of the ditch. The woman is sobbing by now, frantically crossing herself with her right hand. "Let's rape the old hag," says Ron. "That's what she really wants us to do anyway." Instead, Ron is dispatched to reposition the Black Lady so that her headlights will better illuminate the ditch and the buried wheel. Meanwhile, Kevin slides behind the wheel of the Model T, shifts into low gear, and tries to ease the car back onto the road.

"No dice," says Mitchell. "It's only cutting the wheel deeper. We'll have to push it out." Saul offers protection from nonexistent traffic, Leo is blissfully asleep, and Kevin's at the wheel, leaving the rest of us to try to rescue the car. Grunting, straining, slipping, cursing. Finally, the offending wheel comes free and the car lurches forward. "Hurrah!" says Mitchell. And Kevin is quick on the gas as the car slowly crawls up the shallow ditch before shuddering to an ominous stop.

"Son of a bitch!" says Brooks. "What now?"

Kevin leaves the cockpit to crawl in the snow-crusted mud, reporting that the rear axle is caught up on a rock, that the same damn wheel is now suspended off the ground. More pushing and lifting have no effect except that the old woman is now shrieking: *"Aliyam! Schlavakah! Aliyam!"*

"We'll have to dig it out," Mitchell says mournfully.

The shovels are stashed under the mattresses, and Leo is distinctly unhappy at being awakened from his kindly dreams. As Leo climbs from the crypt spewing maledictions, the old lady is certain she's witnessing the devil's own resurrection and she scrabbles in her purse for her rosary beads.

It takes well over an hour to dig around the huge stone, a tricky business lest the axle slip unawares and crush a carelessly exposed limb. We take turns shoveling, two at a time, but our snarling curses, the woman's yelping, and Mitchell's annoying instructions continue unabated.

"Fucking car! Fucking snow! Whose fucking idea was this?"

"Shasta! K'vich! Aieee!"

"A little more to the left there. Careful, don't break the shovel."

Actually, I enjoy the digging, the sweating in the open air, the crude rhythm of the mindless labor . . . At last, the stone falls backward and the car rolls free. Kevin plots an escape route and we push, pull and drive the stubborn old car back onto the road. As soon as she can, the woman leaps into the car and flees from the devil's legions with nary a word of thanks. Leaving us by the roadside, sweating and panting.

"Fuck her," says Leo. "We should've left her there."

Back inside the Black Lady, Ron produces a soggy grocery bag containing a thick, shiny tube of bologna, a loaf of white bread, and a quart of milk. Several cans of cat food and a box of steel wool are tossed out the window. As Mitchell chews on a dry bologna sandwich, he says, "Good job, Ron." And Brooks can't help laughing.

We get turned around and lost in Buffalo. The heavy snowfall has virtually cleared the streets of pedestrians, and the few we encounter are unable to locate St. Jude's High School. We pull to the curb near a neat brick house in a residential neighborhood to ask directions from an old man out shoveling his walk. He answers our question with one of his own: "You fellers lookin' for a church to bomb or sumpin'? There's one 'bout five blocks southa here on Niles Street you might be int'rested in. A jigaboo church. Cross my heart 'n' swear to Jesus I won' tell nobody."

We finally find an open-for-business gas station. "Just about to close on up," the proprietor says, a mustachioed middle-aged man wearing a green plaid mackinaw. "Sarey rings me up on the tellyphone an' tells me when dinner's almost ready, an' that's when I lock up an' go on home."

We've still got a half-tankful of gas, but Mitchell insists on a fill-up "just in case." The air bubbles blurp and gurgle in the red-dyed gasoline bowl atop the pump. *Ching!* the meter chimes as each gallon registers. "Sure enough," the gaskeeper says, and he directs us the four miles from here to there.

We arrive at St. Jude's at 6:35, barely twenty-five minutes before the scheduled game time. It's an old, massive gray-bricked structure, replete with a bell tower and looking more like a cathedral than a school. As in Glens Falls, there's a clergyman waiting for us on the front steps. This one is enormously fat beneath his black, fur-trimmed coat. He seems almost immobile, and there's some clogging of breath in the depths of him, some wheeze of depravity and avarice.

"Where the hell've you guys been?" he asks, and his face reddens from the effort. "Everybody's getting tired of waiting for you. C'mon, hustle it up."

He leads us toward a locker room in the basement, points at the door, then huffs and puffs his way back up the stairs. The room is cold, dark and dank as a dungeon. The lockers are fit for midgets and the dressing benches are barely shin-high. But several signs taped to the gray, peeling walls indicate that the school's football team uses this same space:

A HARD HIT IS JUST LIKE A XMAS PRESENT—

BETTER TO GIVE THAN RECEIVE.

JESUS IS A WINNER—ARE YOU?

Our uniforms are still wet, and Kevin rushes to get dressed. "Slow down," Mitchell counsels. "Relax. They can't start without us."

"That's right," Brooks adds. "Take your time. The other team has been gearing up all day for a seven o'clock start. The longer we can make them wait, the sooner their legs'll turn to rubber. We want to stall, to keep them moving around the court as long as possible."

We're just about ready to go when Ron enters the room (nobody realized he was gone) and delivers his scouting report: About two thousand spectators at a buck each and there are uniformed cops at every turning. The home team is small and slow, but built like weight lifters. They have only two reliable shooters, #17 and #33. "And the court," says Ron, "is surrounded by a thick chicken-wire fence."

"Oh, shit!" Mitchell moans. "A fucking cage."

The cage apparatus is a relic from the late teens and early twenties. Normally, the taut wire fencing (or sometimes rope netting) was set up contiguous with the court's boundary lines and secured by a combination of poles and cables. Originally, the idea was to prevent overly rambunctious fans from storming the court and assaulting players and/or referees. Because the fencing was considered part of the playing area, the ball was constantly in play. Teams that habitually competed inside cages became adept at advancing the ball by throwing unexpected passes high off the fencing. Cage basketball was also notorious for being a much rougher style of play. A careless player was apt to be sent crashing against the fence like a hockey player being checked into the sideboards.

Most importantly, the cage also permitted the home teams to install several extra rows of expensive courtside seats. I can remember an old "cager" who used to play at Henry Street when I was a mere hoopling. With the slightest prompting, he would gladly testify to the dangers of playing basketball inside a cage, swearing that he once required surgery after an infection resulted when an overzealous fan reached through the fence and stuck him in the ass with a hat pin. On the flip side, any team fortunate enough to win on the road had the option of remaining safely within the cage until the irate fans left the building.

There's a caged court still extant in Erie, Pennsylvania, where Mitchell, Brooks, and I played a money tournament just last spring. And Brooks tells the uninitiated among us of the special strategies involved in cage ball. "Keep the ball in the middle of the court," he advises. "And if you can, try to stay away from the fence. However, under the basket it *is* possible to push off the fence to help create a rebounding space for yourself. Let's try . . ."

At this point we are interrupted by the wheezing priest, choking on his white collar and sweating under a magnificently flowing gown. "C'mon!" he says, clapping his meaty hands in a frenzy. "Right now, or I'll declare the game null and forfeit!" An empty threat, but we hurry up the steps and follow the noise into the gym. It's already seven-twenty.

We must forge our way through the crowd to reach a small

gateway into the cage. They boo us all along the way, calling us "Sheenies" and "Christ killers." Our sense that there is some risk seems plausible and we feel like sacrificial lambs. None of the cops are on hand as several obstreperous fans reach out to manhandle us. Following Brooks's lead, we form a flying wedge and quickly bust into the cage.

Once inside, we exchange curious glances with the home team. In their blood-red uniforms, they look especially vicious. Most of the players have pig-bristle haircuts, several have tattoos on the shanks of their muscular arms (in various combinations, a flaming cross, a snake, and a broken heart). Their tallest player is only six-five, but they all show bulging bodies, a Viking horde only halfheartedly converted to the Cross of Pain.

The two refs are in striped shirts, and as we investigate our end of the cage, they're both shooting layups along with the St. Jude's Jaspars. Brooks approaches one of the refs, insisting that since the visitors' bench lies outside the cage, a cop be positioned to protect Saul and Kevin. With remarkable foresight, Brooks also requests that someone be sent at game's end to oversee the safety of our car. "Could be," says the ref, a delicate-boned man, beaky, vigilant, like a well-groomed vulture. Forthwith, the ref confers with #17, who nods his approval, and a squat policeman is summoned to sit on one of the five folding chairs provided for us. This #17 has red hair and an oft-broken nose that doglegs to the left. A sharpshooter with a built-in head fake.

We huddle inside the cage. "Don't take any shit from these guys," Brooks says. "And remember, there's a hundred-dollar bonus for winning."

There are no pregame introductions, so we simply assume our customary positions for the opening tip-off. I extend my hand across the circle to #17, but he rudely disregards my offer and says, "Fuck you, Jew bastard." Subsequently, I feel more than justified to ignore the thin-boned ref as he tosses the ball into the air. Instead of leaping in contention for the game's initial possession, I whip my right elbow at #17's face. The bone whizzes just short of his nose and he clumsily taps the ball to #33.

On offense, the Jaspars run a three-man weave, with #17 and another big man picking for each other across the lane in a high-low variation. Sometimes, one of the bigs steps back and picks for a guard. After #17 sets a pick, he wants to flash toward the ball and either catch and shoot or catch and go. It's easy enough for us to stuff their offense and, in their impatience, they'll readily throw up hasty shots, then storm the boards.

On defense they play a compact 2-1-2, the universal zone. The difference tonight is that whenever one of us tries cutting through the middle, we get slammed from all sides like the steel pellet in a pinball machine. Their obvious strategy is to restrict our offense to long shots from the perimeter.

An average college team will convert approximately one of three outside shots. Pro teams are expected to shoot thirty-five to thirty-eight percent. With Leo and Mitchell as our top-gunners we anticipated shooting forty to forty-two percent from long range. Unfortunately, the home team provides the basketball, and this old leather model is blackened by age, its pebbled surface worn smooth and its laces raised and loosened to discourage any passing fancies.

"The ball's too fucking heavy," Leo complains, and it is, subtracting perhaps two or even three feet from our normal long-range attack.

When he overhears Leo bitching, #17 laughs lightly and says, "It's the home-court advantage." Curiously, #17 says nothing directly to me, and even though he continues blasting away at my teammates, he exhibits perfect sportsmanlike behavior whenever I'm in his vicinity.

Leo does hit a twenty-foot set shot, Brooks drives the baseline for an off-balance flipper, Mitchell bottoms the net with a running hook, and after stealing a sloppy pass, Ron beats everybody downcourt. That's all the scoring we can accomplish in the first ten minutes of play.

At the other end, they pound us on the offensive boards, jumping over our backs in cahoots with the refs. "Shut up and play," the thin ref sneers when we protest. "One more word and you're outta here."

It's a slow-paced, bruising ball game, their rhythm, not ours. Even though we're the beneficiary of several questionable palming and traveling calls, we trail 9–8 at the quarter break.

"A bad sign," Brooks says in the huddle. "They'll get all the calls in the second half. Hey, big guys. We've got to box out."

The crowd is ornery, booing whenever we score. On those rare occasions when we're attempting free throws, the fans hold their noses and loudly honk. For the entire ball game we shoot 1–6 from the foul line.

Midway through the second quarter, as I foolishly run along the sideline, #33 bumps me into one of the support poles. I'm trying to find my legs when somebody tosses a cupful of soda into my face, stinging my eyes. While I stagger into the attack zone, a routine pass bounces off my hands, giving #17 a breakaway layup.

Leo can't piss in the ocean. Poor Saul can't move two steps without getting elbowed, pushed, or tripped. "Kike!" the crowd chants. "Kike! Kike!" We switch our defensive assignments after #17 connects with two long set shots and Ron shuts him down. For the rest of the game, Ron and #17 snarl at one another, eager for an excuse to fight.

Meanwhile, I am shotless and scoreless. Meanwhile, the old-timey carbon lights flicker and crackle overhead. Every so often, a small piece of carbon ash descends to anoint my head and adhere to my sweaty shoulders. During time-outs a small red-haired youngster sweeps the floor with a splintered broom.

Number 33 is a cheap-shot artist and I am forced to protect my teammates: Off the ball, away from the officials' scrutiny, I present #33 with my specialty—the point of my right elbow expertly pronged against the wedge of cartilage attached beneath his sternum, thereby raising a lump that will make his every breath painful for at least a week.

Despite this minor satisfaction, we trail 20–13 when we regroup in the locker room at halftime.

"We obviously can't use our wheel against their zone," Brooks says. "They're just knocking us off our routes. Let's try spotting up in a one-three-one alignment. Leo's at the point. Ron and Mitchell at the wings. I'll play the high post, and Aaron, you follow the ball in the pivot. Let's just whip that fucking medicine ball around and see what we can find. No sense taking a beating for nothing. And yes, I know they're fouling us, but we've still got to seal the boards. Aaron, Saul, everybody. We've also got to pick up the pace on defense, create some turnovers so we can uptempo and steal some easy baskets. Hell, Number Twenty-nine can't score with a fucking pencil. Let's double-team Thirty-three and Seventeen and let Twenty-nine shoot till he comes in his pants. Let's go after it, guys. A hundred smackers is a lot of dough."

On my way back to the cage a black-haired boy about ten years old steps up and proffers his hand. He wears patched overalls and worn boots both oversized and laceless. Smiling, I pause to extend my right hand, but the kid reaches up and pulls hard on my beard. "Ouch!" I yelp. "You little fucker!"

All the fans within listening range are instantly alarmed, advancing toward me, shouting insults. A stout wart-faced woman menaces me with an upraised umbrella. "Dirty Jew!" she squeals.

"Leave the kid alone. All's he's tryin' to do is have himself a good time." Saying nothing, I scoot back into the cage.

The game resumes with #17 backing away from the tip-off and Mitchell getting us going with a step-back setter from twenty-five feet. Mitchell stays on-target, and for a time our defensive intensity rewards us with several broken-court situations. As we battle for the lead, the referees' bias becomes more blatant.

Kevin checks in to give Brooks a breather. When Kevin shoots his favorite one-hander, he is low-bridged by #33 and sent tumbling to the floor. "All ball," says the cadaverous ref, and he dares us to challenge his judgment. Kevin uses the fence to pull himself erect, and a loyal Jaspars' rooter reaches through the diamond-shaped links to scorch Kevin's shoulder with the glowing end of a cigar.

As the game progresses, the fans begin to shake the basket stanchions whenever we launch a long shot. After three quarters, the home team's lead is 28–25.

Saul replaces me to start the last ten-minute session, easily capturing the center-jump. Everybody's tired now, and after our early third-quarter spurt the contest has slowed to a walk. When Ron misfires on a running one-hander, Saul reaches over #17 to snatch the offensive rebound, catching and shooting in the same motion. Just before Saul releases the ball, he is out-and-out punched in the ear by #17. The thin ref waves off the basket, saying "Walking! He shuffled his feet before he was hit!"

Saul is bleeding from his ear and I'm compelled to replace him, my "rest" totaling exactly forty seconds.

Moving the ball (instead of our bodies) on offense, we seem to be somewhat quicker to the play as the game winds down. Mitchell and Brooks finally carry us over the top, and our first lead is 32–30. If the

Jaspars are slower to react, they compensate by playing with an increased recklessness. Conversely, we can't scratch our asses without being whistled for a foul. With twenty-eight seconds remaining, #17 hits a driving hook to put them ahead 37–36.

Brooks calls a time-out. In the huddle, Mitchell and Leo each campaign for the privilege of attempting the last shot. "I'm hot," says Mitchell, "and you're as cold as Santa Claus's dick."

"That only means that you're due to miss and I'm due to hit," Leo counters. "It's a question of mathematics. Probability and percentages."

We all trust Brooks's knowledge and instincts. We also understand that in Leo's heart of hearts he has no inclination to chance the gamer. "Here's what we'll do," Brooks decides. "Set up in a one-two-two and spread the floor. Leo's up top. Mitchell's wide on the right wing in Number Twenty-nine's zone. Ron's on the left wing. Me and Aaron are wide on the baseline. I'm on the right side—Aaron, you take the left. Leo, I know you can beat Twenty-nine to the middle. He's slow to begin with, and by now he's totally exhausted. That's the key to the play. Mitchell and Ron? Start low then pop to the elbow when Leo makes his move. Draw and kick, Leo. Look for Mitchell first. Next, look for me on the baseline. If nothing's there, find Ron. Understand? Only as a last resort do you shoot, Leo. Y'hear? I guarantee that Mitchell will be wide-open. Leo, start your move with eight seconds left. Saul and Kevin? Stand up and yell 'Red' when the clock's down to ten. Everybody understand? After the shot goes up, we're all climbing the boards. Let's do it, guys. A hundred-dollar shot."

The crowd is berserk as Leo kills the clock, dribbling behind his back, under his asshole, until he fakes #29 hard right and plunges into the bosom of the Jaspars' zone. The trick is to unload the ball before getting clobbered, and there it is, just as Brooks predicted, a nifty behind-the-back pass to Mitchell popping free at the right elbow . . . .

Mitchell's two-handed release is smooth, the ball rides high, spinning tightly, then falling under the weight of so many hopes and fears, falling short.

But #17 has forgotten about me, has neglected to box me out, so I slide along the baseline and jump to touch the sky. The ball comes to me like a trained dog, and I lay it gently off the backboard and through the ring. Only after the ball tickles the net and bounces once off the floor does the buzzer explode.

"No good!" the gaunt ref shouts. "The buzzer beat the shot!"

The crowd gasps, confused, then emits a weak, tentative cheer. But #17 grabs the ref by his shirtfront and yells something into his leansome face. The ref shakes his head, resisting, until #17 shoves him and shakes a threatening fist. Then the ref shrugs, turns to the scoring table, and reverses his call, indicating with meek hands that the shot does count and the ball game is over. Now the crowd hoots just as feebly as it cheered.

We are milling about at centercourt and here comes #17, offering his hand. So far I'm 0-for-2 in handshakes, but I take another chance. "You guys are tough," #17 says with a hearty grunt. "You beat us fair and square." On his own, he escorts us safely through the baffled crowd to the stairwell leading to the locker room. "Good luck," he says in parting, "and God bless."

We're too bone-weary to celebrate, but we share quiet handshakes and perfunctory hugs. I've never scored a game-winner before—my only shot, my only basket. "It's not how many," Brooks says. "It's when."

Our shoulders, arms, and legs are scratched and bruised from our encounters with the fence. Saul is still bleeding from his red, swollen ear, yet he insists that he's "fine." There's a small circle of oozing raw flesh on Kevin's shoulder.

Otherwise, Mitchell is obviously pissed that he missed the last shot, but he's easily consoled. And the rest of us hurry through our normal postgame routines. "Hey," says Ron. "Where's the fucking tape cutter?" Mitchell opens the medical kit and swabs Kevin's wound with Mercurochrome. For Saul's ear, Mitchell prescribes a towelful of snow. We shower quickly, anxious to get paid and get gone.

We're fully clothed when the fat priest enters, saying, "Here's your money."

Mitchell carefully counts and re-counts the bills. "There's only two hundred here. Where's our bonus for winning?"

They squabble, the priest claiming that the outcome of the game is still under dispute. "Bullshit," says Mitchell.

"How dare you?" the priest says, his beefy face reddening as he slowly squeezes out each word. A heart attack seems imminent.

"Thou shalt not steal," says Mitchell.

And the priest's resistance collapses like a dead balloon. With enormous effort he reaches under his gown and peels three crinkled twenties from a thick roll of bills. Then he slaps the money down on the nearest bench and says, "I'm deducting for the hot water. Also to pay for the security guards. If you guys were good Christian people, we wouldn't've needed a houseful of cops."

"If we *were* good Christian people," Leo snaps, "then you wouldn't've had a house."

"Heathens," the priest snorts, then he hauls his saintly flesh back up the stairs.

We search the streets of Buffalo for an hour looking for a place to eat. All we can find is a twenty-four-hour diner across the tracks in the Negro neighborhood. It's nearly midnight and the joint is still jumping, sharpsters in brightly checkered suits, whores all slinky in fake furs, bookies, runners, cab drivers, and assorted wiseguys. They laugh when we come in: "Hey, rabbi! Ain't no docked dicks in here!" After which they mercifully abandon us to our own company.

Our waitress introduces herself as Wanda, a stringy old bird, but helpful and polite. When we stand and recite the *broche* over our food, several other customers also stand and bow their heads. "Amen," says a fat lady from a nearby table.

Following Wanda's suggestion, we engorge ourselves on family-style platters of fried chicken and fish, on bowls of coleslaw, meaty fried potatoes, and greasy greens that taste suspiciously and deliciously of bacon drippings. Saul munches the greens without protest.

Just as we're helping ourselves to a deep dish of peach cobbler, Ron laughs for no discernible reason. Our attention caught, he reaches under his coat and pulls out a slick black leather basketball, slashed near the laces and flattened unto death. "It's the game ball," he says, and we howl with delight.

The future seems rosy: Our next stop is Cleveland tomorrow night. The snow's slackened off and the drive will be a mere one hundred miles. Playing against the Dallas Redheads for a whopping five hundred dollars. Should be a breeze.

Later, we ease the car into a parking lot behind a synagogue, Beth Israel, hidden from the street and out of the wind. For an expenditure of only thirty-two cents (two gallons of gas) we'll run the motor (and the heater) all through the night. Because of their injuries, Saul and Kevin are voted two-thirds of a mattress each in the crypt. My reward for being a hero is to sleep between them on the seam.

And I'm certain that I'm tired enough to sleep peacefully. But my slumber is haunted by smoky visions of a ten-foot-high gallows with a peach basket nailed to the crossbar.

From Mitchell's Log:
Day Two — January 7, 1936 — Monday

	Today	Total
Mileage	273	510
Expenses	$10.95	$15.11
Income	$260.00	$360.00

Net Income - $344.89
Average Share - $49.27

Won - 2
Lost - 0

God and his angels are watching me, squinting down from heaven, searching my heart, tapping on the window. I rub my eyes open to see a minyan of old men surrounding the car, peering in at us. Brooks sees them too—and the old men scatter when he turns the key and slowly noses the Black Lady out of the parking lot.

It's still dark at 6:39 A.M., and the car in motion wakes everybody except Saul. Our bodies are sore, our legs stiff and strained. I've a few new bruises myself, plus a slight yet ominous tenderness inside my left knee that I've never felt before. Oh, shit. A dreaded pain in the "devil's triangle"—a small area bounded by the articulation of dem dry knee bones, where cartilage tears.

Nobody has anything to say. Then, just two blocks from St. Jude's High School, we come upon the Trolley Diner. We've already seen several of this type: A long, narrow structure designed to approximate a railroad dining car, a trolley or a bus. Always the illusion of movement, of accomplishment.

"Looks good enough."

"Yeah."

"Okay."

"Anybody need to vote?"

"Fuck it," says Leo. "Long as they got a bathroom."

I must forcibly shake Saul to rouse him. There's some kind of pinkish fluid that's caked in his right ear and also crusted around his nostrils, yet as he sits up, Saul complains only of a slight headache and insists that he's fine. He forgoes his morning prayers, settling for a pair of aspirin that Mitchell digs from the medical kit. These Saul gulps down dry as we enter the diner.

Inside, chrome-trimmed stools at a matching counter, in harmony with the booths slotted along the windows. A few heads turn, several fingers point in our direction. As our waitress leads us to a table, a young man sitting at the counter says, "I told you so," to his buddies, all of them wearing yellow hard hats and blue industrial-strength jumpsuits. "I told you guys last night that their beards were for real."

We've been seated quickly in the rear, around a short corner from the kitchen and the bathrooms. Our waitress is a sagging brunette who wears too much makeup, and by the time she's ready to transcribe our orders, we've each completed our pit stops and ablutions. We'll have the usual all around—except that Saul only wants "a glass of tea" (which he gets) and Leo orders oatmeal.

We're subdued until our meal is served and Saul gropes his way through the blessing, straining to recollect the familiar words. Brooks and I exchange worried looks. Apparently Saul has a concussion, of what degree we can't begin to guess.

"Okay," Mitchell says abruptly. "There's several ways we can go. One way is to drive to Cleveland right now, getting there in two and a half, maybe three, hours. Then we can rent rooms in a cheap hotel and sleep all day until game time."

Everybody murmurs their general assent, still too sleepy to indulge in any form of abstract thinking. We've already grown accustomed to having Mitchell make most of our off-court decisions. "Hold on," Mitchell snaps. "Not so fast, guys. There's another possibility to explore."

"No, no," Leo protests softly. "Let's take a vote to see if we want to take a vote."

Mitchell continues: "After we drive straight through to Cleveland, we could also find ourselves a movie theater that's showing a matinee. Think of it. Soft, cushiony seats, a flickering hypnotic darkness that induces sweet dreams. For those so inclined, you can stay awake and watch the movie. The best thing is the admission price. Five cents? A dime, tops? As opposed to more than a dollar a head for a hotel room."

"We're tired," Brooks says, trying to energize himself for another debate, "and we had a windfall last night. Why not spring for a few measly bucks to hole up in a hotel and make things easier on ourselves?"

Mitchell licks his thin lips, flicking his tongue like a lizard attacking a bug. "Follow my argument," he dares us. "We've got an easy game tonight against a bunch of women. Right? What if we do the movie this afternoon, play the game, then drive to Sing Sing overnight and get there by daylight. *Now* we rent the hotel rooms. Now we have *all* day to futz around until the ball game. Or do we want to get into the expensive habit of renting hotel rooms by the hour every time we need a nap."

"Makes sense to me," Brooks decides. "We'd certainly make better time driving overnight with no traffic. And I'm all for saving money. The less we spend now, the more we'll each of us have in California. A dollar here, a dollar there. I can eat two good meals on a dollar."

"What're we getting for the prison game?" I ask.

"Fifty bucks each," Mitchell says. "Listen, we've got to think ahead, guys. There's a lot of ball games to be played over this coming weekend. A big payday in Chicago and a major money tournament in Indianapolis. By the way, the tournament is double-elimination, so we might even have to play two games in one day. Right now we're still early in the tour. Dammit, it's only the third day, and relative to what's ahead of us we should still be fresh and lively-legged. Believe me, guys, the injuries, the weariness, they're going to pile up as we move farther and farther west. That's why the longer we can postpone spending money on hotels, the more we'll appreciate it later on." Mitchell's broadening pointy-toothed smile is meant to prove that his logic is irrefutable. "Now," he says, "I think we're ready for a vote."

Leo reluctantly swallows a spoonful of oatmeal as though it was a lump of somebody else's shit. "Wait up," he says drily. "Not so fast." Then he drains half his glass of water. "I want to go to Niagara Falls. It's only twenty-two miles away." Kevin's face brightens in agreement, but he says nothing.

"Why not?" I say. "Long as we're in the neighborhood."

"Twenty-two miles there," Mitchell points out, "and twenty-two miles back. That's at least an extra two hours of driving time."

"Leo," Saul says with a small smile, "you want to see Niagara Falls? Get married."

Everybody laughs, then Brooks, Ron, and I vote along with Leo against Mitchell and the two rookies.

"Hey, Kevin," says Leo. "Don't let Frankenstein tell you how to vote."

"I didn't. I just don't want to go there."

"Please don't call me Frankenstein."

Meanwhile, we're still here eating breakfast in Buffalo and Leo already starts lobbying to see Greta Garbo in *Anna Karenina*. Ron wants to see *Captain Blood* with Errol Flynn because he loves pirates. Kevin likes Laurel and Hardy. "Fat and skinny." I opt for a return trip to the men's room.

Imagine my surprise when I see somebody I know rinsing his hands at the sink. Instead of a striped shirt he now wears a soiled, sleeveless undershirt, also green gabardine pants, and a filthy full-length apron. His shoes are shabby, and, as he moves toward a roll of paper towels mounted on the wall, the sole flaps loose under his right shoe like an empty, hungry mouth.

"You!" I say, and his gaunt face turns into a death mask.

"Oh, shit!" he moans. His hands catch his weight behind him as he slumps backward against the sink. "Let me explain . . ."

His name is Viktor Lukazewski and in real life he's a dishwasher here at the Trolley Diner, "a shit job" paying $10.50 for a backbreaking sixty-hour week, not nearly enough to support his wife and their three kids. It seems that the wheeze-bag priest is Father Szkoda, Viktor's wife's brother. Jon Szkoda is his "other brother-in-law."

"Who?"

Number 17, "a really nice guy," says Viktor, who tried to intimidate me only because Father Szkoda promised each Jaspar an additional ten dollars if they beat us.

Anyway, Viktor gets two dollars a pop to officiate the Jaspars' home games. They usually play once every week at St. Jude's, earning Viktor enough to get him "over the top." Last night, Father Szkoda also promised Viktor and the other ref ("Gregor, my other brother-in-law") another twenty dollars each if the home team won.

I wonder if there was a point spread. The Jaspars minus 3? Minus 5?

"I know I screwed you guys," Viktor says, "but how could I turn the deal down? My kids are all the time hungry. I'm four months behind on my mortgage. And every single tire on my old wreck of a car is so bald that I'm afraid to drive anywheres with the kids."

We stare into each other's eyes. His are a soft brown fading at the edges into black. His eyes moisten and he quickly looks away.

"Well," I say, embarrassed, "we won anyway."

His face lights up. "Yeah. Everything sure came out okay, didn't it? Father Szkoda said it really wasn't our fault that the Jaspars lost, so me and Gregor still got our extra money." His reflex is to cross himself twice, touching his forehead, then his bellybutton and both shoulders, once for justice, once for charity. Then remembers where he is and to whom he's confessing, so he hides his right hand in his pocket.

"Number five," he says, pointing with his left hand at my chest. "That's you, ain't it? It was you that scored the winning bucket."

I nod and turn to leave, uncomfortable, unpeed.

"Please," he says, "don't tell the other guys I'm in here."

"Sure."

"And, hey. Any chance you got a spare cigarette?"

No. But I hand him a dollar bill.

Mitchell drives north while the rest of us sleep. Sweet, swift, dreamless sleep.

Sure, the falls are magnificent, the cold wind and the wild, rushing water are primitive powers to be either worshiped or avoided. Or else, in the twentieth century, controlled. And indeed, the huge turbines near the falls and the menacing fields of towers and crackling wires are just as magnificent.

In the town itself and at all approaches to the falls archetypical honeymoon cottages are clustered. Picket fences, fireplaces, heart-shaped beds. All empty now in the loveless depths of winter.

"I wonder," Leo says, "if maybe they got some special place around here where a single guy can go to jerk off."

Saul and I stand beside each other, leaning on the railing, staring down into the rough, roiling water. The wind hammers at my back and I must wrap my arm around the top railing to keep from tilting too far forward.

"It'd be real easy to commit suicide from up here, wouldn't it?" Saul says casually. "One quick step and take the plunge. You'd probably freeze in about five seconds, long before you'd ever drown. And this time of year the water's so cold that you wouldn't even feel anything. No pain, no nothing. This is the way to do it."

And for a moment I can easily imagine myself climbing the rail, jumping, flying .... But I push myself away from the edge and turn to see Saul, his eyes unfocused, his broad shoulders sagging. And I can also see him in twenty years, with braces on his legs, working in a sideshow on Coney Island.

"It's no big deal," he says. "Just theoretical speculation."

Mitchell says it's Leo's turn to drive, so before we embark for Cleveland I arrange for Saul and me to be paired in the backseat. We begin a conversation about basketball, about last night's nightmare game, about Saul's progress, his strengths and deficiencies.

"Keep at it," I advise him. "For a guy your size you've got considerable skills. You're so young and you're still growing into your body. So be patient with yourself. Brooks says that you're the shape of things to come, and when it comes to basketball, Brooks is never wrong."

"You really think so?" he asks. "You don't think I'm just some kind of freak? A freak whose freakiness just happens to coincide with the dimensions of some crazy ball game?"

"You're a person, not a freak. But if you don't love the game . . ."

"I love the game," he says. "It's so quick and geometric. There's a certain flow, a synchronicity . . . . I don't know how to really describe it. I'm still learning and there's so much to learn. But, yeah, I do love the game."

"Look at this," I say, and even in the limited confines of the backseat I'm able to demonstrate various forearm techniques that can maximize the effectiveness of a pick. We talk about angles and leverage until gradually the conversation becomes more personal.

Saul first became interested in basketball at an Hasidic bungalow colony upstate near Liberty, New York. The previous owners of the colony were goyim and there was a basket nailed to a hickory tree in a small clearing on the far side of the lake. In the absence of a ball, Saul used a variety of round and even oval-shaped fieldstones. If any of the Hasids had discovered him secretly shot-putting his neophyte layups, his father would have been embarrassed . . . . Throwing rocks at a circle nailed to a tree. What does this *mishegoss* have to do with Torah?

Then I can't see Saul's eyes, and he's quiet for so long that I'm afraid he's fallen asleep, so I pump him. "I imagine it must have been an interesting experience growing up in an Hasidic community."

Saul startles me with the passion of his response. "*Interesting* isn't exactly the word I'd use," he says, turning toward me, his green eyes flashing. "The Hasids believe that we, that they, are the only enlightened people in the world. Everybody else is living in the dark. Even those Jews who aren't Hasids. Shit, even other rival Hasidic sects are dismissed as being *goyisher*. It's crazy."

He shakes his head and his long, curly beard rustles against his coat. Then he's silent for another moment, and I get the feeling that he's deciding how much he can trust me. "My father was a *tzaddik*," he finally says. "A loose translation would be a 'prophet.' My father was believed to be as real, as divinely inspired, as Isaiah or Zachariah. His followers numbered in the tens of thousands, both here and in Poland. They sent him money, they waited on him hand and foot. None of his disciples would ever get married without consulting my father. Or change jobs, or move to a different city. God speaks to a *tzaddik,* unlocking the secrets of the past and unfolding the future. That's what they believe."

"And you? What do you believe?"

"That my father was a good man. Wise, pious, scholarly, and compassionate. He was famous for being so compassionate. At the same time, he was narrow-minded and intolerant. It's a major contradiction, I know. There was also something abstract about him. Something very fragile at the heart of his being. I used to think it was because he knew that he was destined to disappoint his disciples' expectations. I think he was always very aware of his own humanness. And he did grant me permission to play basketball, which in its own way was as big a miracle as the parting of the Red Sea."

"What do you mean?"

"Because being a *tzaddik* is usually a hereditary title. Not always, but most of the time. Especially when one of the sons, usually but not exclusively the eldest . . . when one of the sons manifests some extraordinary devotion to the Torah."

"Like you?"

"Like me. I was a prodigy. At age five I had committed the entire Torah to memory. I was the crown prince. Even before my bar mitzvah there were people already sucking up to me, currying favor against the time when I would be acclaimed by my father to succeed him. Teachers, grocers, tailors. Old Mr. Solomon who owned the candy store would always rush out into the street whenever he saw me pass by and press candy into my hands. Parents with infant daughters still in swaddling bands were constantly trying to arrange marriages. My own playmates used to spy on me. It was sad. It was like living inside a closed, stuffy room."

The right side of his face twitched. "And the studying," he says. "Reading until two or three o'clock in the morning. All of those crooked words and backward sentences chasing themselves around and around inside my head. Those volumes of ancient commentaries, the dense arguments and counterarguments. It was all so incestuous. And then my father dropped dead on the sidewalk like a peasant. He was a *tzaddik*. How could he not have known when he was going to die? Maybe it was all God's judgment on them. What a disaster! His disciples were tearing their hair out, crying hysterically for days and days. But for me, my father was never what I always wanted him to be, needed him to be. He was too distant, too holy. The surprise is that the old man knew before anyone else did that I wasn't up to following in his footsteps. So at least I respected him. I mourned him like a loving son and I suffered for my mother's heartfelt grief. Mostly, though, I was confused."

He shifts in his seat and softly rubs the temple above his injured ear. "Of course," he says, "by that time I was playing basketball in school, so it was already too late for me to replace him. Even if my father had officially named me to be the next in line, which he didn't do anyway because his death was so sudden . . . . Even if he had named me, the congregation would have rejected me out of hand. My disenchantment with Hasidism, with Judaism, was already a scandal by then. My mind wandered when I read from the Torah. Sometimes I skipped over words, sometimes whole paragraphs. Once, while reading from the pulpit, I started on the wrong page. *'Gevalt!'* they said. *'Gevalt!'* But I didn't really care anymore. I was fed up, disgusted with the racial arrogance, the whole concept of *yiddisher kop*, the notion that Jewish brainpower is so superior. Everything was so unbearable about the Chosen People and their covenant with Jehovah, the Master of the Universe. No matter how much they prayed, their faith seemed bogus to me. All good deeds were mercenary. Except perhaps for a few really pious men like my father, showing compassion was just another way of scoring points in God's ledger. Instead of worshiping the spirit of man, they worshiped words and customs. I was relieved when somebody else was named to succeed my father, an ass-kissing cousin of mine named Yonkel. So I withdrew completely. I devoted my full attention to basketball. And then my mother married my uncle Shloimie, another lazy, greedy *putz*. I couldn't even stand going to *shul*. But in spite of what I know and what I feel, the words are still a part of me. The prayers. The mumbo and the jumbo. With my empty prayers, I'm as bad as them. Does that always happen? That more and more you come to resemble those you hate? Ha! You know something, Aaron? Everybody thinks I'm just a kid, but I feel like I'm five thousand years old."

He pauses to gently rub his eyes. "Today was the first day since my bar mitzvah when I haven't said the *Shema*. It's funny. They called me an apostate and worse. Had they only known the truth, they'd have stoned me. For real."

He coughs and turns to face me. "Three years ago I started reading the New Testament. If my father ever knew, he'd be spinning in his grave. If my mother ever found out she'd *plotz* on the spot. And, you know? I think Jesus was right about a lot of things. About the Jews being slaves to the letter of the law and oblivious to the spirit. It's still true almost two thousand years later. We've learned nothing. We still can't see the forest for the trees. Bah! Jews! A plague take us! Wipe us off the face of the earth and make us start all over again. I love God, Aaron, but I hate being a Jew. Does that make any sense?"

He breathes a mighty sigh, one that he's been suppressing for eternity. His eyes are moist as he says, "My head aches, Aaron. I'm dog-tired." Then he leans back, and the poor guy is asleep in an instant.

Just what the world needs—another crazy, self-tormented Jew. No wonder I like him.

To Brooks's delight we come across an authentic Hebrew National delicatessen in downtown Cleveland. His joy is so unrestrained that our vote is perfunctory and unanimous.

Most of the customers are old men and none of them look twice as we parade through the door. Then a waiter with a beard longer than Saul's points us to a table in the front section, a first for us. The waiter's another old man, this one is wearing greasy brown pants, a gray cardigan sweater, and shuffling along in brown slippers. The top of his head is covered with a black leather yarmulke that fits him like a thick scab. He also wears gray woollen gloves with all the fingers cut away, the better to carry hot plates out of the kitchen. Humming an ancient melody, he tosses a stack of menus on our table, then leaves.

At the front of the room, adjacent to a large plate-glass window that looks out onto Madison Street, there's a sizzling metal grill loaded with fastidious rows of frankfurters, potato, kasha, and liver knishes and thick, gelatinous slices of stuffed derma. Also resting on the grill is a small metal bowl of sauerkraut. A steam cabinet below holds slabs of pastrami, corned beef, flanken, and tongue. On a nearby shelf, a ceramic pot of mustard is meant to be stirred and schmeared with a wooden dowel that leans half-submerged in the grainy yellow-brown goo. Next to the mustard are four stately stacks of sliced rye bread and a small wooden barrel of sour pickles. The glass display cases are loaded with salamis, bolognas, and other more esoteric cold cuts. There's even a kitchen in the back where the specialties are prepared—potato latkes, stuffed cabbage, kasha varnishkes.

I breathe deeply the briny, fatty odors, as close to orthodoxy as my family ever came. "It's good to be home," I say aloud.

The tables and chairs are stolidly fashioned of wood, the floor is a puzzle of tiny white hexagonal tiles, and the walls are glazed in white plaster. The wall opposite our table shows an electric clock in white and blue with a red-scripted legend on the face: PEPSI-COLA HITS THE SPOT. Another sign offers three carefully crafted Hebrew letters, which Saul translates as "strictly kosher." At the table nearest us another old man sips hot tea from a saucer.

Outside, the snowplows have been busy. Up and down the sidewalks several shopkeepers are also shoveling their own pathways. But the weather has blown the normal workaday traffic off the street. A woman ducks into the wind, pulling a two-wheeled shopping cart behind her. On the corner, a shivering man in ragged clothing sells apples for a penny.

The waiter returns, flips open his order pad, and says something in Yiddish. *"No comprende,"* says Brooks. Whereupon the waiter delivers an immense shrug of total indifference.

We order franks slathered with mustard and sauerkraut. We order every variety of knish, also meat sandwiches with mustard and coleslaw on rye. Saul wants a bowl of chicken soup. "You're from back east, huh?" the waiter says.

Dr. Brown's Cel-Ray is the beverage of our choice. "Celery soda?" Kevin says, astonished. "How about an asparagus egg cream?" It's his first attempt at a joke, so we all laugh too hard and too loud.

There's a used newspaper, which Ron commandeers from the top of an unoccupied table, peeling off a page or two for each of us to read until our food is ready.

South Africa: 19 killed by giant hailstones
Ethiopia: Daggha Bur razed by Italian bombs
Washington, D.C.: U.S. Supreme Court denies Hauptmann appeal
Berlin: Jewish doctors forced to resign from private hospitals under Nuremberg Laws

"Who's got the schwartz section?"

Pasadena: Stanford wins Rose Bowl 7–0 over SMU
Chicago: Brown Bomber readies for title defense against Charley Retzlaff
Detroit: Lions defeat Packers in third annual professional-league championship

"Hey! There's something in here about us!"

Cleveland: The popular Dallas Redheads bring their feminine version of roundball to the Erie County Convention Center tonight at 7:00. The Redheads, led by star center Mildred Didrikson, are undefeated in their last 87 ball games, an amazing feat that, according to the team's manager, Charley Simmons, includes victories over several of the country's top-caliber pro and semipro men's teams. Tonight's opponents are the House of Moses All-Stars, a team of pro players from New York who have been undefeated since their inception. Looks like something's got to give. Tickets are $1.50 on sale at the box office.

"Eighty-seven games," says Leo. "Who the fuck have they been playing? Singer's midgets?"

Our waiter returns and casually slides the plates of food around the table like he's dealing cards. When we stand to recite the blessing, he laughs and says, "Greenhorns."

Leo is muttering as we seat ourselves. "It's stupid to say the *broche* like that," he says. "It's embarrassing. Why do we have to keep doing it?"

"Tradition," says Mitchell. "Publicity. It's in the bylaws."

"Well, let's change the bylaws."

"Impossible. That takes a unanimous vote. Why does it bother you? Leo, you're ashamed to be a Jew?"

"Eh," Leo says, and hides his face inside a page of newsprint.

More than the news that's shaking the world, more than the sports, our immediate concern is the local movie listings. Brooks wants to see Clark Gable in *Mutiny on the Bounty,* claiming we'd all benefit from witnessing the successful revolution of "freedom over tyranny." Ron reiterates his fondness for *Captain Blood,* starring the swashbuckling Errol Flynn. "It'll get us up for the game," he argues. Leo is now "dying" to see Carole Lombard emote her way through *Hands Across the Table*. His reason? "Blond pussy is the best." After considerable confusion, we settle on *Night at the Opera* with the Marx brothers, mainly because the Fenwick Theatre is only two blocks away.

Like every other moving picture venue in the country, the Fenwick Theatre used to be a vaudeville house. The huge hall is appropriately dim and musty, and all the seats are angled toward the stage, where the silver screen is framed by lush velvet curtains. Early on a snowy weekday afternoon, the showing is sparsely attended and we can sit where we please. Brooks, Mitchell, and Saul are intent upon serious snoozing, so they retreat to the balcony. Leo and Kevin sit wide-eyed in the front row. Ron disappears into the darkness, while I find the middle seat of the middle row in the middle section, leaving my field of fire clean and unimpeded.

But try as I might, whatever the film, now and forever, I can never be duped into believing that a curtain of shadows only one atom thick has anything to do with reality.

"Mr. Driftwood," says Margaret Dumont, "you invited me to dine with you at seven o'clock. It is now eight o'clock and no dinner."

Groucho sits at an adjoining table, facing his preferred dinner companion, a blond bombshell. There's a linen napkin tucked into his shirt collar. Turning in his chair to face "Mrs. Claypool," he leers and peeps at the bodice of the dowager's black-spangled dress. "What do you mean, no dinner?" he asks. "I just had one of the biggest meals I ever ate in my life, and no thanks to you, either."

"I've been sitting here since seven o'clock," she says haughtily.

"Yes," says Groucho, "with your back to me. When I invite a woman to dinner, I expect her to look at my face. That's the price she has to pay."

When the waiter eventually hands Groucho the check for the dinner he did eat, he stands and says to the blonde, "Nine dollars and forty cents! This is an outrage! If I were you, I wouldn't pay it."

And so on, until I drift into a fitful sleep.

When Judy returned home from the hospital, she either slept, wept, or walked around the apartment in a daze. I stayed home from school to shop and clean, to cook simple meals (meat loaf, bacon and eggs, spaghetti) that she merely tasted. Judy was convinced that the fault was all hers. The "baby" (she never called her by her name) lived inside her own body for so long, the two of them sharing the same breath, the same life, the same secret deformities of flesh and spirit. She'd cry herself to sleep and wouldn't let me touch her, console her.

After two miserable nights, I gave up and took to sleeping on the couch.

One morning after she'd been home for a week, she suddenly started screaming at me while we sat across the kitchen table staring at our breakfast. "You bastid!" she said. "You burned her like a piece of garbage!" Then she swept the dishes to the floor with one wild swing of her arm and ran crying into the bedroom.

The doctor told me to be patient. "Right now," he advised, "your main concern is to keep your wife from destroying herself."

"You mean . . .?"

"Yes," he said gravely. "Suicide is a distinct possibility."

So I hid my razor blades, her hand mirrors, the kitchen knives. Could she possibly slash her wrists with a broken light bulb? I served our meals on paper plates. I disposed of the tin-can lids (baked beans, soups, tomato sauce) by carefully compacting them and flushing them down the toilet. I *X*'d all the windows with strips of adhesive tape and kept the curtains closed. I threw out the aspirin, the bottle of iodine. I stayed awake through the night, tiptoeing in to check on her every fifteen minutes. When she finally felt well enough to go visit her parents overnight, I slept for twenty-eight hours.

Naturally, Cy and Sylvia attributed the catastrophe to me. (Strictly a lucky guess.) After all, Cy's ancestors came from Poland, wealthy jewelers who "dealt with royalty." Sylvia's relatives were Sephardic Jews, driven from Spain in 1492 and eventually settling in Greece. "Artists and artisans" is how she described them. "My great-great-grandfather painted a very famous portrait of King Nikos."

Q: Aaron, where did you say your family immigrated from?

A: Russia.

Q: And what was their "occupation?"

A: They were peasants.

"Perhaps you and Judy should consider adoption," my father-in-law suggested. "It's certainly not worth risking Judy's mental and physical well-being for her to bear another child."

Cy was also upset over the cremation. I had "cheated" them of a "proper funeral," of the chance to mourn their granddaughter. It was "selfish" of me.

Clearly, neither Cy nor Sylvia would be overly distraught if I simply vanished. Once, after drinking too much wine, Cy asked if I was "cohabiting" with his daughter. Perhaps, he said with a crude smirk, I should find myself a "girlfriend on the side." I was puzzled until I figured out that the only legal grounds for divorce in New York State was adultery. After three weeks I went back to school.

"Hey, wait," says Chico. "What does this say here?"

"Oh, that?" says Groucho. "That's the usual clause. That's in every contract. If any of the parties participating in this contract is shown not to be in their right mind, the entire agreement is automatically nullified."

"Well, I don't know."

"It's all right. That's what they call a sanity clause."

"Oh, no," says Chico. "You can't fool me. There ain't no Sanity Clause!"

The Movie-Tone newsreel is next. Gabriel Heater highlighting the Rose Bowl. Also the unveiling of the Douglas DC-3, "an airliner capable of carrying twenty-one passengers at nearly one hundred and sixty miles an hour."

Then a lengthy preview of the 1936 Berlin Olympics: Massive stadia under construction, new roads, swimming pools, luxury hotels. Hitler strutting around like a demented popinjay. "Hitler," brays the announcer, "who has injected new energy into Germany's tired economy." Then a closeup of several gigantic flapping banners with news that the Reich has added the swastika to the official German flag, "an ancient and respected symbol." Footage of thousands of uniformed children doing perfectly synchronized calisthenics. "For the first time in Olympic competition, a gold medal will also be awarded in the American sport of basketball." Here's a layup line of German players, awkwardly dribbling downcourt as though each ball was a bomb on the verge of exploding. Then a crowd shot, a busy street in Berlin, a passing Jew wearing a large Star of David sewn to the front of his coat. Hitler promises to remove all anti-Jewish slogans during the Olympics. The announcer claims that a group of American Protestants who are asking for an Olympic boycott are, in reality, seeking to "deny Germany this extraordinary opportunity to raise her head proudly among the world's community of peaceful nations."

Since we're lighting out for Ossining right after the game, we decide to return to the deli and buy sandwiches and sodas to go, the idea being to save time and trouble by eating *en transit*.

Both Leo and Kevin express their eagerness to become members of the Olympic basketball squad. "Yeah, sure," says Brooks. "Your only hope is that Henry Street secedes from the Union and enters its own team."

The Erie County Convention Center is a decrepit building that the U.S. Army utilized as a training center and storage depot during the Great War. We are greeted at the stage entrance by the Redheads' manager, Charley Simmons. He's a petite five foot two inches, wearing a thick red plaid overcoat with a yellow muffler draped around his neck. Despite the frigid weather, his coat is unbuttoned to reveal a matching red plaid sports jacket, a white shirt, white trousers, a red necktie, red belt, and red leather shoes. Perched precariously atop his head is a ridiculous straw hat trimmed with a red plaid band. A garish outfit, no doubt a trademark uniform of his.

Probably in his midfifties, he also shows blue eyes watery and half-closed with slack pendules of flesh hanging down his cheeks. His hands move slightly and without purpose as he manages a mechanical smile. "Howdy, boys," he says. "Who's in charge here?" A thin string of spittle connects his upper and lower incisors.

We can't help being offended by his air of condescension, but Brooks nods and Mitchell steps forward. Not bothering to present his open, weaponless right hand, Simmons merely grunts and says, "Follow me." He leads us inside the building through a thick steel door, past a dozing guard, along a dark, narrow hallway, and down a tight circle of metal steps. The entire building reeks of animal droppings, causing Simmons to curl his upper lip and say, "The rodayo just left town, boys. Smells like they also left us a little something to remember them by."

We follow him into the locker room, a cramped, cold space, the floor littered with broken beer bottles. He removes his boater and his coat and leans lightly against the wall. Bare-headed, Simmons reveals a cheap hairpiece that's much too small to cover his still-expanding Friar Tuck bald spot.

"Nice gimmick you boys got yourselves," he says. "What're y'all supposed to be? Some of Hauptmann's buddies? Some of them Bolshevik annykists?"

"Something like that," says Mitchell, kicking aside the fractured bottles from the floor near the locker he has chosen. "This is a real classy place."

"What can you do?" says Simmons, then his eyes sharpen. "I assume you boys know the deal?"

"The deal?" Mitchell says. "Sure. We get five hundred bucks."

Simmons flares up like a match struck in a dark room. "Don't be so fucking cute, mister. I've been promoting events like this for over thirty years, so there's no curveball you all can throw me that I can't sock out of the ballpark."

"I don't know what you're talking about," Mitchell says, bending to unlace his street shoes. And Leo is always itching to get involved in a belligerency contest, so he adds, "Yeah, shorty. What's your fucking problem?"

Simmons slaps his right hand against the wall, softly but efficiently with a cupped palm to produce a loud slam-bang noise, obviously a practiced gesture. "Gad dang it!" he barks. "That fucking New York Jew of a booking agent. What's his name? He didn't tell y'all?"

"Tell us what?" Leo says, taking a menacing step forward. But the little man will not be unnerved. With his left hand he pats the bulging right breast pocket of his jacket, then he points a warning finger at Leo, cocking his thumb and shooting point-blank. Leo clenches both his fists before retreating.

"Don't you boys read the local newspapers?" Simmons says, cocky now, spinning his hat on his left index finger in a tight, quick circle. "Those Redheads of mine are undefeated. We never lose. Never."

"Not until tonight," Leo says with a pale defiance.

"No, no, boys. This here's the real deal. The Redheads are good, real good. They cuss like men. They drink like men. They play like men. The Dallas Redheads never lose, boys. 'Quoth the raven, "Nevermore."'"

"You must be drunk your own self," Leo pipes. "I don't care how good you think they are. No way a bunch of girls can beat us. That's impossible."

"Tonight they will," Simmons says coldly.

"A fix," Mitchell says with sudden understanding. "He wants us to dump the game."

Simmons nods and cranks up his automatic smile. "Now y'all's got it. You lose. We win. That's the deal."

"Wait a minute," Leo says. "Why should we let some cunts beat us? You must be crazy."

Simmons only laughs. "Why else do y'all think I'm paying five hundred bucks? So the yokels here in Cleveland can see you boys play like hot shots? Shit 'round these parts they never even heard of you boys. Y'all're here today and gone tomorrow. And we play here in this same building twice every year to good houses. It's all about cash-money, boys. Moola. Frog skins. How else could we beat teams like the Celtics? The Phillips Sixty-sixers? Even the Renaissance Big Five? What're you boys, virgins? None of y'all ever did business before? Hell, this here ain't even a real ball game. It's just an exhibition. So who gives a flying fuck? Win. Lose. Five hundred dollars, boys. Read your contract."

"What contract?"

"Call that booking agent of yours, whatever the fuck his name is. He'll put you wise. Y'all lose, I pay up the five hundred. Y'all win, you get an instant nationwide reputation for being unreliable fuckups. And I want a real game, boys. Not no fucking rollover." He jams his hat onto his head and scurries from the room, muttering, "Fucking amateurs."

Ron has left on his fact-finding mission, Mitchell is angry, Brooks is amused and I really don't give a hoot. After last night's rough-and-tumble game I could use a forty-minute vacation. So could Saul, and the plan is to have him dressed but keep him bench-bound tonight. Kevin is wide-eyed—here's another turn of events he'd never dreamed was possible. Deliberately losing a ball game!

Leo loves the idea. His antagonism toward Simmons is instantly forgotten because shaving and dumping are Leo's specialties. "We should have asked the little jerk exactly how many points he wants us to lose by," Leo says. "Maybe we could've gotten us a bonus for hitting the point spread right on the nose."

Then Ron comes in and offers his pregame briefing: The playing court is raised some two feet above the level of the floor. The apron is narrow on all sides, so we cannot be reckless in pursuit of loose balls heading out of bounds. The baskets are loose, "sewers" he calls them, so any rebounds are apt to be short ones. Ron estimates a hearty crowd of five thousand. Beer is on sale tonight at the main concession booth at the bargain rate of only two cents per cup. "Be careful," says Ron. "Most of the fans are already drunk and rowdy."

The Redheads are short and weak, but on the quick side. Their best player is #13, who can shoot, drive hard, and operate effectively near the basket. At about five foot ten, she's also their tallest player. Her teammates can hit layups and free throws. "Period." Also, we're to play eight-minute quarters instead of ten, and both referees are female. "We'll beat them without breaking a sweat," Ron concludes. "It's up to us to name the score."

When Mitchell informs him of "the deal," Ron fumes. "That's bullshit!" Ron and Mitchell shake their heads and grimace, sharing their outrage.

Just before we leave the locker room, Leo steps out of the bathroom, flashing a big smile. "Thanks for the tip," he says to me. "That oatmeal stuff smells like cat puke and tastes like wet cardboard. But I've been as regular as Il Douchebag's train schedules."

All the girls have dyed red hair to match their uniforms—short-sleeved V-neck jerseys, puffy bloomers, and flared, pleated skirts. Their athletic shoes are dyed a darker red.

There's #13, rehearsing her hook shots. Several of the others shoot lunging one-handers and wrong-footed layups. Apparently, they have their breasts strapped flat against their chests, except for #38 (her bust size?), who flops and bounces as she runs about. They also seem particularly arrogant while they warm up, all laughing and casual, knowing that their victory is a lock.

"Holy shit," says Mitchell. "They look like lesbians."

"No kidding?" Kevin is flabbergasted. "I thought they were from Dallas."

Both teams are introduced with recorded trumpet trills and high-pitched enthusiasm from the public-address announcer. Leo is nervous when his real name is used. "Hey," he says to me after joining the rest of us along the foul line. "There's a lot of wops in Cleveland. Maybe one of them's a cousin or something of the wop I double-crossed in Jersey. Aaron, do me a big favor. Switch jerseys with me? Please?"

We are roundly booed by the raucous crowd, but it's a good-natured razzing with no religious epithets that we can hear. The loudest cheer is meant for #13, Mildred "Babe" Didrikson, introduced as "an internationally renowned golfer, tennis player, and track star."

"Never heard of her," says Leo.

Back in the huddle, I yield to Leo's urgent entreaties and we exchange shirts. Ugh! His is smaller and wetter than mine. Then, just after a canned recording of "The Star-Spangled Banner," one of the refs (wearing gold hoop earrings and a bristling butch haircut) awards the Redheads two technical foul shots because Leo and I are wearing "illegal numbers."

"Say what?" Brooks asks.

"Their names and numbers don't match the names and numbers in the scorebook," the referette says. "Play ball!"

For the center-jump I am paired with a pert, freckle-faced girl who stands about four foot ten. I smile and extend my hand, but she slaps it away, saying, "Just do what I tell you, buster." Then she straightens up and shouts, "Hey! Your shoelace is untied!"

I look down at my shoes, then laugh along with the crowd when she steals the tip.

As the game is under way, the Redheads constantly talk to us, cuing us in on their copy of the script. "Go for the fake," #38 tells Brooks. He obliges, and with her tits unbound, she drives for a layup. Later, when #3 is putting on a dribbling exhibition, she orders Leo to "dive on the floor." He does so, tripping and stumbling to please the crowd. "Let me block your shot," says #8. "Let me steal the ball." All the while, Ron and Mitchell get hotter and hotter.

Babe and I are guarding each other, and she plays her game without issuing any imperatives, just hustling and moving like a bona fide athlete. I try to stay away from her, and the only shots I attempt are experimental one-handers that clang off the rim and bounce awry. When Babe sinks a hook shot that I could've easily blocked, she says, "Thanks."

After the first quarter the score is Redheads—12, Beards—6.

Several of the girls taunt us as we move toward our bench. "What's the matter, fistfuckers? Can't get it up?" Their laughter is bass-toned and abrasive. "What's your real name, fellas? The dickless wonders?"

We're all riled up as we huddle. "Fuck them," says Mitchell. "And fuck that little twerp of a manager." The consensus is that we should play the rest of the game on the level. Saul calculates that it's easily worth forfeiting $70.43 each to "humble those bitches." The vote is 5–0 with Brooks and me abstaining, but both of us agree to implement the majority's policy.

Accordingly, we punish them on the boards as the second quarter commences. Our defense is fierce, our picks rattle the Redheads' teeth and untie their shoelaces. We make steals and score easy layups. The fans are brought to the edge of a riot when Ron gratuitously blasts Babe with a savage elbow to her chest, sending her sprawling over the endline. *Tweet!* "That's a foul!" The refs call every possible foul against us, every possible turnover both real and imaginary. Still the score mounts.

When #3 hits an unexpected set shot, Leo casually pats her ass. "Faggot!" she says.

"Dike!" he counters.

"Suck my dick!" Ron suggests to #38.

"I would if I could find it," she responds, "but I left my microscope home."

"How come your fingers smell like fish?" Mitchell asks the four-foot-ten center-jumper.

"How come there's hair in your teeth?" she returns.

Just before halftime, as Ron and Babe are chasing the ball downcourt, #38 unleashes a vicious elbow that bloodies Ron's lip. The crowd roars its approval. We lead 26–16 at the intermission, and as we head offcourt, Ron delivers a parting insult: "Hey, girls! Can I come into your locker room and watch you play lickity-split with each other?"

"Fuck you, asshole."

Simmons is waiting for us in the locker room and he's on us like stink on shit. "What the fuck're y'all doing?" he shouts. "You're making a travesty of the game. Listen up, boys. There's better ballplayers than y'all standing on breadlines outside in the cold. There's hardworking men who don't earn five hundred dollars in a month of Sundays. I thought you Jew-boys'd do anything for money! By Gad, I'll have y'all tarred and feathered! Ingrates! Morons! Fucking, cocksucking, motherfucking, shit for brains . . .!"

Calmly, Mitchell says that if Simmons withholds our five hundred dollars, we'll tell the newspapers that the Redheads are a fraud. That all of their eighty-seven victories were rigged.

Simmons threatens to have us arrested for inciting the riot that will "undoubtedly" ensue should we win the game. He'll also have us arrested for breach of contract. "I swear on my sainted mother's grave," he vows in a shrill voice. "I guarantee y'all that the rest of the dates on your tour will be canceled as of midnight. Every single one. You can all go on home and sell rags from a pushcart." Then he stomps out of the room.

We're left to stew in our own angry juices. Until Brooks finally says, "He's right, you know. He may be a repulsive little creep, but he's right. We're here to make money, not to win meaningless ball games. And I'm sure he does have the influence to have our tour aborted. Lookit, I pushed a cart around the neighborhood not so long ago. Remember? I'm here to tell you it wasn't any fun. Lookit. We've already made our point by thrashing them in the second quarter. Let's just finish up, get our money, and get the fuck out of town. Let's be reasonable.

Even Ron and Mitchell are forced to agree.

Just to make sure, the refs conspire to foul Ron and Mitchell out of the ball game early in the third quarter. And Ron's fifth foul is a beaut: He fakes a set shot, and when #3 sees she's been suckered off balance, she simply continues moving forward and attempts to thrust her knee into Ron's nuts. But he's too quick. Dropping the ball, he grabs her extended leg and flips #3 onto her back. *Tweet!* says the earringed ref, and Ron is penalized for "tripping." Shortly thereafter, Mitchell is nailed with his fifth for setting a "moving pick" even though there's three feet of daylight between him and the ostensible pickee. In truth, both Ron and Mitchell are relieved to be honorably discharged from an embarrassing situation.

So it is that Saul is forced into the fray, weak and wobbly, but still six foot ten. On three consecutive possessions, Saul meekly relinquishes the ball to Babe's quick, thieving hands. He does manage to put back an offensive rebound, then another bounces off his head and veers out of bounds.

With the leading mutineers banished to the bench, Leo takes over the ball game. Leo, the master of the slightly errant pass, the ring-rimming missed shot, the slick-fingered bobble. Zigging when a zag is the appropriate strategy. Diving headlong for the futile interception and permitting a layup instead. The Redheads catch up and pass us early in the fourth quarter.

Emboldened by their rally, the Redheads resume their abuse. When I wheel, deal, and miss a complicated layup, #8 says, "Nice move, Ex-Lax." And Saul is the new butt of their jokes. He juggles one pass and loses another, prompting #3 to say, "Big man, little peter." And #38 adds, "But you've got a sweet ass, sugar. I'll bet you're your teammates' favorite corn-hole."

Leo makes a clumsy attempt to steal away #38's dribble, falling off-balance and snatching a handful of her bountiful left breast instead. Both refs choke on their whistles and no foul is signaled. But #38 makes her own call, slapping Leo's face hard and loud. Leo plays to the fans, putting up his dukes and backpeddling like a punch-drunk boxer.

With Leo orchestrating the outcome, the Redheads prevail by 39–36, close enough to give the fans a thrill. Babe and I pause to shake hands. I say, "Good game," while she's saying, "Good luck." Everyone else makes a beeline for the locker room.

As before, Simmons is waiting for us. "Good job," he says, handing Mitchell a fistful of twenty-dollar bills. "I liked the way you controlled the score. You boys are real good."

"Years of practice," says Leo.

A postgame quiz reveals no fresh injuries (except to Ron's and Mitchell's pride). Kevin's burn is still leaking but looks clean. Saul says he's somewhat dizzy but he feels fine, the run having cleared the "tumbleweeds" from his head.

But Mitchell won't let go. "Fucking cunts," he rages. "Worthless slits. Chain 'em to the fucking stove and chain 'em to the bed. That's all they're good for."

Most of us mumble in vague agreement, except for Saul, who says this: "You're wrong, Mitchell. Or does all of our talk about freedom and equality apply only to men? Half the population of the entire world is—"

"Yeah, yeah," Mitchell snaps. "I get your fucking point . . . Hey, Aaron! Don't use all the fucking hot water!"

Because of the shattered beer bottles we must wear our shoes to and from the shower. Nevertheless, we're done and gone by ten o'clock.

Mitchell decrees that we drive to Ossining in two-hour shifts, he'll bat leadoff. He also complains that the seating-sleeping rotation is "all bollixed up" and he asks for volunteers. After a brief consultation, Saul, Leo, and Kevin are allowed to start off in the crypt. I'll ride shotgun, then man the helm from midnight till two A.M.

"I don't care about the bylaws," I tell Mitchell. "If I can fall asleep, I will."

"Of course," he says, his voice curling with sarcasm. "Why not?"

Before setting off, we empty one of our spare five-gallon cans of gas into the tank, which moves the needle to *F.* Then Mitchell finds his way back to the highway while we all greedily consume our cold sandwiches and warm sodas. "Watch the crumbs!" Mitchell chides us. "Careful where you put your greasy hands." We've neglected to bring paper napkins from the deli and are forced to use our wet towels. "Laundry tonight," Mitchell announces. "We'll have a lottery to see who gets the first detail."

No one objects when Mitchell twirls the radio dial and finds some dance music on NBC-blue. "Be sure it's true when you say I love you . . ." Mitchell slides his window open a crack to help keep himself awake and he mercifully blasts the heater to help the rest of us get slow-brained and sleepy. Our legs are dead, and amid a chorus of belches and farts, inhaling the stench of twice-dead meat, we drift off one by one.

And here comes my inevitable nightmare: There's a barrel hoop nailed to a tree beside a soft, glossy lake. And I fill the rustic circle with hook shots, right and left, with set shots from the edge of the clearing (I can't miss!), shooting heavy stones and dead babies.

From Mitchell's Log:
Day Three — January 8, 1936 — Tuesday

	Today	Total
Mileage	234	744
Expenses	$10.02	$25.13
Income	$500.00	$860.00

Net Income - $834.87.
Average Share - $119.27

Won - 2
Lost - 1

DAY 4

The car swerves sharply, waking me, raising sepulchral moans from the crypt. "Dead dog on the road," Mitchell explains. I yawn and reach to rub my aching knees, my sore legs.

Mitchell is muttering softly to himself and shaking his head. Another car whizzes past from the opposite direction, headlights quickly brightening into a false dawn, then flashing into oblivion, consumed by the relentless night. "It's the whole trip," Mitchell finally says in a sudden rush. "Everything's all fucked up."

I turn to watch him in the darkness, his face glowing redly in the meager light of the illuminated dials and gauges. Should Mitchell lose his enthusiasm, we are doomed.

"This game tomorrow night is a ballbuster," he says. "Five hundred miles tonight and just about eight hundred miles overnight Thursday from Ossining to Chicago. And for what? Fifty measly bucks a piece? Minus the added expense?"

"Fifty bucks is a lot of money," I say. "Fifty bucks can feed and shelter me for a month. I know we've got plenty of money in the strong box, Mitchell, but that's the situation right now. Who knows what? Tomorrow's another day."

"Aaron, what are you saying? You sound like you expect something bad's going to happen."

"To whom?"

"To all of us. To any of us."

I have to think for only a moment. "It probably will, Mitchell. Shit. Let's be honest about it. Look at how fucked up we are. All of us."

"I know it," he says quickly. "Ron is a real criminal, isn't he? I was right about that."

"I like Ron. He's also a better player than I thought. That was Brooksie's call."

"No matter," says Mitchell. "So far Ron's been a benevolent criminal—for the time being. But do you really trust him? Who the fuck knows how long Ron can keep his hands out of *our* pockets? It's an unhealthy situation . . . . Brooks is gambling with our safety. And nobody's more fucked up than your pal Brooksie."

"*Our* pal Brooksie."

"Brooksie's never changed. Lunatic on the loose, then lunatic from a dame, then a political lunatic. The only place he's not a lunatic is on a basketball court. He'll wind up yet in a straitjacket in Bellevue. In the rubber room between yours and mine. We'll have our own revolution."

"Brooks is playing better than ever, Mitchell. And you know it."

"No argument here. Brooks never makes a mistake on the court. You move without the ball, bang, it's there. He never takes a bad shot and his instincts are sensational. I love to hoop with Brooks. He even plays defense."

"So does Kevin. The rookie saved your ass when Babe the Blue Ox beat you on the baseline that time. Zip! The kid was there to close the lane. And he hung in there with those strong-arm nutcakes in the fucking cage."

"From henceforth," Mitchell says in a stately tone, "and from now on, the apparatus in which we played in Buffalo shall be known as 'the fucking cage.'"

"I agree. The vote is two to nothing, with five abstentions."

"Damn," he says sharply. "I wish I had a beer .... We're still talking about Kevin, right? And, yeah, I do like the way he plays. But, personally, I have to question Kevin's intelligence. His competence. After all, Kevin did cast in his lot with six madmen."

I twiddle my fingers across my lips to suggest a maniac's incoherent blubbering.

"And if memory serves," Mitchell says, "big Saul was another of Brooksie's calls. The Frankenstein Monster. Can he chew gum and clap his hands at the same time? Now, don't get me wrong, Aaron. I pray the kid isn't brain-damaged or something and that he heals overnight. Like a divine intervention. And if by some other miracle, I was as big as him? Forget it! I'd be the best basketball player in history. Which Saul might someday, conceivably, still turn out to be. Who knows? He's certainly done some things I like. He hustles, especially on defense. He's got good hands. He's strong as an ox, but he has to learn how to use his advantages. I'd like to see him get mean."

"Saul's just a young kid. Coming from a very strange and close-minded background. The Hasids. There's something so ancient about their view of the world. There's something dynamic about it, too, an ardor for the Messiah. Give the kid a chance, Mitchell."

"That's what I said. Someday, maybe he'll turn out to be who knows how good? But before that happens, Saul's got to figure out whether he wants to be Albert Einstein or Joe Lapchick."

Mitchell tosses his head, recoiling from a hard laugh. Then he coughs and says, "Then there's Leo."

"Shhh, Mitchell. His ears'll start to burn and he'll wake up."

"Leo is crazy altogether," Mitchell says. "I thought he was *especially* despicable tonight."

"One thing I can always say about Leo. Crazy as he is, Leo is always Leo. He's not a phony. You know?"

"I agree. Leo is for real. Ninety-nine and forty-four one-hundredths percent pure. Pure crazy. Leo forever after." Mitchell smiles grimly and continues: "And you, Aaron? You're even more fucked up than Leo. You always were. Even back when you were a kid. Remember? You used to shinny up the lampposts and swing from the tops like a monkey. Remember the time you climbed on the roof of the D train and rode it all the way out to Coney Island? And how many times did you put on your roller skates and hitch rides at the back of trolley cars and taxicabs? Whoever thought you'd live this long when you were a kid? You were always fucked up, Aaron. Even before the baby died."

"I don't want to talk about it."

"It wasn't your fault, Aaron. It wasn't Judy's fault. It wasn't anybody's fault. It was God's fault."

"It's not God's fault, Mitchell. . ."

We approach a railroad crossing, so Mitchell slows down, darts a dozen quick looks in each direction (including up), then accelerates and bumps the Black Lady over the tracks. Nobody misses a snore behind us.

"Those guys could sleep through a four-alarm fire," I say, and Mitchell, another light sleeper, readily agrees.

The headlights seem so weak, the road reaching into darkness. The white line writhing like a segmented snake.

"You know?" Mitchell says. "I get real nervous with all this cash on hand. Even in the strongbox. I can't wait to get to Ossining and wire some money to Max for safekeeping. Shit. We've also got a laundry to do."

"Make the rookies do it. Saul and Kevin. Don't tell Brooks I said this, but we do need to establish an underprivileged class if our little gas-powered utopia is going to work."

Mitchell grunts and says nothing.

The clouds hang low, hiding the moonlight. Mitchell's doing forty miles per hour over a crushed-stone section of road. A WPA project for shovel leaners.

"Jesus H. Christ," Mitchell says as the pebbles rattle against the Black Lady's underpinnings. "Only fourteen more days to go. Almost four thousand more miles. *Damn*. I need a fucking beer. I need a fucking ball game. *Je*sus. I'm worse than Brooks."

The radio dial remains lit long after the station is off the air, now broadcasting a low hum, an electronic *oooohhmmmm* to hypnotize us into misbelieving we've achieved Nirvana.

"Let me ask you something, Mitchell. If this ball game in Sing Sing is such a pain in the balls, then why are we heading, even as I speak, toward the biggest fucking jailhouse north of the Mason-Dixon Line?"

Mitchell laughs. "Ask your brother, Max."

The story is that some do-gooders in the upper echelons of a newly formed federal agency, the United States Department of Correctional Facilities, have a brand-new buzzword—*rehabilitation*. That's why numerous programs have lately been established and funded to try to connect hard-core prisoners with the outside world. "Amen," says Mitchell. "I'm all for it. Give the poor fuckers in the can another chance, even if it *is* a waste of taxpayers' money." Classes offered for high school and college credit. Even a wide variety of athletic competition.

Anyhow, some other barnstorming hoopers unexpectedly reneged on their commitment and Sing Sing needed a basketball team in a hurry. For the new prison agency, canceling the scheduled game would have "undermined the inmates' morale and increased their distrust of legitimate authority." We had the open date, and our booking agent, Gabe Livinski, promised to add two "lucrative" games out west if we'd squeeze this one in.

"It seemed like a shitty idea at the time," says Mitchell, "but your brother, Max, insisted. He agreed with you that fifty bucks is a lot. He said that he didn't intend to lose his shirt on this deal. That's the word he used, 'deal.'"

"No kidding?"

I had never considered the possibility that this excursion was in any way a "deal" to Max. He's my brother, isn't he? Just being brotherly? . . . Maybe Charley Simmons's red-plaid dealings have me cross-wired. Or maybe Max is getting a cut somewhere along the line that I don't know about.

"Fuckall," says Mitchell. "Now we have to drive almost due east through the entire very large state of Pennsylvania. Speed limit thirty-five, a cop behind every tree. Son of a bitch. And I'm worried plenty about our fuel. No telling where we'll find a gas station. No chance we find one around here that's open all night. We may have to detour miles and miles to gas up. Actually, we're okay for now. We should be able to handle this leg. Heading out to Illinois, though, will definitely be an adventure."

Now Mitchell reaches to fiddle with the radio dial, finding the music of the spheres at a lower frequency than before.

"And tonight's ball game was another son of a bitch," Mitchell continues. "I don't care if everybody else in the living world thinks it *was* a meaningless exhibition. You know the truth, Aaron. That I'm always out there competing for all I'm worth. It's this play, then another play, then the next play. That's why I love basketball, because it exists on its own terms. Either you put the ball through the basket or you don't. Yeah, yeah. Referees are a necessary evil, they don't count. So, you play hard. You play smart. And you play fair. That's the way you play, Aaron, and I respect you for that. You leave your heart on the court and you walk away, win or lose, knowing you've done your best. That's why tonight was such a fucking disaster for me. That's why I never tanked a game in my life. Damn."

Mitchell thinks he picks his nose unobserved in the red darkness, rolling a hard crust into a ball between his left thumb and index finger. He twitches, about to toss the pellet into his mouth, then he remembers he's not really alone. Have I seen him? Will I tell the others?

"It's aggravating, Aaron," he says softly. "I just don't understand it."

"It?"

"The way you play," he says. "As hard as you hustle . . . How could you ever have shaved points?"

I laugh. "We'll need a much longer ride than from here to Sing Sing to air that one out." Actually, now that I think about it, Brooks and I've never totally agreed on what really *did* happen back then.

"Anyways," Mitchell says, trying to find a station, or at least change the pitch of the static. "You'll survive. I'll survive. *Nosotros surviveemos*. There's another ball game tomorrow night."

He drives slowly through the center of Mercer, Pa., population 1,204. Everything buttoned up for the night, even the daytime stop-and-go traffic light has been switched to a blinking yellow for caution. A police car emerges from behind a billboard (DUZ DOES EVERYTHING!) and escorts us out of town. "The son of a bitch," says Mitchell. The cop U-turns at the margin of a snow-encrusted oak and maple forest.

Once we've made our getaway, Mitchell speeds up and says, "This trip . . . it's not what I hoped it'd be. It's starting to come loose at the seams . . . How much can we spend for lunch? Who sits where? Who drives? Who navigates? Who gets to sleep in the back? Such trivialities they worry about. They don't understand the basic concepts of how to make decisions that are both rational and popular. It's getting all tangled up and everybody's got a bitch with me. If they're uncomfortable, it's my fault. One mattress is lumpier than the other, so Leo blames me. Yeah, okay. I know I've made some mistakes. I forgot to pack a can opener. I forgot matches. Everybody makes mistakes. But somebody's got to look after the details. Otherwise . . . Yeah, Aaron, I know. I'm a *nudnik*. I'm a perfectionist. But fuck Leo. If him or any of you want the job, you can have it."

He reaches forth to activate the windshield wipers and erase a small rivulet of melting snow.

"You're doing a great job, Mitchell. We'd be floundering without you. And we all appreciate your efforts. Sure, it's easy to blame you if something gets fucked up. You're the one with the information, with the blueprint. It's only human nature, Mitchell. But maybe, just maybe, you do overdo it from time to time. C'mon, Mitchell. Sometimes you do. You know it's true."

"Sometimes," he says tightly.

“Mitchell, you’ve known me since we were kids. I mean, what the fuck do I know about anything? What to do? How to live? How to plan ahead? All I know is this: that none of us has as much control over our own lives as we think we do. Doesn’t life just seem to happen to us? Like trying to look at the passing scenery when you’re driving at night. What-izz-it? Where-amm-I? So fuck it, Mitchell. We probably all need to just relax a little. Jeez. I can’t wait to sleep in a hotel bed.”

A car overtakes us from behind, racing past at fifty-five or more, a souped-up Caddy, its red lights swiftly shrinking ahead, snuffed out by a bend in the road.

“You know something, Aaron? You know what the real trouble is? It’s simple .... Nothing ever comes out the right way in this fucking country. Everything out of Uncle Sam’s Ass always turns out to be shit. And, Aaron, don’t be fooled by that Roosevelt character. He’s helping the English and the Arabs to keep Jews out of Palestine. He’s just another member of the club. And when push comes to punch, the working slob is still going to end up with a pocketful of nothing. With *bupkes*. If the slob’s lucky, he’ll wind up somewhere in Germany with a bullet in his head, a dead hero in a rich man’s war. But that’s not really a bad way to go. At least his widow and kids’ll get some kind of pension money. Aaron, I’ve got to get the fuck out of here before the bombs start falling and I get drafted into a foxhole .... Anyway, I’ve got to take a leak. Lookie here, it’s almost two o’clock. Your turn to drive, and then some.”

Nobody else stirs while we stop and pee on the roadside. I fit myself behind the wheel, then click off the radio once Mitchell begins to snore. The snow has finally stopped. Gas foot, brake foot, clutch foot, wheeling through small towns and ghostly white fields. Past an all-night diner in Falls Creek, two A & P trucks parked in the lot with their motors coughing. I’ll bet the truckers know where there’s gas available. Past a high school in Du Bois, its windows silver, black, and blind. White puffs of smoke rising peacefully from the chimney.

I returned to work the thankless Monday after Thanksgiving. Seward Park High School, a massive, ominous castle ensconced behind an iron fence, each slender fence pole mounted with a crude, wrought-iron fleur-de-lis. The front doors are huge, forbidding portals, slowly opening and closing with enormous rusty screams.

Through these portals the students enter in subdued, deferential postures, children of serfs permitted and compelled to attend the pleasure of the baron. Most of "Sewage Park's" students are either immigrants themselves or first-generation Americans. Predominantly young Jewlings come from Russia and Eastern Europe, working to secure "professional" careers as teachers, social workers, lawyers, accountants, or, best of all, governmental clerks. Add a handful of coloreds who keep to themselves. Plus a large contingent of Italians and Irish striving mightily for a high school diploma, a ride on the Magic Carpet, delighted to sweep the city's streets, put out its fires, sort the mail, shovel the shit. The girls all want to find a husband.

There are few disciplinary problems here. A mere threat to call a parent into school for "a conference" is sufficient to thwart the most outrageous classroom buffoonery. Unlucky the child whose misbehavior forces Mom and/or Dad to forfeit a day of work, a precious day's pay. The strap will move, raising welts on tender asses. Or the shoe. And to the immigrant, a summons from a schoolteacher speaks with terrible authority over their meek lives. When occasionally, some scions of the Black Hand extort lunch money from four-eyed geeks for "protection," a brief phone call is usually enough to drive the extortion off school grounds.

Inside the building, the passing faces blended, the secretaries in the main office, my fellow teachers, the young girls neat in blouses and skirts, the boys in ties, home-knit sweaters. I passed among them like a blighting cloud, a biblical curse, turning smiles to frowns, causing light bulbs to flicker, potted plants to wilt.

"I'm sorry . . ."

"Thanks."

"I'm really sorry, Aaron . . ."

"Thanks."

"I'm really sorry, Aaron, to hear about the baby."

"Thanks."

"How's Judy?"

"Fine. Thanks."

There was only one face, one body, one voice that could eat my pain. Did I want her still? Even now? Did she want me?

In my homeroom, the children were hushed. There was a hand-drawn note of sympathy on my desk. I mumbled my appreciation and called the roll. Here. Here. Present. Here. Then I looked through the lesson plans left by the substitute teachers: My second-period class was on page 144 in *Ivanhoe*. My third-period had only reached page 119. The fourth-period seniors had started reading *Julius Caesar,* Act II, scene i, and the sixth-period had kept pace. My seventh-period honors class would be submitting original poems to be read aloud and discussed.

I had hall duty for the first period, interrogating every student I intercepted, scrutinizing their passes, bursting into the boys' bathrooms trying to apprehend somebody smoking a cigarette. I also had Debra's class schedule memorized—she had trigonometry, Room 217—so I glanced through the wire-grilled window at the back door, angled so that she couldn't see me. There she was, leaning forward, her green-shirted breasts splayed atop her desk. She yawned at the problems her teacher wrote on the blackboard, then she bent to her notes, chewing on the eraser-end of her pencil. I turned away before I was discovered, more confused, more guilty than ever.

According to my second-period class, there were three different substitute teachers during my absence. For three weeks, the subs instructed the students to read aloud from the text, pausing only to discuss any archaic language by citing the glossary at the bottom of each page. The kids seemed pleased to see me and were eager to get to the bottom of *Ivanhoe*.

Throughout the summer I had studied and prepared for the curriculum I would be expected to teach. Long, glazed hours prowling through the 42nd Street Library looking for interpretive criticism that made sense. Anything to mitigate the possibility of facing a classroom full of bright kids who could easily have been more studied, more literate, than I was supposed to be. I was afraid of opening my mouth and having nothing come out except dust and feathers.

So I told my second-period students to close their books, to do their reading at home. Then I spoke about Sir Walter Scott's usage of precise social details to promote "verisimilitude," about the romantic and Romantic context of the novel. The self versus society. I defined terms. I emphasized the character of Isaac the Jew, torn between his love of money and his love for his daughter. The material versus the spiritual. (I watched them taking notes, nodding at each of my platitudes like puppets with broken spines.) I sat on the desk and discussed Scott's unique methodology, having fictional characters discuss actual historical figures. Robin Hood. Prince John. King Richard. I discussed the Crusades and the Holy Land of the Christians, Jews, and Muslims.

Toward the end of the period, a freckle-faced boy (whose name I couldn't recall) raised his hand and buried me with questions: "What does it all mean, Mr. Steiner? I mean, I read and I understand most of what happens. But what's the point? What's the relevance to the modern reader in modern times? Is it just a story? Then what's the difference between *Ivanhoe* and 'Prince Valiant,' in the funny papers?"

The self versus the spiritual versus society versus money versus love . . . . They all looked up at me with their pencils poised. Would I dismiss the red-speckled boy as a wiseguy? Or would I uncloud the glass of their dim understanding with some magic metaphor? The bell rang. Still the students looked at me with eager, trusting faces. I stepped back behind my desk, an oaken barrier between us, and I said, "It means nothing. Nothing. Class dismissed."

I abandoned the fruits of my summer researches during my third-period class and had them read aloud:

> **"Meanwhile, stand up, ye Saxon churls," said the fiery Prince; "for, by the light of heaven, since I have said it, the Jew shall have his seat amongst ye!"**
>
> **"By no means, an it please your grace—it is not fit for such as we to sit with the rulers of the land," said the Jew, whose ambition for precedence, though it had led him to dispute place with the extenuated and impoverished descendant of the line of Montdidier, by no means stimulated him to an intrusion upon the privileges of the wealthy Saxons.**
>
> **"Up, infidel dog, when I command you," said Prince John, "or I will have they swarthy hide stript off, and tanned for horse-furniture!"**
>
> **Thus urged, the Jew began to ascend the steep and narrow steps which led up to the gallery.**
>
> **"Let me see," said the Prince, "who dare stop him!" fixing his eye on Cedric, whose attitude intimated his intention to hurl the Jew down headlong.**

"Next."

> **The catastrophe was prevented by the clown Wamba, who, springing betwixt his master and Isaac,**

and exclaiming, in answer to the Prince's defiance, "Marry, that will I!" opposed to the beard of the Jew a shield of brawn, which he plucked from beneath his cloak, and with which, doubtless, he had furnished himself, lest the tournament should have proved longer than his appetite could endure abstinence. Finding the abomination of his tribe opposed to his very nose, while the Jester at the same time, flourished his wooden sword above his head, the Jew recoiled, missed his footing, and rolled down the steps,—an excellent jest, in which Prince John and his attendants heartily joined.

I left the building during my free period, lunching on an apple and an orange bought from a pushcart vendor on Delancey Street. I walked quickly through streets already clotted with garbage, with holiday shoppers, with a steaming pile of shit plopped by the junkman's horse. There was a kosher butcher shop on Mott Street showing a Christmas wreath nailed to the front door and a Hanukkah menorah hung in the window. Most of the shopkeepers simply displayed "Happy Holidays" signs. Ashamed (or afraid) to be Jews even in their own neighborhood.

Wandering unawares, I was surprised to find myself standing in front of the apartment building on Pitt Street where Debra lived with her parents. Pausing to wonder, my hoop-trained peripheral vision caught a small movement over my left shoulder. A blindside pick? A surprise double-team?

It was a short, shifty-footed man in a derby hat and a long brown overcoat. As I glanced in his direction, he quickly spread open a copy of the *Daily News*, turned at random to somewhere in the sports section, and began reading. Now, everybody I know reads the *Daily News* like a Hebrew book of prayers, always starting from the back page, then methodically reading one page at a time until the sports news gives way to the want ads. The only exceptions are the horseplayers, who never read a newspaper without wielding a pencil. No question, the guy was a detective.

So I faked left and went right. I cut sharply around a substantial pick set by another apartment building and turned the corner at Division Street. Then I crossed over, east to west, and concealed myself behind a black Packard, angling over the front fender to observe the passing lanes. Sure enough. He came peeping around the corner, only to be startled when I was nowhere in sight. Then he sprinted down the block, slowing to sneak a look into each storefront window before disappearing south back onto Delancey.

A detective, hired by Cy to catch me in the act. Certainly nothing less than I deserved.

Back in school, I faced my fifth-period class, thumbed open my copy of *Julius Caesar*, and tried again. Talking about Shakespeare this time, and introducing my students to the intricacies of Elizabethan philosophy: The entire universe was thought to be ordered in a perfect chain of existence reaching from God at one extreme down to the devil at the other. Just below God were the heavenly angels, precisely 144 of them, conscientiously named and ranked by contemporary metaphysicians. There were Archangels and Spirits. There was Peter at God's right hand, straight on down to Golub, barely more angelic than the most regal and righteous human being.

Mankind is the next category, ranked from kings and emperors down to the lowest beggars and miscreants. And, it must be noted, the Elizabethans assigned man a higher cosmic position than woman. At which information, the boys in the class cheered and the girls said, "Boo!"

The animal world followed the human—from soaring eagles to blind moles furrowing through the earth. The hierarchy in plant life began with roses and descended to weeds. Gold was the perfect metal, lead the most gross.

And of all the classifications, the only one in which disorder was possible was mankind. Emperors assassinated, wives not heeding their husbands, children usurping their parents' authority. And whenever there was some manifestation of disorder among humans, then the entire chain of being was disrupted, the natural order turning wild, random, and chaotic.

Consider what happens just before Julius Caesar goes forth to the Senate to be murdered by his underlings. His empress, Calpurnia, implores him to stay home, reporting dire and unmistakable omens of the world turned upside down:

"A lioness hath whelped in the streets,
And graves have yawned and yielded up their dead.
Fierce fiery warriors fought upon the clouds
In ranks and squadrons and right form of war,
Which drizzled blood upon the Capitol."

And even as I lectured, I questioned myself: What *does* this stuff mean? Shakespeare. To the modern reader in modern times. Is the sheer poetry enough to be meaningful? The now-exotic "world order"? Or alas, is the Shakespearean canon simply a collection of cultural knickknacks and high-sailed curiosities? All right, what about reading the characters strictly as psychological studies? Why people do things. But forsooth, what people? Kings, emperors, blind soothsayers. Doing what? Regicide. Romantic mayhem. Deeds.

So then ... We have the fiercest of beasts tamed. The dead come alive. Bloody strife in the heavens. God's own pure rain turned to blood ... The meaning of *Julius Caesar*? Some people are better than others. Therefore, at all costs, the status quo must be maintained.

In the sixth period, I abandoned my philoso-babble and instructed the students to read aloud from the text.

"O, pardon me, thou bleeding piece of earth,
That I am meek and gentle with these butchers!
Thou are the ruins of the noblest man
That ever lived in the tide of times.
Woe to the hand that shed this costly blood!
Over thy wounds do I now prophesy
(Which, like dumb mouths, do ope their ruby lips
To beg the voice and utterance of my tongue),
A curse shall light upon the limbs of men;
Domestic fury and fierce civil strife
Shall cumber all the parts of Italy;
Blood and destruction shall be soon in use
And dreadful objects so familiar
That mothers shall but smile when they behold
Their infants quartered with the hands of war,
All pity choked with custom of fell deeds;
And Caesar's spirit, ranging for revenge,
With Até by his side come hot from hell,
Shall in these confines with a monarch's voice
Cry 'Havoc!' and let slip the dogs of war,
That this foul deed shall smell above the earth
With carrion men, groaning for burial."

"Next? Who's next?"

Then my last class, seventh period, creative writing. The one I've been anticipating and dreading all day long. In the "passing period," while the students lawfully moved through the hallways, I visited the faculty men's room to wash my hands and face, to rinse my breath, to stare at myself in the mirror. At a jester running footloose and jangling in a darkening kingdom.

When I reentered my room, I immediately noticed that Debra had shifted her seat, her posture, sitting in the back row, her knees primly pressed together. We avoided eye contact as the class genius, Arthur Schleigleman, handed out mimeographed copies of his latest poem.

Then Arthur stood at the front of the room—with the wings on his white shirt collar flying in opposite directions, his red necktie knotted askew, a blot of ink above his heart pocket, his thick-rimmed glasses sliding down his nose, his hair swept wild by some private windstorm. "The name of the poem," he said, "is 'Ode to Autumn.' Ahem." Then he read with a slight lisp:

"So silently has another equinox slowly turned the world—
gray leaves twirling flying already dead
Only a few blazing flowers to survive the frosty curtain
of nightfall
Runny noses
winter cough
Sturm und *screen*
The fearsome nocturnal sigh of an oil burner coming alive
The hawkwind whipping your face
Wild ducks arrowing southward and blackly under sere gray
clouds of doom
Vitamin C and thermal undies
Snow tires and tired batteries

So silently does death come upon us—
dancing our imaginary lives macabre upon
the crumbling edge of despair
Turning the earth to stone

Spring seems so far from here—
escaping like a warm tailfeather of a dream from a
cold and rheumy morning

Even so—
some joyful someday

shall the barren heart-stones of winter
suddenly burst forth into luminous blossoms"

I tried to catch Debra's eye while Arthur read, but she stubbornly kept her attention dropped to her copy of the poem. After the reading, somebody raised a hand to ask about *macabre* and Arthur was happy to connect it with *dancing*. Somebody else wanted an explanation of "*Sturm und* screen," and once more Arthur was glad to oblige.

"Thank you, Arthur," I said. "That was wonderful." All right, so the kid's a fucking genius. That's *his* problem.

When the bell rang, my plan was to remain safely planted behind my desk, pretending to grade the other poems, and not make a move until (unless) Debra took the initiative. The fault and the guilt would then be hers.

Even so—my heart knew otherwise, poised there in its net of veins like a stone in a sling.

Debra stalled after the bell rang, "accidentally" dropping her books, then restooping to tie her shoelaces. "We've got to talk," she said when I approached, so I led her into a storage room behind the gymnasium. Indian clubs on a rack, a broken set of parallel bars, torn volleyball nets, and piles of tumbling mats, soft and plump.

I locked the door, and without another word we tore into each other, unable, unwilling to restrain ourselves, grabbing at clothing, pushing, moaning, wetly fucking frontward, backward and sideways. Both of us sweating, sobbing, exhausted after only fifteen minutes.

Still weeping, sad-eyed and speechless, she left the room before I did, fluids exchanged, heat and pain, but no other words.

Beyond the cold windowglass, the pole-wires tirelessly stitch the night into a shroud. Past the town of Bellefonte the snow has changed to rain, and we pass a cemetery, the cold drizzle falling on a newly dug grave.

Now Brooks taps my shoulder with an urgent need to pee. I stop the car by the roadside and, quietly as I can, I empty the rest of our spare gasoline into the tank, which gurgles and foams like piss in a bottle. It's Brooks's turn to drive, so I curl into the backseat, knowing that should I sleep, I'll die. Dreamless. Falling. Too late, too weary, to climb from the dark, enveloping gravehole. My eyes bound with night.

I am resurrected in Ossining, New York, on Greene Street to be precise, in front of a four-story wooden building, weathered gray and sagging, the Half-Moon Hotel. Up and down both sides of the empty street, most of the other commercial buildings are boarded up—a jewelry store, a notions shoppe, a tailor, Flora's Flowers, Tony's Restaurant. Their doors and show windows are crisscrossed with long, rough-cut slats pried loose from shipping crates and secured with secondhand nails, all rusty and bent. In the gaps between the boards, black stars have been stoned through the glass. Another desolate street in another dying town. Could Mitchell be correct? Is war the only thing that can save us?

"The half-ass hotel." Leo smirks.

"How appropriate," says Brooks. "How'd you find this place, Mitchell?"

"A New York guy tipped me off. It's where the families stay when they come up to visit the jailbirds. During the week the place is empty. And like the birdie says, 'Cheep. Cheep.'"

There's just a thin, dappled frost on the cobblestoned street, which we crunch and stamp, trying to revive our balky legs.

"Holy Moses!" says Saul, flexing his knees. "Feels like rigor mortis. Is this what you old guys feel every morning?"

Mitchell snorts his annoyance. At age thirty-three he is the oldest and the most sensitive. "There are no old guys on this team," he snaps. "Only some who are more experienced and game-wise than others. Now, listen. This is important. I think the cash box is safer in the car than in the hotel. Anybody disagree? Okay, don't forget to bring in all your wet stuff and hang it on the radiator to dry. And rookies! Saul and Kevin, that's you. The rookies. You two have the first laundry detail. Find a washing machine somewhere, or else wash the stuff by hand in your room. Everybody bring your dirty clothes to *their* room. Sorry, boys. That's why God created rookies."

"A vote," Saul says.

"Rookies can't request a vote," says Brooks. "Read the fine print."

The hotel is flanked by a bar, the Red Roost, and a pawnshop, Blue's Buy & Sell, Inc., two thriving establishments. Across the street on the far corner, Joe's Sandwich Nook is open for business twenty-four hours every day. Even now, at 8:57 A.M., there are police cars parked in front of Joe's, and cops aplenty walking in and out with paper cups of coffee, with doughnuts, a buttered roll, maybe a danish, but probably not. As they pass us in cars and on foot, the cops pause to check us out.

The circus is in town. Seven jumbo Jews, staggering like drunkards, bent and stiff-kneed, into the lobby.

Inside, the cramped lobby is enclosed by yellow-papered walls, grime-streaked and peeling. Not so far above our heads hovers a tin ceiling whose curlicues and vaguely floral designs are either clogged with black grease or disintegrating into reddish brown flakes. The carpet is mostly brown, except for the untrod beige patches under the two colonial rockers and a matching redwood end table. There's a sparkling new coin-operated cigarette machine near the elevator, "Walk a Mile for a Camel," only ten cents a pack. A calendar on the wall and the electric clock above it both advertise O'BRIEN'S FUNERAL PARLOR.

The front desk is fashioned of solid oak, worn, chipped, and scratched, but a monument to the good old days. To the high-life politicians and gangsters who used to stay here overnight. The big-shot lawyers and traveling salesmen. So close to the train station, so close to New York City. Nowadays, in its slow eclipse, the Half-Moon looks more like a flophouse than a hotel.

Thumbtacked to the desk front are several notices crudely crayoned on sections of gray cardboard, the kind that's used to hold the shape of dry-cleaned shirts: Checkout time is noon. IN GOD WE TRUST. ALL OTHERS PAY CASH. Single rooms cost $1.25. Doubles are $1.75.

Behind the counter an old woman sits motionless in a rocking chair, her watery blue eyes peeping over the counter, her gray hair pulled into a tight bun, her shoulders thin and shivering beneath a black widow's shawl. She is toothless, and as she absently licks her gums, her sharp nose threatens to stab her chin. The lobby smells like her underwear—rusty-pissy-fishy.

"I'll bet you guys a sawbuck each," Leo says, "the old hag's got a sawed-off shotgun pointed at us right now."

"It's the cheapest place in town," Mitchell brags, and we believe him.

Leo picks the lucky number to get the single room, and Saul and Kevin want to bunk together. Brooks and I are an obvious pairing, but Mitchell whispers to me that "under no circumstances" will he room with Ron. "I'd stay awake all night," Mitchell predicts. "How could I sleep holding my wallet in one hand and the key to the strongbox in the other? Do me a favor, Aaron."

Sure.

In the guest book, Leo identifies himself as "O. Leo Leahy." After we're checked in, Mitchell and Brooks are off to gas-up the car and have the tires inspected. "Just in case we picked up a nail or a sharp rock." Then they'll find the Western Union Office and wire six hundred dollars to Max.

"It's fi strees notha here," the old lady gloms. "Raht ova there, nes doah to where tha ole Fi-delty Bank uster be."

We'll all convene in the lobby in three hours for lunch and "general decision making." Mitchell seems to have more ants in his pants than usual.

"Have a nice life, guys," Brooks says over his shoulder as they head for the car. "Mitchell and me are absconding with the funds. *Hasta la vista.* See you in Havana."

Ron and I are on the third floor overlooking Greene Street. All the houses, all the loose-shingled rooftops, lean gently downhill. The street still swarms with java-sucking coppers.

"I don't like cops," I say. "They're weaklings, bullies with a club and a gun."

Ron walks over to have a look out the room's only window. "These guys are worse than cops," he says, pointing his chin at the street below. "Imagine what kind of guy wants to work *inside* the pen, bossing around crooks and killers. Believe me, prison screws are the *big*gest cowards. The meanest cops you'll find. Stay the fuck away from those blue-ball bastards."

Several blocks away, looking out the only window eastward and downhill, the Hudson River stretches dimly white and frozen from bank to bank. There are no inspiring vistas inside the room, not a picture hanging on the walls, not even a calendar. Just peeling floral wallpaper and a damp, musty odor. The beds are swaybacked antiques set side by side, metal-framed and covered with faded yellow bedspreads. Without looking, without wanting to know for sure, I'd guess that both mattresses are fouled with seeping yellow stains. At least the beds have no footboards, so I'll be able to stretch out without banging my feet.

Beyond the beds there's a doorless closet, a dusty incubator for breeding and hatching wire clothes hangers. Our only dresser has been freshly painted a glossy yellow, and two of its four drawers are swollen shut. The bathroom offers a cracked toilet seat, a moldy tub, and, for contrast, a shiny new sink. Hanging from the ceiling above the toilet, and likewise centered above each bed, are three long ribbons of flypaper, stretched and weighted with clusters of gummy corpses.

Ron jumps onto the bed nearest the window, flopping on his back, saying, "There's no place like home," then falling asleep as soon as his eyes close.

I drop off our dirty clothes at the rookies' room, then head for the lobby to call Max collect from a pay phone.

"Where the hell've you been?" he demands to know. "I've been worried sick."

I mutter a generic apology and manufacture several vague excuses, then he asks about the ball games in Buffalo and Cleveland. He laughs when I describe the fiasco against the Redheads. Then I ask him, shooting from the hip, exactly how much money he has invested in the trip. "For the car, supplies, the booking agent . . . including everything."

"Almost a thousand dollars," he says. "Nine hundred ninety-five, to be exact. And sixty-four cents."

"Max. Tell me the truth. Why are you doing all this? Financing the trip."

"I told you already," he says with a little snuffling laugh. "It's cheaper than paying the bills for you in Bellevue. Because that was where you were headed, Aaron. With all that crazy *mishigoss* you were doing . . . Going back to school for one day. For one day! And then disappearing like you did. Right off the face of the earth. No telephone call, no letter, no nothing. Making us all crazy. Judy, her parents. Everybody. We called the police. We called the hospitals. We even called the FBI."

"Max . . ."

"Aaron. I know you were upset and, believe me, you had every right to be upset. We were all upset. But, my God . . ."

"Don't, Max."

"Living in the Bowery like a bum! Daddy, God rest his soul, would be turning over in his grave."

"Max. Enough already . . . Hey, there's the guys. I've got to go."

"Go? Where you going? You don't play until tomorrow night."

"To go get something to eat. We've been driving all night . . . Max. Please tell me why this game was scheduled in the first place. It seems totally unnecessary. You have no idea what it's like traveling like this."

"It's business," Max says, an edge in his voice now. "If it was easy to do, then everyone would do it and nobody would pay you nothing."

"What kind of business?"

"Aaron. Business is business. *Torah* and *srorah*. God's business and man's business."

"Cut the crap, Max. I want to know why we're playing this ball game. Why am I voluntarily walking into Sing Sing tomorrow night? Yeah, I know. Fifty bucks is a lot of money. Fifty bucks is business."

"Wait, Aaron. Wait until you see the games Livinski gave us in Oklahoma City and Los Angeles. You won't believe the money. Especially in L.A."

"How much money won't I believe?"

"Well, I'm still working out the details. It's a complicated deal. But in the neighborhood?"

"Yeah, Max. Park Place or Baltic Avenue?"

"I'd guess maybe a grand for each of you. Maybe more . . . Oops, there's a call I've *gotta* take. So, are you feeling okay? No injuries? Judy's staying with her parents, such lovely people . . . Go get something to eat. Get some rest. If you want, you can call me collect at home tonight. Bye-bye, *boychik*."

I hang up and lean back against the wall . . . $995. *And sixty-four cents.* He knows his outlay to the penny. What the fuck's going on? I'll have to quiz Mitchell in private about Oklahoma City and Los Angeles.

I buy a newspaper, the Ossining *Gazette,* from the old woman, then as I turn toward the elevator, a man and a woman burst into the lobby from the street. He's a gray-haired gent wearing a bowler and a fancy tweed overcoat. The woman is younger, a peroxide blonde with Jean Harlow overtones. She clutches his arm and laughs. "Hold the elevator, big boy," she calls to me as the electric doors slide open. Laughing still, she prompts her escort into a stiff-legged skip through the lobby and they're soon giggling like virgins as they cozy into a corner of the elevator car . . . Wires thrumming, cables in motion, lifting us and our rattling cage off the ground.

"Just getting ya warmed up," she says to the man, who smiles and glances at his watch, suddenly embarrassed by my presence. Maybe he thinks I'm a rabbi.

Then she presses closely against the old man, enclosing him inside the huge wings of her green-checkered coat. She giggles when the old man loses his balance and the elevator car rocks side to side, clanging up against a taut steel cable. I must do a quick defensive slide step to keep my feet.

"Hey, there," I say. "Easy does it."

She turns to laugh in my face, her red-limned mouth pulling away from her crooked yellow teeth, and she boldly opens her coat to show red-sweatered tits. "Looks like the big fella here is afraid of riding in the elevator," she says. Then she swings her hips and bangs them against the wall, causing the car to sway again. "What else're you afraid of, big boy?" She shows her teeth and laughs again.

Maybe I'll pay two dollars and fuck her when the old man's done. Maybe she's the only kind of woman I should be allowed to touch. But she's older than she appears, her thick makeup dissolving into dust on her shoulders. Maybe I'd be better off living unfucked, self-fucked, until I die.

The elevator stops and the door opens. "Woopie do," she says to the old man, turning her back on me. "Here we are, honey. Second floor. Lady's underthings. Bedding. Hardware. Nuts and bolts. Hammers and screws."

Ron is awake when I walk shoeless and softly into the room. "That wasn't much of a nap," I say.

"I'm all right. I slept good in the car. That a newspaper? Lemme see the sports when you're done. Will ya?"

But the *Gazette* is a weekly and the only sports info deals with local bowling leagues, dart tournaments, and a recap of last weekend's high school basketball games. The Ossining Owls "trounced archrival" Yonkers High by 26–12.

"Lemme see it anyway," says Ron.

On the front page, news of promotions and retirements among the prison guards. The budget's being trimmed. The warden vacationed last week at the Grand Canyon. There were three inmates executed over the weekend. The "world news" is on page five, "national news" on page six.

"I have to laugh," Ron says, rustling the sports section. "Even though it ain't so funny."

"What's that?"

"I probably know maybe thirty, forty guys doing time in here. I'll betcha I know a couple guys on the basketball team. Joey Altoona and Nicky Nagle, for sure. I used to run with those two in Brownsville. Small-time stuff. Gas stations. Drugstores. Those two numb-nuts got nabbed trying to hit the payroll at a furniture factory in Long Island City. Three-time losers, both of 'em. I swear, doing Big House time is for chumps."

"I'd guess it's not something most guys plan on doing."

"Don't be so sure," Ron says, dropping the newspaper across his chest. "There are plenty of guys who can't live outside. Old guys who've been in so long they can't wipe their ass without asking somebody's permission. Some young guys too. You're locked up, of course, and it's down and dirty in a max joint like Sing Sing. But the rules are easy to learn and you don't have to worry about pounding the pavement and trying to find a job. It's dangerous, but in a crazy way it's also secure."

"Like being in the army."

"Exactly," he says brightly. Then he pauses, threatening to say something else. After a moment, he lifts the newspaper and resumes his reading.

So do I . . . War rages in . . . Poland gives amnesty to twenty-seven thousand political . . . Hitler says . . . Goebbels says . . . Denied parity in London naval talks, the Japanese delegation . . . U.S. Supreme Court finds Agricultural Adjustment Act . . . Rudyard Kipling dies at age . . .

I turn my head slightly to look at Ron: Teammate. Roomie. With his derby hat parked at the foot of his bed. His thick brown unruly hair. His scowling smile, his quick-eyed felon's squint. Below a chronically broken nose, fleshy lips tremble, forming each word as he labors to read. Does Ron really have a bloodstained ax in his gym bag? Or is he just like the rest of us, a lost fart in a windstorm?

"That was some screwball game last night," I say. "I've never seen anything like it."

"Actually," he says, "it was kind of fun. I like being that close to girls' bodies. Sometimes, near the boards, or when one of them posted up, it was almost like dancing. And I don't care if they *were* lezzies or whatever. There were a couple of them babes I wouldn't've thrown out of bed. Know what I mean?"

Establishing a common ground. A wolfpack mentality. Girls are born for guys like us to fuck, pluck, and plunder. Ball games are tests of life and death. Living brave, free, and rapacious.

"The little one," he continues. "The one who jumped center? I could've jumped her. Spun her around on my dick like a helicopter."

"Zoom," I say, laughing despite myself. Then we settle quickly into the silent comfort of real beds, until I say, "By the way, Ron. Just for the record. I sure do admire the way you play defense. No fucking lie. But I also think you should be shooting the ball more. The way you're shooting now, you seem very tentative. Like you're afraid to miss."

"Except for open layups," he says, "Mitchell doesn't like it when I shoot. Mitchell's in charge, ain't he? I mean, all that bylaws stuff's just bullshit. Right?"

"Well, Mitchell's very good on details, on planning ahead. But that doesn't mean he's in charge, especially on the court. Brooks is the coach. And as hard as you've been working on the other end, you've earned the right to shoot . . . Provided that you take good shots. Ones you know you can make. For example, that diving hook shot you like. Just don't force your offense. Let the game come to you."

"I understand what you're saying. Alla you guys are so easy to play with, except sometimes for Leo. So I'm having the time of my life. I loved the game in that fucking cage. Rock 'em, sock 'em. Show no mercy. I can't wait to play in those big-money games."

"I feel the same way." Whatever else he is, the kid's a warrior. "But, Ron? It didn't bother you that we had to throw the game in

Cleveland?"

"Shit, no," he says. "Didn't bother me one bit. If we're playing to win, I'm right on it. Nobody wants to win more than me. On the other hand, I don't mind taking it easy for a freak show like last night. What'd that little jerkoff call it? An 'exhibition.' But I could never tone myself down in a real game. Although, you know . . . nobody's ever asked me. I mean, if somebody were to wave some significant green in my face, who knows? Right?"

"Money is the root."

"Amen," he says, reopening the newspaper.

Suddenly, I'm very tired. In the depths of the concave bed I curl into a fetal position and sleep.

We meet in the lobby and everybody's pissed at Mitchell. "What a fucking dump," Leo complains. "A vacation resort for cockaroaches." Mitchell says that the only other hotel in town is supposed to be "a lot nicer," but it costs three times as much.

Then Mitchell digs into his pocket and extracts seven five-dollar bills. "It's time for everybody to start being responsible for themselves," he says. "It's time for a new regime."

"Long live the revolution," Brooks says.

"Revolutions aren't necessary in democracies," Mitchell says, "and what *we're* all about is a true enlightened democracy. Anyhow, this is your spending money. You're responsible for feeding yourselves while we're here. Get it? You're on your own. If you run short, I'll gladly advance you from your total share of the kitty. From now on, we each get five dollars every three days for food and for personal incidentals. The bank still pays for laundry and for sleeping quarters, when and if. Everybody got it?"

"Yeah," says Leo. "Sure. Fuck it. Where're we going to eat lunch at?"

Joe's Sandwich? Too many cops around. So we pile into the car and poke around town until we find a Chinese restaurant.

Along with the menus, a small yellow man places a basket of white bread on the table. I order Hot and Sour soup and Mu Shu Shrimp. Everybody has a favorite except for Kevin, who complains of "cat's tails," then asks the waiter for "a plate of Chinks."

"Don't fuck with these guys," Leo warns. "Somebody'll come running out of the kitchen with a cleaver."

"The Chinese," Mitchell says grandly, "were the world's first Jews. Never underestimate them. They work hard and they're smarter than they look. The Chinese believe that all human behavior can be seen in terms of tactics and strategy. It's like warfare. You have to know the terrain. You don't destroy the terrain, you deal with it. The Chinese can adapt to any country, they can thrive in any culture. Like the Jews, they get along by making little deals and alliances with one another and with the indigenous population."

"But they have yellow skin," Leo interjects. "And Chink women have cunts that slant the other way."

"Someday," Mitchell says, "it'll come down to us and them. The whites and the yellows. There's so many of them over in China. Five, six hundred million? It's a good thing they don't let too many of them into the country. They'd take over the whole shebang."

"Whatever," Leo says. "What's to do in this here burg?"

We're quiet when the waiter returns with our food and sets it on the table. Kevin is served a combination plate of rice, egg roll, and Chicken Chow Mein.

"Yeah," Ron says after the waiter leaves. "We've got a free night. Let's use it."

Everybody's noticed that the hotel's crawling with whores. "Naw," says Leo. "Too raunchy." What else? Movies? What's playing? Mitchell suggests that we catch up on our sleep. Brooks asks about the Red Roost.

Leo has something else in mind: "There's a train station down the hill and three streets over. Only a forty-five-minute ride into Grand Central Station."

Mitchell almost chokes on his Egg Foo Young. "Absolutely not," he sputters. "You'll miss the game and we'll all be up the creek."

Right or wrong, we're getting used to voting against Mitchell's pontifications. (Another bulletin—with no further fuss, Kevin has been totally enfranchised ever since the breakfast vote on Sunday morning. He simply raises his hand pro or con along with the rest of us.) But this time I support Mitchell because I don't trust Leo. No matter, a vote of 5–2 empowers Leo to depart for the city.

"We're out of the hotel tomorrow at noon," Mitchell says, "and we have to be at the prison's rear gate at exactly six o'clock. If you're late checking out, you pay the difference. If you're late to the prison, they won't let you in. I'm warning you, Leo. Fuck up and we'll leave for Chicago without you. Miss tomorrow's game and you're out, Leo. You'll forfeit your entire share of everything we've earned so far. Understand? Right now we're talking about a hundred and twenty bucks per man."

Leo crosses his heart. "I swear I'll be back on time. If I'm lying, I'm dying."

"You know something?" Ron says out of nowhere. "I'm getting kind of nervous hanging around here. All these cops and all. I think I'll head for the bright lights along with Leo."

We return to the hotel, then Leo and Ron hotfoot on down to the train station. Mitchell tries reasoning with the old lady at the front desk, explaining that Leo only occupied his room for four hours. "One sixth of a dollar seventy-five," he says, "is only twenty-nine point two, let's make it thirty cents. Here, let me show you the figures."

The old woman clucks her tongue against her bald gums and says, "No refuns, mista. Still gotta clean the room."

Saul, Kevin, and Mitchell plan to see a movie. Brooks is bone-weary, and the two of us arrange to meet later on at the Red Roost.

I decide to take a walk, heading downhill toward the river: The entire town is built on the slope of the riverbank, and somewhere above us is the penitentiary, its high walls bulging like a dam under pressure, liable to rupture at any time and flood the town with bloody mischief.

As I walk down North Avenue, the sunlight pierces the clouds and the day warms up some. A car moves slowly past me, a black Oldsmobile. Then a bakery truck rumbles over the slick cobblestones. I pass a row of wood-shingled houses and see a man standing on a porch. He wears black trousers over stained winter underclothes, his suspenders dangling from his hips, a battered felt hat crouched on his head. He sips a cup of coffee, warming his hands against the bowl in a soft, caressing motion. "Howdy," I say, but he only stares vacantly at me, not bothering to turn his head and track my progress down the street.

There's a ten-foot-high wire fence at the bottom of the hill and a double set of railroad tracks, then the river. Two teenage kids in overlarge coats stand by the fence, eagerly eyeing the tracks, hopeful of seeing a passing train, and we nod at one another. "No school today, eh?" I ask in a friendly tone, and they both shrug their indifference to school, to me.

The river narrows here, a slick sheeting of ice. Halfway across, an arm extends from a rude cardboard shack to suspend a fishing line over an ax-hacked hole.

Within minutes, a train appears, picking up speed out of the station and heading north. The boys wave at the engineer, then yank hard at the air above their heads. The engineer returns their greeting, tooting the train's sharp whistle twice as the short line of coaches powers past us. The sound fills my head, loud and colossal as a bomb exploding.

Once the train is out of sight, the kids shuck their coats and lay them carefully across the barbed-wire strands atop the fence. Climbing the fence, they scour the tracks for loose chunks of coal.

I return to the hotel to reread the *Gazette*, to doze and redoze until it's time to meet Brooks.

The bar is warm and burnished in pine with colonial-type chairs and tables nestled in small groups under dim lights. There's even a moose head mounted on the wall above the bar. Nearly all the customers are in uniform, (they are guards coming off duty), and their curiosity is politely piqued at the first sight of me and Brooks.

No, we're not here to visit anybody in the pen. Yes, we're the basketball team for tomorrow's ball game. "Are you real players?" a red-faced old man asks, his eyes like two pissholes in the snow. "Yeah? Then go out and kick those assholes' asses. I've got a finn bet on yiz."

A younger man with short brown hair offers a scouting report: The rapist is a great shooter. The child molester doesn't box out. The arsonist can't go left. Neither of the murderers play defense. We are further informed that the home team is favored by 3 points, that "amongst the population" the prisoners habitually bet cigarettes on ball games. The stakes are especially high in those games pitting the convicts and "outsiders." Sometimes the cons wager cigarettes against the use of somebody's "homo." After exhorting us to "kick their asses" once more, the guards return to their drinking, leaving me and Brooks to settle behind a nearby table.

"Jeez!" says Brooks. "This is the best-tasting beer I've ever had. What the hell is it? Genesee? Never heard of it. Hey, Aaron, don't be such a fucking mope. Leo and Ron'll be back in plenty of time. Wagging their tails behind them."

We can overhear the guards talking at the next table over. Their subject is politics, and the yellow-eyed old man loves Roosevelt. FDR is *for* the working "stiff" and he will get the country "right" again.

The young brown-haired cop is from Nebraska and he argues for the Townsend Plan as opposed to FDR's recently enacted counterplan, Social Security. "A two-percent income tax on everybody with no exceptions," he enthuses. "The money goes to old folks over sixty, to the blind and disabled, to mothers of dependent children. The only catch is that everybody who receives this money has to spend it all within thirty days. That's to stimulate the economy. Dr. Townsend's a great man, fellas. The savior of our country. He's not one of the silver-spoon set, like the President. Just a plain ol' country doctor from Omaha. Roosevelt's Social Security plan is okay as far as it goes, but it doesn't go far enough. Townsend's plan is the only way out."

"Shit," says the old-timer. "Doesn't matter much either ways. One or t'other, the money eventually winds up back in the rich man's pockets."

Brooks and I are enjoying our beers, delighted to mind our own business, casually eavesdropping as the guards' conversation embraces a Ku Klux Klan meeting scheduled to be held in some farmer's barn on Saturday. "What's right about Sing Sing," one of the guards says, "is that the niggers're in jail, where they belong."

"Say, did you see them niggers shit their britches Sunday morning when the lights got dimmed cause ol' man Hankus got sparked?"

"Sure enough. And on Monday, Cookie, he serves them up some fried gristle-burgers with a barbecue sauce that sure as shit looked like nigger blood. None of them fuckers ate worth a lick."

They all laugh to beat the band.

Brooks and I drink several more beers in near silence. The only thing Brooks has to say is this: "Well, it looks like Mitchell is starting to crack.

I thought he'd be able to hold himself together for longer than this."

We toast Mitchell's mental health with our last dregs of beer, then we duck into the night to buy sandwiches at Joe's before turning in.

"Tomorrow's game is going to be interesting," Brooks says as we cross the street. "I've never played inside a prison before. Have you?"

"Me neither. You scared at all? Just a little?"

"Yes. A little."

"Me too."

I dream that I'm alone in the car, driving on a nighttime road, lost and baffled. I seem to be driving in circles, passing the same church, the same cemetery, twice, three times. I feel an obscure sense of urgency, somebody's chasing me and there's someplace I have to get to soon, but I can't recollect the particulars. Then the highway loops like a roller coaster, around and around. I push the gas pedal to the floor, racing faster and faster. Should I slow down, I'll fall off the road and keep falling. The church, the cemetery, spinning past. Then the road levels and I continue as before, driving headlong into the night.

From Mitchell's Log:
Day Four — January 9, 1936 — Wednesday

	Today	Total
Mileage	409	1,153
Expenses	$44.47	$69.60
Income	0	$860.00

Net Income - $790.40
Average Share - $112.91

Won - 2
Lost - 1

I sleep late and wake with a headache. Staggering to my feet, I enter the bathroom and pull the light cord. And there on the floor, scurrying and glinting in the yellow light, is a congress of cockroaches. Most of them vanish through an aperture where the floor doesn't quite meet the base of the toilet bowl. One roach is caught inside the bowl, feasting on the brown crud that adheres to the porcelain just above the water line. I literally piss him off, then use him for target practice before subjecting him to the Big Flush.

The roach will doubtless survive, likely to crawl out of the washbasin's faucet and greet the next tenant.

I pack my gear, Ron's as well, and tote it down to the lobby. It's only 11:07 A.M., and Mitchell is there, stalking about, wringing his hands. He points to the redwood table, which is neatly piled with clean clothes. I can distinguish each pile by the folded uniform on top. Number 2 is Mitchell's pile, twice as high as anyone else's. Everybody's had their towel washed except Leo and Ron. Leo's All-Star uniform is the only one that's missing, also his socks and jocks. There are faded shit stains on Leo's top-of-the-pile boxer shorts.

"These're yours," Mitchell says. "These're Ron's. Here's the keys to the car, Aaron. It's parked right outside. Pack yours and Ron's laundry away, then go load your bags into the car. Okay? Don't forget to lock up when you're done."

"Where is everybody?"

"Well, I hate to tell you I told you so, but there's no sign of our delinquents." Mitchell shrugs, hugely and helplessly. "As far as the rookies are concerned, they're out and about somewhere. Brooks is still sleeping. I'm giving him another fifteen minutes before I go get him. That old hag at the desk will probably charge us for a full day if we're a minute late.

"What's on tap?"

"Another movie for Saul and Kevin. *Captain Blood.* There's a matinee at one and they're leaving at a quarter-to if you're interested. Personally, I wouldn't cross the street to see a pirate movie. My own plan is to wait here in the lobby for Ron and Leo. Calm, cool,and collected, that's me. If I get too stir-crazy, I'll walk down to the train station and wait there. What're you up to?"

"I don't know. Walk around for a while."

"Remember," he says. "We're meeting here . . ."

"Mitchell. Mitchell. Take it easy. You're making me nervous." Mitchell, who loves to offer advice and reminders in the imperative tense.

"Well, fuck it, then," he says, his hairy black eyebrows going up in flames. "So we'll leave whenever we leave. I don't care."

"Okay. Okay . . . How far is it to the prison from here, Mitchell? Do you have directions?"

"Yeah. From Joe Sandwich. He said to go uphill along First Avenue and we can't miss it. Ten minutes from here. So we should leave from the lobby at a quarter-to-six sharp. With or without those two putzes.

Across the street from the hotel is a pawnshop, a eunuch pawnshop with no visible balls. Just the name painted on the window, BLUE'S BUY & SELL, INC. No iron bars, no gate to protect the show window. Not even a decal to warn potential burglars that the premises are wired with an alarm system.

In the front window are the usual broken-hearted relics of the usual sweet dreams gone sour. Here are acoustic guitars and gleaming saxophones, trumpets, clarinets, accordions, bowling balls. Several console radios and Victrolas, a row of wire-winged toasters. There's an old sewing machine and a glittering assortment of crystal vases and bowls.

A brass bell clanks above the door as I push my way inside. More of the same junk on shelves, racks, stands, and behind glass display cases. An old colored man comes shuffling into view through a curtain of stringed and glossy glass beads.

"Yassa," he says. "Yassa."

His skin is black as a moonless midnight. He wears shiny black police shoes, green drawstring pants, and a ratty blue sweater. His bald head is rotated a few degrees toward his right shoulder and cocked slightly downward, imparting a mischievous cast to his sharp brown eyes. He scuttles toward me, moving with a hippity-hop limp, and it's clear that his neck is locked into its quizzical angle.

"Yassa," he says, turning his entire body so that he can catch me eye to eye. "Can I help you?"

"Just browsing around."

"Yassa. Go right on ahead."

He slowly eases his body into a tattered leather chair set near the beaded curtain, then he taps a pinch of tobacco into a well-used corncob pipe. "Yassa."

I peruse the wedding bands, hundreds of them, ringed around a dozen display poles. Fourteen-karat gold or gold-plated, studded with diamonds or with glass chips. Reminding me of my own wedding band, long-gone too, lying at the bottom of the East River.

Here's one entire case holding watches. Another for candlesticks. Gold-plated fountain-pen-and-pencil sets. Men's rings mounted with rubies or garnets. Pearl necklaces, jade brooches, cameo pins.

"Yassa," the old man says to himself, exhaling a gust of fragrant white smoke.

"Excuse me," I say. "Is any of this stuff ever redeemed? Looks like you've got a lot of big-city merchandise for such a small town."

"Used to be a lively town," he says from his chair. "The exey-cutions used to draw the high-tone society folks up here from the city. Mobsters be up here in those days, throwing they monies around like water. Those that were inside doing easy time. Rich man's time. Having parties the likes of which you ain't *never* seen. Night-calling womens walking around all brazen and such. Bootleg whiskey. Funny-weed. Whatever you could afford, that's what you could get. Mayors, senators, gubbners, all acoming up to here for their privacy. You unnerstand? To keep their own business to theirselves. Ain't no stool pigeons 'round here on the outside of those walls. Plenty on the inside. Yassa. Town used to name Sing Sing until they changed it back to Ossining in Nineteen-and-twenty. Sin Sin is ack-chly what it was called. But in these times, these later days? Stuff what goes in hock, stays in hock. Yassa. Say, you one of them basketballers here to play the fellers, ain't that right?"

I introduce myself, walking over and shaking his gnarled and bony hand. Then he tells me his story.

His daddy was a slave in "Alabamy" who wandered north after the Civil War looking for "the Jubilee land," eventually making his way to New York City. "Daddy took up with a round-heeled woman. Nine months later out I come. And there she go. Leaving Daddy and her baby boy behind. But Daddy done me right. Teetched me a trade, one that's good anytime, anywheres. What they calls a cutpurse and a pickity pocket."

Blue and his father worked the baseball games up in Coogan's Bluff, the fights at Sunnyside, the vaudeville shows at the Hippodrome. Easy pickings. When Blue was fourteen, his father was shot trying to lift a wallet from an off-duty cop. Blue supported himself for another three years. "I could cut the bottom of your pocket with my razor and you wouldn't feel not a thing. Then I'd just pick up your wallet or your money clip, right up from the sidewalk like pennies from heaven. I was a good'un. Like to steal the eyes outen your head without you missing 'em till the next *day*."

Young Blue was finally apprehended when a scrupulously Catholic pawnbroker called "the cheese" on him. "It was a *in*-scribed gold watch I was aiming to sell. My regular fence-man, he was temporarily in the hoosegow, and seeing as how the names on the back of that watch was 'To Cardinal Morley' and 'From John F. Tweed,' that there hockerman had me arrested. Thang of it is, I din't even steal the dang watch. I done bought it from a colleague for five dollah, 'cause it had this here big cross on the front and I felt sure enough it was good luck. Jesus luck. I carried that there watch for a entire year afore times got so bad that I hadda sell it. I'll never forget that watch. Thanks to Jesus."

Blue was sentenced to Sing Sing for a five-year stretch. "Nigger's sentence and nigger's time." Halfway through his stint, Blue got involved in a "fracas" with another con, who tried to pilfer a sharpened teaspoon that Blue counted among his valuables. "I cotched that nigger with his hand in my shoe while he thought I was sleeping. And I had to cut his throat. Yassa. I did."

For this, Blue was condemned to hang. "This was back in Eighteen-and-double-eight, two years afore they discovered the lectrizity chair." But a miracle happened instead. The hangman's knot was looser than it "ought," and Blue was saved. "I jes dangled around there for a while, choking and gasping. Yassa. 'Twas Jesus luck for sure." He was cut down and set free on a legal technicality, "double leopardy."

Loose on the town, his neck crooked but still functional, Blue became a local symbol of good luck "in a place where most everybody's luck is bad. They done rub the nap right offa my head." Blue found employment in this very pawnshop, owned back then by "Mista Jimbalbo, a Eye-talian man, a ol' man with a hearta gold." Ten years ago, Mr. Jimbalbo went to his reward, leaving no heirs, no creditors, and willing the business and the paid-up mortgage to Blue. "Yassa."

The old man climbs from his chair and beckons me over to another glass showcase along the back wall. "Specialties of the house," he says. "Look here. Got sebenteen Ka-*gresh*nal Medals a Honor. They's five dollah each one. Silber Stars, here they is. A dollah each one. And here's my prize that ain't for sale at no price. No matter what."

He unlocks a small metal box and shows me a gold medallion. Reverently he removes the medallion from its bed of purple velvet, and the gleaming disk trails a long blue and white ribbon. There's a garland of laurel leaves decorating the front surface, and these words: OLYMPIC GAMES. SWEDEN. 1912. DECATHLON.

"Yassa. This here's one of the gold medals the U.S. gubbmint stole back from that Indian boy, Jim Thorpe, 'cause they said he wasn't no amachure. Don't aks me how I got it and don't try to buy it. Yassa. This here medal gonna be hanging ' round my own crooked-as-a-ram-horn neck when I'm finally dade and buried."

Blue also shoes me his general collection of pocketknives, Bowie knives, butcher knives, sawtooth skinning knives, and more. Also handguns, derringers, six-shooters, rifles, shotguns, plus a single "elphant gun that ain't for sale." Another huge case contains rows of brass knuckles and blackjacks. "'Saps' is what the po-leece calls 'em." In fact, most of Blue's current trade is in firearms. "Cops buy guns," he says. "My good luck, they buys enough to keep me fed and warm. I don't need much these days. Don't drink no likker no more. These hard days. Yassa. I been saving my monies to buy me a plot for burying in the cemetery out backa the coloreds' church up on Walnut Street. I got my spot all picked out under a big tree. I figure I'll have the proper amount in about three more year. Yassa. Thanks be to Jesus. Yassa. Hard times is here and they's worse yet to come."

Even so, his eyes sparkle with happy expectations, and I'm moved to ask him about the future. Tell me, black-skinned man, saved from the grave, what did you see in the darkness beyond?

"Yassa." He smiles. "I sure do got me a diffint pointa view than most folks, doan I? According to what I figure, someday they's gonna make a prison of the whole country coast to coast. Yassa. A prison without no walls. The wardens and the guards, they still gonna live up on Easy Street just like always. The resta us? They gonna have to feed us, clothe us, and make a roof over our heads. They gonna have to make work for us to do. Digging ditches. Filling ditches. Making roads and highways. All them gubbmint letters? The WPA? CCC? That's the start of it. Yassa. We all be in jail in the by-and-by."

I wander through the dusty artifacts and find a leather belt with a big copper buckle that the old man lets me have for two bits.

"Yassa."

In the hotel lobby, Saul and Kevin are each squeezed into a rocking chair, their long legs stretching into the middle of the floor. Squeaking to and fro, going nowhere, killing time until we leave for the ball game. No, they haven't seen anyone else. Flexing their legs, they clear a path for me, and I take my seat on the redwood table beside Leo's and Brooks's piles of clothing.

Kevin is eager to retell the movie: Buried treasure and damsels with torn bodices. Treachery on the high seas. Good guys and bad guys. *Ship ahoy* and *Land ho* . . . Saul listens to the recital with a slack smile, faintly amused yet sensitive to Kevin's enthusiasm. I'm glad to see the two rookies become friends.

"It should be interesting," says Saul. "Tonight's game, I mean."

Kevin agrees. "I just hope it's not too interesting."

They look to me for advice. For words of encouragement and warning. "You got me." I shrug. "I've been in jail, but I never played ball in one."

"You were in jail?" Saul says. "What for?"

"I once killed a referee. Strangled him."

"Really?" says Kevin. "Where? How?"

"He's kidding us, Kevin. He's never been in jail."

Just then Mitchell enters from the street, his face reddened, his eyes watering from the sudden blast of warmth. "Cold as an Eskimo's pecker out there," he says. Mitchell's just come from Joe's, where he bought enough bologna sandwiches, milk, and beer to "tide us over" on our long trip to Chicago. Everything's already stashed in the car. The tires checked out okay, the gas tank and the spare cans are filled. "I even bought another ten-gallon can," Mitchell says, "just in case."

"Good job, buddy," I tell him, and he beams like a schoolboy receiving a gold star from his teacher.

Then Kevin asks out of nowhere, "You ever play in a jail before, Mitchell?"

"Twice," says Mitchell. "Jailhouse teams are usually in great physical shape. They get three squares, plenty of sleep, and plenty of exercise. That's why all jailbirds look to be so young. Cigarettes can cut their wind, but prison teams usually go fifteen players deep, especially in big houses like this one. You'd also think they'd be rough-and-tough kind of players, wouldn't you? Knock 'em down and drag 'em out. Right?"

The rookies shudder and I try to nod sagely.

"As a matter of fact," says Mitchell, "it's not like that at all. In fact, prison games are powderpuff games. You have to realize that these games are a real treat for the convicts. They know if there's any kind of trouble, a fight, even an argument, then zippo. No more outside teams coming in to play basketball. No more softball games either. Or baseball. Or football. Or even boxing. You see? So the cons are always on their best behavior. We should be the ones to play a physical game, because those guys' hands are tied. They can't fight back. Believe me, it'll be as easy as picking cherries."

The front door opens and the Harlowesque whore steps inside to scan the lobby, looking right through the four of us, then turning back into the street.

"I guess she's not looking for me," Saul says.

Mitchell laughs. "Boy, I'd sure love to prong her. Wouldn't you?"

"Why not?" I say, and the rookies blush and twitch.

"Aha!" Mitchell says in triumph. "What've we got here? A couple of virgins? Yes? Well, we'll have to amend the bylaws. One of our main goals should be to get the rookies laid. Hee!"

The elevator opens and Brooks appears, yawning. "Where the hell were you?" Mitchell says. "I went to your room at a quarter to noon and you weren't there. You haven't been in Joe's. Where'd you go?"

Brooks yawns again and says that he found an empty room unlocked on the second floor, where he's been sleeping all day.

Just then, Ron and Leo make a loud, stumbling entrance from Greene Street. It's five-thirty and Mitchell is overjoyed. "Good going!" he says, and with his right hand he unrolls a thumbs-up.

"Go stick your thumb up your ass," Leo says, red-eyed and obviously drunk.

"Here," Ron says, apparently sober, fishing for something in his wallet. "Look at this, you guys. Here's a driver's license. A longshoreman's card. And even a library card. Look at the name on them. 'Elliot Warshaw.' That's me. They look real, don't they?"

"What'd you do?" Kevin asks. "Steal them?"

"No, dummy." Leo spits. "They're fake I.D.'s. I got some too. Here . . . 'Gregory Dodge.'"

"What for?" Kevin asks.

Leo grunts and shakes his head. "What it's *for* is that Ronnie-boy here has an arrest record under his real name, so they'll never let him inside Sing Sing as a guest. Ain't that right, Ron? And what it's *for* for me, is that I don't want certain parties being able to find out where I am, where I was or where I'm gonna be. That's what *for*."

"Terrific," Mitchell says with a snideways turn of his mouth. "What if they check your fingerprints or something? Then we'll all wind up in the clink."

"Ease off," Ron says, annoyed. "Nobody's checking nobody's fingerprints. I.D.'s all they want to see."

"I'll take your word for it," says Mitchell. "All right. C'mon. Let's get going."

On the short drive uphill and out of town, Leo regales us with tales of his overnight adventures in New York: "We were at the wildest party ever. I'm telling you. Right, Ron? And we met some dames that were really hot to trot. No lie. It was an education, even for me. And you know what I did? For the first time in my life?"

"You fell in love with somebody besides yourself," I suggest.

"You joined the Salvation Army," is Mitchell's guess.

"Fuck you," Leo says at large. "What I did was to fuck this dame up her ass! Heavy on the Vaseline. Here I come, baby! Right up the shit chute! I gotta tell ya! Ain't nothing like it."

We're all laughing and ya-hooing until we see the walls.

The high stone walls look like they'd be cold to the touch even in the summertime, and the machine gunners in the turrets take casual aim at every visitor. Large signs direct "Groups" around to the rear, to a long cinderblock building leaning hard against the wall. We park in a cleared field, then solemnly file into the "Group Prep. Office."

Four uniformed and armed guards stand behind a long green metal counter. The walls and floor are bare cinderblocks on the inside, too, and there's a large gas heater on the cops' side of the counter. All business, the first guard asks each of us for "three pieces" of identification. The second guard prints our names in a logbook—"IN at 5:58"—then he makes a phone call to some central office to discover if any of us is an ex-con or a fugitive from justice. Next up, the third guard empties our gym bags, checking the shoes for false bottoms, slicing the soap bars in half to see if we're smuggling keys or blades. He even puts a small taste of Leo's talcum powder to his lips.

Nobody says a word. The tape scissor in Mitchell's bag is confiscated. So are our belts. Also a straight razor that Brooks carries. Plus both sets of car keys and both keys to the strongbox. To be returned on the way out. Mitchell timidly asks for a receipt and the guards laugh at him.

We are asked to sign, then print, our names on numerous cards and roster sheets. Then our pants pockets are turned inside out, our street shoes are removed, and we are coldly frisked, poked inquisitively in the balls, and jabbed in the ass. Our beards are roughly pulled and fingered. "Open your mouth and lift your tongue," the fourth guard commands us one by one. "Hold still. I'm gonna shine a flashlight up your nose, in your ears."

Another guard escorts us from the shed, and we must walk carefully, holding up our gym bags and our pants. A forty-foot iron gate grinds open and slowly slams shut, a lonesome clanging. From this side of the wall, all the faint breezes smell like rust. We must step smartly around a deep concrete trench used to inspect the undersides of incoming and outgoing vehicles.

"Has anyone ever busted out of here?" Mitchell asks the guard.

"In a hundred and twelve years since it opened," he says proudly, "nobody."

We walk through an open area, a snow-patched field of concrete, surrounded on three sides by five-tiered buildings. Bare hands reach out the windows between the bars, and our passing is signaled with piercing wolf whistles and amplified puckering explosions.

"Shake it, honey! I see you!"

"Hey, Jew-boys!"

"Hey, white meat!"

More gates, more doors, more sheets and cards to sign and countersign. Again we're shaken down and frisked. Again, and once again. "Kick the shit outa them niggers," the guards tell us. Then we're led through another, smaller concrete yard: In the farthest corner a pole-lamp gleams on several inmates who labor at chinning bars, push-up stands, and bench presses. "Thirty thousand pounds of weights," the guard says. "All the workout stations are outdoors. These guys are rugged, man. They don't fuck around."

Through another locked gate and we're introduced to Pete Abrizzi, short and squat in his dapper blues—an unarmed cop wearing an old-timey handlebar mustachio, the director of recreation. "Welcome," he says. "Glad to see you. We sure do appreciate you guys filling in and helping us out of a pinch." Inside this most central building, the pervasive odor is sour cabbage.

Abrizzi is our only protection as we pass through greenly painted corridors that echo with our mild-mannered footfalls and our guide's friendly conversation. There are floor-to-ceiling fences separating the uptown and downtown traffic lanes, and at every intersection, large holding cages are bolted against the wall.

"We play ten-minute quarters," Abrizzi says. He wears a wooden whistle on a lanyard around his neck. "College rules. I'm one of the refs and a con is the other. Between us I promise you'll get a fair shake."

Suddenly there's a loud clattering from around the corner ahead of us and a referee's whistle shrills down the hall. "In here," Abrizzi says, pointing to the nearest cage. Then he locks the door behind him and blows hard on his own whistle. Forthwith, a gang of colored prisoners overtakes and passes us. Fore and aft they are prodded apace by six guards, none of whom show guns, but all six walking with their billy clubs at the ready. The cons are rowdy and yellow of eye, all dressed in dull green pajamas.

“Fucking Jews!” one of them says with disgust. “Hey, Blood! There’s some Jews here.”

“Mr. Warden! Let me out! I won’t be locked up in here with no Jews!”

“Keep moving,” the rearmost guard drones. “Keep moving.”

“White motherfuckers!”

“Pussy-ass bitches!”

They pass out of sight and we remain caged until another whistle sounds. “Don’t mind them,” Abrizzi says. “Those’re just some crazy jigs from Cell Block E fresh off the streets. It’s cell blocks A and D gonna watch the ball game, lifers mostly. Much more domesticated than those jungle bunnies. The pigeons from A and D’ve been inside long enough to be completely institutionalized. They’ll be noisy all right, but harmless.”

More gates, more steel doors. The air seems thicker in here. Have we been moving down a slight incline? Are we above ground or below?

Abrizzi is proud to show us the main gymnasium with its soft, resilient floor, its worn and shot-gobbling rims. The auxiliary gym features a square boxing ring in one corner, also a volleyball setup and a leatherbound pommel horse. There’s a small room centrally situated off a wide hallway between the two gyms. The sign on the door says, AUTHORIZED PERSONNEL ONLY.

“This is your dressing room,” Abrizzi says, fingering the ends of his mustache.

The room’s only window is cut into the door. Aside from the green metal lockers, the furnishings feature a curtainless shower stall, a blackboard mounted on the wall, several green metal folding chairs, and an exposed shitter that faces the window.

“You’ll be safe in here,” Abrizzi says, “but the door doesn’t lock, so I’d take all my belongings with me if I were you. Yeah, there’ll be some traffic along in the hallway here, but those guys’re mostly trustees. They might stick their heads in if the door's left open, but they'd never dare step inside. There's absolutely nothing to worry about. There's always a guard within shouting distance. Just remember, all the cons you'll encounter here have already had their wildness burned out of them by the system. They don't want any more trouble than they've already got. Game time's in about twenty minutes. There'll be oranges at halftime, and towels for you after the game. Let me know if there's anything else you need. Good luck."

We dress quickly, mindful of the occasional curious face pressed to the window, the cackling laughter ringing down the hall. Ron will have no scouting report for us today. Then Brooks calls us to order for his pregame instructions: "They'll most likely want to run the ball up and down and run players in and out. What we've gotta do is slow it down. Make them play defense. Keep them off the boards. The first five minutes are crucial. They'll come out all full of piss and pepper, hoping to stampede us. Ron and Leo? You guys have your heads screwed back on? Saul? You ready to go? Yes? Then let's give them a lesson. Let's show them how professionals play basketball."

Inside the main gym, the bleacher seats are empty on both sides of the court and the home team is also conspicuous by its absence. Abrizzi is here, conferring with the official scorer, a middle-aged man wearing the pine green suit. Abrizzi points out our team bench and bounces three basketballs in our direction, new models with wider seams for better handling and tighter, less obtrusive laces.

Before we can organize ourselves into layup lines, the house team arrives, resplendent in short-sleeved green uniforms. The white block letters on their jersey fronts spell out VARSITY and there are no numbers on the backs. The team is lily white (like us), ranging in size from about five-nine to six-four, a confusing mob of bulging pectorals and massive arms. How to tell them apart?

Closer inspection reveals that our opponents can be most easily differentiated by their various tattoos and facial scars. "Anchor-on-a-Chain" is perhaps the superior shooter-cum-rapist we've been warned about. "Cheekbone-Zipper" is their biggest player. "Flaming-Heart-for-Jesus" turns out to be Joey Altoona, Ron's erstwhile partner in crime.

Ron summons me to midcourt for an introduction. "Nicky's in the hole," Joey says after we greet each other. "Had a run-in with a screw that stole the Christmas cookies Nicky's old lady sent him. Man alive, it's like a loony bin in here. The food is so bad it's dangerous. Macaroni and spaghetti we get. We're all bloated on starches, and some of the older guys are sick all the time with running sores and the drizzling shits. It's disgusting."

"So how are you doing, Joey?" Ron asks.

"Learning the ropes, kid. But Christ Almighty! Some of these guys are wacko to the core. They belong in here. You've really got to watch your step whatever you do. Don't trip over nobody or accidentally touch nobody. Hey, kid. You know who's in here? Big John. Weeli. Hudger. It's like a reunion. But let me tell you something, Ron ol' buddy. J. Edgar Hoover is right. Crime doesn't fucking pay."

"How you doing otherwise?" Ron asks. "You look in pretty good shape."

"Of course," says Joey. "Lights out at twenty-two-hundred, wake-up is at oh-seven-hundred. Smuggled booze is too rich for my budget. There ain't no broads, and I never been into faggotry. What the fuck else is there? I even started lifting weights." He flexes his sturdy right hand and his bicep bunches impressively. "Charles Atlas better watch out. I'll kick his fucking ass when I'm sprung from here."

"How long're you in for?" I ask.

"I got me a seven-year bid and I'm eligible for parole in 1940 if I stay clean. If I stay alive .... That reminds me ... I hear Leo Gilbert is with you guys. Yeah, there he is all right. How come that asshole's running around scot-free and a nice guy like me is in here? ... Anyway, word is out that Leo's ass is grass. I heard he double-crossed some big-shot mobster's favorite nephew. Carmine Sforza out of Jersey City. So there's some big shoulders looking for him. You know? In here is probably the safest place he can be. I hope you guys ain't going to Chicago 'cause that's where Sforza's uncle lives."

"No," says Ron. "We ain't headed nowheres near Chicago. After here, we're headed to Boston and Philly, all up and down the coast."

"Gotta go," Joey says. "My guys're getting pissed. My teammates. Nice to have met you, Aaron. Good luck, Ron, but not too much of it. Tell you what ... after the game, what'd'ya say we go have a couple of beers and shoot the shit?"

The stands remain empty as the game begins. I outjump Cheekbone-Zipper for the first possession and, right away, Mitchell is clobbered while driving for a layup. Abrizzi makes the call: "Foul on Killer Kelly! Number Two shoots two!"

Mitchell fondles the ball as he sets his feet just so on the edge of the foul line. But instead of shooting, Mitchell backs away and says, "Hey, ref! What'd you do? Take this fucking ball out of the box just five minutes ago? This ball is way too slick. It needs to be rubbed down."

"Naked-Lady" motions for the ball, saying, "Lemme see," so Mitchell obediently tosses him a soft bounce-pass. Naked-Lady paws the ball, then sets it behind his back and rubs the ball twice, three times against his own ass. "Here." He laughs, flipping the ball back to Mitchell. "All better."

The Varsity are earnest and quick, but they're too selfish and impatient to offer serious competition. They try to zone us and we move the ball like it was a live grenade, until Brooks or I can sneak behind the defense for easy shots. When they play us man-to-man, they're mesmerized by the bouncing ball, and we backcut for easy layups. At the other end, they're reluctant to pass, suckers for double-teaming.

We're ahead 9–3 when the front door opens and several hundred white men come rushing into the gym, shouting curses, clamoring into the stands behind the home team's bench.

"Hey! This is my fucking seat! I was here first!"

"Move out or you're dead."

Thankfully, they turn their attention to the Varsity players and seem to ignore us.

"You fucking dip-shits losing already?"

"Cocksuckers! I bet a hundred push-ups on you guys!"

As our lead mounts, the Varsity gets more anxious. Whichever player brings the ball across the midcourt line wants to shoot first and never ask questions. Brooks also sics Ron onto Anchor-on-a-Chain, and the Varsity's best shooter never gets to touch the ball. When our margin builds to 17–6, the players start bickering with one another and begin trading barbs with the fans.

"Give up the fucking ball!"

"Fuck you!"

"Fuck *me*? Fuck *you*!"

Near the end of the first quarter, with our lead extended to 24–9, the door opens again, admitting a large number of Negro inmates, who spill into the bleachers behind our bench. Now the insults are tossed crosscourt over our heads, more vicious than before.

"Here come the spearchuckers!"

"Fuck you, white bread!"

"Who these Jew motherfuckers kicking yo' white asses?"

"Spades!"

"Crackers!"

The coloreds root hard for us, keeping us focused, encouraging us to run up the score . . . Kevin is at the free-throw line and Saul takes the inside position along the right-hand lane. They exchange a furtive glance, keying a play we've often discussed but never undertaken. Kevin deliberately overshoots his free throw to his right, enabling Saul to corral the rebound and drop it through the basket. Someday the geniuses who wrote the rule book will decree that only the defensive players be allowed the inside lane-spots during free throws.

We're now up by 31–12 and the colored fans are hopped up. An old black man stands up and shouts, "Go get 'em, Jew-babies!"

To their credit, the Varsity takes their beating with good grace, congratulating us on "nice shots" and accurate passes. As we're running downcourt side by side, "Red-Rose" points up to the ceiling, saying, "See those?" Perhaps a dozen gray canisters hangling loosely from electrical wires wrapped around the girders. "If you beat us by more than twenty points, a screw pushes a button and down they come."

"What are they?"

"Tear gas."

I wonder—are there any Jews incarcerated here? Embezzlers, forgers, racketeers, stockholders in Murder, Incorporated? Are they sequestered in segregated cells? Praying, discussing great literature, preparing legal appeals, lending cigarettes at high interest. Or are they here in the gym, acting like goyim.

Breaking for the half, our lead is 41–19. Indeed, there are succulent sliced oranges awaiting us in the locker room. And mindless of our overnight journey to come, we can't help rejoicing.

"Let's score a hundred," Leo suggests.

"Why not?"

"No," says Brooks. "That's bush. What we're gonna do is just the opposite. Take the air out of the ball and keep the score down. Let's have Saul and Kevin start the second half in place of me and Aaron."

When Saul and Kevin complain of stomach cramps, they get no sympathy. What did they eat for lunch? "Meatball sandwiches." *Goyische* meatballs made with who knows what, maybe sawdust and roach powder. What did they expect?

Mitchell's prescription is simple: "Take a shit and you'll feel better."

The second half is more of the same except that Saul is surprisingly aggressive and controls both backboards. Maybe our little talk at the Falls did him some good. "You high-pockets!" comes a cry from the white section.

Kevin is uncanny with his one-hander and he sheds defenders like a bear shaking off the rain. During a time-out several "homos" and "sweet boys" dance the hootchie-kootchie along the sidelines. In one corner of the colored stands, two woolly-haired criminals quietly play chess.

We can get a layup whenever we please, but under Brooks's orders we commence bombing away from the stratosphere. Mitchell has regained his touch, and after three quarters the score is 56–33.

Back on the bench, Saul is squirming. "I've got the shits again," he says tightly. "It definitely was the meatballs." Saul leaves the gym headed for the locker room and we quickly forget about him.

As the game winds down, Ron apparently trips over the foul line, and on the very next play he gets tangled in his own feet—allowing Joey Altoona two uncontested layups.

Mitchell is furious: "What the fuck are you doing? Now we're only up by seventeen!"

"Up yours," Ron replies.

Brooks must call a time-out to settle their dispute. "Fuck him!" says Mitchell. "He's crooked as a three-dollar bill."

"Fuck you, Mitchell. You shmuck!"

"Shut up!" says Brooks. "Both of you." Mitchell is distressed when Brooks fails to support him. Nor is Mitchell soothed when Brooks banishes him to the bench for the duration.

Our final margin is 74–57 and we are kept oncourt until all the cons in the stands have been herded out the door. Meanwhile, we accept good wishes from the losing team.

"Good job."

"Thanks for the game."

"See ya later, Ronnie boy. Tell Leo to be careful."

When we're finally cleared to walk off the court, I turn to Ron saying, "They seem like such nice guys."

"They are. Until they can't get their own way . . . . See ya, Joey."

We find Saul laying face down on the floor in the locker room, naked, bruised, bleeding lightly from his ass.

While we stand motionless, shocked and uncomprehending, a pair of colored prisoners stick their heads into the still-open doorway. "The brown-hole bandits strike again!" one of them says, and they both laugh.

"Close that door!" I shout to Kevin. "And tape a towel up to cover the window."

Saul sits up slowly. He's crying and his nose is bleeding. "It was four white guys," he says weakly. "My God! What they did to me . . . . !"

Just then a guard shoves the door open and yanks away the towel. "You can't cover the window," he says. "It's against the rules . . . . Hey! What the fuck happened here?"

Within seconds Abrizzi rushes into the room. Apprised of the circumstances, he demands that Saul be taken to the prison hospital. "It's no consolation," Abrizzi says, "but this is a routine occurrence around here. I'll send for some ice and we'll get the doctors to have a look. You may need stitches. After that, we can move all of Cell Block A through a lineup in about thirty minutes tops."

But Saul declines on both counts. "Just get me out of here," he says. "Just get me the fuck out of here!"

Forgoing our showers, we put our clothes on over our wet uniforms. Then, holding our pants up like sad sacks, we hustle through the gates, the lockups, the signature matchups. At the last checkpoint, Abrizzi hands Mitchell our money in an envelope. "I'm sorry this had to happen," Abrizzi says, "and I still think the doctors should check this out. But I understand. And I promise that we'll find out who those bastards were and we'll make sure they get their asses busted."

We find ourselves inside the car—I'm in the backseat with Saul, Mitchell's at the helm—still stunned and brain-locked. For the sake of the noise, Mitchell starts chattering, "I've got baloney sandwiches, beer, and milk. Help yourselves. Here's one with mustard, one with mayo." He shuffles the sandwiches like playing cards. Then he starts talking a mile a minute, raving on the edge of sudden hysteria: "What should we do? Saul? What do you want us to do? Go back to New York? Guys? What do you think? Let's take a vote. I say fuck the trip! Maybe we should all go back."

It's the perfect excuse to abort our venture. Now or never. But Saul doesn't want a vote. "No!" he shrieks. "I won't go back to New York! No!"

"Shhh," I say softly. "Easy. Easy. You're young. You'll live. Saul . . ."

He hugs himself until he stops sobbing. The Black Lady still chugs in neutral.

"What's there for me in New York?" Saul says in tight gasps.

"Nothing. And there's nothing for any of us there. That's why we're here. Please, let's go on. I swear that I'll be okay. Really. Aaron's right. I'm young and I'm still alive. It could have been worse. That's what my father used to say whenever anything bad happened. I'm lucky. It could have been worse."

"Sure," says Leo. "At least you're not pregnant or nothing, right?" Then Leo snorts a thin laugh through his nose.

Later, the night cloven by our headlights, all of us easily succumbing to the familiar roar and ramble of the road, Saul clutches my shoulder and starts weeping again.

"I know why this happened," he groans. "This is how God gets even. It's almost funny, you know? Like He's got nothing else to do . . . Aaron! Aaron! It's not fair. It's . . . it's unforgivable. Look at me, Aaron. Now I've got nothing. There's nothing left inside of me that still belongs to me. What'll I do, Aaron? How can I live like this? You should have let me jump at Niagara Falls."

My sandwich lies untouched on the floor, my beer uncapped. I sit there hopelessly grieving while Saul sobs himself to sleep. Grieving for Saul, for myself, for all of us. And what is there inside of me that's mine? Perhaps I'm afraid to look too closely. I might find nothing more than a seashell sound, the roar of my own blood.

From Mitchell's Log:
Day Five — January 10, 1936 — Thursday

	Today	Total
Mileage	118	1,271
Expenses	$11.58	$81.18
Income	$350.00	$1,210.00

Net Income - $1,128.86
Average Share - $161. 26
Cash on Hand - $528.86
Max Has - $600.00

Won - 3
Lost - 1

DAY 6

After my wondrous fuck-orama with Debra, the last place I wanted to go was back to the apartment. I was disgusted with myself on several counts, mostly because I had enjoyed myself immensely. (And despite her tears, Debra did too.)

Look at it this way—I'll bet that Cy and Sylvia will make sure that their daughter's plenty mean and nasty when she does come back to life. And I knew then, looking at the wet and viscid stains on the tumbling mats, that Judy and I were undone.

By the time I hitched my pants and left the building, most of the students were long gone. The only stragglers were a few "fast" girls and some wiseguys in training, gathered to smoke "coffin nails" just outside the front gate. Look at the girls posing and flexing their tits, the boys trying hard to look tough and suave like George Raft.

And across the street, sitting, slouching on the chipped front steps of a once-fashionable apartment building, casting fugitive glances over the top of his wrinkled newspaper, was my father-in-law's private eye. Mr. Trace, keener than most persons. He did a sudden vaudevillian double take when he spotted me, jerking the newspaper to cover his face, then craftily peeking around the edge. Who was this guy? Somebody's cousin who worked cheap? A retired Keystone Kop?

What did it matter? Now I was forced to go home, a ten-block walk through the busy streets, through the winter's short twilight, the haze of the city all grayed and shot with silver. The schoolkids newly dressed in rough denim pants and patched jackets filtering back into the streets. Old ladies wheeling wire-woven shopping carts behind them. Cars puttering and honking *ahyouga!* Old men holding brown paper shopping bags from the A & P. What's for dinner tonight? A fresh chicken. Some fish. Meat or dairy? A Salvation Army Santa-bum stands on the corner of Livingston and Grand. So I flip four bits into his pot. "Thanks, bud," he says, ringing his bell. "Merry Christmas and God bless you."

God bless me. What a great idea! God Almighty. Master of the Universe. Good God. Nice God. Mr. Jehovah, Sir.

Making a small detour, I led Boston Blackie through Little Italy and stopped in front of Saint Anthony's R.C. Church on Broad Street, all bright and merry with Christmas lights. In the church's frontyard a papier-mâché puppet show: The Baby Jesus with a gold-foil halo, his crudely fashioned idiot's face reminded me of my lost Sarah Pearl. The Holy Virgin and the Wise Men, everybody wearing the same radiant and idiot smiles. Which of the three was the *moyil*? Balthazar? Even the camels were smiling. I'd walk a mile for a savior. A sign above the manger read, BEHOLD! THE KING OF KINGS IS BORN!

The Father, the Son, *and* the Holy Ghost? (Like Three-in-One oil?) All the rosaries and the gilded statues. The fire and candles and miracles with wafers, wine, and water. The goyim are such pagans, even bigger fools than the Jews.

And Dickhead Tracy trailed me home like a flag of toilet paper stuck to the bottom of my shoe.

Number 1775 Reilly Street was still considered a prestigious address. The main entrance was four glorious steps above the lowly sidewalk, and the front stoop was flanked by two regal lion heads cast in pale concrete. Inside the vestibule, a classy two-way speaker system fit above the mailboxes, and the visitors had to be buzzed past the security door by a tenant. The gray-tiled floors were wet-mopped daily by the superintendent, a colored man named Smitty who lived in a basement alcove near the furnace. The building's six floors were also serviced by an elevator. "An Otis elevator," Mrs. Greenblitz, 4A, liked to say. "The very best kind." Other amenities included an incinerator chute on each floor and the considerable distinction of a dentist's office on the ground floor. The dentist paid a hefty $12.00 per month, and our rent was $7.50. Plus utilities.

The elevator moved sluggishly up to the fourth floor, and Mrs. Greenblitz's eye flashed through her peephole as I stepped onto the landing. I tossed a cavalier salute, and in a huff, she winked away. Then I tiptoed over to my apartment, 4C, and listened at the door, overhearing an excited male voice asking a question of the ages: "Can this girl from a mining town in the West find true happiness as the wife of a wealthy and titled Englishman?" It's time for *Our Gal Sunday*, which meant that Judy was home.

I walked up the stairs to the sixth floor, where I pushed open the counterweighted fire door to a separate stairwell and climbed to the roof.... All over the East Side the rooftops were interchangeable, even in Chinatown. Commonly known as Tar Beach, they were the playgrounds of my youth.

When we were kids nobody we knew had air conditioners or electric fans, so Tar Beach was our only antidote to those sweltering August nights when to think was to sweat. After dinner, the kids would be sent up with blankets, pillows, a jarful of water, and an empty jar to piss in. "Behave," we were told. "Mrs. Schwartz on the top floor likes to complain."

Of course we'd also conspire to bring along our secret supplies—balloons to fill with water or piss, the better to bombard passersby. Under Brooks's tutelage we'd also drop handfuls of strike-anywhere wooden matches. About one-third of these incendiary sticklettes would hit the pavement headfirst and crack into brief flames. Especially effective after dark. One of Brooks's most notable boyhood triumphs was when he showered Mrs. Lipschitz with an entire box of matches, frightening her so that she dropped and broke a bottle of milk.

We'd also watch with interest whenever Brooks hurled alley cats to their doom. Much more humane were the spitting contests for distance and accuracy. Mitchell, with his chronic postnasal drip, was the undisputed champ. One time, he launched a wind-aided lunger that splotched against a third-floor apartment window clear across the street.

"That's why roofs exist," Brooks used to say. "To throw things off of."

Brooks would occasionally fetch his father's binoculars and we'd search the lighted windows for naked women. Our best score was finding Mitchell's mother sitting at the kitchen table in her slip and brassiere. Mitchell cursed us roundly and nearly had a duke-out with Brooks, but in the end, he scoped his mom, too, giggling and blushing like the rest of us.

There were no alleyways separating the contiguous apartment houses, no wasted unrentable space, only air shafts in the middle of each square block. That meant we could roam freely along the rooftops, entering somewhere on Mott Street and escaping on Pitt.

It was years since I'd been on a rooftop, the familiar black surface frozen stiff and crunchy underfoot, the belated rooftop sunset in cold metallic gleamings. Several clotheslines sagged wearily as they stretched from the furnace chimney to the topmost overhanging railings of the fire escapes, brick thumbs and iron fingers playing cat's cradle. Then my eyes followed the shadows down into the street and there was Sam Shovel sitting on a stoop just beyond the first splash of light dropped from a streetlamp.

All the neighborhood kitchens were alight, the windows steamed and opaque. Somebody's window was cracked open for ventilation and a radio was too loud:

"Won't you try Wheaties?
They're whole wheat with all of the bran.
Won't you try Wheaties?
For wheat is the best food of man."

A police siren howled up from over on Block Street. Somebody was playing a two-step piano-roll rag. A bar mitzvah boy rehearsed his whining *Adonoi*s and *Kiddush*es. To the east the lights on the Brooklyn Bridge glistened in the darkening sky. I looked up for a twinkling star to wish upon, but found none.

It seemed so peaceful up there. The city sounds and the passing people, so small, the night so close and trembling. I'd always wanted to live on the roof, up there like a hermit on a mountaintop.

Then I heard the flutter and flap of wings and looked up to see a flock of pigeons wheeling overhead. And from two rooftops over, a broken falsetto crooned, "K't'cooo! K't'cooo!" Old man Lombardo at his pigeon coop, orchestrating their flight by waving a ten-foot wooden wand. He didn't see me as I approached, his small head tilted toward the sky. Lombardo was short and gnarly like an Italian cheroot and I didn't know his first name. He wore faded dungarees, a shapeless green coat, and a gray fedora, all of his garments slimy with whitened bird shit.

The coop itself was a lopsided wooden shack built of vagrant boards and screened with mismatched sections of chicken wire. "Who's dat?" the old man said when he finally saw me looming in the near darkness.

"It's Aaron, Mr. Lombardo. Aaron Steiner. Julius' son."

"Oh, yeah. You Julius little boy."

"Not so little anymore."

"I taut you was one of dem forking Irish kids wid dem BB guns come here to shoot my li'l angels. C'mon over here."

The roof nearest the coop was slippery with white droppings, and above us perhaps thirty birds flew and swooped in loose formations, soaring over the street, then on down toward Division Street before they circled back overhead.

"Eh!" the old man said. "Not so far! Columbus! You don't take dem so far! I tole you! Eh! Crazy birt."

The old man coughed and spat over the edge of the roof and the birds quickly changed direction to chase the wobbling clot. Meanwhile, Lombardo kept waving the long baton, to what music I could not hear. And as the flock swarmed through the air, one gray-speckled pigeon flew off on its own down Mott Street.

"Eh! Lulu! Come back here!" The old man looked at me over his shoulder and explained. "Dat's Lulu. She gotta mind of her own. Just like a woman, you know? But Columbus, he no let her get away." Sure enough, the lead bird swooped low, and the flock followed to reclaim the wandering Lulu.

"Dat Columbus," the old man said in rapture, "he the bess birt I ever have. Last week he won me ten dollars. From dat old crook Gallazo, you don't know him, he live in Brookalyn. We have a race, you know? So I take Columbus over to his house in a cage, my brudder-in-law drive me. And Gallazo, he take his birt over here. A ugly dirty brown half-bread dat look like he roll in shit, you know? Then we each go home, me and Gallazo. Then we go up to de roof and put a secret message into de leg band of each odder's birt. Den atta zactly noon on de clock, we let each odder's bird go fly home."

The flock flapped overhead and two birds fell from the sky to alight on the roof of the shack. "Shoo, Enrico!" the old man shouted, beating his arms like wings. "Teresa! Shoo! You lazy birts!"

Without releasing his gaze from the whirring, whirling birds, he resumed his story: "Den we go up de roof and we wait. Me and Gallazo. My wife, she wait in the house by de telephone, and Gallazo's old maid sister, she wait by his telephone, but I call him first: 'Here'sa you secret message, Gallazo. "Viva Il Duce." You lose ten dollars.'"

And still the birds flew, their wings touching above their backs to make a loud clapping sound. Then they'd glide freely with their wings held in a V and their tailfeathers spread.

"See dat clapping?" the old man asked. "Dat mean dey want to get laid .... Eh! Columbus! Get away from dat building! Get away from dem filthy birts! Dat's dat bastid Armenian's coop. He steal my birts and hole dem for randsome. He say dat's what dey all do in Europa."

Then Lombardo bent into the shed, motioning for me to follow. Tucked behind the chicken-wire was a closed space, reeking of shit and whirling with loose feathers. The old man carefully inspected the perpetual dripping from a water bottle and picked a few stray feathers from the basin below. Then with his bare right hand he scratched some crusted shit off a small block of salt. "Dat's iodine salt," he said, "so my angels don't catch a goita and choke to det."

There were wooden roosts and boxes built into every corner and curve of the coop. Several boxes were filled with straw and sticks and topped with nesting birds. "Dey sick," the old man told me, frowning. "Dis one over here, Maria, she gotta canker. I once had a pretty red carnoo, but he died from canker. Dis one, Antonio, he gotta TB. No, donna worry. Itsa no catchy. Whoop! Here dey come!"

Outside, the sky rained birds while Mr. Lombardo smiled and sang, "K't'cooo! K't'cooo!" The birds landed on every side of him and seemed to mimic the old man's cooing. Then several of them bent forward and began to nod their heads as if slowly pecking at the ground. "Dat means dey want to build a nest."

Two birds bobbled forward and begin to peck lightly at each other's head feathers. "Dat's Lorraine and Salvatorey. Dey in love. My angels are good Cat'licks. Dey never get divorced."

Suddenly, a large red-banded bird—Columbus?—ruffled his neck feathers, lowered his head in my direction, and began turning in menacing half circles. "He mad at you. Wanna chase you away. Dat's okay, Columbus. Itsa Julius little boy. He's a frenna mine."

Other birds wiggled their heads and strutted around like peacocks while Lombardo pointed out the different breeds—mostly yellow tumblers, white fantails, and a single pair of white silky fantails. "Columbus, he'sa racing homer. *Columba Livia,* dat's his Italian name. He's like dat famous French messenger birt in de war, Chair Hommy."

Then the old man started cursing Gallazo again: "Dat bastid. He likes to eat young birts. Squabs, dey call 'em. All dark meat. Italian butchers sell dem inna store, but I could never eat one of my angels. Dat rat bastid Gallazo, he sell dem for two bits a piece. He sells his own and eats his own too. Eh! Itsa bad enough de kids come by and steal dem and shoot dem wid BB guns. De rats and de mice eat dem too. De louse-flies get inbetween de feathers and suck out de blood like vampires. Dey get worms too. Dat crazy bastid."

I followed him out of the coop, and somehow Lombardo managed to maneuver all his birds back inside. Then he leaned into the darkness to find a small cage from which he pulled a yowling yellow cat. "No eats de birts," he said, setting the cat down carefully inside the coop. "Eats de mice."

After hooking the coop closed, he wiped his hands on his pants and delivered this *Summa Theologia:* "Dis here is my familia, my angels. I no care about anyting else, 'cept my wife. People, dey gonna lie ana cheat. Breaka you heart. My angels here ain't like dat. Wid people? Italians hate Irish. Irish hate Jews. Everybody hate de nigs. But my angels? Alla birts get along. And looka dis. Just like people, dey can fly wherever dey want to. Up here, down dere, all over the world. But every night, dey come right back and I lock dem inside. You know? . . . Say hallo to you father. Eh?"

Down in the street, Sherlock was still on the beat, so I walked over the rooftops around to Dillon Avenue, took the elevator down, and made good my escape.

En route to Chicago, we change seats, positions, angles, a ritual dance we've already learned to do without thinking. Somebody empties the spare gas into the fuel hole, somebody drives, somebody pees in the roadside weeds. Nobody talks. Saul moves, bent and stiffly like the rest of us. He sits himself with care and his eyes are dead and glazed.

Moving through flat and snow-drifted farmland. Only a stark lonesome tree or silo to disrupt the flat line where the sky cuts against the land. The sun rises behind us and overtakes us near South Bend, Indiana. The highway slices between dull open fields until we reach Gary, then through huge electric grids, factories, and chimneys belching fire and brimstone.

As we close in on Chicago, Brooks makes a reasonable proposal: "I think we should find ourselves a bath house. None of us showered last night, and besides, it's a cheap place to pass the time."

Mitchell opposes the motion. "Taking a steam bath or a hot whirlpool before a game is a bad idea. It takes all the jump out of your legs. It makes you logy and slow to react, more susceptible to an injury." The vote against Mitchell is 6–1.

As the morning brightens, we've been nibbling away at the bologna sandwiches, gluggling the warm beer and the curdling milk. No one is very hungry anyway, and while we fill-er-up at an Esso station, Brooks consults a telephone directory and finds that we have only two choices, Abe's Baths or the White House Baths. We get directions from the pumpmaster and head out for Abe's.

Driving through the nervous streets of the midwestern metropolis. Chasing the busy pitch and clang, the blue tailstar of a trolley. Seeing newspaper vendors stamping their feet for warmth, fingers stirring the coins in their soiled change-aprons. Civilians hurrying to their jobs. Above us, wild pigeons gurgle on ledges and winged shapes flap through the morning haze. Tires rumble over trolley tracks, sounding like vast machines of war.

Abe's Baths is housed inside a large brown-brick building set facing a firehouse on Cantine Street. Inside, the air is moist, warm, and faintly mildewed and we're already sweating as the clerk collects the toll. He has a long beard, side curls, and a yarmulke. He mumbles something in Yiddish and gives Mitchell twenty-five cents change from the two dollars laid on the counter. We also receive seven locker keys fastened to small elastic garters to be worn around the wrist or the ankle. Under our street clothes, our game uniforms are wet again, and yesterday's congealed patches of skin salt start to melt.

We undress quickly in the locker room, then study the signs on the walls:

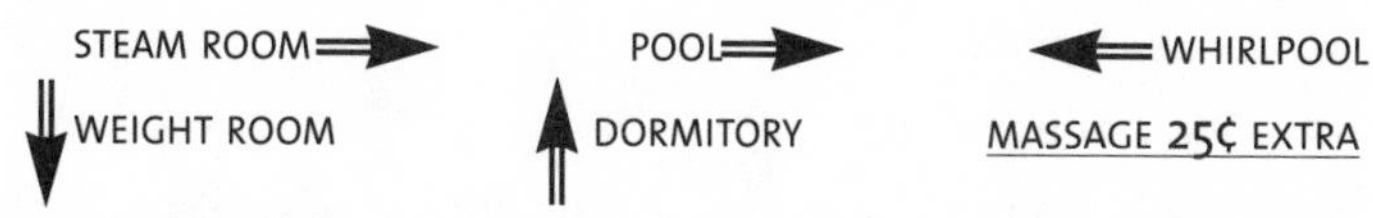

The trickle of blood has dried on Saul's thigh, forming a thin black line like a cancerous vein. We all take showers using the house issue brown bars of coarse soap and raspy towels. Naked old men walk about, their asses sagging, their balls heavy and pendulous, their *putzel*s limp and weary. Saul is off to the whirlpool hoping to find a sitz bath, and Kevin goes along for the company. Ron and Leo disappear while Brooks, Mitchell, and I seek out the steam room.

The hot mist sears my lungs and I breathe deeply and cough. We grope our way toward four rows of wide wooden benches. The top two benches, the hottest spots, are occupied by hazy human shapes. There's a long hose with a pistol-grip nozzle curled on the floor, and a spritz of cold water feels good on my face.

"Where you fellers from?" a disembodied voice asks from the fiery fog. "Hey, you guys are tall."

"New York," says Mitchell, and he might as well trot out the whole spiel. Barnstorming. House of Moses. But the voice is only interested in our home base.

"New York, huh?" As my eyes get used to the climate, I can see a boiled-looking fat man, who chews on a damp cigar stub. On the bench below the fat man, there's a distorted reflection of me, Mitchell, and Brooks—three long-bearded white-limbed Yids. "It's Ruse-velt," says the fat man. "He started that Home Relief program and that's what brought all the *shvartzers* to Chicago and New York." When nobody responds, the fat man says, "Where are you fellers headed, then? Where you been?"

Mitchell reviews our itinerary. "We finish up in Los Angeles in about two weeks."

"And then what?"

"Who knows?" Mitchell shrugs. "Some of us'll probably go back to New York. Brooks here wants to stay in California. I'm hoping to work my way to Palestine."

The fat man grunts politely, but the long-beards show a sudden interest. "Palestine?" says the middle one. "The Holy Land."

"Whatever," says Mitchell.

"Listen," says the Jew on the left. "He says, 'Whatever.' That means he's a Labor Zionist or a Revisionist. So please tell us which."

"I'm a Revisionist," Mitchell says sharply. "I think it's only sensible to want the greatest number of Jews to get into Palestine in the shortest period of time. Not like Weizmann and Ben-Gurion with their legalistic snail's pace, their insistence on the *proper* certification. Nonsense. The Jews have done enough groveling."

The right-most beard says, "Bah! Revisionist. Labor. Zionists are all peas from the same pod. Ben-Gurion and his Jewish goyim will build *Eretz Yisroel*? *Goyishkeit* they will bring to the Holy Land, not Torah. God will build the land, not Ben-Gurion, not you and your Revisionist gangsters. When Messiah comes, we'll have *Eretz Yisroel*, a true Holy Land, not a land contaminated by Jewish goyim. How can you disregard Messiah? How can you ignore the Master of the Universe? A secular Jewish state is a sacrilege. A violation of Torah."

In response, Mitchell laughs cruelly. "Wake up and smell the borscht," he says. "This is the real world and there's a pogrom coming the likes of which you can't even imagine. There's no time to indulge in religious fantasies. There are Jewish lives to be save. Thousands. God forbid. Tens of thousands."

"From where comes such a catastrophe?" the right beard asks. "This pogrom of such worldwide proportions?"

"From the Nazis," says Mitchell. "From Hitler."

"Ha! The Austrian housepainter? That little *shlemiel* with the Charlie Chaplin mustache? Him we should worry about?"

"Yes. Don't you read the newspapers? Don't you know about the Nuremberg Laws?"

"It's nothing," says the middle beard. "*Bupkes.* The process of assimilation. It's nothing new."

"Meanwhile," Mitchell says, his temper flaring, "that crazy Nazi sonofabitch gives them courage even here, all the anti-Semites in America."

"*Oy!* Such language. No wonder . . ."

"No wonder what?"

"It's no use talking with the likes of you."

Mitchell rises to his feet and clenches both fists. "Listen," he says, but his anger is chilled when the door is unsealed and Ron and Leo walk blindly into the room.

"At ease," Leo says when he discerns Mitchell's hostile posture. "Whatta we got here? Some wiseguys giving you trouble?"

"Oy," says the middle beard. "Another one. Another *langa lucksh*. Another meshuggener."

"How's the weather up there?" the fat man asks as he sucks the black juice from his dead cigar.

In answer, Leo grabs his own dick and aims it at the fat man. "What's that you say? I can't hear you from way up here. You'll have to speak into this tube."

We can't help laughing as we leave.

Ten minutes later, as if by some prearranged intelligence, the All-Stars convene in the "Dormitory," a large dry space filled with several rows of canvas cots. There's also a red leather rubdown table in the far corner.

Taking me aside, Saul says that he's sore and swollen but that there are no cuts or splits in the skin. "The bleeding's also stopped. I'll be okay. Physically okay."

Another five minutes and we're all asleep on the cots.

Mitchell wakes us at three o'clock, insisting that we have to "get something in our bellies before it gets too late to properly digest." So we find a deli on Kersey Street, where we have our fill of Chicago-style red-hots—greasy frankfurters piled with fried onions and green peppers. Saul also introduces Kevin to the healing properties of chicken soup while Mitchell previews tonight's ball game.

It's at the Jazz Time Ballroom and there's a dance after the game. We're playing against a team of coloreds."

"A whole team of them?" Leo asks in amazement.

"They're supposed to be real good," Mitchell says. "Our pot is three hundred and that's all I know. Tomorrow and Sunday is the money-time tournament in Nap-Town."

"Niggers," Leo mumbles. And I feel like punching his face.

We all walk lightly around Saul like he's a live bomb, but he insists on driving to the ballroom. And I waive my rights to the crypt for a chance to share the backseat with Mitchell.

We have tenuous directions from the attendant at the bath house, but Saul soon gets us lost. "Make a Jew-turn," says Brooks, and Saul complies.

Then I sidle up to Mitchell and say, "Tell me about the dates we have in Oklahoma City and Los Angeles."

"We're at the fairgrounds in Oklahoma City," Mitchell says. "Some kind of livestock and farm machinery exhibit going on. We're booked for a whole weekend, and the deal is that we take on all comers, ten-point wins for ten bucks a game. Livinski says there's lots of money to be made. The rubes all get drunk and they're ready to challenge the world."

"And Los Angeles?"

"I'm not exactly sure. Some kind of big-money game against some other pros. Livinski says it's a plum. I'm supposed to call him a week ahead."

The slanting light slowly turns to darkness as we find ourselves in a neighborhood of one-story wood-frame houses, ramshackle but immaculate. On the tidy porches there are snow-capped flower boxes left over from the summer. Also in front of every house: burlap sacks over the shrubs in the front yards, neat picket fences, and shiny, undented garbage cans at the curbside. Bicycles are propped against fences, set there in trust. Only the luxurious cars parked in the street don't seem to belong there—Cadillacs, Packards, even a rocket-shaped Mercedes-Benz.

"Niggertown," Leo says. Kevin wants to know how he can tell. "By the smell."

Nobody else smells anything amiss as we find a parking spot two blocks removed from the dance hall and make our way through crisply shoveled snow-paths on the sidewalks . . . . Niggers. Spooks. Jungle bunnies. Who are these strange people? Sure, I've played against Tarzan Spencer and Foothead Jones. Yes, I've played on a team that beat the coal-black Renaissance Five (and two teams that lost to them). I know the colored with their leaping, hard-driving skills, and I always love the challenge. Playing against Shines. Spades. Spearchuckers. They have even more nasty nicknames than the Jews. How else do I know these brown-skinned people? Joe Louis. Steppin Fetchit. Bojangles. Haile Selassie. Paul Robeson. Louis Armstrong. Amos 'n' Andy are white. Jim Crow . . . Outcasts with a cruel history of slavery instead of pogroms. Bound to the wheel, bound to each other. Somehow my chops are up for this game.

Up ahead, THE JAZZ TIME BALLROOM is written in garish yellow lights on a huge rooftop sign that can be seen blinking in the night for blocks around. The four-story building is also wood-framed and resembles any one of the neighborhood homes swollen to gargantuan proportions.

We walk single-file and silently through the narrow pathway, detouring to slog through the snow as we overtake and pass several couples moving toward the same destination. Leo mutters darkly because all the other pedestrians are colored and variously dressed in expensive coats and fancy feathered hats. One especially dark-complexioned woman wears a foxtail comforter.

As we approach the building, we can read the cornerstone, engraved with a date—January 18, 1900—and a large Star of David. The ballroom was once a synagogue!

Mitchell is upset. "It's a sacrilege."

But Brooks scoffs at him. "As the Jews moved to greener pastures, the Negroes moved in. It's economics."

There's a hand-lettered black-on-white sign posted above the iron-trimmed temple doors: CHICAGO 8-BALLS VERSUS NY JEW TEAM + LICORICE STICK SAM AND THE CANDYMEN. And we're waved down a narrow alley into a side door by a short, bird-faced white man dressed in a tuxedo.

"My name is Carney Jones. Who's in charge of you gentlemen?"

Then he shakes hands all around and leads us briskly down an echoing flight of stairs to our dressing room while talking up a blue streak: "How's your trip been so far, gentlemen? It's a long way from New York, ain't it so? Now, don't take it personal that I sneaked you in the side door. I just don't want the paying clientele to get too good a look at you too early. And I must say that you gentlemen have yourselves a great gimmick. Are the beards real? Thought so. You know, I'm mighty glad you gentlemen are so punctual. Being on time means a lot in this business. Surely does. Time is money and money is time. Any of you gentlemen got change for a half hour? Har!"

We've seen this dressing room before—rickity folding chairs, a few large clothing hooks screwed into the walls at eye level, a rusty-looking shower stall, pipes overhead dripping oil and brown water. "Here's the situation, gentlemen. We've got us a high-rent crowd here tonight. Even this early there must be a hundred of 'em already. Colored swells from uptown, downtown, even out of town. White folks slumming. So we want a nicely played ball game. No fights. No problems. Five hundred dollars, win or lose. Got it?"

He stands in the doorway as we shift around, each of us claiming a chair and a hook, being careful where we step, ready one more time to don the ritual apparel.

"Got it," says Mitchell.

"All right, buddy," Leo says closely under his breath. "Beat it. What's he going to do, stand there and watch us get undressed?"

"Regulation college rules," Carney says. "And one more thing . . . If my boys happen to get way ahead in the ball game? They may pull a few pranks just to please the crowd. Now, don't take it personal. Just remember, most of the clientele is here to see my boys and to see the band. You gentlemen are the stooges. So to speak. Like I say, don't take it personal. Game time's in thirty minutes."

We climb into our uniforms slowly, reluctantly, feeling more like performers than warriors. Is this going to be the same kind of charade as the Redheads' game in Cleveland? Lacing my gym shoes, tightening my knee pads more than usual in deference to the twinge I felt last night. What happened to my enthusiasm?

Saul is sitting next to me, still in his civvies. When I turn to prod him with a glance, he says, "I don't really feel like playing, Aaron. I don't even want to be here. Maybe we should've turned back when we had the chance. There doesn't seem to be any compelling reason for me to be doing this anymore. You know?"

Saul's last interrogative tag line asks me to convince him to stay and play. "No, Saul. You made the right decision. But look. As long as you're here, you might as well be all the way here. I mean, what happened can't be undone. No way, forever and ever. And no matter what anybody tells you, you'll never forget it either. But, Saul, you've got to survive. We've all got to survive. Look. Worse things have happened to people. There's a war being fought in Ethiopia, right? Bombs falling. Bullets flying. Saul, everybody's bleeding somewhere, somehow. I know that sometimes life seems like a booby prize. But we're here, Saul, living one breath at a time."

Then I tell him about Judy and Debra, about Sarah Pearl, in short, unadorned sentences. "And I went to Coney Island and threw her ashes into the sea." Like a newspaper story. "And I took Debra into a back room." Masking my emotions for his benefit. "Then I lived in the Bowery." And here I am.

He nods, comforted perhaps and certainly surprised. Then, bless him, he nods in dreadful sympathy.

"You're young, Saul, and you're in pain. So am I. Sometimes it's hard to see any way out. The idea for both of us is to keep busy. To go through this crazy, misbegotten trip one step at a time. To play each ball game one play at a time. And slowly, steadily, time passes. Not that you ever forget, but things are somehow different."

There are tears welling in his eyes when he says, "Thank you, Aaron." Then he unpacks his gear.

That's when Ron joins us, moving stealthily into the room, and we pay close attention as he delivers his scouting report: "Every high-yeller in town is here. Mink coats, diamond pinkie rings, fat cigars. The whole works. Also some white couples and a pair of real suspicious white guys just nosing around. But there's plenty of security everywhere you look. Probably a dozen Pinkertons, all of them armed with nightsticks. And guess what they're charging at the door? Five bucks a head!"

Mitchell whistles, impressed, then asks, "What does the place hold?"

"Maybe twelve, fifteen hundred."

"What about the Eight-Balls?" says Brooks.

"All colored like advertised. Every one of them quick and fast. Two real big guys about six-five or so. Big gorillas with real big hands that can hold the ball like a grapefruit. I never seen nothing like it before. They look like a *real* good team."

"Bah," Leo says. "Niggers can't shoot. All we gotta do is zone 'em."

Ron continues: "They all have drop shots like Saul does, but they do it much harder. Wham! Even the guards. Man alive! They can jump and almost touch the sky .... Oh, yeah. One white ref and one colored."

"Just make sure you stay away from the niggers' heads," Leo warns. "Niggers got heads of stone."

Then Brooks summons us into a rough circle in the middle of the dim basement room to hear his game plan. "Let's slow it down," Brooks counsels, quickly nodding his approval at Saul in uniform. "We're tired anyway. We'll start out in a one-three-one zone to save our legs and see if they can hit from the corners. We've also got to box them off the boards. This is imperative. No easy shots for them. On offense, we've got to be patient and set solid picks. Our picks have been getting sloppy lately. We've got to head-hunt more. Okay? Now . . . That little guy in the penguin suit was talking about the 'pranks' his boys're going to pull on us. I don't know about you, but I don't like to be played the fool. If we just go out and kick their ass, then the trick's on them."

Leave it to Brooks to find an issue that stokes our competitive gumption.

Upstairs, Ron has the crowd scouted to a tee—but their fancy duds don't prevent them from railing at us when we trot oncourt.

"Look at them Jew-boys with their long beards!"

"They're fake!"

"Is it true you Jew-boys got such big noses 'cause the air is free?"

"C'mon, bloods! Beat them beards right offa them!"

The court surface is old wood, wonderfully soft and springy. The baskets are slightly tilted forward and are loosely bolted to the backboards. Shooter's rims and short rebounds. Striding easily through our warm-ups, my knee feels okay.

Some of the "clientele" crowds around the endlines to get a closer look at us, and two Italian-looking white men position themselves out of bounds under our basket. Gamblers with a point spread in mind? Hustlers checking out the ponies before post time?

With my knee apparently up to speed, I'm once more anxious to play. And soon enough, another game begins in another city. Where are we? Oh, yeah. Chicago . . . My counterpart is #8, who flashes a gold-toothed smile and freely offers his hand as we crouch for the center-jump, which he controls easily, at his high-leaping peak while I'm barely off the floor.

From the get-go, the 8-Balls are clearly quicker and stronger than we are. They're also occasionally self-involved, so whatever advantage we might have depends on our experience and cohesion. On defense, they sic a light-skinned half-breed (#1) on Leo to relentlessly hound him full-court. That means Leo has both hands busy just advancing the ball and trying to initiate our weave offense. Every one of their defenders has swift hands in the passing lanes, and even though they don't bother boxing us off the boards, they're quicker to the ball and limit us to one shot per possession. At the other end, their guards repeatedly dribble into the creases of our zone, and #4 is always there to knock down short one-handers from the baseline.

Brooks calls a strategic time-out with us trailing by 10–2. "Holy shit," he says. "I've never seen a team so quick!" When we switch to a 2-1-2 zone alignment, #4 simply moves his accurate shooting to the foul line extended. And over and over again, they vault over our clumsy attempts to box them out for easy put-backs. Only some hot shooting by Mitchell keeps us competitive.

Ron starts out playing cautiously. "I've never played against an all-nigger team before," he explains in another time-out. "Even in the Harlem schoolyards, the teams are mixed. But don't worry about me. I'm ready to get serious from here on in."

Brooks seems to be spinning his wheels, working hard yet producing nothing but muffed rebounds and missed shots. Number 8 and I just about nullify each other—he's strong, eager, and fundamentally sound. Like me, his joy is playing defense and rebounding. He pins my right arms whenever I have inside rebounding position, a nifty trick I've never seen before. We thump each other in the battle of the boards, elbows held low out of mutual respect, rarely receiving meaningful passes from our teammates, trading an occasional put-back. "Nice box-out," he tells me. "Nice pass," I say to him. He seems like a nice guy—I'd love to share a beer with him after the game and shoot the shit.

The action is clean and flowing, forcing both teams to dig deep into our respective wills to win. The referees are incompetent but equitable. Yes, there's a discernible flow to the ball game, a sharpness and proficiency that threatens to overwhelm me. Yes, a freewheeling sense of brotherhood and communion. As the game progresses, Leo is too busy to showboat or take forced shots, and Ron's normal aggression seems somewhat tempered and under control. *Bang!* Mitchell plays give-and-go with Brooks. *Zip!* Number 4 runs a gorgeous backdoor cut in cahoots with #1. "Nice play!" What's the score? Who cares? There's no anger to distort anybody's energy. We're just ten players playing one ball game. What an unexpected revelation! What fun!

When Leo steps to the line for a free throw, one of the big-shouldered *paisanos* materializes out of the crowd and stands at the edge of the court, smacking a big fist into his open left hand and saying to Leo, "I've got a message for you from Carmine Sforza." Leo says, "Shit!" and misses the free throw. We're behind by 21–17 at the half.

There are six scruffy-looking colored men in our dressing room as we retreat there for the intermission, Licorice Stick Sam and the Candymen, all smiling and friendly. They quickly relinquish the available chairs to us and cluster in a corner to fiddle with several dowdy tuxedos that are framed on wire hangers suspended from the pipes. "You men's from New York?" Licorice Sam asks as he screws together two long tubes that make up his clarinet. "I was born there my own self. In the Bronx, near Crotona Park. Where you be headed? Where you done been?"

Mitchell and Sam compare geographical notes, but the only common ground seems to be Chicago and New York. Sam noodles on his mouthpiece and says, "The road sure is a big place, ain't that the truth?" All of us nod sadly and wisely. Then Sam rejoins the circle of his bandmates to smoke a thin stick of what smells like reefer. Ron inhales the basement air deeply and obviously yearns for a puff.

"No," Mitchell says sternly, but Ron winks at Sam and mouths the word *later*.

"All right," Brooks says. "We've got a game to win . . . . How about we run a pick in the backcourt to ease the pressure on Leo?"

"Fine," I say.

"Do whatever the fuck you want," Leo says. "I'm done. I'm finished. Where's my clothes?"

"What're you talking about?"

"That gangster. That bone breaker. Didn't anybody else see him? Didn't you hear what he told me? Says he's got a message from Carmine Sforza, that wop I short-circuited in Jersey."

"But, Leo," Mitchell says, "what can he do to you in front of all those people? They're just trying to scare you into paying up. Hey, you've got enough money now, don't you? We'll advance you the rest if you need more."

We nod in eager agreement, but Leo says, "No, no," as he rapidly unlaces his shoes. "I owe him two G's. Unh-unh. That guy's here to fuck me up. Lookit. Guys like that don't give a flying fuck about witnesses. Why? You think if he shot me in the middle of the game, somebody in the stands would testify against him? Shit, no. I ain't going back out there, and that's that. Gimme the key to the car and I'll meet you there later on . . . . No, Mitchell, don't try to talk me out of it. It's a matter of life or death. Mine, not any of yours."

So Leo dresses in a rush, and when we return to the court, he sneaks into the street.

Without Leo handling the ball, the home team gradually widens their lead. Ron is just too slow to play the point against #1's quick, thieving hands. Poor Ron gets ripped twice in the backcourt and is constantly forced to pick up his dribble much too soon for us to get into our offense.

"Where's the little guy?" #8 asks.

"He's sick."

"Too bad. He can play real good."

With Ron in Leo's slot, Kevin's in the game to play small forward, but the rookie has fumble-itis. Then for a long stretch, Mitchell is successfully denied the ball by #4's persistent defense, and we have even more trouble than before finding good shots. Finally, we abandon our weave and play a more station-to-station offense, trying to create better spacing. But it's no use. Our deficit stretches to 12 points. Send in the clowns.

Damn! I didn't realize how much we need Leo.

In the stands, I can see the two thugs shouting at each other, arguing over who was responsible for letting the fish escape the net. Saul is our only relief off the bench, and he seems to play in slow motion, losing the ball to fast hands and suffering the indignity of having a hook shot blocked by a guard. The fans laugh at us.

"You Jew-boys go count your monies! Don't be trying to play no ball with the bloods!"

A late-game shooting spree by Mitchell keeps the game close enough so that the 8-Balls are deterred from pranking us. The final score is 45–39, and the handshakes are sincere as we congratulate one another for such an enjoyable run. Turns out the 8-Balls are also entered in the Indianapolis big-stakes tournament. "See you later on," says #8. And they encourage us to stay and hear the band.

Indeed, the band members are dressed and just about leaving as we enter the dressing room. Sam, too, invites us to come upstairs and "have a look-see." Then Ron hobnobs in a dark corner with the bass player, probably sharing some of the reefer he craves.

So Ron is lit and I'm played out, but everyone else seems downtrodden as we shower and dress. "I hate to lose!" says Mitchell. "That fucking Leo! It's his fault!"

"Couldn't be helped," Brooks says in a mild funk. "They're younger, quicker, and well rested. Face it, we were lucky we stayed so close. If you'd had a bad game, Mitchell, we'd probably have lost by twenty. Then who knows what might have happened. Our pants pulled down. Buckets of water dumped on our heads."

"That was a great first half, though," I chime in. "Wasn't it?"

"What're you talking about?" Mitchell snaps. "We lost the first half too."

"Our only real consolation," Brooks notes, "is they had to play us straight."

Back upstairs the joint is jumping. The trumpet bleating and the trombone bending notes in perfect harmony. The drums, bass, and guitar playing intricate rhythms. And Sam piping his black melody stick, now snarling, now cooing, always soaring. The lively music moves the male dancers to cast off their tuxedo jackets and unwind their neckties and the ladies to kick their high-heeled shoes to the sidelines. We behold a courtful of jitterbugs, leaping and writhing in syncopated ecstasies.

"Animals," Mitchell sneers. "Such primitive music."

Brooks laughs. "Ease up, Mitchell. These people are just having themselves a good time."

On a trip to the men's room whom do I meet but #8, with his ever-ready smile proudly showing his glistening gold teeth. His eyes are brown and wide-awake. His black, cavernous nostrils show large beneath a nose that looks like it's been pounded flat by a hammer. Like a long-lost cousin, he playfully cuffs my shoulder. "My man," he says. "Number Six. How you doin'? Havin' a good time?"

"Yeah. It's great."

"Hey," he says, sidling up beside me. "Answer me one question, will ya? Nothin' personal, man. But I always wanted to know somethin'. Okay?"

"Sure. Be glad to help."

"I mean . . . No offense, man, but I always wondered what it was like to be a, you know, a Jew."

"Well, we grew these beards and these side curls just for the tour. Otherwise, you can't hardly tell us from regular white people."

He pinches his flat proboscis into a small peak and says, "Sept for the nose." And we both laugh.

"In New York," I say, "being a Jew's not such a big deal. The prejudice is real subtle. Most of the highfalutin hotels and country clubs exclude Jews and so do certain businesses. But that doesn't affect me anyway. Outside of New York it's a different story. With the beards and the yarmulkes it's like the mark of Cain. A lot of people are afraid of us and that's why they want to hurt us."

"Jes like us. Sept we cain't shave off no beard and pass for white. Our skin don't change color."

"What's that like for you?"

He shrugs. "We mosely stick to our own, you know. It's like you said, real subtle up north. Even in Chicaga. Leastways we don't get jerked up no trees as often as they does down Souff. It's a hard life, man. I'm here to tell you . . . Always being stepped on. Treated like an animal. A colored man's got to be real strong to feel good about hisself. It makes it real hard to raise a fambly and being a proper father. Pres'dent

Rosabelt, he trying to help us along. And, you know, thins gonna have to change some. Cain't get no worser. Glory be, our time is coming. Now, mind you, I'm only a sometimes churchgoing man, but I still look at it thisaway . . . . All our trials and tribulations jes bring us closer to the Lord. That's what keep my people strong. Acourse, there be plenty others that yield up to temptation and fall to the devil. But mostly it's the hard times, man. Dirt-scrabble hard."

I want to know what he does for a living. I want to know about his wife and kids. What does he like to eat? How does a barber cut his kinky hair? I want to ask him a million things.

Off the court, I've never really talked this much with a Negro before. Usually it's been "Keep the change" or "Third floor, please." Sure, there are several Negro players in the Harlem schoolyards. ("Nice pass" or "Good defense.") But sad to say, me and #8 are too far apart. There are actually some places in the land of the free (Chicago?) where coloreds are freely lynched and firebombed. (Only because they're easier to spot than Jews?) Even though he's a ballplayer, I feel more connected to those Old World Hasids I saw in Nyack than with a colored man. In any case, #8 says, "Party time, man. You guys can surely ball. Later on."

"Yeah. See ya."

Back inside the dance hall, Carney finds us to say, "Great game, gentlemen. Very entertaining." And to count out five crisp C-notes into Mitchell's hand. After a few more tunes we remember that Leo is waiting for us and we gather for our leavetaking. There's no sign of the thugs, but Mitchell "strongly" suggests that (except for Ron) we each take possession of a hundred-dollar bill, that we leave singly and make long detours to the car just in case we're followed. Ron has to be yanked from the dance floor, where he's hopping and bopping with some big-assed mama, and I'm the last one out the door.

The famous hawk wind clutches at my face and the night air is frosty and refreshing. It comes to me that I've spent far too much of my life indoors. And suddenly my mind is surprised by the image of Debra . . . . Debra. My victim or my partner? Jesus, maybe I love her! Actually love her. Is that remotely possible? Heat and passion. The itch that only she can scratch. Isn't that what I used to feel about Judy? And if I did in fact really love Debra, wouldn't that change everything? Give me an excuse? Mitigate my circumstances? Maybe. . .

Suddenly a big-shouldered form moves out of a shadow to step behind me and poke something narrow and blunt into the small of my back. "We ain't so stupid as you think," a deep voice boasts. "We know exactly where Leo Gilbert is. We know exactly where the car is parked. What I want you to do is walk to the car. Slowly. We only want Leo. We don't want to hurt nobody else."

He's lying. If he knows where the car is, then what does he need me for? And why wait until we're all there? Why turn 2:1 odds into 2:7? And where's his buddy? So I slowly lead him astray, circling the streets (now crowded more than before with fancy cars), but never moving more than a block or so away from the Black Lady just in case.

Then there's a shout from around the corner, shrill words borne high on the wind: "Carlo! I found it! Over here!" Then from the same direction comes the ringing sound of a gunshot. Quickly, I reach behind me and slam an elbow into my assailant's meaty face. No whistle sounds, no foul is called, just a groaning and the sigh of a big man falling. And I run full-blast toward the car.

The other plug-ugly is standing boldly in the middle of the street, bathed in the Black Lady's headlights, pointing a handgun in front of him and shouting over his shoulder, "Carlo! Is that you? He's in there! Carlo?"

Hugging the shadows, I can see that Mitchell is behind the wheel

. . . but there's some kind of commotion going on inside the car. It's Mitchell and Ron shouting at each other. Then Mitchell sticks his head out the open driver's window and yells in my direction, "Hurry, Aaron! Where the fuck are you?"

The thug in the street aims his gun at where he thinks I am, has second thoughts, then re-aims it at the front of the car. Firing now, a bullet pinging through the right front fender. Then another shot, this one aimed at the tires. Next comes the sound of heavy footsteps behind me, and Carlo takes a potshot at me. Jesus! So I run a change-of-direction zigzag drill toward the car, swiveling like a halfback as another shot cracks the pavement near my feet. Then Ron jumps out of the car with Kevin's gun in his hand and shoots the spotlighted thug somewhere in the leg.

"Carlo! I'm hit! I'm dying!"

As for Carlo, he ducks behind a parked car and returns Ron's fire just as the crypt door swings open and I dive inside headfirst. Now Ron is back inside the car, too, shoving Mitchell into the navigator's seat and stomping the accelerator.

Carlo runs into the street ahead of us, his nose bleeding, assuming a kneeling position near the crumpled and wailing form of his partner, aiming his gun at us, steadily, as the car rushes at him. But Ron reaches out the driver's-side window and fires a wild shot while driving full speed ahead. Carlo is brave no more, diving for his life behind the shelter of another parked car. Ron laughs like a maniac and swerves slightly to run over the outstretched leg of the already leg-shot thug.

And Ron drives recklessly onward, cornering on two wheels, cutting down dark alleyways, running red lights, doing fifty on city streets. A siren yowls behind us, the local cops now on our tail, but Ron easily eludes them. Later, near the edge of town, Ron suddenly steers the car into a blind alley, where we wait for fifteen long minutes until he's sure our pursuers have given up their chase. We finally cross the state line into Indiana, still breathless.

"You fucking madman!" Mitchell screams at Ron. "You could have gotten us all killed!"

And Leo cries, "They'll get me! Wherever I am, they'll come and get me! Now they got blood in their eye, so they'll kill me for sure!"

Meanwhile, Ron just laughs, high and mighty.

From Mitchell's Log:
Day Six — January 11, 1936 — Friday

	Today	Total
Mileage	732	2,003
Expenses	$28.82	$110.00
Income	$500.00	$1,710.00

Net Income - $1,600.00
Average Share - $228.57
Cash on Hand - $1,000.00
Max Has - $600.00

Won - 3
Lost - 2

On second thought, we unanimously decide to skip the money tournament in Indianapolis because of its dangerous proximity to Chicago. Instead, we'll drive straight through to Oshkosh, Wisconsin, a leisurely day on the road.

"And, Leo," says Ron, "whenever we're out in public, you gotta walk ten paces behind us."

Later, when we stop at an all-night roadside diner, Leo says to me, "Could you do me a big favor, buddy? Bring me back a fried-egg sandwich, the eggs over easy, and some black coffee with one and a half cubes of sugar? I ain't moving out of here until I have to. Thanks, Aaron. I'll pay you back later on."

Inside, there's a bell that jingles when Mitchell pushes open the front door. The kitchen is situated behind swinging doors, the wooden tables and chairs are chrome-trimmed. The only other customers are a group of teenagers sitting at two tables pushed together, gawking at us and talking in close whispers.

As Ron and I head for the head, I ask him about the front-seat fracas he had with Mitchell just before the shooting broke out. "Mitchell, he went nutso when I took the gun out of the glove compartment," Ron says with a smirky grin. "There's this goon standing twenty feet in front of the car pointing a gun at us, and Mitchell says that I'm a no-good troublemaker. What a laugh. Brooks? He was in his usual daze. And the rookies were staining their drawers. Leo? Burrowing into the floorboards and screaming that we should get the fuck out of there right now and leave you behind. If I wasn't there, they'd've gotten themselves all killed. Me? I loved it. I love that kind of action."

Ron joins Saul and Kevin while I seat myself at the same table as Brooks and Mitchell (both looking so sleepless and forlorn). I order oatmeal and black coffee from a fat waitress in a clean starched uniform. My two compadres order eggs and bacon.

Then Mitchell unloosens a silently screaming yawn and says, "You know something, Aaron? Me and Brooks were just now saying what a fucking disaster this trip of ours is turning out to be. You know? Nobody gives a fuck about the bylaws anymore. Ron thinks he's hot shit, and the rookies mostly keep to themselves. Of course the thing that happened to Saul was a real tragedy. No question about it. And there's no way any of us can be blamed for that. But what really scares me is last night's fireworks. I mean, we could have tough guys like that trying to hunt us down all across the country. Just think about what a living nightmare that would be. Anyway, maybe we should just give Leo his walking papers. I'm serious, Aaron. I'd certainly breathe easier if he was gone. Anyway, that's my opinion. What do you think, Aaron? Is it worth calling for a vote?"

The waitress brings the food. The oatmeal is lightly dusted with cinnamon and comes with a miniature ceramic pitcher of milk and one of honey. I mix all the ingredients to their proper consistency and deflect the question to Brooks.

"Don't ask me about Leo," Brooks says. "Don't ask me about voting. All I know is that whatever we're doing isn't working." Then he begins methodically to eat his eggs.

The oatmeal is scrumptious. Between mouthfuls, I manage to say this: "I'm upset by some of the things that've happened to us, too. But I also think we've got a long, long way yet to go. And I don't think it's right to abandon Leo. Just like we can't abandon Saul."

"You're probably right," Mitchell admits. "But I just get the feeling that Leo is only getting what he deserves and that we're the innocent bystanders."

"Mitchell," Brooks says somberly. "None of us is innocent."

"And I hope and pray," I add, "that none of us gets what *we* really deserve."

Back in the car, I stretch out, between Saul and Ron, in the middle of the mattresses and I'm happy to fade away into a sinister dream . . . . It's high noon in the Wild West and the wind swirls the dust on Main

Street. It's a showdown. All the stores are closed, the shutters bolted, the law-abiding townsfolk in hiding. And here I am, standing under the hot sun, a pearl-handled six-shooter strapped against my right hip. My hands dangling, my fingers twitching, I'm one-on-one, face-to-face, with my own reflection in a full-length mirror. Finally, my right arm moves like a hydra-headed serpent quickly toward my gun, but my mirror-image has already beaten me to the draw. *Bang!* Now the real me is gut-shot and gasping as I shatter into a million shards of broken black glass.

I wake up with a start and see Saul looking at me with a sad and mournful puss, so I gently inquire about his physical and mental well-being. "I'm okay," he says with a broken smile. "I'm actually doing real good, Aaron. Sure. Now I can forget for maybe a minute at a time. Yeah, I'm doing terrific."

All I can offer is an understanding sigh and the suggestion that he not be so tough on himself.

"Look who's talking," he says before closing his eyes.

We drive through the darkness and away from the rising sun. Our next stop is a Greek diner, where I order a lettuce and tomato sandwich with mayo on toasted rye and a carton of milk to go, please. While I'm waiting for my order to be filled, my attention is nagged by the wall-mounted pay telephone near the bathroom.

Whom can I call? Max? Judy? City Hall? The Answer Man? Debra.

Debra.

Could I really talk myself into loving her? *Putz* that I am! Imbecile! Weakling! Coward! But wouldn't it be nice if I did love her? If we loved each other? . . . I did it for love, Your Honor . . . . Yes, Sarah Pearl, you'll have to excuse your daddy because he fell in love, because he couldn't help himself, because all is fair in love . . . . And wouldn't it be nice if Debra and I could live happily ever after in the land of the Silver Screen? Don't we both deserve it?

That's right, keep on talking to yourself, Aaron. Happily ever after. *Toujours l'amour.* Once upon a time.

So I ask the fat waitress to please cashier three singles into silver, then I ask the telephone operator for long distance . . . . If one of Debra's parents answers, I'll—

"Hello?"

"Hello, Debra? It's me. Aaron. Mr. Steiner."

"Hello? Is it really you? Just a minute . . . . It's for me, Mom! A girlfriend from school about the social studies homework!"

What does the electrified, static-backed sound of her voice do to me? Nothing. Oh, God! Am I finally cracking up? Is there no end to the selfish ways with which I manipulate other people's lives? "Debra, I've been thinking about you. I don't want to, but I am."

"You. Where are you? You vanished into think air just like that Judge Crater . . . . What do you want?"

"I just want to talk to you, that's all. To find out how you've been."

"I'm . . . I don't know. My dad says I got myself in trouble because I tried to act too grown-up. Is that what really happened?"

"Hold on. You say you're 'in trouble'? Debra, are you pregnant or something?"

"No. Absolutely not. But this man came by the apartment. Mr. Goldfarb? Your—your wife's father? And he talked to both my parents. There was a big scene. They wanted me to sign some paper, but I wouldn't do it. Not that it makes much of a difference. Everybody knows in the whole living world. Everybody's watching me now. In school, the juniors are reading *The Scarlet Letter* in English and they all call me Hester. You should hear what they call you."

"Debra, I don't care what—"

Then she breaks down, crying softly, painfully, saying, "Oh, Mr. Steiner! I hate my life! I feel like running away! To somewhere. If my dad knew I was even talking to you, he'd send me away to reform school."

"Debra. I'm in . . . I'm near Chicago and I'm on my way out to Los Angeles."

"California?"

"Yes. Look, I want you to meet me there, Debra. In Los Angeles. I'll send you money for the train fare."

"What do you mean?"

"You say you want to run away. To start all over again, right? Well, here's the chance to do it. For real. I'll be there in Los Angeles in about two weeks. Think about it . . . . We could have a new life together, Debra. It'd be just the two of us. And I'll have plenty of money by then, so we could do whatever we wanted to do."

"California?"

"Picture it . . . the palm trees, the Pacific Ocean."

"The movies."

"That's right."

"You know what? Even when I was a little girl, I always wanted to be a Hollywood actress."

"It could happen, you never know. A pretty girl like you, Debra. At least you'd be giving yourself a chance to find out."

"I don't know . . . You really think I'm pretty?"

"I think you're beautiful, Debra. I love . . . your looks."

"I don't know . . ."

"You mean you really want to stay in New York? With your parents watching you like you're in jail? With Mr. Goldfarb snooping around? And you mean you like going to school?"

"I don't know. I'd be ascared to go."

"Well, I don't know what else I can say, Debra. I want to be with you." (I think. I hope.) "Look. Let me call you back in a few days. I've got to go now. Think about it and don't tell anybody."

"No, I won't. I mean, I will think about it, but, no, I won't tell nobody."

"Okay."

"Are you really serious about this, Mr. Steiner? You're not just teasing me?"

"I'm serious, Debra. I've got to go now. I'll call you next week."

"Bye-bye."

(And I hate myself all over again.)

Leo has gotten us lost and is squabbling with Mitchell in the front seat. I'm in the backseat with Brooks, both of us sharing a newspaper purchased at the Greek diner. "Don't you know right from left?" Mitchell is shouting. Quietly, I reach forward and slide the chauffeur's window shut.

Let's see—in the comics section, Dick Tracy aims his sharp profile at a closed door, saying, "Open up in there! I've got a tommy gun in my hand and it's in a barking mood!" In sports, Joe Louis is a prohibitive 10–1 favorite to defend his heavyweight title against this month's bum, Charley Retzlaff, next week back in Chicago. Here's another group of Protestant clergy calling for the United States to boycott the Berlin Olympics because of the Third Reich's Nuremberg Laws. In South Dakota, Albert Stevens and Orvil Anderson have set an altitude record, floating to seventy-four thousand feet in a hot-air balloon . . . . And I can't help peeking at Brooks over the top of the page. He looks ten years older than he did a week ago, his eyes are watery, his teeth are yellower, and I swear that his black beard is now flecked with gray. After a while, Brooks gets twitchy and expectant, aware that I'm staring at him. "What?" he asks.

"What?"

"You know what, Aaron. Ask me what you want to ask me."

"What what? Which what? What the fuck's wrong with you lately?"

"Aha! That's the what I'm talking about."

"So talk about it, Brooks .... Yeah, yeah, I know what you're gonna say .... Everything's fucked up. Saul and Leo. The trip. The world .... So you have plenty of good reasons to be feeling sorry for yourself and moping around like a fucking zombie."

He sighs like a witness under interrogation and about to confess to murder. "I'm such a fool, Aaron. I really thought that we could be an example or something. Some kind of proof that certain things were possible. Brotherhood. Equality. *Viva la revolución!* But all we're doing is playing out a selfish little adventure that means nothing to anybody except ourselves. We're mercenaries, Aaron. Whores on wheels. And meanwhile, nothing changes. Corruption, poverty, exploitation. Mussolini and his fascists bombing the shit out of Ethiopia."

"So? What else is new? So the world is a big bad place and none of us are saints. You want something to change because seven meshuggeners are driving a hearse and playing basketball games from coast to coast? Grow up, Brooks. We're doing what we're doing."

"Tell me, Aaron. Please. Exactly what are we really doing?"

"We're making money for ourselves, Brooks, and there's nothing wrong with that. Poverty isn't holy. And we're also rolling the dice. Trying to rescue ourselves from our own lives. That's good enough for me."

He laughs rudely. "When is this rescue supposed to happen? And where do we get to read the devil's bones? Here in Illinois? Maybe in Wisconsin or Iowa? Or in Hollywood, where stupid dreams come true? ... C'mon Aaron. We're just farting around."

"What's your remedy, then? What should we be doing that we're not doing?"

"Making a commitment," he says quickly.

“To what, Brooks? Making a commitment to what? The revolution? Tell me where it is and I’ll go there.”

He erases my words with a careless wave of his hand. “A commitment to ideals,” he says. “A commitment to something bigger than ourselves. The idea of communism. The idea of labor unionism.”

“Sounds very Platonic, Brooks. Have your pie in the sky and eat it too.”

“Make jokes, Aaron. But mark my words, I’ll know it when I find it. And I’ll be ready to pay the price.”

“Brooksie, my bosom buddy and boon of my childhood . . . why can’t we just roll with the punches like we’re doing now? We’re on the move away from something and toward something else. Why can’t that be good enough? For you, for me, for us? We can’t save the world, Brooks. It’s all we can do to try to save ourselves.”

“Now look who’s lecturing.”

“Fuck you, Brooks.”

Why are we all so hungry? Is it fear? A sense of incompleteness? Brooks suggests we’ve picked up some intestinal parasite from “the good folks” in Glens Falls. Mitchell makes some cursory objections to our spending too much money on food, but we ignore him.

One more pit stop, one more phone call. This one to Max, collect at his sumptuous Greenwich Village apartment.

“*Nu, boychik.* What’s new? Where’ve you been? I almost called out the FBI to go find you.”

We’ve been hither and yon, winning and losing and making money. I don’t tell him about bypassing Indianapolis, but I do supply the harsh facts about Saul. And Leo.

“My God,” Max says. “This is serious. But I hope you didn’t call the police about this Leo business.”

"Are you kidding, Max? We have an unregistered gun, a concealed weapon, which we used to shoot somebody. And there's nothing we can do about Saul."

"Good thinking. You don't ever want to get the police involved if you can help it. And here's another thing, little brother. You tell Mitchell that Monday morning, bright and early, I want him to wire me some more of the money, because I still get nervous with you guys carrying around so much. Understand?"

Yes, Max .... Yes, I feel fine .... Yes, the car is fine .... Yes, Saul will be fine .... When I tell him how much I'm looking forward to Los Angeles, he doesn't respond, so I pump him. "Max, some of us are wondering exactly what the arrangements are for the game in L.A."

"Don't worry, little brother. I promise you'll love it .... Ooops! There's the doorbell. Got to go. Don't forget to tell Mitchell to send me some more money."

We reach Oshkosh in midafternoon and are directed by a gas station attendant to the Lakeside Manor, a magnificent hotel in the Euro-Rube tradition. The Lake in the title is Winnebago, and the Manor is an approximation of a Swiss chalet replete with white-trimmed gables and window peaks, and a fleur-de-lis painted in white above the crosshatched main entrance. The air smells like cold smoke, and as we pull ourselves out of the hearse, I can hear Mitchell murmuring, "I'm gonna kill that fucking Leo."

Inside, there are long leather couches in the lobby, antlered heads of deer, and glass-eyed elk mounted high on the walls. Some local wag has inserted a meerschaum pipe into the savage-toothed grin of a bear's head. The fieldstone fireplace glows with the warmth and crackle of hardwood logs aflame. Standing in the lobby, I feel like an uninvited guest in a rich man's house.

An alert young man sits behind a gleaming mahogany counter-top. He wears spectacles, a crisp white shirt with blue bow tie, and he informs us that a "convention of sign-language teachers has just about cleared out" and that off-season rates are currently in effect. Singles cost $4.00 per night, doubles are $2.50. A "continental breakfast is *gratis*" from six to ten A.M. in the restaurant.

And Mitchell celebrates our escape from Chicago by granting all of us the option to room alone. "Hear! Hear!" says Brooks with a wry wrinkling of his brow.

Even Leo gets the message and offers no resistance. "Okay. That'll be no problem. I'll just have to sign the guest book with my left hand and register under a phony name."

The rookies are the only pair wishing to bunk together, and for total privacy we insist that none of our rooms be contiguous. Game time is seven o'clock tomorrow night, and we'll meet in the lobby an hour before. Then Mitchell distributes five dollars each for our personal expenses here and in Cedar Rapids before he's "off to hit the sack."

My room features graceful and intricately carved cherrywood furniture. The bed, a chair, a table, and a dresser are beautifully handcrafted, their corners and curves joined by wooden pegs. The filaments in the wall-mounted lantern-shaped lamps flicker in imitation of lively leaping flames. Too bad the bed is way too short and blocked at the far end by a solid wooden footboard engraved with vines and grape clusters.

The only window is framed with gingham curtains and overlooks the frozen expanse of Lake Winnebago, now glinting and glimmering in the silver sunshine. Far offshore, I think I see a yellow dot of light dancing in and out of a shadow. A mirage? An hallucination? A Martian spaceship? I'm too tired for further speculation, so I move the mattress to the floor and plunge headfirst into a deep slumber like a lead-booted diver falling to the bottom of the sea.

In my dreams, I'm caught in the wash of a gentle black tide, floating among sprightly water ferns, friendly squid, and kindly turtles. The most restful sleep I've had since we left New York.

From Mitchell's Log:
Day Seven — January 12, 1936 — Saturday

	Today	Total
Mileage	291	2,294
Expenses	$52.25	$162.25
Income	0	$1,710.00

Net Income - $1,547.75
Average Share - $221.11
Cash on Hand - $947.75
Max Has - $600.00

Won - 3
Lost - 2

DAY 8

I don't wake up until the next morning just after seven bells. Despite my restful ease, my legs are stiff and aching as if I've been beaten with a rubber hose. Go figure.

The white porcelain bathtub rests on brass lions' paws and the tap handles are lions' heads in full roar. There's a small glass bottle of a nameless (but *gratis*) shampoo on a shelf near the sink, also a vial of bubble bath. How can I resist? So I draw a scalding-hot bath while I'm happily perched on the throne.

Shortly thereafter, I slowly lower myself into the steaming bathwater, luxurious, even though my long legs must be flexed at an awkward angle in the short and slippery tub. When the water cools, I pull myself onto dry land, relaxed and soothed and already anticipating a long afternoon's nap.

I dress in clean dungarees, a clean-enough T-shirt, and a thick green sweater that Judy's mother once knit for me. Then I gaze out the window at the frozen lake, haphazardly looking in the direction of the blinking light I thought I saw last night. And there it is . . . inside or nearby some kind of manmade structure. A tent? A shed? The light must be a fire. Fire and ice. The substances of Dante's hellpit and lair of the devil. So I don an extra sweatshirt against the cold and find a back staircase that leads down to the waterfront.

Outside near the shoreline, snow trees rise white and thin and the air smells like ice. Clouds float overhead like icebergs in a dense sea-colored sky. A white-slatted wooden dock and a barrel-buoyant raft have both been hauled ashore and stranded high on a narrow strip of snow-crusted sand. The surface of the lake itself seems to be frozen solid, while a cutting wind swirls the loose snow crystals to reveal the green-tinted ice beneath. I find it easier to slide my way forward than to step, falling only once as I approach the strange light.

The man-crafted enclosure is canvas-backed and khaki brown, a half-cylindric shape most likely propped inside by curved lengths of wood or specially torqued metal rods. The hut seems to rest on the ice with no visible pegs or lines to secure its position. The small hemispheric side that faces the hotel is only partially blocked by a canvas curtain, rolled up nearly to the curve of the roof, and the ice in front of this opening is licked by a tongue of pinkish light.

I slide to a smooth stop opposite the entrance and bend forward to see what I can see . . . . The shelter is perhaps four feet high in the middle, four feet wide, and eight feet long. The light comes from a short-legged brazier heaped with glowing coals. Set dead center directly atop the coal mound is a battered and charred copper teakettle. Behind the brazier a bearded human figure crouches and points a double-barreled shotgun precisely at my face.

"Hello there," I say, real friendly like.

It's a wild-eyed hermit, wearing what used to be an expensive leather coat trimmed with fur at the collar and cuffs, but now scruffy and ragged. The man's long brown beard is likewise unkempt, and the skin hangs in loose folds from his neck like turkey wattles. He could be forty years old, he could be sixty, squinting hard at me, then lifting the shotgun in a menacing gesture, and saying, "Who are you? Jeremiah? Ezekiel? A prophet or a thief?"

Bravely standing my ground, I say, "My name is Aaron Steiner."

"Aaron, you say? What's your business here?"

"I'm with a traveling basketball team out of New York City. The House of Moses All-Stars."

Imagine my surprise when he lowers and cracks open the barrel of the shotgun, then falls to his knees in an attitude of amazement and justification, showing small pointed teeth inside a lopsided grin. "Aaron from the House of Moses," he says, his chest swelling with pride. "Behold! I am delivered!" From under the whites of his slightly protruding eyeballs peeks a rim of the red madness that rages inside his head. "Is it true? Are you indeed Aaron? Also known as the Illumined? The Enlightener? Aaron, the brother of Moses? Of the Israelitish tribe of Levi, and the first high priest of Israel? Welcome to the tent of the meeting. Come and enter in God's peace."

I bend through the doorway, my knee twinging as I squat inside a musty reeking of rotten fish. Crunching brittle fish bones with every cramped slide and half-step forward, already apologizing, "My name is Aaron Steiner, like I said, but the House of Moses doesn't really mean anything. It's just a gimmick."

Still beckoning to me, he points to a small wooden stool near the brazier that he'd obviously been sitting on. Then he hunkers down on his right leg and says, "I've been waiting for you." With great dignity, he removes the kettle from the coals, grasping the naked copper handle with his bare right hand and pouring what appears to be hot water into a dented tin cup. "Please," he says, reaching behind him into the darkness to find and offer a slick and frozen fish head. I accept only the cup and sip carefully at its contents—hot water.

"Silver tea," he says, pouring himself another cup, grunting with pleasure.

Now I can see that the shed owes its rolled shape to several hand-cut saplings lashed together with baling wire. There's a small smoke-hole crudely gashed into the rooftop, and an old army-issue sleeping bag is tucked into the far corner. Behind the fire a rough egg-shaped hole has been hacked through the ice, most likely by the same hand ax that's propped against the stool. A large stick is set on the ice to span the widest diameter of the hole. A thin gray string tied to the stick descends into the black waters beneath us.

"I am Jesse," the madman says. "Which is interpreted as meaning 'upstanding,' 'firm,' 'strong,' 'He who is.' I am the son of Abed. Grandson of Boaz and Ruth, and father of David."

"Pleased to meet you, Jesse."

"It is the end-time," he says. "The apocalypse is nigh."

"I agree with you, Jesse. Absolutely."

"The kingdoms of this world are bankrupt," he continues.

"Decent men are downtrodden, and sinners are exalted."

"This is also true." The wind gusts into the little hut and whips the coals into a brief flaming. "You're a wise man, Jesse."

"And you, Aaron, were a fool and an apostate," he says, "when you fashioned the Golden Calf in the wilderness. O ye of little faith."

This guy may be nutty as pecan pie, and he may be armed to the teeth, but his madness seems harmless, and in no way do I feel threatened. Is it, however, time to change the subject? "Do you catch many fish, Jesse?"

"Sufficient unto my needs."

"This place sure looks lived in. Do you spend the whole winter here?"

"So long as the ice holds," he says, mostly sucking the fishsicle meant for me. "The rest of the time I roam the hills and dells, eating berries and succulent roots and tubers. Sometimes I fish up north near the falls. The only things I need from town are coal for the winter and some matches. Mostly, I can barter fish for everything."

"How long have you been living like this? In the wilds."

Still squatting on his haunches, he rotates the stick so that the line is wrapped and shorted and the bare hook is lifted from the water. He reaches into the shadows again, this time for a large lidless tin can, from which he extracts what looks like a frozen worm that he threads onto the hook before unwinding the line again.

"How long I've been here depends on what day it is, what month, and what year . . . . No, no. Don't tell me. I really don't care to know." Then he's silent for a moment, searching for his own reflection in the fiery coals. And he seems more lucid, more normal, when he finally says, "It was after the crash. I had put my faith in Mammon, just as you did, Aaron, with your golden idol. I had a career I was so proud of, a profession. Yes. I was the head accountant for the Mays' department store over on Spruce Street. Working with numbers and ledgers. Producing nothing real, nothing useful. Poring over chicken scratches on a white page. Worshiping black ink. Living in fear of numbers written in red. No wife. No family." He sighs like a dying man trying to remember how to breathe. "I was so proud of my fancy car, my house up on Greene Hill. Why, this coat I'm wearing cost twenty dollars brand-new. I had tens of thousands of dollars in the bank. I thought that I was king of the world. A lynchpin in a great economic empire. Little did I know . . . When the bank failed, I was ruined . . . . And you see my world now. A better world. A true one. Living off God's bounty. Measuring my life by the stars glistening in the night sky, by the beauty of a sunset, by the martial music of a thunderstorm. The only ledger I'm interested in nowadays is the Good Book."

From inside his coat he produces a well-thumbed leatherbound Bible. I wouldn't have been surprised had he produced a live rabbit or a human skull. Then he opens the pages and reads apparently at random: "And the fifth angel sounded, and I saw a star fall from heaven unto the earth: and to him was given the key of the bottomless pit. And he opened the bottomless pit; and there arose a smoke out of the pit, as the smoke of a great furnace; and the sun and the air were darkened by reason of the smoke of the pit. And there came out of the smoke locusts upon the earth: and unto them was given power, as the scorpions of the earth have power." Then solemnly he closes the book and says, "Amen."

Now he changes his position, doing a slow-motion *kazatzki* and folding his left leg under his body. "So," he says, as though some formality has been completed. "I've welcomed you to my home and hearth. I've fed you as best I'm able . . . . "

"Yes. Thanks. I sure do appreciate your hospitality." I'm about to rise up and retreat to a more rational universe, but his fevered glance paralyzes me.

"So, then, Aaron. Also known as Aharon, the Unknown. Aaron, son of Amran and Jochebed. Aaron, who will die on Mount Hor. Aaron, who, like his brother, Moses, will not be permitted to enter the Promised Land. Aaron, whose trust in God was insufficient. So, then, Aaron . . . Why have you sought me out?"

"Sought you out?"

"Yes. What is the message you carry to me?"

"Sure . . . Ummm . . . The message is this . . . Keep up the good work, Jesse, son of Abed. When the Savior comes in his glory, blazing forth through the heavens in a chariot of fire, then you, Jesse, shall sit upon his left hand."

Now he's sobbing, reaching out to grab my right hand and covering my knuckles with kisses, tears, and globs of shnotz. Then he drops his face into his opened palms, still crying and moaning in a madman's ecstasy. Time enough for me to exit stage left.

Back outside, the graying clouds anoint me with fresh snow, and the cold air stabs the bottom of my lungs. Jesse, the poor loony bastard. Yet I feel strangely peaceful as I slide and sashay my way back toward the hotel. Yes, I do—because I've taken nothing from Jesse except a cupful of boiled snow and, even in the depths of his madness, I've brought him a small, insane measure of hope.

Several of my teammates are whiling away their time in the cheery, wood-fragrant lobby—Leo, Ron, Saul, and Kevin. Seated with them in the same grouping of plump leather couches are three pretty girls wearing pleated slacks and fully-bosomed sweaters. Leo is laughing to beat the band and chatting with the middle girl (always the prettiest). Leo acting the fool again, mugging with raised eyebrows, fluttering his eyelashes, and running his words together in an outrageous rapid-fire monologue: "I loveyoubabyandIwanttosuckyourbigtitties . . . That's right . . . I'manallnightloverandI'llmakeyourpussyspeakintonguesandsayUncle . . . All right? You like that?"

The three girls share a quizzical look and break into a shrill riff of giggling.

"Leo," I say harshly. "What the hell are you doing? . . . Girls, you'll have to excuse my friend here. He must be drunk or something."

Leo shakes his head. "Save your breath, Aaron. They can't hear a word you're saying."

"They're dummies," Ron says.

"What?"

"They're mutes," Saul explains. "There was a convention here over the weekend. Remember the desk clerk told us about it when we checked in? Sign-language teachers."

Leo laughs and randomly wriggles his fingers. "This is how deaf-and-dumb people talk to each other." The girls burst into a fresh chorus of silvery giggles, and Leo looks at his own writhing fingers. "What'd I do? Tell a joke or something?"

Now the girls are communicating in their private digital code. And on second glance, their pretty faces seem vacuous and puzzled, even stupefied. Could it be that, deprived of a normal involvement in the human family, they are somehow incomplete? Their powers of expression so circumscribed that their intellectual prowess is also stunted? Are they therefore more liable to be sinners, or saints?

"Listen to them when they try to talk," Leo says. He points to his chest and says, "Leo. Lee-oh."

The girl in the middle mimics him and identifies herself as "Moonaw."

"Mona," says Saul.

And I'm reminded of how gruesome is Leo's full-throated laughter, a braying, choking sound.

"Don't they read lips?" I ask Saul.

"Not very well."

Saul's long face twitches with conflicting desires: He can't stand the proximity of Leo, yet he's so obviously fascinated by the full-bodied and guileless young girls.

Then Leo says, "Watch this . . . Okay, ladies. Read my lips . . . Vacuum! Vacuum!" The girls get red-faced and scandalized until Leo pushes and pulls an imaginary vacuum cleaner across the carpet. "They thought I said 'Fuck you,'" he chortles.

"You're a laugh riot, Leo," I say. Then I ask Saul if he's eaten in the hotel's restaurant.

"I had a grilled-cheese sandwich and a chef's salad. Not bad. And Kevin really liked his hamburger."

"All right, then. See you boys and girls later."

The waitress wears a pin on her collar identifying her as "Amelia." She's rather short-legged and stumpy-armed, but her face is pleasant, with pencil-thin eyebrows above light blue eyes, delicate cheekbones, and red-glossed pouty lips. Her white uniform fronted with a prim black apron does nothing to conceal her bountiful curves.

"What'll it be, big fella?"

"What's good? Any specials today?"

She casts her ice-blue eyes quickly around the large brown-carpeted room, taking in the blocky wooden chairs and tables, haughtily regarding another waitress, who carries a tray of bluish milk and shredded wheat to an elderly couple in the far corner. Then Amelia snaps her gum like a Broadway moll and says, "I'm the only thing special around here in this dump."

And I can smell her heat, her boredom, her desperation. If I asked her to run away with me to California (or even to Cedar Rapids), she'd never refuse. Nor would she say me nay if I invited her upstairs to my room for a mere matinee's mayhem. Not such a bad idea. Actually, I haven't gotten laid since . . . since Debra.

"You know what, Amelia? I'll have me a grilled-cheese sandwich and a chef's salad to go."

She tosses her head back and huffs out her ample chest. "Suit yourself," she says.

Crossing the lobby on my way back to my room, I see that only Leo and the middle girl are still there. Leo is now sitting right beside her, breathing hotly into her face. His left thumb and forefinger are curled into a circle and his right forefinger is rigid and intent on penetrating that circle. What a classy guy.

Up in my room, I devour my meal then pick up the telephone and ask the hotel operator for long distance. New York City. Murray Hill 2-1839 . . . . But a woman answers. "Hello?" Of course, it's too early and Debra's still in school. So I fake a *Yiddisher* accent.

"Alloo? Dis is Yahooey? Yes?"

"Who?"

"Yahooey? Dis is you?"

"Sorry, there's nobody here by that name. You must have a wrong number." And she hangs up.

Then I sleep deeply, knowing that Mitchell will dutifully make his rounds and wake me on time. And I dream of a gigantic interplanetary penisoid life-form that invades the earth, fucking mine shafts and subway tunnels, flooding the countryside with rivers of jism.

The game is at Winnebago High School on the other side of town. Mitchell drives us there, his directions scribbled on a sheet of hotel stationery, as we move under bright streetlamps through narrow, snow-banked avenues. We pass gingerbread houses with storybook picket fences and snow-drifted lawns. There's the Oshkosh Grange Hall and the local 4-H Club.

"What're those?" Saul asks, pointing portside out the back window. "They look like chalk marks on the sides of some of the houses. Look, there's another one. Two parallel marks. A house on the last block had three marks. Anybody know what they signify?"

Ron does. "It's the hoboes' sign language. There must be a train station here in town. Three stripes means the people who live in that house will let you work for a meal. Chopping wood. Cleaning out the rain gutters on the roof. Shoveling snow. Mowing the grass. And they'll feed you like a king. Two stripes means you can get maybe a sandwich or a piece of pie or some leftovers for free. One stripe means you get a boot in the ass."

"You rode the rails?" Mitchell asks.

"Just for a few weeks a couple of summers ago."

Mitchell interrupts our discussion to "get our minds back on basketball." Tonight's payoff is $350 with a $150 bonus should we win. And Mitchell "guaranfuckingtees" that the Oshkosh Lakers we'll see tonight will be "a damn sight better'n any other team we've played so far." And by the way, Mitchell has also wired another $1,000 back to Max for safekeeping.

Another rural red-brick high school—how many of these have I played in? The trophy cases in the main lobby proudly displaying blackened basketballs from noteworthy ball games, regional championships, or perhaps a state tourney. There's one dated January 18, 1928, commemorating a 12–6 victory over J. W. Riley H.S. There's a withered football dating from October 15, 1918, inscribed with the same opponent and the same score. Here's the standard golf trophy, and a yellowed baseball signed by the county champs. The usual signs are also posted on the walls: VISITORS MUST REPORT TO THE MAIN OFFICE. NO GUM CHEWING ALLOWED.

We find the locker room on our own—the familiar rows of dented green lockers. As always, the varsity hoopsters are awarded the full-length lockers, their names proudly printed on white strips of adhesive tape: JUMPING JOE KLUCAS. DEAD-EYE DAVE SMITH. The overhead light bulbs are protected by small wire cages. Inspirational hand-lettered posters decorate the green-painted walls: IT'S NOT THE SIZE OF THE DOG IN THE FIGHT. IT'S THE SIZE OF THE FIGHT IN THE DOG. High school locker rooms smell from sweat, mildew, roachicide, and pimple cream.

As road-weary as we might be, we've still got our chops up to play the famous Oshkosh Lakers. I can personally testify to the excellence of the mighty Lakers: When I played for the Trenton Tigers in the defunct American Professional Basketball League, the Lakers were always booked for a preseason "exhibition" game in Trenton for a thousand dollars, winner takes all. The Lakers drew fans out of the woodwork, at least two thousand spectators and sometimes more, by far the largest crowds of the season. We beat them three out of the four games I played against them and every game was a rip-snorter. That was years ago and I'm sure their roster has changed since then.

And here's Ron's scouting report: "There's about fifteen hundred bumpkins in the stands at a dollar a head. We must be the only show in town. Relax, Leo, I didn't see any professional bone breakers unless they're disguised as hicks or boobs. There's no cops. No private security. All the cash is dumped in a paper bag. A fucking paper bag. It'd be an easy caper, believe me. Anyways, all the guards can shoot and one of them, Number Twelve, looks real shifty with the ball. All their big guys are mooses with muscles on their muscles. Everybody's quick except for one really big guy, who's almost as big as Saul. The court itself is long and the surface is soft. The rims are honest, but the nets are cut real short. That's a new one on me."

Brooks knows the reason why. "So that when the ball goes through the basket, it doesn't get squeezed and slowed down by a long net. It means that the Lakers want an up-tempo ball game. Strictly midwestern style basketball. They like to run, run, run. They'll be physical on offense, but pussycats on defense. Expect a standard two-one-two zone. Expect great shooters and poor ball handlers who hate to play half-court basketball."

"Wait just a minute," says Saul. "I don't understand how you can characterize a style of play for an entire geographical region." These are the first words Saul's spoken to the group at large since he refused our offer to abandon the trip in Ossining. A good sign.

"Well," Brooks says, and a flush of animation brightens his eyes, "basketball gyms in the East are usually small and narrow because the buildings are so old and space is at a premium. That's why ballhandling is so developed in the East. Same thing for half-court possession-style offense. Also, good defense and any kind of maneuvering in close quarters. Pivot play, for example, is more refined in the East. Out here, so many of the basketball courts are in newer buildings like this one, so there's more room to run. More room to spread the game out."

Then, just as Brooks is about to outline tonight's specific strategy, our meeting is invaded by the Lakers' manager, Pippy Clune. The same gray-haired old man I remember and still wearing the same shiny blue serge suit.

"Sorry to butt in," Clune says with an oily grin, "but I've got a little proposition for you boys. Just 'cause I like you. Just 'cause I know what a powerhouse team you have. Just 'cause I know some of you boys from the old American League . . . . Leo, how are ya? Brooks. Mitchell. Aaron

. . . . And I'm sure you other boys are mighty good players too. So, here's the deal . . . You're supposed to get three-fifty plus another one-fifty if you win, right? Now, what if we play you double or nothing? . . . If you win, now you get a grand. If you lose, you get zip. How's that sound, boys? What it amounts to is betting three-fifty against a thousand . . . . No, no. Discuss it amongst yourselves and tell me upstairs."

Just before Clune pushes out the door, he turns to face us again and adds, "Tell you what I'm gonna do, boys. The point spread being offered around town is the Lakers minus one and a half. To show you how fair-minded I am, if you do decide to take the double or nothing bet, then I'll let you boys have the points. How's that? An extra free throw and a half for a thousand bucks. Boys, you can't go wrong."

Mitchell laughs. "That's very generous of you. But who's reffing the game. Your brother and your uncle?"

Now it's Clune's turn to chuckle. "No, sir. The game will be impartially officiated by the justice of the peace and the Unitarian minister."

"In a pig's eye," says Mitchell.

We need only a brief moment to debate the proposal. Naturally, Leo wants to accept the wager. "What're you guys—chicken?"

"It's a setup," Mitchell says. "Don't be a sucker, Leo."

The vote is 6–1.

Afterward, Brooks proposes another patient game plan. "What we don't want to do," he says, "is get into a track meet with these guys."

The Lakers' center is at least six foot eight and 250 pounds, wide as a doorway, immovable in the pivot as the Statue of Liberty. I may be quicker, but he's still too big for me to circumnavigate. Yeah, now I remember him. Richie Dalzell. He kicked my ass one long night in Newark.

"Hiya, Richie."

"What d'ya say, Aaron?"

And as the game moves along, my legs seem too loose and wobbly. What was I thinking of to take a hot bath on a game day? A bone-headed rookie move. I can hardly lift myself off the floor, and Richie beats me to nearly every rebound.

As promised, their guards are swift-footed sharpshooters and their forwards jump like kangaroos. So the game is fierce right away as each team attempts to impose its own cadence.

For us, Leo reverts to his sticky-finger mode and we don't have nearly the ball movement we need on offense. Mitchell is shooting well enough, but Leo seems to be snubbing him. Is Leo simply pissed that we voted against accepting the wager? Or is there something more sinister in the works?

One of the Lakers' guards (the #12 that Ron warned us about) commands a tricky head fake, an up-and-go move, that continually lifts Mitchell to his toes, thereby allowing #12 entry into the guts of our defense. When Brooks or I have to move over to plug the penetration, #12 neatly dinks a pass to one of the big men sliding behind us. "Stay down!" Brooks finally yells at Mitchell. "What're you, a fucking piece of popcorn? A Mexican jumping bean? Let him shoot from way out there!"

Brooks plays with a calm desperation, shooting well and ravaging the boards. His intensity is inspirational. However, one of the Lakers' pet plays is a baseline crosspick, and Brooks's man always seems to get a solid piece of me. When I call "Switch!" Brooks ignores my plea and Richie gets a wide-open layup. "Goddammit!" I shout. "Time-out!" And I'm still livid in the huddle, screaming at Brooks. "I called a fucking switch! So switch! How many layups are we gonna let them have?"

Brooks takes my measure with a frigid stare. "You guard your man, Aaron. And I'll guard mine."

And it's Ron who keeps us in the game, driving furiously to the hoop and converting his free throws. The Lakers' careless arrogance also keeps the score tight: Whenever they forge to a 5- or 6-point lead, they'll cast some showboat passes that mainly wind up intercepted or in the stands.

We complete the first half lucky to be down by only 3 points—22–19—and everybody is touchy and bitchy when we trudge into the locker room.

Mitchell has a beef with Leo: "What've you got, glue on your fingers? I need more shots, dammit! Or kiss the game goodbye!"

Leo is just as hot on Mitchell's case: "That fucking guy you're supposed to be checking's got you on a string. Shit! You couldn't even guard your own shadow!"

Meanwhile, Brooks and I continue our debate over the Lakers' crosspick and how to neutralize it: "That big guy's tossing you around, Aaron, like you're made out of straw."

"Well, fuck you, Mister Charles Atlas. Why don't you try guarding him?"

"We'd all be playing much better," says Leo, "if there was a thousand bucks at stake."

Back on the court warming up—and I notice Leo standing near the sideline, visiting with the Lakers' blue-serge manager. At the time, the circumstances seem innocent enough.

As the second half is under way, the All-Stars play like we're strangers. There's no cohesion to our offense, and our defense is even more disjointed. In disgust, Brooks removes himself from the game, with the Lakers comfortably ahead 36–27. "Saul! Come in for me! I don't want to play with these assholes!"

And just like that, Saul turns the game around. Paired against Richie, Saul puts the big man's offense in a cage. Here's Saul wrestling the ball away from Richie, then rocketing off the floorboards to shove the ball through the hoop. And here he is again—clawing through the crosspick and slapping Richie's bid for a layup into Ron's eager hands. What's the difference in Saul tonight? I'd say it's anger—a fury that's been slowly building since Ossining, exploding at last in Oshkosh.

Without having to worry about banging heads with Richie, I begin to assert myself, and the game turns into a brawl. Much to our delight, the homestanding refs let both teams play hard as long as we're playing clean. But as much as we scrap and hustle, we can't quite get over the hump. Leo misses an easy scoop shot at a critical juncture. Then Ron makes a foolish gamble on defense, leaving his man unguarded for a short-range popper.

With only two ticks left on the game clock, the Oshkoshers are up 46–44 and Leo is due for a single free throw. We have one last time-out at our disposal, and Brooks's strategy is obvious:

"You have to miss the free throw, Leo. One point doesn't do us any good. Try to knock it off the right side of the rim, where Saul's got the inside rebounding slot. Remember, Saul . . . there's a hometown timer at the scorers' table, so I doubt if you can bring the rebound down and then go back up for the shot. Right? Everybody else will crash the boards. Right, Leo. Overshoot to the right. Let's go."

A perfect scheme with only one flaw in the execution: Leo steps to the line and calmly sinks the shot. *BZZZT!* And we lose 46–45.

Stunned, we stumble into the locker room and sag on to the benches. Not until the Lakers' manager arrives with our $350 and begins to praise our "valiant effort" do we suddenly revive.

"Get out!" Brooks shouts at him. "Get the fuck out of here!"

When we're alone again, Mitchell simply says, "Leo . . . ?"

"It slipped," Leo lies in self-defense. "Look. It's hard for a good foul shooter like me to miss on purpose . . . . I don't know . . . Maybe I forgot to miss. Maybe my competitive instinct took over."

After Leo escapes into the shower room, Mitchell, Brooks, and I see the light at the same time.

"Fucking Leo!" I fume.

"I'll kill the bastard!" says Brooks.

"It was the point spread," Mitchell says. "The cocksucker made his own deal."

That's why we're waiting for him when Leo comes out of the shower, crowding him against his open locker door. "Hey, you guys! Give me some room. What the fuck's going on here?"

"We're wise to you, Leo," Brooks says. "No, no. Don't say a fucking word. We're not interested in any more of your lying excuses. Just shut your fucking trap and listen."

"What'd I do?" Leo says, turning his innocent palms to the ceiling.

"I said to shut the fuck up!" Brooks barks. "I mean it!"

Now it's Mitchell's turn. "One more fuck-up," he says grimly, "and you're finished, Leo. We'll leave you high and dry wherever we happen to be. We'll leave you with no money, no nothing. We've had it up to here."

When we finally turn and walk away, Leo whimpers, "But, guys, you got me all wrong!"

It's only 147 miles to Cedar Rapids, Iowa. Mitchell drives and I ride shotgun—and the radio is tuned to "Father Charles E. Coughlin's Freedom Forum," broadcast nationally out of the Shrine of the Little Flower in Royal Oak, Michigan. Fulminating against "the Jewish bankers" and railing against "Franklin D.-for-Double-Crossing Roosevelt," Coughlin frequently reminds his listeners that a onetime one-dollar fee will enlist them in his own National Union for Social Justice.

"Mitchell," I say. "What are we listening to this shit?"

"Shhh! It's a portent of the future. Listen . . ."

The highlight of tonight's program is Father Coughlin's revelations about "the true character" of Hollywood: He goes on to claim that Edward G. Robinson's real name is Nathan Schwartzman, that Paul Muni and John Garfield are also "secret Jews."

Mitchell gnashes his teeth as he drives, and even though I am technically prohibited from falling asleep, I can't help myself as Coughlin babbles on:

"I say to the good Jews of America, be not indulgent with the irreligious, atheistic Jews, who promote the cause of persecution in the land of the Communists, the same ones who promote the cause of atheism in America. Yes, be not lenient with your high financiers and politicians, who assisted at the birth of Russia, the only system in all civilization that adopted atheism as its religion and slavery as its liberty."

And what dreams arise like rank mushrooms in the night-forests within my skull! Dreams of ice daggers pointed at my throat. Dreams of fire wheels whirling in the sky.

From Mitchell's Log:
Day Eight — January 13, 1936 — Sunday

	Today	Total
Mileage	76	2,370
Expenses	$57.50	$219.75
Income	$350.00	$2,060.00

Net Income - $1,840.25
Average Share - $262.89
Cash on Hand - $240.25
Max Has - $1,600.00

Won - 3
Lost - 3

We switch seats after a gas-and-piss stop near Madison, so that Brooks moves behind the wheel, Leo navigates, Mitchell and I are in the backseat, with Ron and the rookies occupying the crypt. Then sometime after midnight, Ron wakes up and says, “I’m hungry.” And we realize all at once that, because of tonight’s turmoil and tumult, we’ve forgotten to eat.

When a cursory tour through several small towns offers no succor, we decide to tap our store of canned foods. Baked beans, peach halves, and evaporated milk. "Evaporated milk!" says Leo. "What the fuck?"

As always, Mitchell has a rational explanation: "Concentrated nutrients, Leo, that can keep us alive just in case we get stranded somewhere."

Kevin works the can opener and we soon discover that Mitchell's inventory doesn't include any eating utensils. Most of us merely tilt the cans (being mindful of the jagged lids still attached) and bottoms-up our main course, dessert, and beverage. But not the ever-fastidious Mitchell, who fishes around in a cardboard box that's stuffed underneath the backseat for a twelve-inch wooden ruler. He spits into his handkerchief and wipes the ruler's sides and edges before using the upper two inches to scoop the beans into his mouth (the peaches are too slippery).

"Mitchell," I chide him. "Why on earth did you pack a ruler?"

"That's a stupid question . . . It's for just in case we have to measure something."

"Like what?"

"How do I know? Maybe the clearance under a tunnel or a railroad trestle or something."

Then Ron wisecracks from the crypt: "Maybe Mitchell brought it along so's we could have a dick-measuring contest."

This draws a grudging laugh all around and this predictable boast from Leo: "Well, if Mitchell wants to measure my dick, he should've brought a yardstick."

"And if Mitchell's going to measure his own dick," Brooks adds, "he should've brought a micrometer."

Even Mitchell has to laugh and our mood brightens until Leo cranks open the shotgun window and casually tosses his empty bean can onto the road.

"Hey!" Mitchell shouts. "What the fuck're you doing, Leo? There's a sharp edge on that can. What if a car runs over it? It could easily cut through a tire. Then you'd have a high-speed blowout and somebody could get killed."

"Mitchell," I say. "You're making something out of nothing." But our spark of jocular camaraderie has already been doused.

After prowling around Cedar Rapids, we finally locate a hotel that's both open for business and showing a vacancy sign out front. The Hawkeye House. We grab our gear and move slowly through a front door made of thick glass with brass trimmings, admitting us into a plush lobby. The space is brightly lit by a huge crystal chandelier. White marbleized pillars rise to the gold-flecked ceiling, and the couches, upholstered in brown velveteen, match the soft carpeting underfoot.

Behind the reception desk, an old man in a green Alpine sweater has been awakened by the small breath of night wind we've brought along with us. He's apparently a respectable citizen of Iowa, sitting unmoved, sour-pussed, and taciturn as the Elders of Zion stomp their filthy boots on the carpet. Stomping to raise the devil? Or merely to revive our cold, slow-blooded limbs? Then he rubs his old man's eyes and says, "Yes, sir." He's annoyed at our untimely intrusion. "What can I do for you? Would someone please shut that door?"

Depend on Mitchell to always make the first contact with civilians. "The sign outside says you have vacancies, right?"

"Yes, sir. We surely do." Then a low-voltage light bulb switches on behind his eyes, and he regards us with increasing apprehension, as though we were a stickup gang.

Indeed, Ron saunters up to the front desk and leans over the countertop, looking for a cashbox or loose change. And Mitchell is aggressive in his contempt of this dim-witted hayseed desk clerk, saying, "We need four rooms overnight. It doesn't matter where they are or what they cost."

"Just one moment, sir," the old man says as he reaches for a telephone at hand. "I'll have to check something first." The skin sagging from his sharp cheekbones has recently been shaved with either a shaking hand or a dull razor and there's one red-dotted bit of toilet paper plastered to his Adam's apple.

"What's the problem?" Mitchell demands to know. "Hurry it up. We're falling-down tired."

"Just one moment, sir."

Mitchell and Ron hover over the front desk while the rest of our troupe flops onto the cushiony couches and chairs, carelessly eavesdropping while the old man talks into the receiver: "Yes, Mr. Hoyt . . . Yes, sir . . . They're here now . . . Yes, sir . . . I'll tell them . . . . " When he hangs up, the old man seems more fidgety than before and he says to Mitchell, "The manager will be right down. Sir."

"The manager? Who the hell needs the manager? What's the big deal? All we want is four rooms."

"Yes, sir. The manager's name is Mr. Hoyt and he says he'll be right with you."

"What the hell!" Mitchell says, flapping his arms once to try to shake his mounting frustration.

Presently, a pair of copper-burnished elevator doors slide open and a distinguished-looking personage emerges into the lobby. He wears a long smoking jacket of some crinkled purple material that's highlighted with gold-colored thread. A white silk cravat protects his throat from any vagrant drafts, his hair is neatly slicked back, and his sharp-featured face is dominated by a thin black ridge of hair growing on his upper lip.

"Good evening, gentlemen," Mr. Hoyt says without introducing himself. "Or should I say 'Good morning'?" He speaks to the seven of us, now clustered there before the desk, like a nobleman showing off his manners to a delegation of low-born petitioners.

"Good whichever to you too," Mitchell says brusquely. "We want four rooms, pronto, and we're paying cash on the barrelhead."

"Excuse me, gentlemen, please. I just have one question, if you don't mind."

"What?" Mitchell snaps.

"Would you gentlemen possibly be of a Judaic persuasion?"

"What?" says Brooks, softly wincing.

But Mitchell's eyes flash with sudden understanding. "Now I get it," he says, slapping the top of his head to chastise his own ignorance.

"Precisely," says Hoyt. "I'm terribly sorry, gentlemen. This is a restricted hotel and we can't help you."

"Restricted to what?" Leo says. "Stuffed shirts like you?"

"Restricted to gentiles," Hoyt says smoothly.

"No, no," Ron says. "You got it all wrong, mister. We ain't Jews. We're Armenians .... Hey, pal. We've been on the road for over a week and we need to get some shut-eye. Don't be such a dick."

"Sorry, gentlemen."

As we buzz with discontent and push closer to the counter, the manager reaches inside some hidden drawer and grabs something in his right hand, holding the object out of sight below the level of the countertop. "I'll have to insist," he says evenly, "that you gentlemen immediately vacate the premises. Please."

Mitchell flies off the handle. "You fucking anti-Semite Nazi cocksucker!"

The manager calmly turns to his subordinate and says, "Mr. Poplowski, would you kindly telephone the police station and notify Sergeant Blackshaw of our little problem?"

"Yes, sir."

More than the implied weapon that's still hidden from sight, the explicit threat of calling in the law pushes us toward the front door, all the while shouting abuse over our shoulders.

"You pompous ass!"

"Fucking douchebag!"

"*A choleryeh!* You shmuck with ears!"

Just before we're out of there, Leo unbuttons his pants and defiantly pisses into a potted palm. Then we run, laughing, to the car like schoolboys who've just stolen some trinkets from the five-and-ten. Ron drives the getaway car, revving the engine, squeezing the horn—*Ahyoogah!*—as we make good our escape.

We agree that our only viable alternative is to sleep in the car, so Ron tools through the moonlit streets heading toward the outskirts of town and then down toward the river. "If you can," Ron says, "always camp out near running water."

Before very long we find ourselves approaching what Ron identifies as a "hobo jungle," a loose gathering of tin-roofed shacks and wooden lean-tos, of patched canvas and oilcloth tents, scattered through a small riverside clearing. The ground snow is black and littered with empty food wrappers and rusted tin cans. Several meager fires have long since faded into smoking gray ashes. There are no visible people, just a pack of mangy dogs scouring the area for a forgotten chicken bone or castoff shoe.

From somewhere in the cold-edged darkness, a stone is thrown our way, noisily bouncing high off the front hood. "We'd better leave," Ron says, throwing the clutch in reverse. "Don't ever believe that hoboes are just peaceful down-and-outers rejected by society. Not on your life. Most of them are so desperate, they'll gladly kill you for a piece of bread. But we can park around the bend, behind those trees over there.

The hoboes won't wander that far at night, and when daylight comes, they'll be moving toward town. So we should be perfectly safe."

Ron maneuvers the Black Lady off the road and just a few yards down an old logging trail, until we're concealed behind a stand of poplars. Mitchell wants us to go outside and obliterate our tire tracks, "just in case," but Ron laughs and says, "Relax." And we quickly settle into the moon-hidden darkness, pulling our dreams around us like thick and downy blankets.

The darkness of night is still triumphant when something fractures our peaceful dreams, something hard and clanging against the roof of the car. Then, in a sudden flickering firelight, the car is violently shaken from side to side, and angry voices freeze our blood.

"Open the fucking doors!"

"Come out where we can see you!"

"Who the hell are you men?"

We're surrounded by a vigilante mob, armed with baseball bats, flaming tar-dipped torches, and who knows what else.

"Oh, shit!" Leo despairs. "They found me and I'm a dead man."

Slowly, under the mob's insistent urging, we relinquish our fools' sanctuary and stand shivering in the wavering torchlight. Ron holds his right hand hidden within the folds of his pea coat and I'll bet dollars to doughnuts he has the gun.

"All right," says a large bearded man in a dark-colored coat. "Identify yourselves. What's this Moses shit painted on your car here?"

Mitchell's quick explanation seems to dampen their hostility.

"A basketball team, eh?" the bearded leader says. "Well, you boys are sure tall enough. Look at the size of that one! Ain't that the biggest damn Jew you ever did see?" A round of gargling, drunken laughter ensues. "Well, I myself ain't never been real partial to Jews, unnerstand?

But we got no real quarrel with you. It's them bums we're after. Dirty, chicken-stealing, lazy, good-for-nothing pieces of shit. Cut your throat for a penny. Rob your clean clothes right off the line. Whyn't you boys get back in your vehicle there and just clear on out? We'll forget we saw you and you forget you saw us."

They laugh again, boisterous and proud, then tramp off in a gang toward the river.

"What'll we do now?" Kevin asks, wide-eyed and thrilled by the possibilities.

"What we'll do now," says Leo, "is get the flying fuck out of here!"

But Brooks isn't so sure. "How about those poor fucks sleeping down by the river? We can't just stand idly by and let them get beat up."

"Why not?" says Mitchell. "Better them than us .... But hell, if you have to do something, we can maybe honk the horn or even fire off a shot to warn them. But we'd better hurry."

"That's not enough," says Brooks, and he leans into the car, reaching under the front seat and coming out with a Louisville slugger, Hank Greenberg model, thirty-eight inches long and weighing forty ounces. "The revolution starts here," Brooks says tightly. Then he trots off after the vigilantes.

"Wait!" Ron shouts as he grabs another bat. "Brooks! I'm coming with you!"

"Yeah!" I cry out. "Me too! Gimme one of those!"

The rookies also want to play hero. Mitchell and Leo volunteer to stay behind and "guard the car."

We easily trace the hurried footsteps through the woods while Ron gives us a quick course in home-run warfare. "I can handle myself, but the rest of you should split up in twos so's you can protect each other's backs. When you go after somebody, aim for the arm that's holding the bat and hit the elbow if you can. Don't forget you can jab with the heavy end of the bat too. If someone is swinging at you, the best thing to do is dive to the ground and whack him in the knee. If you can't do that, then move close to him to crowd his swing. Stay away from head shots. We don't want to kill anybody unless we have to. Now, listen . . . I've got the gun right here, so if you're in real trouble, call out my name and I'll get there. All right . . . Let's go bust up some rednecks."

We hear shouts from up ahead and violent shrieks of pain. Running now, we emerge from the clearing to see several shabby figures running for their lives and several prone and writhing. Most of the flimsy shelters are already in flames. And the midnight ambushers go about their ruthless business having the times of their lives, shouting with delight.

"Pow! A line-drive double down the third baseline!"

"Look at this guy, Ethan. I just about knocked his head clean off!"

Brooks and I partner up and, along with the rookies and Ron, we attack the vigilantes from three separate directions. "Kill the bastards!" Ron yelps as he thwacks his bat into somebody's elbow. The bushwhackers are unprepared for any resistance. Confused, they scamper out of our reach.

"It's those fucking Jews!" someone shouts. "We should've beat their heads when we had the chanst! Let's get 'em, boys. Spread out and surround 'em!"

They threaten us with curses and slowly wave their wooden swords, but they remain out of harm's way. Until their bearded leader steps forward to oppose me. "I ain't afraid of no fucking Jews," he says, then he winds up and tries to knock my head out of the ballpark.

I step back and feel the whoosh of strike one swinging. *"Fuck!"* I scream, and we attack each other, bat sent crashing against bat, living or dying on a single test of might. The ultimate phallic challenge! And mine is bigger than his .... His is a Pie Traynor model, designed for line-drive power, mine is built to reach the grandstand seats. With a sharp *crack!* the smaller weapon is knocked loose, then I use a backhanded uppercut to bonk the night-stalker's ribs.

"At 'em, boys!" someone else hollers. "There's more of us than them!"

One of them attacks Ron with a swinging torch and gets his wrist smashed to smithereens. The rest are wary of our long arms and the wide, sweeping arcs of our home-run capability. But they do outnumber us by about three to one, so they soon isolate us and attack in force. Back to back, Brooks and I battle the heathen hordes. Like medieval knights with a bloodlust in our eyes. Any blows we do receive seem weak and incidental, while our own puissant strokes crack bone and cartilage.

The conflict is soon decided in our favor and the enemy is retreating, when from behind my left shoulder I glimpse a desperate swing aimed at my head. Too late to duck, I can only move my own weapon around to try to parry the blow. The incoming war club glances off the upperpart of my right index finger, bludgeoning the fingernail and certainly breaking the bone. I counter with a crosshanded swipe that blasts my assailant's right knee to a bloody pulp. And I hit him again on the hip .... That's for the restricted hotel .... And again, mashing his pleading outstretched fingers .... That's for Ossining. And for the "fucking cage." And I fracture his mouth for baby Sarah .... He groans and cries, still alive. And my finger throbs with unbearable pain as I turn and look for someone to kill.

A sudden gunshot pierces the graying darkness and, just as quickly, the battle is done. The vigilantes have taken flight, sobbing, shrieking, running crookedly on shattered limbs. The beaten hoboes have likewise vanished. And the five All-Stars meet in the middle of the field, red-eyed and sweating, panting with an evil glee.

"Goddamn!" Saul says. "That was fun!"

"Let's vamoose," Ron suggests, "before they come back with reinforcements."

We take a damage survey while we're hustling back to the car: Brooks has a head wound but the bleeding is minimal. Ron has been bashed on his left shoulder. "Nothing serious," he says. "All I need's some ice and there's acres of it right here and free for the taking." Saul's legs are banged up and his left elbow is rapidly swelling. Kevin has received a slight blow to his forehead, but nothing seems to be broken. My finger is an agonizing mess.

"Your shooting hand?" Brooks says. "That means only one thing, Aaron. More shots for me."

We laugh. We howl. We're a wolf pack. We're blood brothers. Leo and Mitchell are strangers.

Leo drives us toward town slowly and unobtrusively on back roads and country lanes as the white sun frosts the edge of the darkness. Mitchell has the first-aid kit, dispensing gauze pads, adhesive tape, aspirins, bandages, and liberal splashes of iodine. In lieu of a splint I tape my injured digit to the nearest healthy one.

"Stupid," says Mitchell. "Totally unnecessary. How many games will this childish little adventure cost us? How much money?"

"Mitchell," Saul says politely. "Blow it out your ass."

We could use a doctor or at least a bathhouse. But we settle for chunks of ice hacked from the roadside as we seek out the ivy-covered walls and scholarly bowers of Fulton College.

Of course, Leo gets lost and we drive smack through the middle of town: Early on a workaday morning the streets are surprisingly empty. There's a haberdashery, an old-time feed and grain store, Lena's

Luncheonette (nobody's hungry), a hardware shop, all two-story wood-framed buildings with residences on the top floors. We cross a jouncing wooden bridge over the rigid white river, not a rapids nor a cedar tree in sight. A few open-backed pickup trucks are parked outside another restaurant (Walt's), and here comes a wagon (Fred's Coal Company) down the center of the street drawn by a gray-dappled horse and loaded to the brim with frosted unshucked ears of corn.

"What a crazy fucking country," Brooks says. "People are starving everywhere. And in Cedar-fucking-Rapids the farmers are burning corn because it's cheaper than burning coal. Money is more important than lives."

The tallest building in downtown Cedar Rapids is six floors high and a huge long-barreled artillery piece from the Great War is set on the rooftop. The roof also supports a colossal billboard that can be seen from both ends of Main Street, depicting the benevolent face and tricornered hat of an eighteenth-century patriot. Below this, the company's motto—SHOT FROM GUNS—and name, QUAKER OATS.

After much ado and many false trails we find the college and pull into a small auxiliary parking field near the northern edge of the campus.

"Game time," says Mitchell, "is seven-thirty. That's seven-three-oh. Let's meet in the gym at six-four-five. The bad guys tonight are an All-Fraternity team, whatever the hell that means. The pay is three hundred, win or lose. Till then, I say it's everybody roll your own. Whoever wants to scout around for a hotel can take the car keys, and good luck to you. If you think you need a sawbones, go find one and I'll reimburse you if you bring me a proper receipt. Brooks and Aaron? I strongly suggest you two try to find some medical attention."

Brooks's response is to spit a frothy white globule to the ground equidistant between Mitchell's shoes.

But Mitchell is not so easily insulted. "What I intend to do," he says, "is hang around the college. Find some cozy spot in some empty room and catch up on my beauty rest."

Ron, Brooks, and the rookies are inclined to find an unrestricted hotel and take a meal in town. Leo aims to offer himself up for adoption at the nearest sorority house. As for me, I'll just flit around like an evil wind.

And there's plenty of space for the wind to blow freely around here. The various buildings that house the offices, classrooms, and student residences are squat, white-shingled structures that hug the ground. The occasional tree is a white-boned skeleton. A line of shrubs around the library is stunted and leaning away from the keening wind.

My long rabbi's beard is frozen stiff and my toes are becoming numb. Then my path is crossed by two coeds bundled in rich fur coats, their faces swathed in gaily colored mufflers, and they desperately clutch each other's hands to keep from falling as they hurry to class. Here's a freshman pledgling, books in one hand, his other hand holding a blue beanie to his head as the wind spins the tiny cap-top propellor and threatens to send the poor shnook flying up into the sky.

On a whim, I trail the two girls into a classroom building, then down a corridor, through an open door and into a large lecture hall. The curving rows of seats form a quarter circle that faces a modest blond mahogany desk and a portable blackboard set on a slightly raised platform. There's a rear door behind the desk. (Every lecture hall at Metro had one, and I'd always imagined that the secret chambers behind these doors was where young lovelies auditioned for A's and B's.)

Perhaps fifty students are already in their seats, scribbling furiously into opened notebooks, while the professor pointedly ignores the three latecomers. The professor wears a brown corduroy jacket with black leather elbow patches. His bow tie is brown, his white shirt collar is starched, and so is his neck. The professor sits behind his desk as though ensconced on a throne, tapping a lighted cigarette on a teetering, chit-marked stack of books. Gazing at his disciples with a fragile benevolence, not quite forgiving them for being such ignorant clods. A sheaf of the professor's thin brown hair has fallen from grace, and his bony right hand strokes it back into place. Unfortunately, the professor has forgotten that the very same hand holds a burning cigarette, so he must pause to decline the ashes that now anoint his brow.

Just what the world needs, a professional genius.

And the great man speaks: "As I was saying before I was so rudely interrupted . . . The significant tool here is allegoresis . . . which is a nifty way of saying that something means anything other than what it appears to mean. Allegoresis. The word itself has a persuasive ring to it. Like Marlovian. Lofty verse. The sinews of poetry. But let me ask you a rhetorical question, class . . . That means you don't have to answer it. Who can tell me . . . ? What's the difference between a rooster crowing and a shyster lawyer? . . . A crowing cock, you know, is a daily reminder of the Resurrection of Christ. Faustus, of course, was also a lawyer, even though he wasn't Jewish. Faustus says, if you recall, that the law is 'a mercenary drudge,' concerned only with 'paltry legacies.' Marlowe takes pains to bag philosophy as well. 'To dispute well is logic's chiefest end.' Big deal, says Faustus. But the Bible, Jerome's Bible, is 'hard,' says Faustus. 'The reward of sin is death.' Yet Faustus resists, and chastens God's omnipotence by not permitting Jesus to save him. And finally, Faustus turns the world 'upsodoun' and sodomizes the devil . . . . But as to Marlowe's poem, 'Hero and Leander,' the subject of today's assignment . . ."

The professor torches another cigarette, selects a book from the pile on his desk, and opens to a chit-marked page.

"The pivotal figure, of course, is Hero herself. Marlowe gives it away when he refers to her as 'Venus' nun,' Elizabethan slang for a whore. Pardon my French. Along the same lines, Marlow also likens her to a mermaid, also considered to be a licentious creature. Sometimes Marlowe gets carried away and writes pure burlesque . . .

She, overcome with shame and sallow fear,
Blah, blah, blah, blah,
Being suddenly betrayed, dived down to hide her,
And, as her silver body downward went,
With both her hands she made the bed a tent.
Blither, blither, blither.
Yet ever, as he greedily assayed
To touch those dainties, she the harpy played,
And every limb did, as a soldier stout,
Defend the fort, and keep the foeman out.

Hot stuff, ain't it? . . . That's all for today, ladies and gentlemen."

Several students grab their books and bolt for the front door but the professor never stirs. Finally, he stands up and writes the names of several books on the blackboard. "See y'all tomorrow," he says. "Oh, yes. A rooster clucks defiance." Then he walks briskly out the rear exit and slams the door behind him.

And as I continue my meanderings through halls and winter walkways that seem almost familiar, I wax nostalgic for my undergraduate days at Metro University . . . . I certainly enjoyed being a campus celebrity—my picture was once in the *Daily News* when I scored the winning basket against LIU. How could I have known they'd be the best days of my life?

I was a physical education (*fizz ed*) major only because the athletic department had more control over its own staff than over the "fruits" who taught history or English, and my profs were all pressured to grant me a "gentleman's C." Whatever the class, I was always allowed unlimited cuts to accommodate practices and road trips. The athletic department also provided tutors, who wrote all of my term papers and sometimes even took tests in my name. The point-shaving money (the *hot* money) burned a hole in my pockets. The girls, the parties, the pleasures of privilege that I thought would last forever.

Looking back, I can hardly recall anything that I learned in any classroom. Oh, yes . . . The temperature in a locker room should be maintained at seventy-two degrees. And from my anatomy class—the hand bone connected to the dick bone.

Now here I am at Fulton College, and what a real sanctuary this place is! There's no Depression here. No hard time. No hoboes desperate for food and shelter. Just look at these happy youngsters, striding confidently from one classroom to another. Joyfully stuffing their lives with useless information. Look at their fresh faces—when they smile, little lights play inside their eyes. And if Mitchell is correct in his forecast of global war (and I fear he is), how many of these young men will die in foreign lands?

God. I'm so tired and empty. And if I can't fill the black vacuum ("Fuck you") in my soul, I can at least fill my belly and find someplace to sleep.

There's Leo in the cafeteria, sitting alone at a table, munching a sliced-egg sandwich and staring bug-eyed at the girls. "Hey, Aaron," he says brightly. "Take off your coat. Have a seat and come rest your bones."

"Don't mind if I do, Leo. Let me get something to eat before I get too comfortable."

The Stephen J. Solomunde Memorial Cafeteria is a large pale-yellow hall, crowded and noisy, with yellow-and-black-tiled floors, and cheap wooden tables and chairs painted a glossy black. Fortunately there's only a short line filing past the food counter and I take my place behind two bookwormy girls. Their pinched faces crease into automatic smiles when they initially identify me as a living male. I return their smile and doff my yarmulke. How quickly they consign me to oblivion and resume their own conversation.

"How'd you do on the eco test?"

"I got an A-minus. I messed up a little on the essay question about buying on margin. I said you needed thirty percent down instead of twenty. What'd you get?"

"An A. But it's bullshit, you know."

"What is?"

"The whole thing. They still don't know why the bottom fell out in the first place. And they don't know what to do so that it won't happen again."

"Yeah. Probably. But I love Professor Glasel anyway."

"I know what you mean. He's a doll."

There's a middle-aged black woman doling out portions of meat loaf, fried chicken, mashed potatoes, and the like from behind a long steam table. She wears a white uniform and a sparkly, teasing smile. When she sees me inspecting the food, she has to laugh and say, "Tell me, Mr. Hep Cat . . . what fraternity you in?"

"Phelta Beta Thi."

Then she laughs again and tells me to stay away from the meat loaf.

I bring a cellophane-wrapped chicken salad sandwich, a "fresh garden salad," and a paper cup of hot tea back to the table. "Looks good," Leo says as he moves his tray to make room for mine. "Mmmm, look at those big red radishes in your salad. I love radishes. They're good for your blood. Most people hate them. What about you?"

"Here, Leo. Take them."

"I knew it. Most people hate radishes."

My sandwich is awful—the chicken's been boiled, then ground

into mush, then mixed with some kind of *goyisher* mayonnaise and pasted onto white bread. But the salad's fresh and tasty.

"I've been wanting to talk to you, Aaron." There's a strain on Leo's face, a tightening together of his eyebrows. He looks melancholy and preposterously sincere. "I know most of you guys think I'm an asshole," he says, "and I kind of understand why. But I want you to know that deep down, I really am a nice guy."

"How deep, Leo?"

He sighs, a prelude to a sob. "Pretty deep, I guess . . . But, Aaron . . . I'm just a product of my environment, you know?"

"Ain't we all?"

"No, Aaron. I'm serious. Lookit. My mom died in a trolley-car accident when I was a real little kid. And my dad, he went broke paying out his money to crooked lawyers and trying to sue City Hall. What a dreamer he was. Then he had a heart attack at work when I was nine. He was a pants presser on Arthur Avenue in the Bronx. So after he died, that's when I moved in with my aunt, Laura, on Clinton Street in the neighborhood. My father's older sister. You knew I was an orphan, right?"

"No, Leo. I never knew anything about your family. You were just another kid who showed up for punchball games in the street and basketball games in the schoolyard."

"Anyway, it's true . . . My sister, Marilyn, she went to live with my father's other sister, Sadie the Spinster, down in Baltimore. I ain't heard from Marilyn in maybe ten years. My aunt, Laura, she was a nice old broad, but her husband had died and she was, you know, fooling around, trying to catch another fish on the line. What'd she want a snot-nosed kid like me around for? That's why I was always hanging around in the streets. The only money I ever got was when some guy would come over to the apartment and say, 'Here, kid. Here's a dime. Whyn't you go to a movie or something. There's a double feature at the Loews.' See? Nobody wanted me around."

I'm touched in spite of myself. "That's a really tough situation, Leo. For a kid to grow up like that."

"Yeah, it was tough . . . But playing basketball saved my life, you know? It made me feel important. I was the point guard. The guy who controlled the ball. Then I got to Saint Anthony's and I was the big cheese. You know how it was, Aaron. It was the same thing with you guys at Metro."

"Yeah." Now it's my turn to sigh.

"And coming here," he says, looking around the noisy, littered hall like he was a visiting Staten Island Catholic seeing the inside of St. Paddy's Cathedral for the first time. "It made me think about what I really learned back at Saint Anthony's. I was a stupid kid back then, but I did learn certain things."

"For example?"

"For example, that you need an edge to get ahead. For example, that the Golden Rule is really this: You should do unto others before they do it unto you. For example, that honesty is the worst policy. That cheaters never lose. That's what I learned, Aaron. And that's why everybody thinks I'm such a *putz*. Really, Aaron. I ain't so bad. I'm just trying to get by the only way I know how."

Is Leo lying? . . . I want to believe him. I want to believe he's just another victim.

"Okay, Leo," I say, extending the hand of friendship. "Let's start all over, you and me. That's the best I can do."

"Great," he says, nearly jumping out of his pants. "You won't regret it, Aaron. Here's two bucks for the money I owe you. See? I'm turning over a new leaf starting as of right now."

"I hope so, Leo."

He squints at a wall clock, then wipes his thin lips with a paper napkin. "I was by the gym before, just to size it up like Ron does, you know? And I met the basketball coach. His name is Whitaker. And he knew about our game tonight. So he invited me to come over and watch the varsity practice. They started about ten minutes ago. What d'ya say?"

"Sounds okay by me."

It's a cavernous gym with a high-girded ceiling and atrocious acoustics, wherein every dribble, every whistle and shout, endlessly echoes and reechoes. The gym at St. Francis College in Brooklyn is similar and there's some kind of discombobulating effect on the inner ear that certain players are sensitive to—like me. Oh well, my mangled finger (which I've been religiously icing) will screw up my game anyway.

So there's Coach Whitaker in his gray gym shorts and gray FULTON COLLEGE T-shirt, with his sweat socks pulled up to his knees to give his skinny bird legs the illusion of muscular bulk. He has a large, triangular-shaped face with wide-set brown eyes and a tiny red gash of a mouth. "Run, you pansies!" he yells as his charges do wind sprints. "Faster!"

Most of the practice session consists of ridiculous drills, culled, no doubt, from some coaches' how-to magazine. Here's an especially silly one: The players are each given an inflated balloon and required to run the length of the court while tipping the balloon ahead of them. "Fingertips!" the coach screams. "Walker! Don't let that balloon get below your shoulders!" When this exercise is finally completed, Whitaker waves a genial welcome to where Leo and I are seated in the otherwise empty bleachers and shouts, "That's one of my favorites! It develops a good shooting touch!"

Next up, the Fulton Falcons dummy their offense. My God, they must have a hundred plays, each as complicated as a Chinese fire drill. Shuffle cuts and back screens, curls and dives, with near-impossible passing angles. And the coach jumps up and down in a froth—"You dunce! You lamebrain!"—whenever a player deviates six inches to either side of his prescribed route.

As the players prance through their paces, it's clear that Whitaker doesn't know their names. He continually calls his center "Big Boy." His point guard is "Hey You." A leansome forward is "Slim." Another guard is "You There." And his players just as obviously hate his guts.

Never at any time are his players allowed a water break. When one of them timidly raises his hand to say he's thirsty, Whitaker has another shit-fit. "Water is for pansies! Are you a pansy, Miller? It's a proven medical fact, Miller, that drinking water during strenuous exercise will bring on cramps. Now give me fifty push-ups for being such a pansy!"

One of the drills covers the fine art of setting picks, and Whitaker personally demonstrates his approved methodology: Knees slightly bent, feet at shoulder width, and both hands cupped to protect the picker's genitals. Even Leo knows better. "What would you do, Aaron, if somebody set a pick like that on you? What would you break first? His chest bone or his nose?"

Now it's time for more sprints. Then foul-shooting practice. For the grand finale, Whitaker lets his team scrimmage, during which time "You There's" defender missteps and goes down with a sprained ankle. "You There" alertly cuts to the hoop, is fed the ball, and scores the easy layup. But Whitaker nearly ruptures a lung screaming abuse at poor "You There" for freelancing and abandoning a "tried-and-true offensive pattern." When the whole team is forced to run more (and more and more) punitive sprints, I've seen enough.

"See you later, Leo. I'm glad we had a chance to talk."

"Me too, pal."

I find a soft chair in the basement of the library, just behind a stack of *Erasmus Review* back issues. And I nap undisturbed, dreaming of food—of a lovely lyrical poem ground into dust, then mixed with brain jelly and troweled between two slices of white bread—a sonnet sandwich.

Some inner alarm wakes me in plenty of time to rendezvous with my teammates in the gym.

Ron's pregame report: "The admission charge is two bits, and that's about twenty-four cents too much because these guys are a joke. I saw half of them just now in the weight room, pumping and flexing so that they'll look good in layup lines. They're musclebound pretty boys, slow and stiff. If we don't beat them by thirty points, I'll eat shit in Macy's window."

Brooks has a bandage on his right ear and a fresh bruise on his cheekbone. "This sounds like an easy one," he says. "Let's just play loose and have some fun. And let's none of us get hurt." He glances at the rookies—both of them proudly sporting welts and discolored blemishes on their heads, shoulders, and arms. Kevin has a chipped tooth I hadn't noticed before. "You two," Brooks commands. "Be ready."

Just as we're about to undertake our final peeings, shoelace tightenings and jock adjustments, Leo calls for our attention. "I just want to apologize to everybody for a lot of things too numerous to mention that I've done on this trip. You all know what I mean. And I want to especially apologize to Saul for being such an asshole and a fuckhead. And I want to make this announcement: To pay back Saul for any embarrassment I've caused him, for calling him 'Frankenstein,' I solemnly promise that before this trip is over, I personally will make sure and arrange for you, Saul, to get laid."

That's why we take the court laughing.

The bleachers are crammed with boisterous, celebrating young people, rich kids already drunk and sneaking nips from pocket flasks.

"Don't step on your beards!" one of them calls out.

"Nice shot, matzo ball!"

"Look at that nose! It's a horn of plenty!"

It seems to be pledge week, and one corner of the stands has been set aside for several dozen slaphappy boys, each wearing a dead fish on a string around his neck. Several fraternity big shots parade the sidelines wielding long wooden paddles painted blue and embossed with various Greek letters. And Ron's scouting report is entirely accurate—the Fraternity All-Stars are more interested in posing than in playing basketball. They shoot layups with crooked arms and stiff-handed follow-throughs like they were throwing shit against a wall.

We are collectively introduced to the jeering crowd as "The Undefeated House of Moses from New York, New York, New York." Then comes an affable handshake with a six-foot-two weight lifter, who says with a wholesome toothsome smile, "Please take it easy on us. We're terrible." I win the tip-off and we score the game's first ten points.

My battered finger is taped as tightly as I can stand it and I studiously avoid touching the ball with my right hand. Brooks is also in a passive mood, and neither of us really wants to play. But Mitchell is earnest as ever, Leo is playful and admirably unselfish. Ron is intent on knocking somebody's teeth out, until Brooks orders him to cool down.

The student body erupts in a wild cheer when one of their own hits an improbable one-and-a-half-handed set shot to make the score 10–2. Later, we're up 17–2 and the frat boys call a time-out.

Brooks takes the opportunity to mercifully substitute the rookies for himself and for me. "Easy does it," Brooks says. "Let's lighten up on defense and let these kids score every so often. Leo? How about a dribbling exhibition? We've got a green light for behind-the-back passes and trick shots." Before we break, we notice Coach Whitaker seated just behind our bench diligently taking notes and charting our plays.

Leo, of course, his "new leaf" notwithstanding, can't resist playing the hambone—flipping an under-the-asshole scoop shot that miraculously plops through the net, then shooting with his eyes closed and barely missing a free throw. Even Mitchell attempts (and misses) a thirty-foot lefty hook. And our clowning around soon gains the crowd's approval. Ron has settled down, contenting himself with passing the ball to Leo and enjoying the show. Through all the buffoonery, the rookies make sure to ream the backboards, and the rich kids gasp when Saul unleashes his drop shot.

Our lead at the half is 35–12, so we relax on the bench and watch the halftime entertainment: There's an exercise in precision drilling by the ROTC, a tumbling exhibition, even jugglers and magicians. But Mitchell is concerned that nobody has officially welcomed us. Who, then, will pay us?

Early in the second half, the jovial weight lifter asks a favor: "My sweetheart is here and she'd love me to death if I could score a basket. What do you think?"

Sure. I let him catch a pass and whisper for him to fake a hook shot, whereupon I leap into the air to swat at an invisible basketball. One dribble and he has an open shot—which he misses, but he puts in the rebound.

Our lead stretches to 41–20, and we play the last ten minutes of the game four-against-five. Even so, Saul, Kevin, Leo, and Ron actually increase our advantage, and the final count is 63–32.

Back in the locker room, Mitchell is frantic. "Where's our money? I don't even know who to ask." Then the door opens to admit

Coach Whitaker, and Mitchell jumps into his face. "Are you the one with our money?"

"You lads sure get right to the point," the coach says. "Actually I'm here to tender you lads an offer. I'd like to recruit you to come play for me next season. All of you, or one of you, or however many of you want to come to Fulton. Yes. Yes. I know that some of you've already played a full quota of college basketball back east, but that hardly matters around here. Nobody keeps tabs on that sort of thing. We'd just supply you with a phony name and a phony high school transcript and nobody would be the wiser." Then he points at me, Mitchell, Brooks, and Leo. "For some of you older lads we could rig up some kind of military record. Which one of you wants the Congressional Medal of Honor?"

"What's in it for us?" Ron asks.

"A four-year holiday. No classes, easy pussy, and free money. And you won't have to shave points to get paid like you do in New York. Here's your chance, lads, to relive those golden, carefree days of yore."

"And afterward?" Mitchell asks. "After our eligibility is used up?"

"Then you're on your own. Hell, do I look like Father Flanagan? Good compensation for services rendered, that's the deal. Think on it. I'll be right upstairs awaiting the word. Fulton College is most likely a far sight better'n anything you might be doing come next September. Just consider your alternatives and you can't turn me down."

Ron is very interested (and for about thirty seconds, so am I). "Shit," says Ron. "I've already got that false I.D. that me and Leo picked up in New York." But Leo tells Ron about this afternoon's practice and Ron's interest quickly fades. "Balloons?"

The door opens again and this time a pimply-faced youth wearing a smelly fish pendant enters and says, "Here. Who gets this?"

Our three hundred dollars.

Then we locate a basement exit to avoid another encounter with the coach. And when we enter the car, Mitchell surprises us with a cargo of sandwiches and beer. Then we're off to Oklahoma.

"Yippee-ti-yi-yay," Ron hoots. "We're gonna tame the Wild, Wild West."

From Mitchell's Log:
Day Nine — January 14, 1936 — Monday

	Today	Total
Mileage	77	2,447
Expenses	$10.29	$230.04
Income	$300.00	$2,360.00

Net Income - $2,129.96
Average Share - $304.28
Cash on Hand - $529.96
Max Has - $1,600.00

Won - 4
Lost - 3

I insist on driving, and the pain keeps me awake and draws my attention forward, to my torturous finger, to the steering wheel, to the road. Interstate 61 going southwest toward St. Louis. Nobody knew how to search out an unrestricted hotel in Iowa, so the plan is to maybe find someplace to rest in Missouri (if things are any different there), only 75 miles away. The choice is

Brooks's (riding shotgun) and mine—where to stop and when, or perhaps motoring through to St. Loo. We're not scheduled to play next until Thursday morning in Oklahoma City (756 miles from Cedar Rapids), so there's no immediate timetable nor any sense of urgency.

Just the urgent throbbing of this goddamn finger. My favorite finger—imparting the last touch and spin to my hook shot. My most dependable nose picker, ear scratcher, and pussy tickler. But now? I've half a mind to chop the fucking thing off.

The pain is soothed some when the entire hand is elevated, like when I hook my right thumb into my collar and drive lefty. But as soon as the throbbing subsides, I get dreary-eyed and sleepy. Behind the first door is pain, a dagger stabbing with each heartbeat, as the Black Lady crawls along through the slow, rumbling miles. Behind the second door is the time-obliterating swiftness of sleep, painless and going nowhere.

Why did I ever volunteer to drive in the first place? Mr. Bigshot. Mr. Maccabee clothed in righteousness and wearing a six-pointed badge.

But I know I can't go on much longer—and Brooks, fast asleep, is no help. So I try to find a hand position of minimal pain, barely enough to keep me from dozing at the wheel. The dullest edge to lean against. What if I raise my hand just an inch higher? . . . Yes, that's better . . . No! Wake up, you fool! Wake up and suffer.

My bladder's been bloated by the beer, and right there's a rest area—with picnic tables and a brick shithouse, but no other vehicles. The perfect excuse for a time-out. I ease the car to a soft landing, then sit for a moment with the motor running. But only Mitchell stirs. "Whazzit?"

"Nothing, Mitchell. Pee time. Go back to sleep."

I lift myself out of the car and quietly click the door shut behind me. For the moment, the chill air is refreshing. Then I step away from the car and piss lefthanded into a patch of virgin snow, trying to script my name, petering out on the upside of the *r*. And I hear a crunching noise behind me, ominous footsteps, but it's only Saul.

"Halleluja," he says softly, moving to stand a free throw away from me and facing into the darkness. He pees slowly, holding his left elbow at a rigid angle and, like me, he tries to button his pants wrong-handed.

"Maybe Mitchell was right," I say. "Maybe we should've both seen a doctor."

Saul disagrees, shaking his head, his long beard swinging in opposition. "And what would a doctor have done? Told you your finger is broken? You already know that. Put a splint on it so you couldn't play ball for a month? Who needs it?"

"What about your elbow?"

"The joint is all soft and puffy, so I'm pretty sure it's a ruptured bursa sac. I had the same thing two years ago back in school. I'll live."

I breathe deeply and, between the high gray clouds, I look for a star to wish upon. "Star light," I say. "Star bright. Not a fucking star in sight." Both of us are reluctant to crawl back into the hearse. "So how's it going, Saul?"

"It's going," he says somberly. "At least my asshole's no longer the only part of my body that's hurting." Now he laughs silently, deeply, bottoming out with a moist and heaving sigh. "Aaron? I know this might sound stupid . . . but do you think Leo was serious? About getting me laid?"

"Probably as serious as Leo ever is."

"Because I need to, Aaron. To get laid. To prove something to myself. Does that make any sense?"

"Totally."

Again I sniff the night air and try to find a star. Then I bend down and gather a handful of snow to pack around my finger. Maybe I can induce frostbite and it'll just turn black and fall off.

"Aaron? . . . Do you have any regrets about beating up those rednecks? Some of them were hurt pretty bad."

"Absolutely not. Those fucking peckerwoods got exactly what they deserved."

"I guess so," he says. "But it's pretty upsetting now that I think back on it. And not only because they were hurt as bad as they were. But mainly because I enjoyed doing it so much. Beating them up. They were going to beat up the hoboes and we beat up on them. So, Aaron . . . tell me, what's the difference between us and them?"

"Saul. You know better than that. The difference is in the motive. They were cowards and bullies. We were putting our hides on the line to protect some innocent people. We were also outnumbered, remember? We were surrounded. And shit yeah, I enjoyed it too. It was a catharsis. A redemption through blood."

"Aaron, Aaron . . . why is there always so much blood? When does the bleeding ever stop?"

I try to shape an exhaled cloud of breath vapor into a circle, but all I can manage is a dying gasp. "Sometimes," I say, "the blood flows in a righteous cause. Sometimes. Like when David slew Goliath."

Saul laughs out loud, an unexpected night sound, sharp and cruel. "You forget whom you're talking to, Aaron . . . I'm Goliath, remember?" Then he spits into the night. "I'm getting chilled, Aaron. I'm going back inside."

Behind the wheel again, my frozen finger melting and painful with a vengeance. I need another time-out. After all, we do have a travel day. So why knock myself out? What's the rush? Saul is already snoozing and I'm sure that nobody else wants to abandon their sweet dreams and drive.

The vote is 1–0 with six abstentions. So I place the gun in my lap, then close my eyes and will myself to sleep.

So I left Mr. Lombardo and his "birts." Then I crossed the rooftops and came downstairs onto Dillon Street, leaving Sam Spade to his own foolish vigil, alone there on Division Street leaning against a streetlamp. And I kept walking until I found myself on the Bowery, where I stayed for nearly two weeks.

I slept in the Moonlight Hotel, where a bed in the huge dormitory hall cost two cents per night. But I had some money in my wallet, so I rented one of the small partitioned rooms for thirty-five cents a week. Either way the beds were the same, thin straw-filled pads swarming with vermin and set upon rusty springs that shrieked whenever somebody's limbs twitched in the throes of some chronic nightmare. And the sour, stale smells, the bad breath, and the putrefying infections, overwhelmed the entire building. I remember the night sounds too—racking winter coughs and chest-deep wheezings, the groans and heavings of despair, the occasional grunting yip of somebody whacking off.

And I belonged there among the failures and the guilt-ridden minions, among the red-faced consumptives and the walking pneumoniacs. I wallowed in my sins, in my own selfish culpabilities. What else could I cling to?

Nobody talked much, but I did encounter several men who were ruined by the crash and had simply given up. Men whose only purpose was to die quietly and obscurely. I also met desperate ratlike men who stole apples from pushcarts and hawked them in the streets, who fought other desperate men for the choicest street corners—42nd Street and Times Square, any intersection near Grand Central Station or Madison Square Garden.

When I awoke one morning to discover that my wallet had been lifted, I learned to hang around fish stores and vegetable stalls waiting for late-night discards and handouts. I also waited on soup lines at church doors, then suffered through the sermons. (Here's where the downtrodden derelicts showed their only kindness to one another. The beadles were eager to rap a nodding head with long knob-ended sticks, and the bums would poke each other awake whenever chins bounced against chests.) The preachers told us that "this life" was unimportant, that the more we suffered "here," the better our chances of entering heaven in "the hereafter."

Always mindful of the cops, the toughest, most veteran bums begged in front of the fanciest restaurants, in front of Broadway theaters and illegal gambling casinos. (Here's a nickel to make you go away, to impress the little lady, to keep the fancy, fat-rich food from being vomited on the sidewalk, to celebrate the winning of a daily double.) But I was too big to panhandle. People were afraid and crossed the street to avoid me. I still wore my brown slacks and brown herringbone jacket that I'd taught in (so long ago), fraying now and filthy, but good enough for me to gain entrance into crowded restaurants at the tail end of lunch hour, where I stole waiters' tips from atop the tables. Quick hands and quick feet. On Thursdays and Fridays (collection days), I followed the young boys who delivered the afternoon newspapers from door to door. The *New York Post*, the *World-Telegraph,* the *Brooklyn Eagle,* even the *Daily Forward.* Then I threatened them into handing over their hard-earned pennies and nickels. "Don't fuck with me, kid. I'll wring your scrawny little neck." Whenever the kids cried, I let them keep a dime. And I believed I'd live like this until somebody killed me or I caught some wasting disease.

Then one evening, I was sitting in the "recreation room" at the flophouse, listening to the radio along with several of my peers, listening to the ever-popular *Amos 'n' Andy Show* . . .

—Now, Lightnin, dis is de reason I ast yo' to pay some o' yo' dues dat yo' is back in. De record show dat yo' ain't paid but thirty-five cents in de last two years, an' dat's a disregrace to de Mystic Knights o' de Sea Lodge dat's puttectin' yo' like it is.

—Yessah, well, I is behind wid ev'rything. My coffin money's even back now. Insurance man come oveh dis mornin' lookin' fo' ten cents. I had to duck de man. I just ain't got it, Kingfish. If yo' would lend me some money, I would pay de lodge.

—Whut yo' mean, *me* lend yo' some money? I is flat as a pancake. I got about fifteen cents, an' I gotta git a dollar by tonight somewhere. Me an' Sapphire goin' have comp'ny fo' supper. De butcher done tighten up on me. I can't ast de people comin' to supper to eat gravy *all* de time . . .

. . . when suddenly I spied someone familiar walking into the room—my father-in-law's inept private eye. The other friendless and kithless men immediately recognized him as some kind of lawman and they scurried into the hallway.

"Howdy," the detective said, his beefy face showing a practiced smile, a smile about as lively as a split seam. "Mr. Steiner. My name's Herbert Williams, and I must say, you're a hard man to find." He seated himself beside me, poked a cigarette out of a gold-plated case, and triggered a gold-plated lighter to set it afire. "But find you I did, and here we are."

"Leave me alone," I said peevishly, my voice cracking like a teenager on the verge of puberty. Aside from the desk clerk and a few fearful newsboys, it occurred to me that I hadn't much spoken to anyone since I'd been there.

"I wish I could leave you alone," he said, exhaling his cigarette smoke away from my face. "I really do, Mr. Steiner. I'm a big basketball fan and I followed your career at Metro. You were a hell of a player back then. But I've got a job to do."

I ignored him and stared at my shoes.

"You're in big trouble," he said. "My employer, Mr. Goldfarb, is out to get you. He wants to see you destroyed."

I laughed sourly. "Tell him he's too late."

"I'm talking about a jail sentence, Mr. Steiner. He wants to put you away."

"What for? For cremating the baby? For fucking a student?"

"For rape, Mr. Steiner. He's been after the girl . . ." Here Williams broke eye contact to consult a notepad. ". . . Debra Goodman, and her parents too. Offering them lots of money if they'll get the girl to sign a complaint of rape against you."

"That's bullshit. Debra was . . . she was just as willing as I was."

He nodded his head, causing his jowls to ripple. "That's the way I figure it too. But she is a minor. Of course, the parents could file a complaint by themselves, but without the girl's cooperation they don't have much of a case."

"Debra would never go along with something like that. Would she?"

"Not yet. But Goldfarb keeps raising the jackpot. It's up to two hundred dollars as of yesterday. Debra's father is an unemployed carpenter and he's putting some pressure on the girl. I've got to hand it to her, though. I think her old man's been slapping her around some, but she's a toughie and she's sticking to her guns. The way I see it, the father thinks he can get a lot more loot out of Goldfarb, so he's giving the girl some leeway. So far, that is. I don't know how long she can hold out."

"So what do you want from me? Should I confess to something I didn't do? Should I turn myself in? I don't understand."

He shifted in his seat, looking for stray lice on the cuffs of his clean shirt, blowing a perfect smoke ring toward the ceiling. "Well, I'll tell you what, Mr. Steiner. All's I'm supposed to do is to find you and keep an eye out so that if and when the rape charges are filed, the cops can arrest you right off. But . . ."

"But what?"

"But something I could never figure out in the first place is why guys like you start fooling around with the young girls. What're you, afraid of getting old or something? If you're so pussy-whipped, whyn't you use the services of a professional? That way nobody gets hurt. Why get yourself involved with a piece of jailbait? To say nothing about cheating on your wife. You know what I mean?"

"I don't know nothing. That's why I'm in a fucking flophouse."

"Ah, shit. Why am I asking you questions I know you can't answer? . . . Anyway, the kicker is that this guy Goldfarb is such a nasty fucker. A gold-plated asshole. He reminds me of my stepfather, but that's another story."

"So?"

"So, I'm an old fool and I'm gonna let you off the hook . . . . I interviewed the girl and I think she's waiting for you to come riding up on a white horse and sweep her off her feet. Actually, she's a nice enough kid. But like I said, I don't know how much longer she can hold out."

"So?"

"So this . . . I'm gonna tell Goldfarb that I can't locate you and that my investigation's still continuing. I figure I can milk him for another couple of weeks' work anyway."

"So?"

"Jesus, you're a real disagreeable bastard, ain't you? Here I am, trying to save your miserable ass and you're busting my nuts . . . . Jesus, my wife's right. I've been in this bullshit business too long . . . . Anyway, if I were you, Mr. Steiner, I'd get the hell out of town before I change my mind and the shit hits the fan . . . . By the way, I ain't the only one looking for you." Once again he scanned his notebook. "Your brother, Max, number one. And number two is . . . Here it is . . . Some guy named Leo Gilbert. You know him?"

"Yeah. It's a business matter."

"Anyway." He stood up and brushed the ashes from his coat. "The sooner you're gone, the better for you. Out of state would be best. Okay?"

"Thanks."

"And by the way . . . It's none of my business, but I figure it's about time you stopped kicking yourself in the ass. What happened to your baby, it wasn't your fault. Believe me. My oldest, Herbert Junior, is mentally retarded. You know?"

So I telephoned Max and met him at his apartment, where he yelled and complained about everything from my abandoned job to the dirt under my fingernails. When he finally calmed down, he encouraged me to "join Leo's tour," which was leaving in four days with only six players. "Go with them," Max said. "That's the only reason I backed Leo because I knew eventually you'd be going too. Hell, if you'd have shown up after they left, I would've paid for a bus ticket so you could join them. You're my little brother, Aaron. It's my job to look after you."

While Max contacted Leo and finalized the arrangements with Livitski, the booking agent, I cleaned myself up, stuffed my belly with steaks, milk, and fruit juices, and to get back into shape, I ran the six flights of stairs in Max's building at least twenty times each day. "You don't know how happy I am," Max said over and over, "that you're going on the trip."

Then on the day before we left, Mitchell dropped off a cardboard suitcase, all the luggage I was allowed. And I returned "home" to pick up some clothing and my basketball gear.

Once again, the radio was blaring so I knew Judy was home.

> **"*One Man's Family* is dedicated to the Mothers and Fathers of the Younger Generation and to their Bewildering Off-spring. Today we bring you Chapter Ten, Book Twenty-Three, entitled "Two Million Dollars at Stake." Phillip Spencer was killed in a private-aeroplane crash while en route to San Francisco to try to prove that he was the father of David, infant son of his ex-wife Beth Holly . . . "**

This time I used my key to quietly unlock the door and sneak into the apartment. There she was, sitting in her favorite rocking chair and staring enrapt at the console radio. She wore a blue terry cloth bathrobe. Her brown hair was longer than before, all tangled and greasy. She looked thinner and worn out. Her brown eyes were red-veined and raw.

> **"Beth has declared that Spencer was not her child's father and was ready to go to any extreme to fight it. Now Spencer is gone and the danger is passed, but circumstances are not willing to let it go at that. Now the attorneys for Spencer's estate announce that the deceased has left funds and properties to the value of . . ."**

When she looked up and saw me, one hand moved to grip the front of her robe while her right hand covered her heart. "What do you want?" she said softly. "You sonofabitchbastard! Come sneaking in here like a thief!"

"I need some clothing."

She rose from her chair (which still rocked in a ghostly rhythm) and moved closer to the radio. "Don't touch me," she said. "I'll call the police."

"I'm not going to touch you or hurt you, Judy. I just have to collect some of my things." Shit! What if she'd thrown them out? She followed me into the bedroom. No, everything seemed to be there, even my dirty shirts had been washed and ironed.

> **". . . San Francisco to Hong Kong on the *China Clipper* for their honeymoon! This happened last night at the engagement shower . . . and now the family is at breakfast . . ."**
>
> **"Now Clifford, eat your breakfast like a normal human being."**
>
> **"But, Mom . . ."**

She sat nervously at the edge of our nuptial bed while I packed what I required. "You're a weakling," she said. "You're pathetic. You should be neutered like a dog." She spoke her maledictions with no rancor, each word turned over in her imagination, polished and memorized since she last saw me. "You're a selfish bastard . . . Men, you're all alike. Little boys who only want the newest, shiniest toy. You think you run the world but you'll throw your life away for a puny five-second thrill. My life. My baby's life. I'd hate to think of how miserable the world would be if men had the kind of climaxes women do. You jerkoff."

"I won't argue with you, Judy."

"You can't. Because you know I'm right."

"I don't know what's right anymore. All I know is that I'm wrong and so are you."

> **"Well, if I'd known what a goose he was going to be, I'd have put my foot down when your father wanted to buy the tickets . . ."**

"He hasn't talked about anything else . . ."

"But you folks don't get it . . . Ann and I are going to fly the Pacific Ocean . . . "

Then she struggled to her feet and pointed at me as if she was an avenging angel. "I curse you, Aaron. You evil man! You lump of shit! I curse you! You'll wander forever and ever and your sins will poison your dreams. You'll grow old and sick and feeble. But you'll never find rest until your miserable life is over and you die in pain. A long and painful death. That's my curse, Aaron. I hate that you've made me a witch! I hate it! But I swear that my witch's curse will come true!"

Looking away from her (but chilled by her cold vehemence), I forced the suitcase shut.

"Well, it should have worn off a little by this morning . . . I'm going to be worn to a frazzle if this hilarity keeps up . . . "

Then she looked at me kind of sideways, sly and devious, saying, "Where are you going that you need all this junk?"

"I've got a job on a ship, a freighter, bound for Australia. I'm sailing tomorrow."

Then she left the room and I heard her frantically dialing the telephone in the kitchen. On my way out, I peeked into the spare bedroom, the nursery, to see the baby's crib, the pink blankets and flouncy pillows still there, the bunny rabbits on the wallpaper and the little lambies. And as I walked out the front door, she rushed to slam it behind me, screaming so even that the neighbors could hear, "Murderer! God will punish you!"

Mitchell wakes up screaming: "How come we're not moving? What's wrong?"

I explain that I was fearful of falling asleep while driving, that sometime early that morning I'd pulled over for what was supposed to be a short nap. "Everybody else was sleeping so soundly that I didn't feel right waking one of you to take over. We have all day to get there, Mitchell. I didn't think it was worthwhile to push so hard."

"Where are we? Missouri? What time is it?"

"We're still in Iowa. The last town I remember driving through was Pemberton. And the time is eight-one-four."

By now everybody's awake and the Black Lady is putrid with the gaseous remains of last night's beer-feast. Another round of roadside pissing is in order, to say nothing of shitting in the woods.

"In the spring," Saul says as he admires his own steaming mound, "a beautiful flower will grow here."

Only three miles up the road I pull over and park in front of another bus-shaped diner, Woody's Place. There are pickup trucks and even tractors parked outside. There's a well-preserved tin lizzie and several bicycles. Inside, the familiar chromium decor, the same old countertop and greasy grill. The cook wears a St. Louis Cardinals baseball cap and a stained undershirt. The waitress is a thin peroxide blonde with black roots showing near her skull. The other customers look like hard-handed farmers, gulping down generous portions of grits, eggs, and pig meat along with smoking mugs of coffee.

We move in a line toward a long table at the back end, when the cook pops out from behind the counter shouting, "Hey! Hey! What're you people doing? Where do you think you're going?"

We stare at him dumbly . . . . Could it be? A greasy spoon that's restricted?

One of the customers speaks up, a beer-bellied oaf chewing on hash and eggs. "You fellers' what? Niggers? Redskins? Polacks? I know you ain't Chinks. Ain't that right, Woody?"

Mitchell smiles at the fat man (anybody who's so fat these days *must* be rich), and I restrain Ron with a secure hand on his shoulder. "We're pilgrims," Mitchell says. "Just passing through."

"Well," says the cook. "Keep right on passing, then. Whatever the hell you be, you cain't eat in here. Tarnation! You'll scare the appetite outta my customers." His motion is seconded by a vote of side-splitting, food-spitting laughter. "I'll do this for you, though," he continues, "outta the goodness of my heart .... Send just one of you in with the orders for you all. Let's do it thata way. Ain't that fair enough?"

Mitchell shrugs and says, "I guess we'll just have to take our business elsewhere."

The cook laughs and informs us that this here is vacation time hereabouts for those what can afford it, and we won't likely find another open roadside eatery until we reach St. Looie.

So we retreat into the car, where we consider our options. "I'm hungry," says Leo.

"Me too."

"Me three."

Then we dictate our individual requests to Kevin. Brooks wants tuna salad on whole wheat toast. Leo wants his fried egg (over easy) on a seeded roll. Someone else will have roast beef (rare), a BLT, grilled cheese, coffee black, coffee with cream, with three lumps of sugar, with one and a half, apple pie, a whole wheat muffin, a danish? Mitchell hands Kevin a five-dollar bill and says, "The bank's paying."

But Kevin returns barely two minutes later with a sad story. Seems that the cook balked at the diversity and complexity of our orders—"Too much work for a bunch of foreigners." The cook "suggests" that we all order the same thing—seven BLTs or whatever. Naturally, this leads to a fierce debate with Leo filibustering for fried-egg sandwiches (over easy) and Mitchell lobbying for roast beef (rare).

"Fuck you!" Leo says to Mitchell.

"Fuck *me*? Fuck *you*!"

Then Brooks says, "Fuck the both of you!" and unilaterally tells Kevin to get fourteen tuna salads on hard rolls plus seven black coffees and a handful of sugar cubes.

"Who died and left you boss?" Mitchell says but Brooks ignores him.

While everybody else waits and grumps in silence, Brooks has something more to say: "Actually, I'm kind of glad we're still in Iowa . . . . Leo, hand me that map, will ya? . . . Let's see . . . we're only about twenty-five miles from the Amana Colonies."

Who? What? Where? Okay, Brooks, we give up.

The seven Amana Colonies, founded in 1854 as centralized, planned, and patterned villages where farming was the principal activity. The original eight hundred Amana settlers, of German, Swiss, and Alsatian ancestry, came to Iowa to escape persecution and pursue a visionary faith called the Community of the True Inspirationalists (more than implying that everyone else's inspiration was false). The Amanites' adopted lifestyle embraced the concept of "communal enterprises," a blend of brotherhood and economics, with each individual contributing what he or she did best. The result was "a pure democracy" plus an extraordinary variety of finely crafted nineteenth-century pioneer furniture, clocks, embroidery, calico dresses, hand-loomed woolen items, whole-grain cereals, Westphalia-style smoked meats, wines of German character, and exceptional Old World baked offerings from a number of community kitchens. "It's now mostly a museum," Brooks says, "with a store full of imported goods that caters to the tourists. It's still worth seeing, even though the actual working commune itself broke up just before the war."

Mitchell admits being attracted to "the concept," but he objects to making "a long trip longer for some wild-goose chase." Leo tries to be diplomatic, but the vote goes 5–2, the stouthearted warriors against the lily-livered cowards.

And the tuna sandwiches are swell—mixed with mayo, chopped celery, and bits of sweet relish. The coffee is hot and strong—and I'm tempted to plunge my aching finger into the scalding liquid, maybe to cauterize the damn thing, rendering it useless but painless. A fair trade.

Anyway, the twenty-five miles to the Amana Colonies turns out to be forty-two miles, and guess what? All we see is a high wooden fence around a compound of old-fashioned houses, and atop the fence a big sign: OPEN APRIL 1 – NOVEMBER 30. Two hours out of our way for naught. And Mitchell gloats as he routinely collects and bags the empty coffee cups and the waxed-paper sandwich wrappings. "I hate to say I told you so," he says, and for a moment he struggles to contain himself .... "But I told you so. I did. Remember?"

Mitchell's reward is to replace me behind the wheel and have Leo riding shotgun. I wind up in the crypt with the rookies and quickly fall asleep.

I wake up when we stop for gas. And the highway cuts through downtown St. Louis—grimy buildings, blinking traffic lights, people in a blind rush, buses farting black smoke, garbage decomposing in the streets. On the sidewalk, an elderly woman in a shabby mink coat walks an elderly schnauzer. The dog pauses by the curb, sniffs in a slow circle, then squats and squeezes out two small Tootsie Rolls. The woman pulls a tissue from her purse, bends down and wipes her doggie's ass. The woman looks up and down the street to see if she's being observed, then she daintily kicks some loose snow over the tissue and the turds.

The sun turns warm on the car windows and there's no longer any tufts of snow along the roadside as we switch onto Interstate 44 and zip through Springfield, Missouri. Into the countryside now, and in the distance, the fields and trees have gradually lost their ice shirts and snow cover. Then, just about a mile inside the Oklahoma state line, we're suddenly chased by a flashing red light, and a wailing siren jerks everybody awake.

"It's a cop," Brooks says. "Mitchell, how fast are you going?"

"The speed limit. Forty on the nose. Here . . . I'll pull over and let him pass. Probably he's late for a lunch date or something."

But the black-and-white cruiser noses in front of us and urges us onto the shoulder. The door opens and a state trooper climbs out, adjusting his wide-brimmed felt hat, proud of his high black boots and bloused pants, looking sinister as a Nazi. He walks a slow circle around the Black Lady, noting the New York plates, the lettering on the driver's side, also the bullet holes. Then he unbuttons the top flap of his holster and raps on the driver's window with his club.

Mitchell affects his most agreeable smile as he rolls the window down and says, "Good morning, officer."

"Somebody been shooting at you boys?" the trooper asks with a leering grin. "Or mebbe y'all just been driving through some big ol' hailstorm. Lemme see your driver's license and the registration for this here vehicle."

Mitchell pulls his license from his wallet and dutifully opens the glove compartment to locate the registration. "No!" Ron yelps. "Oh, shit . . . ."

When the cop glimpses the gun nestled there inside, he draws his own weapon and says, "All right! Nobody move in there!" Still pointing his handgun at us, he backtracks to his car, reaching behind him and quickly exchanging his pistol for a shotgun.

"All right!" he barks. "Come on outa there one by one! No monkey business! You, the driver! You come out first! Slowly! Let me always see your hands! Easy, boys! This thang's got a hairy trigger!"

Mitchell carefully works his way out of the car and is pushed into a spread-eagle posture leaning over the front hood. The cop is briskly frisking Mitchell, when to everybody's surprise, Kevin boldly speaks up, saying this: "Officer, my name is Kevin McCray and my father is a sergeant in the New York Police Department, Thirty-Fourth Precinct in Harlem. The gun is his and I also have his gold badge in my wallet. Now, I'm going to put my right hand into my pocket, real slow .... All right, here it is .... Now what you should do is call Central and have them contact New York and verify this, okay? Here's the badge."

The cop is obviously impressed by the gleaming badge and he wants to know who the hell we are anyway, so Mitchell goes through the usual explanation, adding some cock-and-bull story about a certain gambler who bet against us in Chicago and tried to scare us into dumping the ball game.

"y'all expect me to believe that pile of booshit?" the cop says. Then he commands Mitchell to "stay put and don't move a damn muscle" while the call is made to headquarters.

The rest of us wait anxiously, afraid to make any sudden movements. And Kevin has something to tell me: "The only reason he stopped us is the Jewish stars on the side of the car."

"You're probably right."

"And you know something else? From what I've seen so far, I guess it's not so easy to be a Jew. But there's one thing I don't understand, Aaron, and Saul doesn't really talk about it so's I can understand him. I mean, I don't even know what a Jew is. I know that I'm an Irish Catholic, right? I know that being Irish is my nationality and being Catholic is my religion. So what is being Jewish? A religion? A nationality? If it's a religion, then what do you get out of it that's worth all the trouble? Look, I'm not trying to be a wiseguy. But why be a Jew if you don't have to be one?"

Saul, eavesdropping, is tickled with laughter. "Being a Jew," he says, "is a state of mind."

"See what I mean?" Kevin says to me.

But Saul persists: "Above all, being Jewish means being stubborn. In the Old Testament, how many times are Jews called hard-necked and iron-necked? We're also arrogant, clannish, and devoted to meaningless rituals, although we sure don't have a monopoly on this. Being Jewish means waiting your whole life for the other shoe to drop. Then having it land right on top of your head."

"I still don't understand .... Aaron?"

"Saul knows more about it than I do. I was raised as a gastronomical Jew. We ate boiled chicken on Friday night, matzo brei on Passover, potato latkes on Hanukkah .... To me the whole thing's a setup designed to make you feel guilty about being a normal human being. And I'll say this ... It sure does work."

"What's the advantage, then?"

I pull a handkerchief from my pocket and loudly blow my nose. Still talking into his two-way radios the cop sees me and wiggles the shotgun in my direction. "The advantage, Kevin, is that the world is full of Jews, some who are rich, some who are related to you, and some who are both rich and related."

"The main advantage," says Saul, "is that stubbornness goes a long way."

Kevin considers our quixotic explanations and makes his decision: "I'm glad that I'm not really Jewish."

Meanwhile, the cop has finished communicating with his superiors and, clearly disappointed, he replaces his shotgun in the patrol car before returning the gold badge to Kevin.

"Y'all's story checks out," the cop says, his eyes hidden behind reflective sunglasses. "I just don't know how or why the son of a twenty-year man could get mixed up with these people. Tell me, son . . . don't y'all go to church? Don't y'all know it was the Jews killed Christ?"

Kevin shakes his head. "Not these Jews."

"All right," the cop says, hitching up his belt. "Tell me where y'all're headed and how long y'all're gonna be in Oklahoma."

Mitchell has the specifics: "We're playing at the Farm Fair in Oklahoma City tomorrow. Then on Thursday we're playing at a Cherokee reservation near Tulsa. After that, we're headed for Colorado."

The cop glares and snaps shut the flap of his holster. "We'll sure be watching y'all whilst yer in our jurisdiction. Get out of line once and y'all's ass is in a sling. You hear? If anybody else so much as sees that gun of yours, it's curtains for y'all. And don't say that I didn't warn you. Now, get the hell out of my sight."

"Thank you, officer."

A few miles down the roads we stop and switch places. Now it's Saul's turn to drive and I'm in the backseat with Mitchell.

"Okay," Mitchell says, taking charge again. "Nice work, Kevin. Now we've got an important decision to make. Either we stop soon and get something to eat, or we bust straight through to Oklahoma City. Looks like we've got maybe two hundred miles yet."

The verdict is unanimous—"Go!"

Around and about Tulsa in the eastern section of the state, the highway is bordered by oak trees and green sloping hillocks. The sun is high and warm, tapping sweetly on the landscape like a soft yellow drum. Saul disengages the heater and we eagerly shed our winter coats and crack open the windows.

"A *mechaieh*," Mitchell says, then translates for Kevin. "A real pleasure."

We doze luxuriously as the Black Lady moves inexorably west. And slowly the roadside horizons flatten and dry out. The trees give way to scraggly bushes, the hillocks to gradual dunes of red dust. Red dust nattering against the front windshield, red dust swirling over the road.

"Look!" says Ron. "There's a fucking tumbleweed!"

We're passing through a desert where even the sparse shrubbery is chiseled to the root by the relentless red dust. We see abandoned farms and the dust-blown skeletons of cattle. Strands of barbed wire float on the sands. A weathered sign says, FOR SALE. THIS PLACE AND COW. CHEAP. Cars and trucks pass by in both directions, driving in midafternoon with their headlights on. Police cars slow down to let us know they've seen us. Then we see a huge fenced-in area off to the left and a sign: SITE OF THE BLACKFOOT RESERVATION—1876–1919. And several miles away, another: SITE OF THE CROW RESERVATION—1882–1913. Suddenly the wind gets lively and the sky is filled with dark, scudding clouds.

"Tornado alley," Mitchell says. "Kansas, Nebraska, Texas, and Oklahoma."

Ron is excited. "I'd love to see a real live tornado! I want to be in the middle of one! Stuff flying around . . . ! What a sight that must be!"

In the dusty fields, we see large T-shaped machines, only some of them moving, the crossbars rocking noisily on their pivots like broken and lunatic crucifixes.

"Pumping oil," says Mitchell.

Then gradually we see the gleaming silhouette of Oklahoma City rising from the earth like some darkly jeweled enchanted kingdom. By the time we reach the outskirts, the smokelike storm clouds have blown away.

Looking for a hotel, we pass the same kind of wood-framed

houses we've seen everywhere. Occasionally a small barbed-wire field encloses an emaciated horse or a rib-strutted milk cow. More abandoned farms, splintered barns, and rusting oil pumpers.

Near the intersection of Route 66 and Interstate 44, we pull into the graveled parking lot of the OKC Rodeo House—one large four-story building surrounded by several dozen cottages of varying dimensions. The ubiquitous red dust has been temporarily buried under a thin layer of gravel, the pathways are outlined with splitrail fences, and each of the guest cottages lies within its own corral. There's a tall wooden Indian guarding the entrance to the main building, and Leo says, "How."

Inside, the lobby is lit by one huge wagon-wheel chandelier. Buffalo heads, silver spurs, and uncoiled lassos are secured to the walls. The wooden floor is decorated with small woven rugs of geometric Indian designs. The couches and chairs are rough-hewn and their cushions match the rugs. There's an old lacquered saddle propped in a corner, and a brass spittoon lurks at every turning.

"This is the real thing." Leo beams, happy as a birthday boy.

Several cowboys walk briskly through the lobby, dressed like movie extras in ten-gallon hats, blue jeans, pearl-buttoned shirts, and intricately scrolled high leather boots. One of them carries a briefcase. Another wears a western-cut blue business suit. Ron is disappointed that none of them is armed.

We approach the front desk with some trepidation . . . . Were there rabbis in the Wild West? Are there Stars of David planted up on Boot Hill? But a sunny-faced cowgirl is congenial and very helpful. The cost of the cottages ranges from three dollars to five dollars, the rooms upstairs in the main building go for one dollar for doubles and a dollar-fifty for singles. As before, the rookies will share a room and, after Mitchell distributes our expense money, the rest of us choose the singles.

My room has the same corny frontier motif as the lobby. Bunkhouse furniture and above the bed an amateurish painting of a cowhand riding a bucking bronco. From my window I can distinguish the natural curvature of the earth.

After a short nap, I cross the highway to a BBQ joint, Panhandle Paul's—The Best in the West. The decor seems to be a replica of some imaginary outdoors scene—shellacked picnic tables, varnished trees planted in wooden tubs. Sprightly green carpeting. The "Bill of Fair" is posted on the wall behind the counter—ribs, chicken, sausage, brisket of beef (flanken!), fried okra, coleslaw, plus a local specialty, BBQ bologna, as well as Panhandle Paul's deluxe baked beans, a sweet, gummy mess of undifferentiated fart pods. I order a double-combo platter and a beer.

On my way back through the lobby, I ask the friendly cowgirl to give me four dollars worth of change and to direct me to the nearest telephone. Then I call New York.

"Hello?" Yes, it's her. My only love and atonement.

"Debra. It's me."

"Oh. I expected to hear from you sooner. Where are you?"

"Oklahoma City."

"That sounds so far away. I wish I was there. I wish I was anywhere but here."

"Then you've thought about Los Angeles?"

"Sure. What do I have to lose? Actually, it'll be good to . . . to see you again. Aaron."

"Great. Same here."

Then I figure out when we're scheduled to reach L.A.—on or about January 24th. Debra knows of a Western Union office on Grand Street. "Great." I'll find out what the coast-to-coast train fare costs, somehow pry the money out of Mitchell, and have it wired on to Debra in time to be collected tomorrow on her way home from school. Then I'll call again when we reach Colorado to find out exactly when she's arriving.

"No second thoughts?" she says.

"I was going to ask you the same thing."

"It's what I really want to do, Aaron. I swear it."

"Me too." And upon what collateral should I base my vow? My life? Hers?

Most of the guys are headed out to Oklahoma City's only movie theater, where a George Raft feature is playing. But I'd rather spend the waning evening alone.

In the rear of the main building, the Hoot 'n' Holler Bar features sawdust-strewn floors and barrels of free peanuts. I find myself a lonely table and order a pitcher of beer. From time to time, I even dip my afflicted finger into the beer for the antiseptic splash of alcohol. And the slight stinging is somehow reassuring.

There's a small platform in front of the room, lit by a single white spotlight. And without benefit of a microphone, a nervous and sickly-looking young man serenades the numerous customers, singing in his thin, yodeling voice over the strident laughter and the tinkling of glasses. The young singer wears denim overalls, a stiff-collared white shirt, and a straw hat. He has a long nose, big ears, sallow cheeks, and he strums a battered guitar.

I can hear the clickity-clack of the train
Taking me far away from here
As the rain
Falls through the boxcar door

He sings of train whistles at midnight, of railroad tracks leading to nowhere, of unrequited love, of cold nights in the jailhouse. His plaintive warbling leaves me feeling dissatisfied and unsettled.

A piece of stone for my pillow
As I sleep in these shackles and chains

Vay iz mir! I just got here, in this room, in this city, and already I want to leave. *Woe is me.* Perhaps it's not the arriving that's significant. *Yodel-ay-ee-hoo.* Perhaps the only meaning lies in the journey.

From Mitchell's Log:
Day Ten — January 15, 1936 — Tuesday

	Today	Total
Mileage	503	2,950
Expenses	$52.19	$282.23
Income	0	$2,360.00

Net Income - $2,077.77
Average Share - $296.82
Cash on Hand - $477.77
Max Has - $1,600.00

Won - 4
Lost - 3

DAY 11

I sleep late, seeking long, peaceful dreams, finding only dark and coiling shapes hiding inside my own shadow that's cast by a black sun. Waking to find my body still weary and my finger hurting about two percent less than yesterday. At this rate, I'll be healed by St. Valentine's Massacre Day.

Then I eat breakfast at Panhandle Paul's—ham, eggs, and grits.

(And what's all the fuss about hominy grits? It's only kasha, southern style. Like soft and chewy grains of sand, lily-white and tasteless.) Outside, the weather is perfect for hooping—high, bluish clouds to absorb the sunshine, the temperature deliciously cool, yet warm enough to draw a good sweat. The air smells raw and expectant here in Oklahoma, like the world's been newly hatched. I catch just a whiff of blood, though, and something burning in the distance.

Back in the hotel lobby, I call the train station downtown and I'm quoted a price of $87.42 one-way from New York to Los Angeles. And I can't help repeating the amount to the attendant. "Eighty-seven-forty-two, eh? Why not forty-three or forty-one? Exactly how is this price determined? The passenger's weight times distance multiplied by the coefficient of fuel consumption?"

"Ain't my department, mister. I just read the right numbers off the right chart. Probbly been figured out by some smartass New York Jew."

Then at nine o'clock it's time to meet my playmates in the lobby for the short ride over to the fairgrounds. Everyone else seems to be hale and hearty.

"I hope we're playing outdoors," Kevin says. "I like playing basketball in the sunlight."

Brooks absolutely disagrees. "Pounding my feet on a hard, hot surface? Not me. Ever take a bad fall outside, Kevin? The asphalt or cement just rips your skin off. If you fall on wood, the worst you get's a floor burn."

Mitchell has the directions, driving through residential neighborhoods toward the eastern end of town. White stucco homes, their rain gutters overflowing with sand. Streets blown clean by the wayward winds. A few clattering old cars, an old man riding a mule, thin women hanging wash on their lines, all the bedsheets and pillowcases tinged a dusty pink.

Along the way, Mitchell confesses his ignorance about today's program. "All I know is we're supposed to meet a Mr. Colfax at the basketball court and that this is supposed to be a big payday for us."

The fairgrounds are sealed behind a ten-foot-high storm fence and shielded from the road by a long file of sun-dusted black-stemmed cedars. And the whole operation gets off on the wrong foot when some bristly-chinned old clodhopper won't allow us entrance through the exhibitors' gate.

"The House of Moses All-Stars?" he says from under his low-slung cowpuncher's hat, more than happy to give us a hard time. "Nope. Nothing like that on this here list. Nice try, boys. Got to go pay your fifty cents admission like ever-body else."

Mitchell is confounded. "That's impossible. There must be some mistake. We're supposed to meet Mr. Colfax."

"Never herder him."

"Who's in charge here?" Mitchell says.

The rube shows us a shit-eating grin, then he drawls, "You're looking at him."

And Brooks intercedes, calm as a judge. "Wait a minute. Maybe the name's so long it just got turned around. What about 'All-Stars'? Or 'Moses'? Or even 'Basketball Team'?"

"Nope . . . Nope . . . And nope. Time to move along, boys. There's a line awaiting behind you."

"All right," says Brooks, still trying to play the name game. "See if we're listed under 'Jews.'"

"Nope . . . No Jews . . . I was wondering myself what ezactly you boys were. Thought maybe you was Russkies . . . Wait. Hold your horses . . . How 'bout this'n? 'The Wandering Jews'?"

Mitchell beams. "That's us to a tee."

And we're given more directions: Make a left at the sheep pens, a right at the chicken coops, another right . . . . Passing through rows of buckling wooden barns, corrugated metal sheds, and blue-and-white-striped tents. Goats in stalls, hutches of rabbits, also cattle, chickens, and hogs. There are tractors on display, plowers, balers, and other large-wheeled contraptions that look like machines of war. (War against the earth, against the sun, against fire and water.) There are no Ferris wheels here, no roller coasters. No sideshows or freak shows either. But the fairway is lined with games of chance—vertical roulette wheels, a large boxful of colored holes to catch a tossed and bouncing rubber ball—red pays 2:1, yellow 4:1 . . . . Come try your luck. Knock the iron bottles over with a baseball. Swing the sledgehammer, ring the bell, and win a seegar. For three cents a Gypsy will tell my fortune. And there's a beer garden at every corner. Two cents a mug. Food stalls too—four cents buys a platter of chicken-fried steak with cream gravy. Pickles are a penny each. Cotton candy, corn dogs, pickled eggs. We don't see many paying customers, but it's still hours before noon, too early for the lunch crowd.

Mitchell brakes beside a high-roofed open-sided building made of corrugated steel slates, all of them rusting to the same red color as the dust underfoot. Exiting the car, we investigate the basketball court—a soft, portable floor, the backboards are mounted on rubber wheels, and the bent rims promise a shooter's wet dream come true. Set along one side of the court, a rattling rack of metal bleachers can accommodate perhaps a hundred onlookers. And there's someone waiting for us, leaning against a corner of the bleachers, stepping out a live cigarette butt before coming over to introduce himself.

"Wilson Colfax. Promoter extraordinaire. Speculator. Wheeler and dealer."

He's a big man—six-foot-two, maybe 220 pounds—and he looks like he was once a player. He wears a double-breasted gray gabardine suit, along with brown needle-toed cowboy boots, a black string tie, and the obligatory white sheriff's hat. He shakes hands with each of us and asks our names. Under duress, I offer up my left hand, which he accepts with undisguised irritation. "Around here," he says meanly, "it's left hands for niggers." But he's easily mollified when I display my injured finger. Then he sits us down in the bleachers and explains "the whole shebang."

We've been "contracted to work" for twelve hours, from ten to ten, and we're scheduled to play four ball games each and every hour. He points to a long sheet of oaktag taped to a red-flaking steel post, "the sign-up board," where the names of our opponents have been penned by the team captains. THE BUCKIES, THE SHETKICKERS, THE OAKIES—some of the awkward letters written backward.

In any case, the duration of each contest is only five minutes stop-time. "Short and sweet." Since we're the "house team," the other guys get the ball to start every game. Any necessary overtimes will be sudden death, the first team to score 3 points wins. During regulation time, each team is allotted one time-out, and a player committing two personal fouls will be disqualified.

"Only two?" Mitchell asks. "All we have is seven players."

"Don't fret none. That just gives the refs a handle on the rowdies. I promise none of you will foul out. Believe me, I own the refs lock-stock-and-barrel. You'll get every call that you need."

Brooks and I trade slit-lidded glances. This guy's a bullshitter. And Mitchell wants to know about the money.

Colfax starts to guffaw, gets caught on a gasp, and ends up coughing. When he catches his breath, he says, "Ain't you heard? It's the root of all evil."

Turns out our opponents have paid $10 for the privilege, and should they beat us they'll be awarded $100. Our "honorarium" is $150—"Fifty of it payable right now to prove my good faith, right soon's we're done palaverin'"—plus $5 for every game we win. Should we lose a game, our "account" will be debited $50.

Mitchell does some quick mental calculations and comes up with some very unsatisfactory figures—should we "survive" the day undefeated, we'll have earned $240 plus our $150 guarantee. That totals only $390 for forty-eight ball games.

"Five-minute ball games," Colfax reminds him.

"Okay," says Mitchell. "That still amounts to three hundred and ninety bucks for the equivalent of six regulation forty-minute ball games. So what's the big deal? We'll be exhausted. And if we lose a couple of games, we've got *bupkes*. I don't understand. I was told this was a big-money payday."

Colfax inserts an unlit cigarette into the corner of his mouth. "The big money," he says, "is strictly under the table. Most of the fellas you'll be playing against will want to make a side bet with you, and they'll want points. Five and a half points is plenty to give a bad team, three and a half is too much for the better teams. And there'll sure be enough of both kinds. Real bad, real good, and everything in between. Later on, Oklahoma University and Oklahoma State'll have their varsity squads here. Fact is, most of the really top-notch teams wait to play as late as possible to catch you all tuckered out. Now, the gambling part's up to you. But I guarantee some of your games could be worth hundreds of dollars each one."

Mitchell is forever concerned about our monies due. "When do we get paid our five bucks for winning? After each game? At the end?"

"Either way. What's your choice?"

"After every game."

"You got it."

"And the other hundred after the last game, right?"

"That's keerect. If'n you don't lose .... Now let me give you some free advice . . . . Just remember to pace yourselves, that's the most important thing, 'cause the best of the teams come out at night."

I look around and size up the neighborhood—an outhouse, a cardsharp's tent (Three-Card Monte Smith), a wheel of fortune, and a beer parlor. Then I venture to say, "Mr. Colfax, is it okay if we leave our car where it's parked? So we can maybe grab a short nap or something? Or store some food?"

"Sure 'nuff. Leave it right there . . . . All rightee, then. First game's in twenty minutes. Good luck. Any problems crop up, I'll be around most of the day."

After he leaves, we caucus to plot possible strategies. "I don't like this betting business," Mitchell declares, and he stares at Leo. "Once you start fucking around with point spreads, who knows where it ends."

Brooks easily brushes aside Mitchell's objection. "We've got to make side bets. Otherwise we're selling ourselves too cheap."

The vote is 6–1 and Leo volunteers to be our "betting agent." Mitchell goes along with the majority, insisting only on "a strict accounting" from Leo after every game. Our fifty-dollar advance will serve as Leo's starting bankroll.

"If you need more," Brooks says, "then you're fired."

Furthermore, we decide to send Kevin to buy up sandwiches (tuna salad only), plus whatever fruits or fruit juices he can find. And our first opponents are already warming up on the court, so here we go.

The Buckies— A collection of gangling farmboys from the boonies. One of them plays in his cowboy boots, another wears jeans. In lieu of uniform jerseys, they have numbers black-painted and dripping on their bare backs. Several are already drunk.

Try as he may, Leo can't interest them in a wager. "Hey, boss," Leo is told, "it was all we could do to scrape up the entry fee. We figure we're your ordinary Oklahoma poor white trash. Just one step ahead of you Jew-boys."

Score: 14–2 **+ $5**

The Dust Bowlers— A high school team in crisp red jerseys from nearby Chandler, who've come with their coach. Leo negotiates a ten-dollar bet, spotting them 3 1/2 points.

The game's first possession is theirs and their scheme is to freeze the ball. We must foul them quickly to conserve the clock—they make the free throw, so it's our ball and we're down by 4 1/2. We score, they freeze, we foul, they convert—now with only 3:15 left, our deficit is still the original 3 1/2. (Refs in the bag or not, with only two fouls per man, this particular pattern could easily bring us to grief.) Our only choice is to press full-court and hope that Colfax's refs give us some leeway to reach, chop, and shove. (They do.) We're up 10–5 and the Dust Bowlers don't even attempt a field goal until their final possession. I'm sent in for defense, but Ron ices the game by stealing a foolhardy pass. The Dust Bowlers' coach throws a tantrum, accusing the refs of "hosing his boys."

Colfax was right—3 1/2 is too much for even a decent team.

Score: 10–5 **+ $20**

The Gunslingers— Composed of Oklahoma state troopers, small, testy, and in good physical shape. Leo talks until he's blue in the face but can only coax five dollars on the side for 2 1/2 points.

Following Brooks's orders, we open up pressing, hoping to forge ahead early and then stall. Brooks forbids us to chance any outside shots—instead we'll drive every possession hard to the hole and then hopefully make our free throws. (Leo, our best ball handler, is also a premier foul-shooter.) Board-power is our usual advantage. "Nice rebound, Saul."

Score: 11–6 **+ $30**

The Baskettes— Sponsored by a suffragette group in Norman. Leo wants to get a few dollars down, "or at least bet a blow job," but we'll play them straight up. The gals are spirited enough, kind of cute-assed too. Remembering the humiliating game against the Redheads in Cleveland, we pound these gals unmercifully.

Score: 24–0 **+ $35**

By now, the bleachers are filling up, presumably with future opponents on hand early to scout us. And so far, we're having fun. The temperature's just right, nearing sixty degrees, just cool enough to keep us fresh and energetic. "I can play all fucking day," Ron boasts—and Leo adds, "Especially against bitches." After every game, Mitchell settles with Leo and locks our profit up in the cashbox.

The Doughboys— Enlisted men from the army base "over to Stillwater," comprising several ex-collegiate players including a pair of six-foot-four twins. The bet is twenty-five dollars and we'll play minus 1 1/2 points. A good team, for sure, but they need two minutes just to get loose. By that time our defensive pressure has turned the ball over, and Leo runs out the clock with his ballhandling and free-throw shooting.

Score: 13–7 **+ $65**

4-H Future Farmers— Teenagers with no discernible basketball skills. "What'll I bet?" Leo asks us. "A pitcher of milk? Anybody want to fuck a sheep?"

Score: 14–4 **+ $70**

The Cowboys— Rodeo wranglers from Dallas. Tough and ornery, but none of them's taller than five-ten and they're all stinking drunk. Even so, they'll take 2 1/2 points for ten dollars.

Another easy game for us. Then just before the final buzzer, Ron exchanges elbows with a mean-eyed steer wrestler, but nothing comes of it. (Interesting how Ron draws violent acts like a magnet, acts that justify—at least to himself—his own retaliatory acts of violence.)

Score: 17–8 **+ $85**

Another advantage for us—a cultural reflex for most of the teams waiting to play us is to pass their idle time drinking beer. And Colfax stops by to fork over another five singles. "Good job, fellas. Remember to pace yourselves."

Mahoney's Marauders— A bar team with a tricky 1-4 flex offense. They're "delighted" to wager five dollars and accept 2 1/2 points. As the game proceeds, one of them says to Kevin, "You! You ain't no kike! You're a son of Erin, sure as I'm born! What're you doing looking like that with that long beard? What're you doing playing with *them*?" Kevin shakes his head as though he doesn't understand, then says, "*Gay kocken offen yam*." Sounds like Saul's been coaching him. We solve their offense by switching and denying the post-to-post pass.

Score: 12–7 **+ $95**

The YMCA Motivators— They have the same loudmouth coach and several of the same players from the Dust Bowlers. Now the bet is twenty dollars and their spot is 1 1/2 points. Sure, we're starting to get tired, but it's still men against boys. Saul sweeps the boards, and Brooks bangs home at least three sidearming baseline hook shots.

Score: 13–8 **+ $120**

The Incumbents— Politicians, mostly Democrats, accompanied by a host of newspapermen. The game is merely an opportunity for the pols to show their constituents what all-American he-men they've elected. The game itself is a running gag, with the politicos pausing to gladhand the spectators and pose with the basketball.

I'm sitting on the bench, minding my own business, when a big-boned Incumbent approaches with a photographer in tow. "You mind?" he asks. "I've got some Jewish folks in my district. Hardworking, responsible people. A credit to their race." While the photog sets ups the smiling baby-kisser tells me exactly how Oklahoma City came to be the state capital: "Used to be the capital was in Guthrie until one fine summer's day in Nineteen-aught-nine, when this here posse of drunken Oklahoma City cowpokes rode into town, took out their shooting irons and proceeded to steal all the official files and papers from the Guthrie city clerks. 'Twas easy as that. Brought everything back here and that's the way it's been ever since . . . Much obliged. You fellas get a speeding ticket or something, be sure to let me know." And he leaves without supplying either his name or his office.

Score: 20–7 **+ $125**

The Coaches— High school basketball and football coaches from Oklahoma City. They're disciplined and (in our depleted state) able to outrun us. They're also sober and properly warmed up. Two and a half points for fifty dollars—too many points. Good thing these guys are so small, topping out at maybe six foot one. And they zone us, but we don't mind—we're losing the willpower and the energy to constantly push the ball hoopward anyway. Mitchell hits some long shots early, Brooks contributes a couple of put-backs, and I score my first bucket of the day—a drop-stepped lefty hook. Also, our earnest opponents are hindered by their point guard, some toupee-wearing ham-handed bumpkin who's obviously the coaches' coach. We sic Ron on him and turn up several steals, including a pair of breakaway baskets. Still, it's a battle to cover the spread until Leo deep-freezes the last minute.

Score: 15–10 **+ $180**

The People— A team of fat and out-of-condition teenaged Indians. One look at them and we tell Leo not to bother. Nice kids, quiet and grim-faced. But terrible players.

Score: 19–5 **+ $185**

The Red Dirt Rangers— Another herd of belligerent and inebriated clodhoppers. They want twenty-five dollars and 3 1/2 points and we gladly oblige. Mitchell and I sit this one out—watching as Ron gets low-bridged on the very first play. It's a rough-and-tumble game but the refs diffuse the situation quickly by fouling out three of their most dangerous players. (So far the fans have been fairly quiet. Now they start booing. According to Colfax, the "smart" money in the bleachers is inevitably bet on the local teams.)

Meanwhile, I tell Mitchell why I need one hundred twenty-five dollars from the cashbox. "Look at it as an advance, Mitchell. Later on, you can subtract it from my share. I promise, I'll square everything up when we reach Los Angeles." Mitchell doesn't much like the "precedent," but he stands up, calls for an immediate time-out, then explains my petition to everybody else and calls for a quick vote—5–0 with abstentions by me and Mitchell.

Score: 16–7 **+ $215**

I inspect the sign-up board and learn that our next opponents are the Ponca City Presbyterian Men's Club, the Enid Rotary, and the Bartlesville American Legion Post 127. So I tell Mitchell that I have to find a Western Union office and I'll be right back. "I don't know," he says. "I hate to see one of us go off on his own like that." What an asshole he's become.

"I'm not asking your permission, Mitchell. I'm just informing you."

The Western Union office is housed in a trim whitewashed wooden shed. Inside, the clerk is an astonishingly lovely girl—long blond hair, a shapely physique, and a beautiful face—except for her long and bulbous nose. She smiles fetchingly as she completes my transaction—and I feel like the best thing I could ever do for her would be to smack her beezer with one solid punch and let some plastic surgeon build her a new one. "Bye."

Then I find a shady spot of ground near a lemonade stand and steal a short nap. By the time I wake up, the early-evening sky is closing in on a bruise-colored sunset.

"What took you so long?" Mitchell asks when I finally return.

"There was a line I had to wait on. A long line. A long long line. All right? What'd I miss?"

"Nothing."

The Aztecs— Short and chunky, drunk and laughing Mexicans who can't play a lick. One of them sidles up beside Saul, and the measuring hand he places atop his own head barely reaches to Saul's nipple. "Howdy wedder," the Mexican says, "up dere?" Everybody is amused except for Saul.

Score: 19–3 **+ $325**

The Young Bucks— From a colored high school in Ringwood, undisciplined and off to the races. They have no spare "greens" to bet and their jerseys are ragtag undershirts hand-lettered with black crayons. We overwhelm them on the boards and frustrate them with our slowdown tactics.

During a free throw, a player black as a bowling ball asks if it's true that we're from New York. (He doesn't inquire about my beard or my yarmulke.) "New York," he says dreamily. "That's where I wanna go."

Score: 10–4 **+ $330**

The Texas Rangers— More lawmen who'd rather bully us than play fair. "That's your car there? The one with the bullet holes? I heard about you boys already. I was you? I'd sure steer clear of Texas." These guys are expert practitioners of blind-side elbows and various cheapshots. Ron won't back down, and twice he must be restrained—while the coppers provoke him with their laughter. For fifty dollars and 2 1/2 points, we'll gladly kick their asses.

Score: 19–6 **+ $385**

The Green Pajamas— Inmates from a mental institution in Duncan (only five miles north of Loco), accompanied by two thick-armed security guards.

The players wear the same kind of institutional uniforms we saw in Sing Sing, with long drawstring pants and long-sleeved shirts. Some of them drool, some gawk, and their point guard has a wild facial tic that serves as a built-in head fake.

"What're you staring at?" one of them says to me, a thin-faced young man with pale crosshatched scars on his cheeks. "You think I'm crazy, do you? Ha! You wish you were only as crazy as me!" Then he laughs like a hiccuping hyena, and says, "The doctor told us that this isn't really a basketball game. No. It's therapy!"

One of them shoots a free throw twenty feet over the backboard, and his teammates gawp in admiration. "Ahhh!" Another's shoe flies off as he runs downcourt, and they all pause to watch it soar. When the shoe lands near midcourt, the one who spoke to me makes a loud noise simulating an explosion—"Poom!"—and two others start screaming. When a sub is put into the game, he curls into a fetal position inside the center-jump circle and softly weeps. And Mitchell says to Leo, "In ten years you'll be playing point guard for these guys." (It's not the crazies, nor the gals, nor the drunken yahoos, but us—the Wandering Jews—who are the freak show.)

Score: 8–0 **+ $390**

The 89ers— The varsity team from Oklahoma State University in Stillwater. The side bet is a whopping one hundred dollars and our handicap is 1 1/2 points. The bleachers are almost full and there seems to be a different crowd on hand, a well-heeled bunch loudly rooting against us.

"Now the joyride is over, Jew-boys!"

Too bad we're dragging our asses. "How many games do we have left?" Leo asks of Mitchell.

"How the fuck do I know? Read the sign-up board for yourself!"

"Eleven," says Saul. "Including an AAU team from Dallas, a team from Little Rock, and one from Kansas City. And you know if a team's traveling that far, they've got to be good. Real good."

Given how exhausted we are, the 89ers are as good an outfit as we want to be playing. And we're learning that farm-raised hoopers are tough enough. Getting up seven days a week in the dark hours of the morning to milk the cows and do their chores. Pulling livestock out of mud holes. Lifting and pushing and baling and digging. With their calloused hands and mulish persistence, doing whatever job must be done, however and whenever.

Right now, the OSU boys are quicker to the ball than we are. They foul us harder than we foul them. They press us full-court and make us grunt to complete a pass, to find a decent shot. They send five to the offensive boards and still recover quickly enough to blunt our heavy-footed not-so-fast breaks. But we suck it up—Mitchell shoots, Ron steals, Leo passes, everybody else defends and rebounds. And we find ourselves trailing by 1 with fourteen seconds left and the ball in our possession . . . *Time-out*.

"This is a complex situation," Brooks says in our huddle, loving it. "We're giving them one and half points, remember, so we could run a last-second pick for Mitchell and let him shoot a set shot. If he hits, that wins the game but not the bet. Or else we could try to score quickly and then foul them quickly. Let's assume they'll make the foul shot. That might still give us a chance either to score again and cover the points or else go to overtime. You guys following me? Now. Do we even want to play an overtime? I've been in these sudden-death situations many times and they have a way of lasting forever. A slow, lingering death . . . . I don't think we can afford to fuck around with overtime. It'll sap whatever strength we have left. So, do we really want to win the game? Or win the bet?"

"Go for the money," Leo says, and even Mitchell agrees.

"Then here's what we do: Leo gets the ball and drives like a maniac to the hoop. Look for a body to hit, Leo. Charge into somebody if you have to. The refs are on our side, right? We want a three-point play, a basket plus the foul. That's the best possible scenario. The only way we can cover the point spread. We'd also settle for a missed shot and two free throws. Right? In that case, we can make the first, deliberately miss the second, and crash for the rebound. Got it, Leo? Don't you dare fuck around with this one."

So Leo plows to the hoop, looking for contact, but the wily 89ers simply run out of his way, leaving Leo to score a layup at the buzzer. We win five dollars, and lose a hundred, narrowly averting losing another fifty-five.

Score: 14–13 **+ $295**

Before the next game, Colfax comes over, saying, "Tough luck, boys. I know you're tired, but hey . . . nobody said this was a walk in the park. I just want to know if you guys have any legs left. Be honest with me. Are you dead? Are you done? Tell me and I'll bet against you. Tell me also if you're interested in any action in that direction. A team can make a bundle betting against themselves. Hey, you got all tough teams from here on in."

"Fuck you," says Ron. "We ain't lost yet and we ain't gonna."

"Okay," Colfax says with a small smile. "Remember I told you to pace yourselves, right?"

"Right up yours," Leo says. "We got plenty left."

After Colfax leaves, Brooks says, "He's only trying to goose us. If we lose, we cost him fifty bucks. Anybody too tired to play, let me know now."

The Sooners— Here's Oklahoma U's varsity, not quite as quick as OSU, but more physical. (The bet is seventy-five dollars and we'll give them 1 1/2.) And right off, we uncover a fatal flaw—their point guard is tipsy. What a dunce. So we trap him, bang him into picks, and run clear-outs for Leo. And we win in a walk.

Score: 16–10 **+ $375**

The Hawks— A rugged AAU squad from Kansas City. Big, quick, talented, and outrageously (even ruthlessly) physical. Moving picks are their specialty. Hard, jarring fouls their delight. And their roster features fourteen players—that's twenty-three fouls to spare. (And where are the refs to rescue us? Have they made another deal? Has Colfax?) The bet is one hundred dollars and their spot is 1 1/2 points.

Near the two-minute mark, we're down by 2 when I surround and capture a defensive rebound (ouch!) and pass to Ron, who's running ahead of the field. Then slam! Ron has his legs taken out from under him by a hurtling body-block from behind. A foul most foul. And Ron comes up swinging, a roundhouse right that knocks his man to the floor. Before long, the two of them are grappling and rolling near the Hawks' bench. The crowd is cheering for blood. But the fisticuffs are limited to Ron and the asshole who clipped him, until one of the Hawks' reserves produces a blackjack and bops Ron on the head. Now we're all milling about, woofing and shoving one another.

"Fuck you, punks! You're not players, you're thugs!"

"Jews!" Just that one word, coldly intoned by some cracker as the worst possible insult.

Then Ron yanks the valuables bag out of Kevin's hands, runs to the car, unlocks the shotgun door—and fetches the gun back to the basketball court.

"I'll kill ya!" Ron screams.

Now everybody's running—and Ron doesn't know whom to shoot first, the guy who fouled him or the guy who clubbed him. So he shoots wildly at the former—once, twice . . . *blam! blam!* . . . then again and again until the gun is empty.

"Time to go," Brooks says, surprisingly calm, and we all dash headlong to the car.

"I don't fucking believe it!" Mitchell yells at Ron. "You crazy bastard! You did it again!"

Ron jumps behind the wheel, and we're off—zooming out of the fairgrounds, racing through the countryside, and generally heading east.

"Where'll we go?" Leo cries. "We ain't got a chance! Every cop in the world is after us!"

"Which way," Brooks says evenly, "is Delancey Street?"

And Saul has a bright idea: "The Indian reservation! The place where we're supposed to play tomorrow. Listen. Nobody can touch us there except maybe some G-men because it's federal property. Head back toward Tulsa. We're going in that direction anyway."

"Good call," I say. "Ron, can you make it?"

"Easy as pie."

Mitchell reads the map and finds a road that parallels Route 66. And Ron leans forward over the steering wheel, his eyes bugging out with a wild gleaming. Action! He's ecstatic! Whizzing through the traffic, lane-humping like Barney Oldfield.

"How fast can this baby go?" Ron asks me.

"It was a rumrunner before it got cracked up. So the engine must've been souped."

"Let 'er loose!" Brooks yowls.

The ribbon speedometer rolls forward and wavers at seventy miles per hour. "Oo wee!" Ron shouts. "I'll need a fucking runway to stop this thing!"

With the speedometer topping out at seventy-two, we're only a few miles from our turnoff when we spot two police cars up ahead. The cops are on the verge of sealing off the eastbound lane, several of them grunting to push a big wooden barricade into place—but Ron speeds through the narrow opening, shrieking, "Ride 'em, cowboy!" Immediately, the cops scurry into their cruisers and take off after us. By the time they match our speed, we've got about a mile head start.

"A right here," Mitchell says. "Now a left."

We're on a moonlit rural road, passing a small-town dump that's locked for the night, but there are paper bags of overflowing garbage piled against the fence, and a constellation of raccoons' eyes are caught in our headlights.

"There it is . . . right up ahead."

Another ten-foot-high storm fence, this one topped with curls of barbed wire. A cracked wooden sign reads, CHEROKEE RESERVATION—NO TRESPASSING UNDER PENALTY OF LAW. As we near the fence, the main gate is swung open and two dark figures seem to be waiting for us. To the rear, the patrol cars have closed to within a quarter-mile. Ron slows down through the gate and one of the figures jumps onto the running board.

It's a rotund young man who almost looks familiar.

"Turn here," he says, pointing to a small tree-lined clearing off the road and only about a hundred yards past the gate. After we stop and switch off the engine, the young man turns to Ron, saying, "By their own foolish laws they are forbidden to enter our land. But they will enter anyway." I recognize him as one of the fat Indians we played against this afternoon.

The police cars halt just inside the gate. Although we may be hidden behind the trees, the stirred-up road dust gives easy witness to our presence here. We hear a door opened, then slammed shut, and we're privy to a loud conversation.

"Okay, Chief. We know they're in here. Just give them up and we won't be bothering you no more."

"You are trespassing here. You have not the right to enter."

"Not so, Chief. Local ordinance four-B, section three . . . We're in pursuit of—"

"Your local laws do not apply here."

Other doors open and we hear the shuffling of booted feet.

"Chief, don't make us use force. These men are dangerous. This is an emergency."

"I am not a chief. You will go from here, where you do not belong and are not wanted."

"Listen up, Chief . . ."

Then from the surrounding shadows comes a strange sound. Metal-winged crickets? . . . No. It's the safety switches being unclicked on innumerable firearms.

"You will go. Now."

"Okay, Chief. Looks like you got the drop on us." Then the lawman raises his voice and throws it toward us. "But we'll get you, you fucking sneaky Jew bastards! Shooting at an unarmed man! We'll be waiting here till hell freezes over. Then you belong to us!"

Doors slam again and tires squeal as the police drive off.

Now we're directed to drive farther along the main road, where the trees soon yield to the same monotonous desert land, much more ominous at night. "Stop here." Then our guide ushers us out of the car and into a long, low wood-boarded lodge. "You will be safe here," he says. "The outhouse is over there . . . . There is food for you . . . Get well rested and tomorrow you will talk with the council."

But Mitchell wants some answers now. "How did you know—?"

"Rest," the guide says and is transformed into a shadow.

Inside, the rectangular building has a hard-packed earthen floor, and besides the leather-hinged door, the only other opening is a smoke hole in the ceiling. In the center of the floor, a neat bed of reddened hardwood embers provides an indistinct light. Light enough to see seven low wooden pallets cushioned with dried corn husks. Light enough to see a large pot set beside the fire and a stack of short-handled wooden bowls.

Leo is the first to scoop and taste the steaming liquid. "It's some kind of broth," he says. "Not bad. Kind of sweet and fatty. Buffalo soup. Scalp soup."

So we eat our fill, visit the shitter, and stretch out, each one on a pallet. "Say," Leo blurts, "isn't there some kind of custom where they get real insulted if you don't fuck their wives?"

Saul laughs and says, "That's Eskimos."

"This bed's hard as a fucking rock," Ron complains.

"I'm so tired," says Brooks, "I could sleep on a bed of nails."

"Jesus!" says Ron. "Wasn't that great! What a ride!"

Mitchell is the pessimist. "But you heard the cop. They'll be waiting for us . . . . What I can't understand is how come the Indians were waiting for us like that?"

"Smoke signals," I say, yawning.

And Mitchell lulls us to sleep with his self-absorbed chatter: "What we got is . . . let's see . . . four-twenty-five. Hopefully, that'll stand bail for all of us . . . . And in case anybody's interested, we're due to play here at four o'clock tomorrow afternoon for two hundred and fifty smackeroos. Should be an easy game, right?"

"Good night, Mitchell," I say.

"You know, I wonder what our record was today. Let's see . . . We started at ten and we played four games every hour . . . That means . . . And that fucking shyster promoter stiffed us a hundred bucks! . . . Four times what . . . ?"

From Mitchell's Log:
Day Eleven — January 16, 1936 — Wednesday

	Today	Total
Mileage	72	3,022
Expenses	$5.75	$287.98
Income	$425.00	$2,785.00

Net Income - $2,497.02
Average Share - $356.72 (Aaron minus $125.00)
Cash on Hand - $772.02
Max Has - $1,600.00

Won - 43
Lost - 3

Startled, we all wake up at the same time, suddenly sensing someone else there inside the lodge, some stealthy presence. (A ghost from someone's nightmare? A cop? A mobster? Or the dark angel of death?) It's a man, an Indian, standing near the door with his arms folded on his chest, saying nothing. So we blink and cough, fart and scratch, gradually remembering where we are. Then the man leaves just as silently as he entered, staying the door behind him so that it doesn't clatter against the frame.

"What the fuck?" says Leo.

Mitchell is suspicious. "He was prowling around looking for something."

But Brooks yawns, pokes at his crotch, and says, "Relax, you two. I think that was our wakeup call."

Then from beside his pallet at the farthest end of the low-ceilinged shelter, we hear Saul wailing, *"Sh'ma Yisroel adonoi eloheinu . . ."* Saul, in a prayerful posture, without his phylacteries, but kneeling and pecking at the darkness with his pigeon-headed devotions. Uncharacteristically praying aloud, making some sort of statement, an affirmation. *"Bawr'chu es adonoi, ham'vorawch . . ."*

The rest of us are slightly embarrassed. (Did I just see Kevin cross himself? His hands are faster than Joe Louis's.) Brooks and I find our shoes and visit the "outhouse"—which is nothing more than a tin roof over a trench. There's a depleted Sears catalog lying on the muddy ground beside a small canvas sack of powdered lime. The air smells surprisingly sweet and tangy.

"I'm starting to enjoy this trip," I say, dropping my pants and straddling the trench. "Suddenly I'm not in such a hurry to reach Los Angeles."

Brooks is behind me, at the other end of the trench. "Not me," he says. "I can't wait to get there."

Brooks, the only best friend I've ever had. "You know something, Brooksie? I think this trip's been good for you too. You seem more assured, you know? More settled in the middle of all this craziness. I mean, it's usually your advice, your suggestions, that we wind up following lately. And Mitchell, he seems to be getting more and more hysterical. Don't you think so?"

Brooks ignores my question. "I seem that way because I've finally made a real commitment. And I know exactly what I'm going to do when we get to L.A."

I wait for him to continue . . . . Meanwhile I wipe my ass with a thin, crinkling page—wedding rings for sale . . . . And then I say, "Okay, Brooks. I give up. What exactly are you going to do when we reach L.A?"

"It's not for talking about," he says as he picks up the bag of lime. "It's for doing."

"Brooksie. It's me you're talking to. How can you not tell me?"

"No, Aaron. You'll find out soon enough."

The sky is bright and cloudless, promising warmer weather than yesterday. And the area around the lodge and the latrine is enclosed within green tangles of bushes and trees, grown tall enough to hide us from whatever's out there waiting.

"Brooks, Brooks, Brooks."

"Aaron, Aaron, Aaron."

I follow him back into the lodge, where Saul has concluded his prayers. The rookies are the last to use the latrine, while the rest of us crouch and slouch around in the semidarkness, fumbling with our travel bags.

"I feel like a rat in a trap," Mitchell says.

"Then go outside," I suggest.

But he stays put, content to grumble about "our hosts'" failure to provide any water to wash ourselves. "Not even a basin or a pitcher. It's disgusting."

"Who's next?" Saul asks as he and Kevin return. But they are the last, and as we huddle dumbly inside the lodge, where a single shaft of light pours through the smoke hole like a beam from heaven, Mitchell has a moment of panic.

"Now what?" he says too quickly. "What're we supposed to do now?"

"Relax," Brooks says. "And wait."

"You actually trust these characters?" Mitchell asks at large. "Well, I don't. I feel like we're being kept prisoner."

So I try calming him: "Actually, Mitchell, I feel really safe here. Safer than anywhere else we've been. And Mitchell, what could they possibly want from us?"

Mitchell laughs tightly through his teeth. "The cashbox, you idiot."

Just then the door opens and the same bloke who guided us last night enters the lodge. Dressed in dungarees, a red flannel shirt, cowboy boots and hat, he's small enough to stand erect in the center of the lodge. Then he walks right up to Saul and says something like this:

"Kadomah neeka homah."

Saul shrugs. "I don't understand."

"Kidmah kull tisha nichamah."

"Sorry," says Saul.

"What was that language?" The Indian asks. "That you were just singing?"

"Hebrew. It was a prayer."

"Another white man's tongue?"

"Sort of."

The Indian grunts to acknowledge the plausibility of Saul's response. Then he says, "Come." Obediently, we follow him down the main road, walking away from the entrance gate, away from the car and the cashbox.

There are fewer trees here, lean and supple wands that dance and bow before the lusty winds. As we proceed, we see that both sides of the road are clustered with buildings, small and shabby wooden cottages whose paint has long since been stolen by the weather. Some of the houses are fenced in with chicken wire or randomly matched lengths of wood. There's a disabled car or red-rusted truck parked in almost every yard. Tattered and spring-sprung car seats serve as porch furniture under swaybacked wooden roofs. There's a wheelless Model T being used as a chicken coop. Most of the yards are scattered with broken beer bottles, rusted cans, and torn papers, just like the hobo jungle in Cedar Rapids. Others are neat and broom-swept.

People stare at us as we shamble by—old men and women, even the children, quietly standing or else hunkered on their haunches. The men wear dungarees and long-sleeved shirts. The women peep at us from behind hand-woven shawls. Their faces are dark red, darker than the dust, older than the dust. A few skeletal dogs rush at us, baring their teeth but making no sounds. "Shoo!" says Mitchell, and the dogs silently retreat. A musty smell arises from the entire landscape, as if some large animal, long dead, hasn't been buried deeply enough.

"I'm hungry," Leo says.

We come to the far margin of the village and a lodge similar to the one we just left—a semicylindrical edifice made of curved wooden planks seasoned gray and wind-smoothed. The second lodge rests on a large mound of earth at the highest point in the village. The guide ushers us inside.

A small fire flickers on the hard earthen floor, casting a dull red light onto a semicircle of old men. Sitting cross-legged and bare-chested, impassive, stone-age men, whose polished, stony eyes reflect the wispy flames.

"Jesus," Kevin says under his breath. "Joseph and Mary." And he does cross himself.

The ancient Indian who sits facing the doorway points to the vacant spaces around the fire and motions for us to sit. He has large, thick-ridged scars on his chest, where the skin looks to have been ripped rather than cut. Like him, all the old men wear greasy leggings and they each have stained leather pouches hanging around their necks on thick strips of dried yellow tendons.

As my eyes grow more accustomed to the dim light, I can see other men sitting motionless in the dark corners. Perhaps fifty all together.

The old man opposite the doorway cradles a long carved wooden pipe in his lap. Now he fills the pipe's large bowl with some dark shreds that he pinches from a small wooden box set beside him on the ground. Then with his bare fingers, he lifts a glowing ember from the fire and lights the shreds in the bowl. He chants something in a wavering glottal language as he gestures with the pipe to the sky and the four corners of the wind. He puffs on the pipe only once, exhales a soft cloud that slowly wafts toward the smoke hole, then passes the pipe to another old Indian, who's sitting to his right. The process is repeated until Mitchell receives the pipe. Mitchell puffs too hard, coughing and gasping as he hands the pipe to me. The smoke is sweet-smelling but has a bitter wooden taste. I inhale a smaller draught than Mitchell (determined not to cough), then pass the pipe to Brooks. Everybody in the circle sucks the smoke into his mouth until the pipe is returned to the headman.

Then the headman speaks: "I am called Sun Dancer and I welcome you to the remnant of the People. This place is called Oklahoma, which means 'Land of the Red Men' in the Cherokee Tongue. This Oklahoma is where the White Man herded us and our brothers after we laid down our weapons many years ago. Herded us like cattle. Those tribes who dwelled in the sacred Black Hills, hunting the buffalo to nourish their generations . . . sent here to die in Oklahoma. Those tribes who dwelled near swiftly running rivers, hunting our water-brothers to nourish their generations . . . sent here to die in Oklahoma.

Those who lived in forests thick with game . . . sent here to die. But we have survived, the People, as you see us now. We the People survive, even though the White Man's school feeds our young people ideas that kill their minds. Even though the White Man nourishes our precious generations with despair to kill our spirits. Even though the food the Bureau gives us so freely is poison to us, the long white and brittle sticks that hot water turns into snakes. Empty food. But we have survived because we are warriors. Because each day we say, 'Today is a good day to die.' Because the old ways are still honored among the People. Among some of us."

A grunting of approval comes from the shadows, like a soft chorusing of *Amen*s from the pews in a colored church.

"There is nothing here for our young men to hunt. There is nothing that will grow in this blood-colored soil. There is little for our young men to do but idle away their lives, sneaking into Tulsa to get drunk and get into trouble. Cursing their own skins."

Then he passes the pipe to another old man sitting to his right—this one's chest is smooth and unblemished. Cradling the pipe in his arms, he speaks with a raspy voice:

"My name is Flying Eagle and I also say welcome. And even though your own skins are white, the White Man seeks to destroy you. This we saw yesterday. Perhaps the reason lies in your beards or your clothing. This we do not know. Perhaps the difference is in your language, which is so much like ours. These things are our common ground. Is this not true?"

Mitchell nods eagerly. "Yes. What you say is true."

"The time will come," Flying Eagle says, "when you and your brothers, when all your tribe of bearded warriors will also be herded into reservations like this one. Driven inside the wire-with-small-knives. Sent there to die. Is this not also true?"

"Yes," Mitchell says with a burst of emotion. "My God, it's true!"

"That is why, in small ways, we must help one another. In small ways that can grow."

"Yes," Mitchell says. "Tell us what we can do."

The pipe is passed to another elder, one whose chest is also smooth and unmarked. "I am called Red Fire and I have seen you play your game of the round bouncing ball and the sacred circle. I have witnessed your skill and your courage. I have seen you victorious."

Now there's a silence, a profound silence. No coughing or sighing, no scuffling sounds as uneasy limbs are repositioned. Not even the sound of breathing. This continues for several minutes, until Red Fire says: "This is what we would have you do: Teach our young men the ways of your game. Those of them who are willing to learn. There is nothing to be gained by competing against one another. This was already done yesterday in Oklahoma City."

Another pause, one that lengthens and is not interrupted even when Leo honks and swallows some seepage from his sinuses. So I say, "Yes. We'd be glad to."

The pipe is passed again and their red granite faces betray nothing, neither surprise nor gratitude.

"I am Winter Hawk and it would be helpful to know where you are to go from here and when you are to leave."

Mitchell laughs. "Our next stop is the hoosegow just as soon's we set foot off the reservation."

Winter Hawk shakes his head. "Have no fear of the white man's law. There are trails leading away from here that are unknown to them."

"We have to be in Pueblo, Colorado," Mitchell says, "by two o'clock tomorrow afternoon. That's about four hundred and fifty miles north-west of here."

Then the pipe is passed hand-to-hand back to Sun Dancer, who slowly refills the bowl with tobacco or shredded bark or whatever it is we've been smoking. Meanwhile, Mitchell raises his hand like a schoolboy asking his teacher's permission to go take a leak. The only acknowledgment is a grunt from Sun Dancer.

"Sirs," Mitchell says carefully. "We certainly appreciate the help you've already given us, keeping the cops off our tails and all. And also your offer to sneak us out of here when the time comes. But there's just one catch: We're supposed to get paid two hundred and fifty dollars for playing a game against you guys . . . against you 'People.' Now, don't get me wrong . . . we'll teach your boys how to dribble and shoot and stuff like that . . . but what about our money?"

Sun Dancer's face betrays no trace of distress—he merely repeats Mitchell's last word: "Money." Then he pauses to let any echo disperse before saying, "We have nothing to do with the white man's greed for money. For frog skins. For that, you must speak to Burnside, the agency man. What he will decide to do is always a puzzle to us."

"Oh," says Mitchell, and his face sags.

Brooks nudges a sharp elbow into Mitchell's shoulder and harshly whispers, "Fuck the money, you asshole!"

Sun Dancer lights the pipe as before and passes it around the circle, clockwise this time. Then someone steps forward from the shadows, moves to the door, and holds it open.

"That must be our cue," Mitchell says, and we push ourselves to our feet. "Thanks a lot, sirs. Like I said, we certainly do appreciate your help." And the council sits stone-faced and unmoving as we file out of the lodge.

Our guide now leads us into the front yard of one of the well-kept weather-grayed bungalows, where a huge iron kettle sits steaming on the bare ground. (Heat without fire? What sorcery is this?)

The guide enters the house and forthwith two middle-aged women come scurrying out the door, each one holding a hot brick in a thick section of cloth. The women wear shapeless homespun dresses. Their hair is braided and greased, their faces impassive as they gently drop the bricks into the soup before retreating back into the house.

"Brick soup," says Saul.

Leo is annoyed about something. "All their talk about the White Man this and the White Man that. Like we're niggers or something."

Brooks just shakes his head, saying, "Nothing like this ever happened on Delancey Street."

Then one of the women reappears with a wooden ladle and a stack of the same kind of wooden bowls we supped from last night. She fills each bowl and serves us individually, bowing and subservient, without even glancing at our bearded faces.

"Thanks," Ron says, then he softly sips at the hot liquid. "Mmm. Not bad at all. It's the same stuff as before. I wonder what it is? What it's made of?"

Through a series of foolish pantomimic gestures and some stuttering pidgin English, Ron succeeds in making his queries known to the woman. She shakes her head and says something in their guttural language. Ron shrugs his ignorance, then her black eyes spark and she starts to growl.

"Grrr!"

"What the fuck!" Leo yelps. "She's got rabies!"

"Grrr!" But another idea seizes her and she wags her hand behind her like a tail.

Saul takes a slow, careful drink from his bowl and says, "Fido soup."

Immediately, Mitchell spits his mouthful to the ground—"Arrghh!"—while Kevin and Leo turn away to vomit—*WAAHYOOP!* But the rest of us continue eating undisturbed.

"I don't care what it is," Brooks says placidly. "It sure tastes better than canned beans."

Silently following our silent guide farther down the dusty main road, we can see the parched horizons dotted here and there with clumps of wildwoods. Silently, we synchronize our steps as we march—like soldiers or jailbirds. Then from behind one stand of slender trees we hear a muted clinking of metal against metal. And we soon come upon a dozen or so young men (our guide's back stiffens as we approach them), rowdy-looking delinquents brazenly drinking from a jug of white lightning and laughing shrilly as they play horseshoes. They say nothing directly to us, aiming their taunts at our silent pathfinder.

"Well, if it ain't our favorite reservation red man. Old-Before-His-Time! Where are you taking those ugly, hairy white men?"

"Hey, old-timer! Want a drink?"

"Look out for their horns!"

"Don't step on their tails!"

When we're safely out of range, Mitchell says, "Who were those creeps?"

"Lost sheep," says Saul.

The basketball court is also partially obscured by a gathering of trees. A crude arena. Each crooked basket is supported by a single post—slim tree trunks, barked, dried, and staked into the ground. The backboards are conglomerated of mismatched scraps of wood with an occasional rusty nailhead protruding. Only the rims are store-bought, with thin strips of sun-bleached rags to serve as nets. The surface of the court itself is the same hard, trampled earth that we found inside the lodges. And as we draw near, several women are hand-sprinkling water from iron pails to settle the dust.

And here are our students, about fifty of them, ranging in age from perhaps twelve to twenty, and dressed in a variety of footwear—laced boots and stovepipe boots, embroidered moccasins and sandals. Some of the younger boys are barefoot. Some wear dungarees or breechcloths, others wear boxer shorts. We recognize several of the older boys from yesterday's game. All are bare-chested, but the older ones have their chests, shoulders, and faces painted with various combinations of black, white, yellow, and blue stripes.

"Jesus," says Leo. "They're on the fucking warpath! If we don't do a good job, we'll be in the next batch of soup!"

"Or else," I say, "they might smear us with honey and stake us to an anthill."

"Jesus!"

The only available ball is lopsided, and the rubber bladder is bursting through the midseam like a strangulated hernia. Kevin is dispatched to the car for our spare basketballs. (Mitchell, of course, asks him to make sure the cashbox is still secure.) Then Brooks organizes us into stations, and the boys are divided into six groups, according to size.

Mitchell's group will explore the basic procedures of set shooting, emphasizing body balance and follow-through. Leo is in charge of ballhandling. Brooks does rebounding and boxing out. Saul teaches hook shots and layups. The lump on Ron's head is subsiding, so he'll do defense while Kevin teaches passing. Because of my tender finger, I'll move freely from station to station and focus on the most awkward and clumsiest pupils.

"Thirty minutes at each station," Brooks says. "Then we'll rotate. Afterward, we'll do some three-on-two drills and let them play for a while."

Most of the youngsters quickly prove to be eager learners, concentrating with all their might on everything we say and do. Concentrating so hard that they make no noise—not a grunt, not a word, not a question—lest they miss something.

Only a few seem reluctant, content to linger on the periphery and watch. Several of them gaze with longing toward the distant ringing of the horseshoes. "Use only your fingers," Leo is saying. "Never let your palms touch the ball." Then off to the side, I see three of the older boys slinking away from the court. Our guide also spies them, but he stands fast with his arms folded against his chest.

Later, I'm working with the set shooters when I carelessly let a ball bounce off my mangled finger. "Damn!" I scream and shake my hand. All the students freeze and turn to stare until their instructors call them to order. And our guide is suddenly beside me, beckoning with a hooked finger and saying, "Come."

As he leads me farther away from the village, tracking through a field of prickly undergrowth, I can't contain my curiosity. "You were one of the guys we played against yesterday, right?"

He nods his head.

"My name's Aaron Steiner. What'd that guy call you? Old-Before-Your-Time?"

Without shifting his eyes from the road, he says, "That is not my name. That is the foolishness of young men who have forgotten who they are."

"So what is your name?"

"According to the White Man my name is Joseph Carlisle. But that is not my name either."

Stubbornly, I persist in my questions. "What's it like living here? On the reservation?" But he just shrugs.

Undaunted, I ask, "How did Sun Dancer get those scars on his chest?"

This time he turns to look at me, his eyes squinting with disdain. "They are scars of honor from the Sun Dance."

"Oh. I get it."

I follow him to a smelly animal-skin tent and he motions me inside through a small, dangling flap. Crawling on my hands and knees, I find myself in a dark, foulsome place, illuminated only by the gray radiance of the sky seeping through the smoke hole and the barest gleaming of ashes beneath. The smell of rancid flesh is powerful. And there's another old man, wrapped in a thick blanket, sitting before the meager fire, beckoning for me to come sit beside him as best I can manage. Then he reaches to lightly grasp my right hand, grunting encouragement and nodding to prove himself worthy of my trust. His fingers feel like smooth, polished bones. His unbound hair is black and stringy and he toothlessly gnaws on something as he carefully examines my finger. After he's satisfied, he lights a short pipe with a flint. Then he puffs slowly, deeply, and blows an acrid, thin smoke into my face—and I'm not exactly sure what happens next, nor how long it takes.

I'm aware of his chanting some hypnotic and gurgling syllables, aware of the smoke in my face, of some kind of fat or salve tenderly applied to my finger, of sipping from a tin cup of bitter tea, of my finger being wrapped in thick, pliant leaves—nothing that shouldn't have taken more than a half hour. (And I also feel that something's floating in the darkness behind my head, something silent and ghostly that's straining to speak . . . . My mother, whose face I never saw? My father, who died of loneliness? Or the unformed yearnings of Sarah Pearl? . . . But I dare not turn around to see.) And by the time I'm returned to the basketball court, the Indian boys are already engaged in a three-on-two drill.

And my finger is blissfully numb.

Heap big medicine.

"No, no. The back man covers-the first pass. Like this . . ."

"Cut on a forty-five degree angle when you reach . . ."

"Stay wide!"

"The man in the middle mustn't go past the foul line!"

"Good!"

"That's the way!"

"Very good!"

All at once, a sporty-looking car drives too quickly through the middle of the village and parks near the baseline—a cream-colored Packard roadster churning up a red dust storm in its wake. The driver steps out, resplendent in a white linen suit, lizard-skin boots, plus a cowboy hat that matches the exact hue of the car. His black eyelashes lie like spiders on his pale cheeks and he looks intensely disreputable—a high-class pimp or at least a real estate swindler. Since everyone else is on the court working with the Indians (could it be that only three dozen of the boys remain?), the visitor finds me and introduces himself. He smiles, but the smile never reaches his eyes. "Howdy. I'm Lucius Burnside from the Bureau of Indian Affairs. And you are . . .?"

"Not the man you're looking for." And I turn my attention back to the court.

"I see. Then who am I looking for?"

I insert two healthy fingers between my teeth and whistle sharply toward Mitchell, who comes running at fastbreak speed.

"Howdy. I'm Lucius Burnside from the Bureau of Indian Affairs. And you are . . .?"

"Mitchell Sloan. I'm kind of the team's spokesman."

"I see." Burnside glances impatiently at his wristwatch, a gem-encrusted treasure that flashes in the sunlight. "Actually, I thought the ball game would be well under way by now." He reaches into an inside pocket of his jacket and retrieves a bulging white envelope. "I even brought your money."

"Great. Terrific." Mitchell reaches for the envelope, but Burnside, with surprisingly deft hands, snatches the envelope and returns it into his interior pocket, leaving Mitchell looking as crestfallen as a little boy whose ice-cream cone has just toppled to the ground.

"What time are you playing?" Burnside asks him.

"Playing?"

"The ball game. That's why both of us are here, ain't it?"

"Yes. It is."

"Tell him, Mitchell," I say.

"Tell me what?"

Mitchell scrapes at the ground with one foot like a circus horse doing sums. But before he can get the words out, Sun Dancer is suddenly there, sumptuously dressed in fringed buckskins, his hair braided with eagle feathers, looking primitive and majestic. Without any pretense of friendly greeting, Sun Dancer says, "There will be no game, Burnside, because we do not wish to have one. We would rather these men teach our young warriors the fundamentals of their sport than engage in useless and one-sided competition. This was our wish and these men have graciously complied."

Burnside laughs and speaks aside to Mitchell as if the two of them were alone. "I like that word. 'Complied.' Ain't it funny how the chief can speak the lingo just like a white man when he's a mind to? Injuns. Just goes to show that you never know what they'll do next." Only then does he turn to face Sun Dancer, saying, "Suit yourself, Chief. All I know's that the Bureau went to a pile of trouble to get these jaspers down here to play against your braves. And if I recollect rightly, last month you was all for it. Chomping at the bit. But what the hell, Chief. Now that you got 'em, you can do with 'em as you please. Ain't no skin offa my pink wrinkled ass. All I know's that the Bureau ain't paying no two hundred dollars for nothing excepting a real live ball game. Get my drift? No tickee, no washee."

Brooks is here, arriving in plenty of time to hear Burnside's disclaimer and to spit lightly on his fancy boots. But the agent only laughs. "Have your jollies while you can, boyos. Just remember, the highway patrol's waiting on you."

With that, Burnside transfers the envelope from his jacket to his pants pocket. Then he drives off in a billowing puff of dust.

"Asshole," says Brooks.

"It is so," says Sun Dancer.

Brooks turns toward the basketball court. "Let's get back to work."

Sometime later, the youngsters are playing an impassioned full-court game (it's impossible to differentiate the offensive team from the defenders), when a quartet of squaws walks unsteadily toward us, careful not to spill their burdens. Two of them carry a large double-handled jug that's sloshing with water, and two others carry heavy wooden trays covered with cloths. Their appearance seems to signal the end of the ball game, and the boys gather unbidden near midcourt. This is when we first notice that the sky is darkening, the sun falling into an effusion of bloody clouds.

One by one, our students step up to face each of us, placing their right hands over their beating hearts, bowing their heads and saying, "*Mitakuye oyasin.*" Then they silently walk off into the reddening darkness.

Our meal is some kind of smoked meat cut and dried in thin strips. Dark and gamey. Chewy as shoe leather. Also thick pancakes of fried dough mixed with small, tart berries.

"Oh, no," says Mitchell. "I'm not eating dogmeat again."

One of the women laughs and says, "Is rabbit."

When we're done eating, we're once again led to the council house, where there's now a small fire stoked to blunt the oncoming sharpness and chill of evening. And Sun Dancer sits there by himself, waiting until we settle before lighting and passing the pipe. Then saying this:

"You are worthy men, this we know, you who choose good deeds over profitable ones. It is true, we have helped you escape from those who would do you harm. It is true, we are your only friends here in this barren wilderness. And it is true, you had no choice. Yet were your hearts open, this we see, and this is all that is important."

He folds his hands on his breast, then opens his palms to us in demonstration of goodwill and sincerity. "We have nothing material to give you in place of the money. But we can tell you of the Great Spirit that moves the world, that lives in every stone-brother, every tree-brother, every living heart. We can tell you to look at the turning of the heavens with a feeling in your heart of mystery and wonder. We can tell you to be humble beneath the stars, the sun and moon. We can tell you to know that the Spirit dwells within you. The Spirit within. The Spirit without. We can tell you not to merely *believe* this is so, because belief wavers like the fingers of flame you see here before you. We can tell you to *know* that this is so. Yes, we can tell you. But you will surely learn these things for yourselves as your journey unfolds."

Now he places his hands on his forehead, then opens his palms to us. "Know that there are worlds within worlds. Of bone and muscle. Of power and illusion. Of Spirit helpers and Spirit destroyers. Worlds of the dead and worlds of the living. Know that we dwell in *all* of these worlds. Know that the Great Spirit *connects* all of these worlds, these many layers of being. This is why when we greet our friends or bid them farewell, we say, '*Mitakuye oyasin.*' Which means, 'We are related.' So we must say to you as you leave us, '*Mitakuye oyasin.*'"

Then silently he refills the pipe, but he holds it in his lap like a sword, still speechless, until it occurs to me to nod at Sun Dancer and say, *"Mitakuye oyasin."* Only when my teammates have repeated this blessing does he light and pass us the pipe.

Shortly thereafter, we are instructed to push the Black Lady (yes, the cashbox is still intact) out of its place of concealment and roll it down the main road away from the entrance gate and toward an antique pickup truck—a 1925 Chevrolet. Then at a signal from our trusty guide, Mitchell turns the key and ignites the engine just as another Indian starts up the truck. (All this to deceive the troopers.) Now the truck is driven toward the front gate while our guide steps on the hearse's running board and directs us in the opposite direction. Still following orders, Mitchell keeps our headlights shut off as he slowly motors along at five miles per hour on a faintly delineated dirt road. Gradually, the landscape thickens with wiry shrubs and stunted trees—until our guide steps in front of the car and leads us forward with motions of his hands through what looks to be a trail no wider than a footpath. Spiky leaves growing on long, sinuous branches brush against both sides of the car, scratching the windows and doors without impeding our progress.

"Where's he taking us?"

"What the fuck?"

After another quarter hour, we nearly bump up against a section of the storm fence that rings the reservation. A closer inspection reveals that several strands of the fence have been cut through and are now twisted together to seal and conceal the opening. Carefully, the guide untwists the links until a wide passageway breaches the fence.

"Mitakuye oyasin," I say to him as we slowly drive through the fence.

"Whatever," he says.

On the other side of the fence, an outcropping of limp-looking bushes that apparently blocks our way seems magically to walk off, carried away then replaced behind us by several of our basketball students.

Finally, directions are whispered to Mitchell, we reach a single-lane paved road, and we're on our way.

"What the fucking fuck!"

"Well, I'll be goddamned!"

And we drive headlong through the night, chasing the yellow oblong of light that our headlamps cast upon the road. All of us hushed and speechless, each one pondering his own private mysteries.

From Mitchell's Log:
Day Twelve — January 17, 1936 — Thursday

	Today	Total
Mileage	129	3,151
Expenses	0	$287.98
Income	0	$2,785.00

Net Income - $2,497.02
Average Share - $356.72 (Aaron minus $125.00)
Cash on Hand - $772.02
Max Has - $1,600.00

Won - 43
Lost - 3

The flatlands of southeastern Colorado, vast and soft as a sweet dream. Driving through what several roadside signs identify as the Comanche Grasslands, a tide of snow-crested plains. The wind blows colder here, but gentler. The sun shines widely. We scan the passing snowscape for buffalo or antelope, but see only a few high-hopping hares. A crushed turtle on the road.

The black crusted remains of some small rodent, pecked to shreds by fat, regal crows that squawk when we drive close, then flap away like thieving beggars.

The hocus-pocus leaves encasing my finger have dried hard as a cast, and the skin beneath itches—a sensation nearly as maddening as the pain. The rumbling and swaying of our steady progress, driving hard and fast along well-paved roads, seems restful by now, and soothing.

Click . . .

"Confidence and courage are the essentials in our plan . . . . *Down in de meddy in a itty bitty-poo* . . . **Now, look here, Allen, I don't care what you say about my singing on your** *own* **program, but after all,** *I've* **got listeners!** . . . **Keep your family out of this** . . . . *Deedle oo-ho-ho, listen to the sound come out* . . . **You must have faith, you must not be stampeded by rumors** . . . *Alone, alone on a night meant for love* . . . **Leapin' lizards! Who says business is bad?** . . . *You're so lovely, never, never change* . . . **Straight shooters always win** . . . **Next week the Jell-O program, starring Mary Livingston** . . . *And the way you look tonight* . . . **wave the flag for Hudson High, boys** . . . *and dey fam and dey fam all over de dam* . . . **Show them how we stand!** . . . *Is it true what they say about Dixie? Does the sun really* . . . **We have provided the machinery to restore our financial system; it is up to you to support and make it work** . . . *Red sails in the sunset, carry my loved one* . . . **The makers of Chase and Sanborn Coffee—the blend of the world's choice coffees—now being sold at a reasonable price** . . . *In the chapel in the moonlight* . . . **are proud to present Constance Bennet, W. C. Fields, Edgar Bergen, and Charlie McCarthy** . . . *Millions of hearts have been broken just because these words were spoken* . . . **This has gone far enough, Mr. Fields** . . . **Go 'way, or I'll sic a**

woodpecker on you . . . *The Flat Foot Floogie with the Floy Floy* . . . **Together we cannot fail."**

We stop at a general store in Millersville—which Saul claims is a "half-a-horse town"—and send Kevin inside to buy sandwiches and beer . . . . Mitchell, sitting beside me in the backseat, has a feverish aspect in his beady blue eyes—like someone on the verge of pneumonia or consumption or a nervous breakdown. "Mitchell, are you feeling okay?"

"Never felt better, Aaron. We've got only about a thousand miles to Los Angeles. Then from there, only another three thousand miles to Palestine."

"Mitchell—"

"What's taking Kevin so long? . . . Hey, Leo! Honk the horn to hustle him up! Time's a-wasting."

The scenery gets rougher, the land scooped out and piled up. Stands of alders and evergreens evolve into forests. The road inclines upward as we enter the foothills of the Rockies. Now the flat fields are cluttered with broken stones and boulders. Horse pastures give way to sheep farms. Small towns are farther and farther apart. Utleyville. Branson. Beshoar Junction. Then, finally, just south of Pueblo, we follow the signs and turn off Route 25 at Fort Evans.

There are numerous signposts bordering the approach road: AUTHORIZED PERSONNEL ONLY. NO TRESPASSING. VIOLATORS ARE SUBJECT TO MILITARY LAW. Here's another fenced-in compound bristling with barbed wire and armed sentries. We pull up at the entrance gate, where a pistol-packing uniformed soldier steps out of a wide-windowed blockhouse, then leans forward toward the driver's open window, to speak crisply and ever so politely, his hand resting lightly against his huge holster: "Can I help you, sir?"

Ron and Mitchell are the only volunteers willing to drive into an armed camp—and Ron is nixed without the formality of a vote. So it's Mitchell, with his own artful innocence, who tells the sentry who we are and why we're here. The sentinel doesn't bother to consult his clipboard, but says instead, "Yes, sir. Colonel Goldberg is expecting you." Then he ducks back into the guardhouse and rouses another soldier, who runs out the door and mounts a nearby motorcycle. "Sir!" the sentry fairly shouts. "Would you please to follow Private Larsen. Sir!" And we're in high spirits as we trail our latest escort through the campgrounds.

"Colonel Goldberg? A Yid?"

"Well, looks like at least Leo's safe in here."

"Fuck you, too, Ron. Shmuck-brother. Sent here to die."

"Leo, you're still as big a *putz* as ever."

"Bigger."

"Fuck you all very much."

There's a parade ground with a gigantic flagpole flying the biggest Old Glory I've ever seen. Also squadrons of soldiers marching in precise formations and raising cloud-tunnels of dust. A heavy trafficking of cars and trucks, all of them painted in green-and-brown-camouflaged swirls, and giving way to us at the hand-waving insistence of Private Larsen.

Looking down a long lane to the eastern edge of the compound, we can see a railroad spur. Everywhere we look the grass is trimmed, the decorative stones edging the pathways painted white. We pass several barracks buildings big as barns and painted brown. White soldiers unloading trucks and wheeling dollies. Colored soldiers digging a ditch behind a small wooden building. Nobody we see is at leisure.

"Even when there's nobody shooting at you," Ron says, "being in the army looks like a hard job."

"All the jerkoffs are in the army," says Mitchell, who last worked in a junk yard near the East River. "The guys that couldn't find work in the real world."

"The worst thing about being in the army," says Leo, "is having to wear a helmet. It makes you go bald."

"You're crazy."

"It's true."

The gigantic compound is dominated by a long row of huge red-brick warehouses—maybe a dozen of them—whose entrances are defended by slow pacing military details.

We continue driving at least a mile beyond the bristling activity, until we turn down a winding gravel driveway that's lined with young and fragile dogwoods. The road leads to a two-story white house, a scaled-down antebellum mansion fronted with Doric columns made of plywood and tangled with strands of climbing ivy.

Dismounting, our escort brushes the dust from his uniform, straightens his helmet, motions us from the car, then walks up to rap his knuckles sharply against the front door, disdaining the brass lion's head knocker. A colored man in a white dress uniform is quick to respond, exchanging whispered information with our escort and then ushering us into the house. Private Larsen snaps to attention and delivers us a stiff-handed salute, which only Leo returns. "Good work, private. You can take the rest of the day off."

The colored doorman leads us into an oak-walled and red-carpeted waiting room. "My name is Jerome," he says. "Colonel Goldberg will be with you shortly." He points to several hard-edged wooden chairs set against the walls. "Please make yourselves comfortable . . . . By the way, have you gentlemen breakfasted yet?"

"No," Leo barks. "I could eat a fucking horse."

Jerome nods and leaves the room, closing the door behind him.

There are several portraits in oil hanging on the walls, of generals whose uniforms date back to the Indian wars. "General who?" says Mitchell, squinting to read a tiny plaque. "Never heard of him."

"General Mayhem," says Saul. "General Malaise."

The walls also showcase crossed sabers and nineteenth-century firearms, also several military banners in red-gold-and-blue to celebrate the valorous 78th Battalion. A glass-fronted case of medals is wall-mounted on black velvet. (I am reminded of Blue's Buy & Sell, Inc., in Ossining.)

We look at each other, suddenly aware that we haven't showered since Cedar Rapids. That we're dusty and grimy, sweaty and stinking. We're reluctant to sit down and soil the chairs, to move our feet and soil the rug. We're even too chagrined to speak.

But our wretched reveries are interrupted when a leansome, bony man wearing a red bathrobe enters the room from an opposite door. There's a monogram on the breast pocket of his robe—an angry eagle whose talons clutch a sword and the 78th Battalion's tricolored flag. The bathrobe is also embroidered at the shoulders with gold epaulettes and a single gold star high on each sleeve. He's fortyish, freshly shaven, and showered (his hair is still wet), with cool gray eyes and cadaverous cheeks, a large humped nose and loose, flopping lips. "Welcome," he says with a professionally endearing smile. "I'm Richard Goldberg. Colonel Goldberg. And I'm sort of the head honcho around here." He seems genuinely happy to see us, and after shaking hands all around and asking our names, he asks, "Well, how's your trip been so far?"

Mitchell does the honors: Summarizing the kindly churchmen in Glens Falls. The "freaking cage" in Buffalo. The Redheads. Glossing over our stay in Ossining, and making no mention of the shootout in

Chicago. The rambunctious game in Oshkosh, the college kids in Cedar Rapids, and "our thirty-nine victories" in Oklahoma City.

"Splendid," says Goldberg, still standing. "It's always good to see some landsmen who are successful at their enterprises. In fact, it's good to see some landsmen period. In fact, as far as I know, I'm the only Jew who's ever set foot on this base. That's right. We have one chaplain, Reverend Witherspoon, who does the Catholic and Protestant services and used to do a synagogue service on Friday nights and Saturday mornings just for me. But I stopped going. Reverend Witherspoon reading the *broche*. It was totally absurd, don't you think?"

We unanimously agree, clucking like chickens.

"There're eight of us," the Colonel says. "Almost a minion. Too bad. That was what I was sort of hoping for." He smiles dreamily, then suddenly comes to his senses. "Pardon my rudeness, gentlemen. Please sit down. Forgive me .... Make yourselves comfortable."

We move gingerly to occupy the straight-backed, forbidding chairs. "Please accept my apologies, too, for the furniture," the Colonel says. "It's standard military procedure to make underlings feel as ill at ease as possible while they wait for an audience with the brass."

The Colonel moves his own chair so that he can face all of us. "It's such a hardship," he says "to deal with nothing but the goyim. Day after day. On the one hand, having to explain every little detail in a hundred different ways. On the other, getting them to show at least a spark of initiative. They have such a linear mentality. They seem so incapable of making an inspired leap."

Once again, my burgeoning curiosity overwhelms whatever the dictates of protocol may be. "Excuse me, Colonel. I was just wondering exactly what goes on here at Fort Evans. I mean, if you're allowed to tell us .... "

It seems that Fort Evans is essentially a supply depot. Uniforms, footwear, and headwear are sent here from various civilian contractors to be wear-tested. "Our current project is a newly designed infantry boot. Strictly hush-hush, you know." In addition, the "Fort" also distributes and replaces all the standard military apparel to the other army bases in the Northwest. "Basically," the Colonel says with a wry twisting of his mouth, "I'm in the garment business."

"As long as we're asking questions," Mitchell says. "How come a Jew is such a big shot in the army?"

The Colonel seems eager to supply the details: He was born and raised in New York City—"Riverdale, the ritzy section of the Bronx"—then moved to Atlanta when he was ten. "My father, may God rest his soul, was a wealthy manufacturer who had to move south for his health. You might have heard of the company—Sea Horse Bath Accessories? Shower curtains, bath mats, even toilet seat covers . . . " His brother, Elliot, still runs the business. We might also be surprised to learn that Atlanta has a sizable and very devout Jewish population. Even so, the Colonel—"call me Richard, please"—never felt welcome there. "What they do to their *shvartzers* you don't want to know. The whippings and the hangings with the Ku Klux Klan. The rapings and the castrations. *Gottenyu!* I always got the feeling that despite my father's money and influence, we were next on the list."

The Colonel's father was fabulously rich—"a mogul"—and a generous contributor to mostly Democratic political campaigns. "But he was still a Jewish father and I still had a Jewish mother, may God rest her soul, so naturally I was spoiled rotten. Anyway, years ago, on my Thanksgiving vacation home from college, I was careless enough to get our upstairs maid pregnant. Matilda her name was and, shame of shame, she was a *shvartzer*. Nobody else was very upset about it, except for my parents. So Father bought her off and bought me a commission in the army. And to circumcise a long story, I fought in the war and got gassed in the Ardennes. But that's ancient history. And here I am, waiting for some twenty-year-old half-breed to come leaping out of a closet or a dark alley and say, 'Daddy!'"

The joke's on him, but his easy laughter encourages us to join him. I think I like this guy.

"It's a pretty good life," he says, patting his flat stomach. "I live like a petty potentate here and I do have a few significant responsibilities. I only have to bow and scrape two or three times every year, when General Brogan visits from Denver. Actually, he's a ramrod career man who couldn't care less about my personal idiosyncrasies as long as I do my job. And for myself, I really don't care what anybody says about me behind my back. My superiors snap the whip and I jump. Or I snap the whip and my subordinates jump. It's all the same .... Power, gentlemen. The exercise of power. Ah, well .... "

The Colonel stares for a moment into the spreading of his palms. Then he drops his hands onto his knees and says, "But I never married, you see, because of one thing and another . . . so I'm here alone. Indubitably alone .... I do have a girlfriend who comes down from Denver one weekend every month to service me. But she's more interested in my star than in me. So I really have no one to talk to. Ah, well ... enough of my petty problems."

Just then, Jerome enters the room and says, "Ready, Colonel."

"So," Goldberg says, springing to his feet. "Jerome here can show you where to wash up and then I'd be delighted if you'd join me for a late breakfast."

The bathroom is all gleaming tiles, mirrors, and stainless steel. There are three toilets and three sinks.

"Looks like he's a regular Joe," says Mitchell.

"You think maybe he's a queer?" Leo asks.

"Naw," says Ron. "He's got a babe that comes once a month to service him. Ain't that rich? Getting serviced in the service? Hey, Leo! You ever been serviced?"

The wood-burnished dining room is long and narrow, built to easily accommodate fifty people at a sitting. There are more sabers on the wall, also portraits of generals from the Great War. High windows are hung with gauzy white curtains. Sturdy, red-cushioned furniture is fashioned of black walnut. *"Baruch ataw adonoi,"* the Colonel chants, aglow with a beatific smile. "*Eloheinu melech ha'olam ha'motzi lechem min ha'awretz* . . . . Blessed art Thou, O Lord our God, King of the universe, who bringeth forth bread from the earth."

And what a feast! Served by a phalanx of Jerome look-alikes in white uniforms and white gloves. Heaping platters of thick sirloin steaks. A multitude of eggs—scrambled, fried, soft-boiled, and even poached. Pitchers of freshly squeezed orange juice. Hash-brown potatoes fried with onions and green peppers. Coffee, milk, half-and-half. Pots of jams and jellies. Butter, cheese, and fruit. Baskets of steaming homemade drop biscuits. "It's a shame," the Colonel says. "Out here I can't get a good bagel to save my life."

We eat leisurely, like rich men with no particular place to go. And the Colonel asks each of us about our families, our backgrounds, our hopes of things to come . . . . The familiar stories of hard times, of parents either dead or dying. Mitchell is still longing for *Eretz Yisroel.* Leo has "job possibilities" in Los Angeles. Ron is looking for "action." The rookies are "out to see the world." I'm escaping "a marriage turned bad." Brooks describes himself as a "seeker and a basketball theorist." Neither Brooks nor I so much as mention what might be in store for us in Los Angeles.

Then, when our recitations are completed, Mitchell has another question to ask: "Do you think, Colonel, that there'll be a war in Europe?"

"Call me Richard. That's an order."

Mitchell blushes. "Okay . . . Richard, if there is a war, do you think we'll be drawn into it?"

The Colonel delicately wipes a yellow smearing of egg from his chin. "I certainly hope not. At least, not for some time. All of the bullet-heads here and in Washington are creaming in their pants for war. Especially the West Pointers. They want the promotions and the glory. Not to mention the fabulous amounts of money to be made in kickbacks and contraband. But the United States military is in no way ready for a full-blown war. You know, of course, that the military brain trust has no respect for FDR. Or for that matter, any other civilian president. But I have to give FDR a lot of credit. He's a very shrewd man with all his vague talk of isolationism. He knows just how poorly trained our armed forces are. How out-of-date our equipment is. And our generals? Everybody knows what doddering morons *they* are. Still rehashing the last war. Hell, some of them are still fighting the Civil War. The trench is still considered to be the ultimate military stratagem. Tanks and poison gas are unfair advantages."

The Colonel sadly shakes his head and waits for Jerome's task force to clear the table before he continues: "But the new war, gentlemen. The new war will be fought in the air. Yes, sir. Air power will be decisive. Decisive. Billy Mitchell's got the right idea, but nobody listens to him. Lindbergh does too, but he's a Nazi sympathizer. And meanwhile? We've got nothing in the air but old men doing loop-de-loops in papier-mâché biplanes. It's Germany that's building an air arm that will revolutionize warfare. Think of it. Death raining from the sky. Inflicting maximal damage with minimal casualties. The only serious drawback is the great expense. What we need to do is to drastically redirect our national priorities. Of course, Germany's not ready either, but they're at least ten years ahead of us. I tell you, the prospects are frightening. Germany could conceivably start a war and finish it before we even get off the ground. So, for a variety of reasons, I think it's imperative that our country establish a wartime economy as soon as possible."

"I knew it!" Mitchell crows. "I told you guys! Didn't I? I told you so!"

"It's true," Goldberg says. "We need to beat our plowshares into swords. But can you imagine FDR proposing something like that right now? Why, he'd be impeached."

"What about Hitler?" Mitchell says. "Can anybody stop him?"

"Nobody. In my opinion, the French are paper soldiers. They believe their Maginot Line is impregnable. Ha! Hitler's aeroplanes can just fly right over them. England has grown soft and flabby. They have no aircraft either and their industry is crumbling. But John Bull does have courage and resiliency. England's only hope is to somehow stall Germany until we're ready. It's a long shot. Russia? Still bleeding from the last war and from Stalin's purges. He's killing millions of people. Millions."

"Jews?" Mitchell asks.

"Plenty of Jews. Who else? . . . Poland, of course, has no chance of stopping Germany. The Poles are still on horseback. The Italians are fascists and will eventually align with Germany, but they're the worst soldiers in the world. Do you know who's the greatest military power in the world right now? The Japanese. They have absolutely fanatical fighting men. Superbly trained and obedient unto death. Japan's only drawbacks are her limited natural resources and her primitive industrial capabilities. Personally, I think Japan can only hope to win a short war. There's probably no real threat to us from Japan, but who the hell knows for certain what's going on there?"

Brooks is sobered by Goldberg's alarming prognosis. "So there's no hope? The fascists are unbeatable?"

"Right now they are. Like I said, the only hope is to get the U.S. ready and into the fight early. Something has to happen to give FDR an excuse. An excuse to save us and save the world."

Goldberg gathers himself to leave, but Mitchell has another question: "What about the future of the Jews in Germany? With the Nuremberg Laws. In some circles there's a fear that Hitler will eventually institute the most devastating pogrom in history."

Goldberg is doubtful: "I think that Hitler's anti-Semitic activities are politically motivated because he still has to pacify certain hard-liners in the Party. Once he consolidates his power, I'm sure he'll reinstate the Jews as full citizens of the Third Reich. Even Hitler knows how many loyal Jews gave their limbs or their lives for the Fatherland in the last war. He may be crazy, but he's not stupid. And all of the American officials who're now in Germany to prepare for the Olympics report that the Jew-baiting propaganda has already ended. You see . . . ?"

Goldberg puts his napkin on the table and pushes his chair back. "I think that Hitler's military ambitions pose the only grave threat to anybody. And I'm afraid that the entire world of nations is headed for a long, dark time. Who knows? Maybe this time the barbarians will breach the gates? . . . Anyway, no offense gentlemen, but you really do need to take showers. What else do you need?"

"Someplace to take a nap," says Brooks. "And someplace to do a laundry."

Goldberg summons Jerome, instructing him to escort us to an empty barracks and to assign a detail to collect and wash our dirty clothing while we're napping. "That was a delight," Goldberg says when he returns his attention back to us. "I hope you'll also dine with me tonight after the ball game. I have a special surprise for you."

We take our showers in a spotless barracks, more tiled surfaces, stainless-steel sinks, and shower stalls. Mitchell is impressed: "Look how clean everything is. You could eat off the floor."

When my green cast gets wet, the leaves soften and peel away. The fingernail has come detached, so I flush it down the toilet—and the finger looks mummified, all drawn and shriveled. I'm afraid to scratch the wrinkled skin, afraid the finger will fall off if touched. A steady, aching pain still remains, dull and acceptable.

Mitchell is upset with himself for not asking "Richard" about our money—$350 for this afternoon's ball game. "I don't care how nice he is, I've been cheated by nice guys too. And I don't care how Jewish he is either."

There's a small room between the bathroom and the sleeping quarters. I peek inside the room to see a bare mattress on an iron cot, a metal chair, a desk—and on the desk, a telephone.

"Operator? I'd like long distance, please. New York . . ."

"Hello?"

"Debra? It's Aaron."

"Oh . . . I'm leaving tomorrow morning from Grand Central Station, and the trip takes three whole days on the train! I can't pack until I leave for school in the morning, but I've got everything all planned. I'm gonna hide my suitcase in the basement . . . . Oh! I'm so excited!"

"Yeah. Me too. When are you arriving in Los Angeles?"

"Monday at three-thirty in the afternoon. Local time. You know? I've never even been in a different time zone before. Just New York time, my whole life."

"Does anybody know you're going? Does anybody suspect anything? Maybe a friend?"

"A friend? Who has one? Not me . . . Shhh . . . Here comes my father. I've got to hang up . . . Bye, Aaron. I love you."

"Yeah. Me too."

"Hello?"

"Max, it's me."

"Good. I'm glad you called. I was getting worried. Listen I'm on my way out, but you should remember this . . . . I'll be meeting you in Los Angeles on Monday afternoon. Don't worry about picking me up or nothing. I'll take a cab. But listen carefully, Aaron, and don't forget: When you get to Los Angeles on Tuesday morning or Monday night, or whenever, you should all check into the Golden Palms Hotel on Vine Street in Hollywood. You got that? Say the name, Aaron."

"Max."

"Say it, Aaron. Humor me. Otherwise I'll be worried all the way cross-country that you forgot and you won't be there when I get there."

"The Golden Palms Hotel on Vine Avenue in Hollywood."

"See? I told you. It's Vine Street. Not Vine Avenue. Vine Street. Okay, *boychik*. I've got to go. But remember one thing from your older brother who loves you: Whatever happens between now and then . . . always remember this . . . It's Vine Street, not Avenue."

In the dormitory the metal cots are too short, so Saul, Brooks, and I move the mattresses to the floor and nap there. And I dream of Armageddon . . . of fire falling from the sky. Of houses suddenly exploding. Of storm troopers squeezing my finger with a thumbscrew. And I want to confess, anything to stop the pain, to save my life . . . But I have no information to give them, except that Fort Evans is testing a new infantry boot.

The game is played inside a gigantic steel-walled hippodrome, and our dressing room is a small but immaculate chamber in the basement. Brooks is unhappy because we ate too much for breakfast. Nor is Brooks cheered by Ron's scouting report: General Brogan has recruited the best available U.S. Army basketball players from Seattle to San Diego and they've been practicing for a week. Our opponents are "big and very good"—and none of them are bald. The playing surface is hard and the rims are rigid. The stands are packed with uniformed soldiers, and the betting line is pick 'em. Ron's also heard that Goldberg's bet "a bundle" on his landsmen.

Brooks's pregame exhortation is delivered with more emotion than we're used to hearing from him: "I know we think we're tired and all that bullshit, but we've just got to tough it out. We're almost there to the Promised Land, and we've come too far to start letting up now. This is a big game for us. We may have to stall. We may have to bang heads. But we're professionals, so we'll do whatever it takes to win. Fellas, let's win it for Goldberg."

Warming up, my legs are leaden and even the ball seems heavy. We're all slow and distracted, missing at least twenty-five percent of our shots on layup lines. "Sharpen up!" Brooks says.

But it's no use.

The Fort Evans War Hawks simply kick our asses from baseline to baseline, from tick to tock. Oh, they're nice about it—smiling and respectful, playing with impeccable sportsmanship, helping us up after knocking us down.

We try stalling, but Leo repeatedly turns the ball over. We try zoning, but they don't miss. We try trapping, but surrender easy layups. We can't do anything right.

With my finger taped, I start the game and force myself to hustle and play hard. But I'm still touchy about shooting right-handed and there's no way I can rebound without imperiling my finger. *Ouch!* I catch a pass awkwardly. *Ooch!* I flub an easy layup. But I'm playing as best I can.

They're too good, too rested, too disciplined, too young. Even on equal terms we'd have a hard time competing. They run precise offensive plays and their defense is strong-armed and stingy. We trail at the half, 26–17, and we're fortunate to be that close.

In the locker room, Brooks accuses us of being "gutless quitters" and we're too tired to argue. "I can't believe it!" he says. "Hey, wait a minute! Are you guys deliberately lying down? Leo! Are you guys doing business? Has that chicken colonel set us up?"

"Take it easy, Brooks," I say as calmly as I can. "Don't get your bowels in an uproar. Nobody's setting anybody up. We're just tired. Dead tired. We have nothing, Brooks. We're just spinning our wheels. Sometimes it happens. And, hey, you're not playing so hot yourself."

"But at least I'm hustling! I'm working my ass off!"

"So are we, Brooks. It's just one of those games."

"Aw, fuck you guys!"

I play most of the second half earnestly, but to no discernible advantage. The soldiers are loud in support of their peers: None of their enthusiasm is aimed at us, out of respect for (or fear of) Colonel Goldberg, who sits opposite both benches, his feet impartially straddling the time line.

For tonight, Mitchell can't piss in the ocean. Ron couldn't guard a telephone pole. Leo gets ripped twice in the backcourt. Brooks can't score with a pencil. Kevin plays like his fingers are greased. Only a late hook-shooting splurge by Saul narrows our final deficit to 58–35.

Nobody has much to say in the postgame locker room. Mitchell doesn't even inquire as to the whereabouts of our money. We've simply had our doors blown off, something we've all suffered many times before. Personally, I'd rather get routed than lose a ball buster at the buzzer. But that's a poor consolation.

While we're dressing, a white-helmeted MP comes into the room and asks that we follow him when we're done. He drives a jeep and leads us to the Colonel's house, where Jerome shows us directly into the dining room.

For the occasion, the Colonel has changed into his dress uniform, complete with gold braid and ceremonial short sword. "I'm sorry about the game," Brooks says to Goldberg. "That's the worst we've ever played. I heard we cost you some money."

"Not to worry," the Colonel says. "I'll make it up on a little shoelace deal I'm working on."

And our promised surprise? For starters, we're served chicken soup with matzo balls (a tad too salty, but good enough). Then comes the flanken and the roast chickens. Also heaps of mashed potatoes moistened with *schmaltz* and seasoned with crispy bits of *greeven*.

"What's this stuff?" Kevin wants to know.

"Chicken fat," says Saul, "and the chewy pieces are rendered chicken skin. Tastes much better than boiled beagle."

Bowls of borscht, platters of matzo-meal latkes. Kasha varnishkes. Noodle kugel. Brussels sprouts in butter sauce. Lettuce and tomatoes with mayonnaise. A thick-crusted rye bread with caraway seeds. And to drink? Cold bottles of Dr. Brown's Cel-Ray.

"Here in Fort Evans," the Colonel says, "we don't keep kosher."

And we reminisce about growing up in New York. About our first pair of long, itchy pants. About our bar mitzvahs. We compare the merits of sidewalk games—box ball and four-box baseball. Off-the-Curb and Kick-the-Can. Johnny-on-the-Pony and Three-Feet-to-Germany. We talk about whose mother made the best gefilte fish and why Jews don't like to swim. "Because," says the Colonel, "you're not allowed to swim until an hour after you've eaten or else you'll get cramps and drown, right? So Jews can't go that long without eating."

Our coffee is served with sponge cake, with ruggaluch, with fruit and nuts. We toast each other's health and good fortune with Manischewitz wine.

"L'chayim."

The party doesn't break up until close to midnight, and Goldberg insists that Jerome pack up the remains of the meal for us to take. Goldberg also hands Mitchell our money. Four hundred dollars!

"You shouldn't have," Mitchell says.

"Don't worry," the Colonel says. "The game did wonders for the morale of my men. Consider it a bonus to show Uncle Schloimie's appreciation."

Goldberg also *shtup*s us with tins of caviar and cans of Vienna sausage and a case of beer on ice. He presents us with a box of heavy-duty athletic socks and some khaki-colored army-issue underwear. While we were playing, the Black Lady was jump-started and driven to the motor pool to be lubed, tuned, and gassed.

Our parting is joyful and hearty. "I can't tell you how thrilled I am to meet you gentlemen," the Colonel enthuses. "If you're ever this way again . . ." We shake hands and exchange manly hugs.

"Shalom."

Later, as we drive out the gate, Brooks says this: "I take back everything I ever said . . . . There *is* a God. And he *is* Jewish."

From Mitchell's Log:
Day Thirteen — January 18, 1936 — Friday

	Today	Total
Mileage	282	3,433
Expenses	$10.12	$298.10
Income	$400.00	$3,185.00

Net Income - $2,886.90

Average Share - $412.41 (Aaron minus $125.00)

Cash on Hand - $1,161.90

Max Has - $1,600.00

Won - 43

Lost - 4

DAY 14

"Las Vegas, here we come!" says Ron. "Whores and booze! Fun in the sun and action all night long!"

"That's right," Mitchell says. "We don't play in Las Vegas until Sunday night, so we can relax around the pool and get ready for whatever Max has planned for us in Los Angeles. The worst is over, guys. Just two more games in four days. Easy traveling, big money, and warm weather. Ooo-wee!"

"Whoa dere, Andy!" Leo says in a broad blackface accent. "We goan to relaxate in de sunshine."

Brooks is driving and without uttering a word he suddenly pulls the car over to the side of the road and switches off the engine.

"What's wrong?" Mitchell asks in a quick panic. "Is it the fuel pump? I knew it! The goddamn fuel pump! . . . Kevin! Go pull up the hood and we'll have a look-see. Where's the flashlight?"

"Hold on," Brooks says. "There's nothing wrong with the car."

"What's that?"

Brooks slowly twists around in his seat so that we can hear him and see him better, his face flickering in the light of passing cars. "Okay, fellas," he says, with the weariness of the bearer of bad news. "We all know this has certainly been a long, crazy ride. The games, the miles, the experiences, the 'fucking cage,' the people . . . things we'll never forget."

"Yeah, yeah," says Leo. "What's all this got to do with the price of tea in China? So what's wrong with the fucking car?"

Brooks sighs and slouches in his seat. 'Nothing's wrong with the car, Leo. Don't talk, okay? Just listen for a minute . . . . We've traveled more than four thousand miles and this is our fourteenth day. Fellas, it's time to think about what it all means . . . . " (Now he pauses for a dramatic moment, about to wax philosophical. Crazy Brooks from the neighborhood untangling the secrets of the universe. What could he possibly know that I don't?) "Sure, we've also made ourselves a pile of money, and money is honey all right. But let me tell you something . . . Someday sooner or someday later, the money's all gonna be spent and gone. Then what'll we be left with?"

"Fancy clothes," Leo jokes. "Big cars. Limp dicks and fat bellies."

Brooks ignores the byplay and continues: "The real question is this: What've we learned from what we've seen and done? What've we taken with us from where we've been and whatever's been done to us?"

We're silent as schoolboys who haven't done their homework .... Is this multiple choice or essay? Does spelling count? ... And what *have* I learned? That I'm as selfish and fucked up as ever, but that essentially I'm a good Joe. That I'm still lost in the Bronx. That something really good had better happen to me in L.A., or else, or else, or else something really bad certainly will.

"Don't you guys get it?" Brooks says. "What we've learned is that people have to be responsible for one another. We've learned that kindness is an obligation."

"So?" says Mitchell, bristling with annoyance. "So what's your point?"

"So last week I happened to telephone a friend of mine back in New York, a guy I know from school, and he asked us to do him a big favor."

"Horowitz," I say, and Brooks repeats, "Horowitz."

Mitchell groans. "I don't know what's doing with this Horowitz character, but already I don't like it."

"There's a furniture factory just north of here," Brooks says, "where the workers are trying to unionize. Naturally, the bosses don't like the idea, so there's been a lockout, there's been a strike, there's been scabs brought into the factory, there's been hell and high water. And the workers are in pretty bad shape. Their children are starving. Their—"

"So we'll mail them a contribution."

"Thanks, Mitchell. I'm sure they'll appreciate the money. But that's not enough."

"So we'll send them two contributions."

"My friend from New York, Horowitz, he wants us to play a ball game to get some publicity and raise some money for the strikers. Now, fellas, listen to me, please .... I know that money is important, sure, but more important is for each of us to make a commitment, to go out of our way, to sacrifice something meaningful. Here's a great opportunity to maybe get back to what some of us were hoping to accomplish with our tour, our journey. Here's an opportunity to validate the democratic ideals of our original bylaws. Mitchell, remember how hard we worked on those?"

But Mitchell is immune to such nostalgia. "This friend of yours," he says, "this Horowitz . . . . He wouldn't be a Party member by any chance?"

"He would, but that's not the issue here. Let's look at it this way: We took something from Sun Dancer, right? In addition to his wisdom, his advice, Sun Dancer also gave us protection, food, and a way to escape from the cops. Face it, without his help we'd all be in jail. And we also took something from Colonel Goldberg. Material things, but also loyalty and fellowship. Well, here's a chance to give something to someone else. It's all about justice, fellas."

"Where is this place?" I ask. "This furniture factory?"

"Casper, Wyoming."

Mitchell studies the map and quickly commands the necessary numbers: "From here to Las Vegas is five hundred and fifty miles. From Las Vegas to Los Angeles is another two hundred ten miles. That's seven hundred sixty miles in three days. A leisurely pace. Now it's three hundred and fifty from here to Casper, six seventy-five from Casper to Las Vegas, then the two-ten from there to L.A. That would make more than twelve hundred miles in the same three days. Nearly five hundred extra miles. A killer of a pace. And I presume we won't be paid anything for playing in Wyoming?"

"Not a red cent."

"Ha!"

There follows a most acrimonious dispute: Leo believes that just because "other people are suckers don't mean we have to be suckers." And besides, how can Leo get Saul laid in "Casper fucking Wyoming"?

Mitchell argues glumly and without much conviction that "we're not in the charity business." But Saul says if we take "the selfish way out, we're spitting in the faces of Sun Dancer and the Colonel." Kevin concurs. Ron doesn't "give a shit." As for me, I'll endorse Brooks as partial repayment of my cosmic debt. (Just in case Brooks is right. Just in case Jesus is.)

So the vote is 4–2 with Ron abstaining. And with a muttering of maledictions and a gnashing of teeth, we change course and ascend the Rocky Mountains on our way to Wyoming.

"Not only do I not know anybody from Wyoming," Saul marvels, "but I don't know anybody who's ever been there, and I don't know anybody who even knows anybody who's ever been there."

"Same here," Kevin says.

Leo is about to say something nasty, but restrains himself and says instead, "Time for my beauty sleep."

Brooks is stubbornly determined to drive throughout the night, and nobody objects. ("It's all about justice, fellas.") And the roadway tilts upward, the car choking and chugging. In the crypt, Mitchell, Leo, and Ron slide backward and downhill, their feet hitting against the loose backdoor. "Sonofabitch!" Leo says. "I'm gonna fall out on the fucking street!"

Then the highway finally curls over the top of a ridge and levels out for a few miles, only to plunge precipitously downhill. As we wildly careen forward in apparent free fall, Brooks shows a mischievous grin and says, "Sorry, fellas. But I don't want to burn out the brakes."

"Downshift to second," Saul says.

And the next hill is always higher than the last. "Who can sleep," Mitchell says in a cranky tone, "on a fucking roller coaster?"

Later, I offer to relieve Brooks as the long night's obscurity is slowly clarified by the first rising of the sun. (Another strange, alien day arriving to replace the incumbent, the one I'd just gotten used to. Where do all these new days come from?) By now, everybody else is finally sleeping, and they remain undisturbed when Brooks parks the car in a turnaround area and we switch seats.

"Brooks?"

"I gotta take a whizz."

He feels that the acceptance of my offer has diminished him. Maybe he's having second thoughts about our detour.

"It'll be okay," I tell him. "Horowitz wouldn't steer you wrong. It's the right thing to do. Don't worry, Brooksie." But Brooks only grunts, already skeptical of his own good intentions.

Back inside the car, he's asleep in an instant, his eyes darting quickly behind closed lids, still searching his dreams for answers. And the thought occurs to me that perhaps Brooks is planning to stay behind in Casper.

As the new day presents itself, I can see the highway slicing through the snow-crowned mountains. The tall virgin forests. The remote patches of smoky fog. The isolated homesteads. A church at the crossroad—St. Mary's of the Snow. A log cabin. The incorporated hamlet of Larkspur comprises three houses and a flashing yellow traffic light. Niverville is a church and a dark-windowed general store. There's a tricky glaze of ice on certain elevated portions of the road, and sharp turnings overlook breakneck cliffs and wondrous vistas of raw wilderness.

At Cheyenne, just across the state line into Wyoming, I stop at another rocket-shaped diner—Flap Jack's Place. And everybody stirs.

"Where the fuck are we?"

"Who?"

"What time is it?"

Leo and Ron choose to go back to sleep and stay snuggled in the crypt. And as the rest of us push through the outer door into the diner, we see a large pegboard mounted on a wall and a sign that reads, PLEASE CHECK YOUR GUNS HERE. But at 6:45 on a Sunday morning, the pegboard is empty.

Inside, the same scintillating chrome fixtures we've seen everywhere, the same booths, the same swivel stools set before the same countertop. The only difference here being that the menu is written in bold red strokes on two large mirrors set over the grill. There is no waitress, only a clean-shaven cook leaning over the counter and reading a newspaper. He looks up, says, "Howdy," then returns to his reading.

Mitchell squints at the reflective price list. "Flapjacks seem to be the specialty de la maison, eh? They're like pancakes, right?"

"That's right. Only better." The cook's smile is totally reassuring, his bright blue eyes promise us the tastiest breakfast we've ever had.

"So be it," I say.

Before long, we're all presented with huge, fluffy stacks of fried dough, doused with butter and maple syrup, served with tasty tubes of sausage and fried potato strips. Yesterday's colossal meals have stretched our stomachs and stimulated our appetites. And the cook simply goes about his business, frying and flipping, not even asking if our vittles are acceptable. Even though there's cash on the line, he knows he's a flapjack genius.

"Delicious."

"Absolutely."

"Yeah."

Only Mitchell grouses as he eats. "Another wild-goose chase."

"Mitchell," says Saul, "we're on our way to help feed some people who're starving. Doesn't that make you feel good? Don't you feel all warm and mushy inside?"

"Yeah, now that you mention it. . . . Must be gas from the flanken."

Casper is situated just north of the Medicine Bow National Forest, between a lofty mountain whose name I never learn and a smaller southern peak, also nameless. The shallow valley is randomly sprouted with squat, spiky bushes and whippet trees as it funnels the wind from east to west, even now stampeding a herd of tumbleweeds toward Idaho. Mule deer wander the residential streets on the outskirts of town, placidly nibbling at lawns and flowerbeds, barely lifting their bearded faces as we rumble past them.

Casper is a hard-worn and humble little town, windswept and cold. There's a used-clothing store on "Broadway." An apothecary. The library. A gas station. Casper Feed & Grain & Hardware. The factory looms over the eastern end of town, with its dozen chimneys aimed at the sky like huge God-killing cannons.

Only the biggest, most central chimney is smoking as we approach the parking lot. There are policemen abounding and ragged men marching in picket lines eyeing one another with evil intent. The signs proclaim ON STRIKE. SUPPORT THE WORKERS. CYRIL McKENZIE IS A FASCIST.

Now the cops turn their hostile glares on us—the Stars of David painted on the doors marking us as Communists. To the strikers, we're most likely just another hefty carload of scabs and company goons. Then a young man abandons the picket line and trots over to greet us.

Horowitz—I haven't seen him in years. The campus radical, forever offering leaflets to read or petitions to sign in the quad. Look at him now. . . . The same horn-rimmed eyeglasses, the same thin lips and big teeth. He wears a black watchcap, also a yellowed and scrofulous leather coat. The drippings from his thin and bony nose are frozen into fragile icicles. Horowitz was only a year ahead of me at Metro, but he could easily pass for a middle-aged man now. Haggard and bleary, in his late forties. Why does he look so old?

"Brooks," he says in his habitual adenoidal honk. "Aaron. The rest of you . . . Thanks for coming. We really appreciate this . . . . And Brooks, how are you? Long time no see."

Then he pokes his face through the driver's opened window and says, "I just got here myself on Friday night, and here's what the situation looks like: Management worked the men like slaves over the summer and into the fall, and when the warehouses were filled, they lowered the workers' wages across the board. From an average of nineteen cents an hour to fifteen cents. Men with families, craftsmen and artists, working sixty hours a week for a measly nine dollars. And if they accidentally saw off a finger, or if a cut gets infected, that's their tough luck. I figure that management can hold out until April maybe, but not the strikers. There are too many infants and old folks who won't survive the winter. That's why your being here is so important. A reporter from the *Denver Post* is supposed to come up and cover the ball game. We also figure we can raise about a hundred dollars for food and medicine. And everything's been arranged. You're playing at three o'clock this afternoon at Saint Stephen's against a team from the factory. We've been selling tickets, Brooks, ever since you gave me the go-ahead two days ago."

"Sonofabitch," Mitchell sputters.

Horowitz nods sympathetically, positive that Mitchell is expressing outrage over the workers' plight. "There's been no advertising in the local newspaper or the radio station," Horowitz says, "because they're both owned by Cyril McKenzie, who also owns the factory. He's a real bad egg. One of the worst. Anyway, the news has been spreading around by word of mouth. Nearly all the church groups will be represented. The workers in the granite quarry will also turn out. We should have a full house."

Here comes a copper, tapping his nightstick lightly against the side of his leg. "You men got legitimate business here?" Then he bounces his stick sharply off the front fender, banging a small dent near one of the bullet holes. "What's this? Who are you?"

"We're a basketball team from out of town," Horowitz says quickly, "here to play an exhibition game. And we were just leaving."

Then Horowitz squeezes into the front seat and offers to show us "the sights." As he directs us eastward and farther out of town, he explains that Casper was named after the first soldier to be killed hereabouts in the Apache Wars. "It looks like a nothing of a town, but don't underestimate McKenzie. He has a total monopoly on millions of acres of prime woodland in Oregon, Washington, even in Michigan. He has ten factories in the Northwest, and this particular one here makes only china cabinets that are supposedly the finest on the market. And with the whole country to chose from, the old man lives in Casper because he loves to fish some secret trout stream just west of here. While he's here, he runs the town with an iron fist."

Horowitz also reports that the very day the workers went on strike, they were forcibly evicted from the company housing. "Those falling-down shacks right over there." Pointing as we drive down a ghostly street. "Gouging the men for fifteen dollars a month rent. It's downright sinful." The doors of the tiny weather-beaten bungalows are unlocked and swinging wildly in the constant wind, banging against the walls, rattling the already broken windows. It looks like nobody's lived there in years, but Horowitz says the strike is only nine weeks old.

He directs us down Main Street, off a side road, and then to another clearing at the eastern tail of town. Here are temporary dwellings made of purloined metal sheeting and scrap wood, ingenious structures. Also simpler sheds with meager cardboard walls and tarpaper roofs—more flimsy than the hoboes' hovels in Cedar Rapids.

Small children are chasing one another, laughing and frolicking. Little girls play jump rope with a length of electrical cord. "My name is Anna and my husband's name is Albert. We come from Alabama and we sell apples." There's a wire clothes hanger shaped into a crude triangular circle and nailed to a tree. And some ragamuffin young boys play basketball with a knotted pillowcase stuffed with dirt.

And a young woman without a coat wanders the main street of Hoovertown, U.S.A., her dress tattered and the armpits rotted away. She cradles a baby in her arms, a baby swaddled in a dirty towel and listlessly sucking some grayish liquid from a nippled bottle. The woman's eyes are wild and distracted, and the baby's face is blue. I stop the car to watch them.

"What's with her?" Mitchell asks. "And what kind of milk is that? Sheep's milk or something?"

"It's not milk," says Horowitz. "It's flour mixed with water. The woman's probably trying to sell her body, but nobody's buying. And the baby? It's dying."

"Jesus." Even Leo is stunned. "Can't anything be done to help them? Home Relief or something?"

"Not a chance. McKenzie has a stranglehold on every member of the city council and on every federal agency operating in Casper and throughout the state."

Mitchell starts rummaging in the crypt. "Look here. We've got some food we can give away. Beans and peaches. Look, we've even got caviar. Ain't that a laugh? . . . Sausages. Even socks and underwear. Spare blankets. We've got a shit load of stuff we don't need anymore. Hey! Where's the basketballs?"

Saul clears his throat. "Kevin and I left them for the Indians."

Horowitz snatches one of the proffered blankets, a can each of sausage and fruit, and takes them to the dazed young mother. Talking softly to her, pointing to the car, gently covering her shivering shoulders with the blanket, transferring some coins from his pants pocket to one of her clenched fists.

"Too late," he says when he returns to the car. "I'm pretty sure the baby's already dead."

(Was it a boy or a girl? What was the shape of its head? Its mouth? What will the mother do with the body?)

We drive to the church and unload the canned food onto the back porch. The resident clergyman welcomes us, a short, angular man, Father Williams, but he must dash inside to answer a ringing telephone. "I'm here alone," he says in hasty apology.

Horowitz says we can sleep in the church basement if we want to until game time. Everybody thinks it's a great idea, except me . . . . Remember Jesus' bloody hands reaching down to me from the cross? Jesus and his ransom of blood. Jesus and his bleeding, distorted face. No thanks. I'll take the car and find something else to do.

"Aaron," Mitchell warns. "Be back in time. And don't forget to lock the door."

So I drive the car as far as possible up the mountain, slowly grinding through the gears, sometimes moving forward and upward at barely five miles per hour, driving up to the snow line. Finally arriving at the crest of the road where there's a small parking area deserted of vehicles, then a footpath that leads farther up. And I remember to lock the car before I set out to climb the rest of the mountain.

Taking the first step on the snow-crusted rain-runneled dirt road, with white-armed trees lining the way and loose stones underfoot, I'm breathing heavily, quickly frothed with sweat. The footing is precarious and I must make small cautious adjustments with every step. My footsteps crunch into the snow, crunching like the sound of my pulse beating in my ear when I'm trying to sleep. I must breathe in thick gasps through my mouth, and the cold mountain air cuts deeply into my chest.

After a while, my second wind kicks in and I find a mulelike, trudging rhythm, mindless and solitary, picking out my next foothold, then the one after. Step by step, my lungs pumping full and easy now, my heart playing bass on its lacework of bloodstrings. Moving relentlessly toward the mountaintop. Soon, my feet are moving automatically, choosing the safest, most advantageous route without having to consult any authority higher than instinct. The body slowly regaining an eminence much older than the mind. Sweating freely, grunting.

At last I reach the windswept summit—an infield-sized space strewn with hardy shrubs, flat boulders, and crushed stone. Third-base-to-first points eastward, home-to-second is north. The shortstop's corridor is overgrown with snow-dusted blueberry bushes. A fire tower rises from the pitcher's mound, at least seventy-five feet high, composed of steel girders with a small roofed cubicle at the top. Several flights of rickety steps zigzag from ground zero to the lookout station, but there are numerous broken gaps, and the way seems unattainable.

The waning afternoon is partially obliterated by a rising mist, and the town itself is tucked out of sight around the curve of the mountain. The clouds hang close, puffy and blotched with lumps of gray, only infrequently pierced by stanchions of weak, insipid sunlight. From up here, a landfill is easily identifiable, a dark brown patch attended by matchbox cars and trucks. But the sharp downhill angle and the tall trees hide most of the roads and the houses below. The world is white and brown, with sloping ridges and sharp-antlered trees. Above me, a hawk lazily rides a thermal draft toward the beckoning sun. There are no other living things in sight. Just flat white landscapes, chill and drear.

And here I am. Not peeking through a secret window at other people's lives. I am here, maybe four thousand feet above sea level, alone, tragically, blissfully alone. And I am suddenly flooded with an unformed anticipation. I turn to face the birthplace of the sun, on the verge of some revelation.

The visitation of a spirit? A bear? A white buffalo?

Perhaps the very expectation is the fulfillment.

My feeling is beyond words. "Words," the dark prince of Denmark once said. "Words, words." Mere crooked fingers staring dumbly at infinity. Instead of words, instead of voices, I am witness to the vast mountain, the earth and the limitless sky, and I am here, of them. Embraced by the cold, cherished by the hidden sun and the incipient stars. Whatever this elusive feeling is, it is real.

Then the words start scratching at my brain, shaping questions, doubts . . . Los Angeles. Debra. Max.

So I turn and head back to the car.

As expected, the way downhill is always easier—my long, lunging strides, my galloping seven-league boots. The temptation is to move faster and faster, and my knees suffer a threatening jolt whenever I'm compelled to brake my own recklessness.

Back in town, I park near a public telephone and scrounge around in my pockets for change. I'm short forty-five cents, so I make an unauthorized withdrawal from the coin pouch that's tied to the radio knobs. And yes, I use the stubby pencil to record the transaction in the log book.

"Operator, give me long distance, please . . . . "

"Hello?"

"Hello? Is Debra there?"

A woman starts screeching and weeping: "My God! He wants to

speak to Debra! It must be a kidnapper! Mister! How much do you want!? We're poor people! But we'll pay anything! Please! Send my little girl—"

And I hang up. Horrified.

I find a parking space near the church and distinctly remember to lock the car doors. Then I meet up with my teammates in another basement locker room, this one overheated and humid.

"You're late, Aaron."

"Where the hell were you?"

"You look like shit."

"Did you remember to lock the car?"

While I'm hurriedly dressing, Ron delivers his scouting report: Hard court, soft court, easy rim, tough rim. My mind's still up on the mountaintop. (What did it feel like up there . . . ?) But Ron's describing the players, yes, the players. "They're filthy," Ron says. "Like they haven't bathed in weeks. Three of them are very good. The three biggest. Six-five. Six-four. Six-four. They all played for the local high school about five years ago when they won the state championship. But even those three guys look all skinny and raunchy. Unhealthy, you know? So whatever you do, don't hit any of them in the teeth, or you might get a case of lockjaw or polio or worse. And I swear the placed is jam-packed with other dirty, unwashed people. I mean, it really stinks up there. The gym smells like a flophouse."

Brooks keeps his remarks brief and conciliatory: "As long as we're here, let's do it right. And thank you, fellas."

The game unfolds like a bad dream: Our opponents play bare-chested. Shirts versus Skins! But they're fierce and angry, playing with a dangerous desperation. Playing with slashing elbows. Eagerly low-bridging us. Hacking at us like they're out to crack our arm bones and amputate our hands.

"Hey," I say to one of the big boys. "Take it easy."

He snarls at me. "Fuck you, Jew. Either play the game or go sit down."

The refs are little more than interested spectators, silently sucking their licorice-candy whistles. The only way to protect ourselves is to retaliate, to viciously beat our opponents until they bleed. To break some poor fucker's nose. But we haven't the heart.

"Are you nuts?" Ron asks his shirtless defender after being sent sprawling on an attempted layup. "We're the good guys, remember?"

During the halftime intermission, with our lead at 21–16, Ron seething. "I don't know about you guys," he says, "but I like my teeth just the way they are."

"Yeah," Leo agrees. "Why should we be the suckers? Let's kick their fucking asses."

But Mitchell says, "No. That wouldn't be appropriate." And Ron's proposition is never brought to a vote.

Throughout most of the ball game, we've maintained a 4- to 5-point lead. And our second-half gameplan is determined by no other strategy than to avoid injury—shooting outside and avoiding contact whenever possible. Yet as we cruise toward the final buzzer, the game stays closer than it should be. That's because the three big boys are still running and jumping like the game's just started.

Meanwhile, the burn scar on Kevin's shoulder begins oozing. Ron tenderly touches the knot on his head. Saul is constantly flexing his bruised elbow. Kevin's ribs, Mitchell's hip, my finger. Even Leo is limping for no apparent reason.

Suddenly, the Skins grab control of the ball game. One of the biggies throws in a couple of flying one-handers and we're behind

32–31 with only ten seconds left.

"Fuck!" Mitchell says as we huddle for a time-out. "How did we let this happen?"

"We can't let these scrubs beat us!" Ron says. "See? I told you we should've laid the wood to them."

Then Saul offers a radical suggestion: "As far as we're concerned, the game really doesn't really count for anything. I mean, we're not getting paid anyway. So why not let these poor bastards win?"

Leo shrugs. "That's fine with me."

"Think about it," Saul adds. "If they did beat us, think how their spirits would soar. There's no question that they'd benefit more with a win than we would."

"No," Brooks says. "If we tank the game, they'll know it and they'll feel even worse. Let's play to win. I've had enough dumping to last the rest of my life."

So we run a play for Mitchell, a set shot from behind a pair of monstrous picks perpetrated by me and Saul. And Mitchell gets the shot off in good form—the ball flicked daintily off his outstretched fingertips, with perfect rotation, spinning high and tight, threatening to rise forever and never land. (Like the madman tried to do in Oklahoma City! Then nobody would win and nobody would lose and the game would last forever.) But the ball always falls faster than it rises, until it glances against the far side of the rim and bounces askew. Bouncing into my almost unwilling hands, then quickly spun off my fingers, the ball caressed by my pain, and dropping through the ring as the buzzer explodes.

We win. Hooray for us.

The crowd boos as we rush off the court. "Heartless!" a woman yells. "How could you be so cruel?"

"Greedy bastards!"

We shower quickly in thin streams of rusty water, and Horowitz comes by to bid us farewell. "Good game," he says grimly. Even he seems upset that we won. "Very entertaining."

And I call his name: "Horowitz! You were always a fucking bookworm! So answer me two questions: What the fuck are you doing in Wyoming? And why were those guys so mad at us?"

He twitches his shoulders and adjusts the nosepiece of his glasses. "I just go wherever I'm told to go," he says. "And those guys were probably just mad at the whole world. Although around here, they think that all Jews are rich .... Anyway, thanks for helping us out, you guys. Even though that reporter from Denver never showed .... And Brooks. Call me when you reach the coast."

Then we walk outside to the car, feeling like we've ravaged somebody, like we've gang-banged an elderly nun .... And we find the car doors wide open!

"Fuck!" Mitchell shouts, and glares at me.

"I locked them, Mitchell! I swear I did!"

There are rough scratches on the bottom of the rear door, and perhaps the faulty lock was jimmied open. But what difference does it make how the Black Lady was violated? Because everything is gone. Everything. The cashbox, the mattresses, the gun, the maps, the baseball bats, even Mitchell's ruler. We're cleaned out. Decimated. Broke.

"Why didn't they just steal the car?" Kevin asks.

"Because," Ron says, "then we'd have to stick around and cause somebody some trouble. This way, we'll get the hell out of here as fast as we can."

We're all upset, but Mitchell is crying unabashed. "It's all been for nothing! The miles! The troubles! All for nothing!"

Now, now, Mitchell. Max still has $1,600 of ours. But Mitchell refuses to be comforted. "*Gevalt! Gevalt!* All for nothing!"

Brooks drives quickly out of town. At a red light, he ominously taps a finger against the gas gauge. So we empty our pockets . . . . I've got $5.22. Brooks has $2.54. Kevin has a $20 bill in his shoe. Leo has $10 pinned to his underwear. Mitchell has $100 in his hatband.

My God. My God.

It's 675 long miles from here to Las Vegas, where we're scheduled for a game tomorrow night against the Rhineland Athletic Club. Nobody likes the sound of it—but the payday is supposed to be three hundred dollars.

Mitchell won't stop crying and cursing his entire life. "Why was I born to suffer? Me and my stupid fucking dreams! All for nothing!" Until he starts on Brooks: "You had to be a do-gooder! You had to be a fucking saint and save the world!" And I'm his next target, Mitchell being convinced that I indeed left the doors unlocked, unmindful of the cashbox chain that's been clipped by some huge industrial tool. *"Gevalt! Gevalt! Oy!-oy-oy-oy-oy . . .!"*

The rest of us are silent, dead silent, reconsidering our own futile dreams and schemes. How will Mitchell ever get to Palestine without enough money to grease the proper palms? What about Brooks? And the rest of us? How will Kevin get back to New York? And what will I do about Debra? What kind of life can we have without the money I promised her?

And what about the peace, the exhilaration that I felt on the mountaintop? Was it a mirage? And why does misery always seem to be more substantial than love, than happiness?

And ultimately, who's to blame for this latest catastrophe? Brooks? Horowitz? Old man McKenzie? Or maybe I *did* forget to lock the door.

Yes? No?

"Gevalt! Gevalt! Vay iz mir!"

From Mitchell's Log:
Day Fourteen — January 19, 1936 — Saturday

	Today	Total
Mileage	608	4,041
Expenses	$12.87	$310.97
Income	0	($3,185.00)

Net Income - $1,600
Average Share - $228.57 (Aaron minus $125.00)
Cash on Hand - $137.76 (A = $5.22, B = $2.54, L = $10.00, K = $20.00, M = $100.00)

Max Has - $1,600.00

Won - 44
Lost - 4

The beginning of the world must have looked like this: A blazing sphere of fire spilling over mountain peaks. Dark stones and deserts howling in the wind. So will the end . . . with ancient seas sunken into the earth's saline crust.

The only visible life-forms bordering the highway are some mesquite bushes and bristling Joshua trees. Brooks is slumped beside me, sleeping on shotgun duty, his face clenched and straining even in his dreams. Leo and Ron snore in the backseat, Mitchell and the rookies are sprawled on the crypt's bare metal floor. And the Black Lady hurtles down the black road, chasing her own headlights. And the earth whirls blindly through the burning stars.

"Where are we?" Mitchell asks from behind me, yawning and stretching. His head twitches to read a traffic sign we pass at sixty miles per hour. LAS VEGAS—9 MILES. He grunts, coughs, and swallows a warm chest-clam. Then suddenly, on the road ahead, we can discern the first dusty outlines of civilization, walls of gray stone piled against the wind. *"Gottenyu,"* Mitchell says. "Another city in the middle of nowhere."

"Hunh?"

"Whazzat?"

"Where . . . ?"

"My fucking leg's still asleep."

"I gotta pee."

The sky behind us brightens as we penetrate the city's streets, passing stuccoed homes with scalloped rooftops, passing wood-boned commercial buildings. GEORGE'S GROCERIES. HARRY'S HARDWARE. DR. DODGE, THE PAINLESS DENTIST. SAL'S SHOE REPAIR—SOLES REPLACED WHILE U WAIT.

"This city ain't real," Leo decides. "These here buildings are cardboard cutouts."

Nearing the business center, we drive by the tallest building in sight, made of peeled timbers and sandstone, the Last Frontier, a reproduction of a Gay Nineties dance hall. There's a balcony over the main entrance, and someone's peeping down at us through a parted curtain. I get it—a waxworks gallery of beckoning whores.

"Oooo!" Leo moans. "Did you see them dames waving at us? Let's stop here . . . . Hey, Aaron! Where the fuck're you taking us?"

Toward Las Vegas Boulevard and Western Avenue, in search of

another low-rent bedbug barrack that Mitchell's heard about from Livinski. Past an old gray-brick warehouse. Wheels thumping over a railroad crossing.

"There it is," Mitchell says brightly. "The Paradise Arms, which I swear won't cost us an arm and a leg."

Into a small parking lot of pitted and crumbling asphalt. In better days than these, the building must have been some kind of factory . . . . Look at the one large smokestack standing cold and black-lipped like some ancient god of sterility. The rows of black windows that swallow the daylight. The iron fence topped with dull points, and at the entrance, a grinding iron door that could seal a blast furnace.

Inside, we find another dowdy lobby smelling of boiled cabbage and DDT, cluttered with swaybacked couches and splintering chairs. Single rooms go for one dollar a night, and an old man behind the front desk watches us sign the guestbook while he calmly picks his nose.

"You fellas headed west?" he asks, rolling a small dry nugget along the tips of his fingers.

"That's right," says Mitchell. "To Los Angeles."

"Figures," says the clerk.

"Hey, bud," I snap at him. "You gonna eat that thing?"

He blushes, flicks his snotball to the floor, and wipes his hands on his pants. "Wisenheimer," he says, then turns away.

There's a slot machine gleaming near the front door, looking like the instrument console on Buck Rogers's spaceship. And while the rest of us caucus to devise a game plan, Leo loses a dollar, a nickel at a time.

From a pile of papers atop the front desk, Mitchell lifts a smeared mimeographed listing of "Sights to See," prepared by the chamber of commerce. "Welcome to Paradise! Have Fun in the Sun!" Saul and Kevin peruse the official suggestions, deciding to visit the Hoover Dam, then see the rock formations in the Valley of Fire. Mitchell has a "system" that he's eager to test in the nearest gambling casino. "The Flat Stakes system," he explains. "It's for playing blackjack and it gives you the longest run for your money . . . . You start off betting a dollar a hand and then you draw a little vertical line every time you lose. Every time you win, you cross out one of the loss lines. If you lose five bets in a row, then you double your bets to two dollars. Now, when you win, you cross off two of the original loss lines. Then anytime you lose another five in a row, you raise your bet to three dollars. Understand?"

"Sure, Mitchell." None of us has the foggiest, but we nod sagely just to shut him up.

Leo rejoins us and scans the list of sites, his interest pricked by "Roxie's Ranch—Nevada's Only Legal Brothel." Brooks wants to nap, and Ron is likewise inclined. I'm too hungry to sleep.

So Mitchell doles out three dollars each for meals and incidentals. "Remember," he says. "We're just about flat broke."

I'm not surprised that everybody feels ornery and cloudy-eyed. I don't feel too chipper myself. But in hopes of brightening our mood, I say, "Mitchell, maybe you'll win a million bucks with your system."

"I hope so," he says earnestly. "For all our sakes . . . . As a matter of fact, I was thinking of calling your brother, Max, collect and having him wire us the money he's holding. Maybe he can have it waiting for us by the time we get to Los Angeles. Just in case."

"No need to bother. Max is on his way to meet us in Los Angeles even as we speak."

"With our money," Mitchell says, a flat-toned statement hiding a question.

"Sure," I'm quick to answer. "Why not?"

"Because," Mitchell says, "I don't trust your brother and I never did. Everybody on the East Side knows he owes his ass to Charlie the Cheat. Face it, Aaron. Your brother, Max, is a bullshit artist."

"Yeah," I'm forced to admit. "I know what you mean."

Then Ron steps up and pumps both his fists too close to my face. "I'll tell you this," he says rudely. "Max better not fuck us."

"He won't," I insist. "But, Ron . . . unless you intend to use those things right here and now, you'd better get your fucking mitts out of my face."

Ron studies me for a chilling moment. If he had the gun, he'd probably shoot me. Then he laughs and moves off to find his room.

Not until Ron is gone does Mitchell say, "So here's what we'll do . . . . Game time is at seven and we'll meet here in the lobby at six. Saul, you and Kevin can take the car if you first drop Leo off at the cathouse. Here's an extra buck, Leo, so you can call a cab when you're done. Saul? Here's three bucks for gas. Don't forget to bring me a receipt. No, not you, Leo."

Before we disperse, Leo has a proposition for Saul: "What if Uncle Leo treats you to a pussy session at Roxie's? I promised I'd get your cherry burst before we reached the coast, didn't I? Well, this is it."

"No thanks, Leo. I've actually been giving a lot of thought to the possibilities, you know? And I've decided that paying for it is kind of sordid. Maybe I'm better off trying to find my own . . . situation. You know?"

Leo shrugs agreeably and waves his hands as though he were washing a window. "Then I'm off the hook," he says. "Right, guys?"

"Yeah, sure."

"Whatever you say."

"Six, everybody. Don't forget."

Outside again, where the sun glares dully off the sand-colored buildings. I stroll past a Chinese hand laundry—Sun Too Thu, Prop. Then the Tumbleweed Inn, with its front door swung open and fragile laughter chiming from the daytime darkness within. Then a barbershop and a drugstore. Here's another grocery with a slot machine near the entrance.

It's breakfast time, yet the street and sidewalks are nearly empty. Just a pair of cowpokes limping along their way and chewing on toothpicks. Here's a bent old lady, probably the town librarian or schoolmarm. An elderly Negro in faded overalls walks in the shadows and humbly studies his every step. A pickup truck loaded with rusted mining tools jounces noisily down the avenue. There's the sheriff and his deputy cruising in a green and white Oldsmobile. They slow down as they pass me, to fire a round of laughter and a glob of spittle.

In the distance, the majestic blue mountains ignore us. And someday we'll all be buried under the slow and sweeping sands.

Two blocks down and one block over, I find The Golden Fork, a storefront eatery that looks clean if not enticing. Inside, the plastered walls are painted pus-yellow and the tin ceiling is smoky black, but the brown linoleum floor is neatly swept. The only other customers are a pair of old biddies and a young priest just finishing their meal at a sunlit table near the window. Somehow their smiles oppress me, and their small, polite laughter rings like fine china breaking on stone steps.

I find my own table in the darkest corner and a harried peroxide-blond waitress shuffles over like her feet are bound. She slaps a menu down in front of me and says, "I'll be with you in a minute, honey."

The single coarse sheet of paper is handwritten from top to bottom in an angular black script, and today's special is chicken-fried steak. Ugh. Then what about the beef stew? Never, because for the goyim, even a cow's asshole qualifies as "beef." Eggs? From a chicken or a vulture? When the waitress returns, I order black coffee and peach pie. "Apple pie," she says. "Do yourself a favor."

Her face is unpowdered and there are dry cracks spreading from the corners of her bleary brown eyes. Even so, her upturned nose draws her upper lip into a moist, lascivious pout. She's bosomy and thin-hipped. I'd guess she was pretty once, but she's grown old too fast.

I watch as she thanks the priest and his harem of crones for their tip—coins only, including several pennies. After removing all their dishes to the kitchen, she swabs the tabletop with a damp brown rag. Back into the kitchen, then reappearing a few moments later to carefully place my cup of coffee before me and to slide the pie across the table like a cardsharp dealing an ace.

The coffee is too acidic, but the pie is first-rate. Then suddenly she's in front of me again and pointing to the empty chair next to mine. "Do you mind?" she asks.

"Not at all." Gallantly, I rise and bow from the waist. "Please do."

"Jesus, I'm beat," she says, slumping heavily into the chair. "Mind if I smoke?" Before I can answer, she's pulled a crumpled pack of Luckies from a pocket in her apron.

"No. Go ahead."

She fingers a chrome-plated lighter, then snaps the tiny wheel and passes her cigarette through the brief blue flame. "Jesus," she says again, kicking off her shoes and reaching under the table to rub her feet. "My dogs are killing me."

"Tough job, huh? But tell me . . . what's a nice girl like you doing in a joint like this?"

"That's too corny," she says, laughing in spite of herself, her weary eyes releasing a few sparks of joy, a twinge of pain. (Ah! Be still my foolish heart! I belong to another.)

Turns out her name is Emily and she's from Easton, Pennsylvania. When she was "a kid," she used to be "a looker." Her boyfriend was captain of the high school football team, and his well-to-do father owned the funeral parlor on Raub Street. "I was supposed to get married, raise a houseful of brats, and live happily never after. But I couldn't go through with it. So the day after our graduation, I ran away from home. Hey, I was seventeen. I wanted to hitchhike to Hollywood and be a famous actress. What the hell did I know?" She slowly exhales a lungful of smoke. "That was almost twenty years ago. And this is as far as I ever got. Las Vegas. The Meadows. That's a laugh."

"Tell you the truth," I say, "I really don't understand this place. I mean, I can understand the slot machines and the gambling. No matter how dumb, how poor, or how ugly you might be, blind luck can strike like lightning, and suddenly you're smart, rich, and beautiful. God bless America. But I can't figure out why this town is here in the first place. A little nothing town in the middle of nowhere."

"Honey," she says. "There's a reason for everything. I'm still here because I was never really pretty enough to make it in the movies. See? My chin is too small and I have this overbite. And believe me, honey, every speck of sand around here has a history."

According to Emily, there used to be some kind of gushing fresh-water spring somewhere in the vicinity where the Ute Indians made their winter camps. The Spaniards also poked around here in the seventeenth century looking for El Dorado. Then the Mormons arrived in the early 1850s to "murder" the Utes and build a small settlement. "Mean people those Mormons. The U.S. Army had to kill some of them to civilize the rest." Eventually, the Mormons moved north after the Civil War. Then silver mines were unearthed in the surrounding mountains, and Las Vegas became the commercial hub and clearing grounds for this precious ore. The railroad came through in 1905, but until the Great War the town was little more than a tent city. The nearest timber stand is still in the Spring Mountains thirty miles north, and the first wooden buildings were gambling houses and whorehouses. When the mines petered out in the early 1920s, most of the folks left behind were the descendants of failed prospectors, assorted welshers, cardsharps, and rusting tinhorns.

"People've been talking lately about a big revival," Emily says. "Mostly because of the Hoover Dam, or call it Boulder Dam if you're a goddamn Democrat. They begun that in 1931 and just completed it last year. That's why they legalized gambling back in '31, and we've been watching the tourists kind of wander through here ever since. But I don't rightly know. Some say this'll be a real hot spot in years to come. Others say the town'll dry up and blow away. Me? Doesn't matter much to me whichever way the wind blows. My feet'll still hurt from standing all day. My face'll still hurt from all the phony smiles. My ass'll still hurt when the truck drivers pinch me. I'll never save enough money to leave here. And anyways, even if I did, my life would be about the same anywheres else. I got a kid, see?"

She lights herself another cigarette, careful to blow the smoke away from my food. "Boo-hoo," she says. "That's my sad story. Now what about yours?"

"How do you know it's a sad one? Maybe I'm a Russian prince with a million rubles in my pocket."

She laughs and her eyes sparkle. "No, no. I can tell by your eyes. I can tell that whatever you're supposed to be in that getup . . . with that beard and those stringy sideburns . . . and that little beanie hat . . . I know it ain't really you."

"How can you know for sure?"

"Honey, reading faces is my business."

So I tell her about my women and my lusts, about my little girl. Boo-hoo. About the cities and the ball games. My life spills into her lap like a tipped bowl of hot borscht.

"Breaks my heart," she says with a hard-edged smile. "But sounds to me like your wife didn't do you right. She shoulda forgot about what the sawbones said. Big belly or not, a woman's got to take care of her man."

I flash her a hungry look, but she glances away to light another cigarette. "So who're you playing against out here? There's the high school kids over in Archer County, but I don't know any other basketball team."

"We're playing the Rhineland Athletic Club. They're not from around here."

She snorts through her nose. "I know those bastards. They came in here for breakfast the other day. Call themselves the Bond, or something like that. Just a goddamned bunch of Nazis is what they are. The whole town is swarming with them. Must be a convention or something. They're nasty guys with busy hands. And lousy tippers too."

The front door swings open and two dusty young men in boots, cowboy shirts, and dungarees make a noisy entrance. "Emily!" one of them shouts. "How you been, dollface?"

"Jesus," she whispers, then she steps on her cigarette, primps her hair, and activates her workaday smile. Without a glance behind, she grabs my menu and leaves me in the dust. "Hi ya doing boys? Long time, no see."

(Don't abandon me, Emily. Please. Come back and let us rescue each other. Come with me, Emily. Please. We're still young, aren't we? It's not too late for either of us.)

But I keep my feelings to myself, dropping a dollar tip on a forty-five cent check and walking toward the door. "See ya, honey," she says quickly on her way to the kitchen. "Come back again."

The Last Frontier is just down the street, the waxed whores still waving from the upstairs rooms still promising lies.

On the other side of the swinging doors is a spacious ballroom brightly lit by massive chandeliers of fractured yellow glass. The red carpeting underfoot is singed with cigarette burns. But the gaming tables are high-class, fashioned of dark and polished woods—and a sign over a long mirror claims that the black mahogany bar was recently shipped "round the Horn from Madagascar." Along each available wall stands a militant row of slot machines. Several large tables in the center of the room support roulette wheels, also green-felt surfaces for tossing dice and laying down cards.

The attendant croupiers and dealers wear black brims over their eyes and black woolen wristers. The gamesters include the same gritty cowboys who prowl the streets, also the same posse of old ladies who breakfasted at the Golden Fork (they've ditched the priest). Here's a young man dressed like a rodeo rider with a white-fringed red shirt and a big white hat. Another young man wears blue overalls and counts his coins from a small leather pouch. There's a woman with her hair in curlers, wearing a bleached-out blue floral housedress and nibbling her fingernails to the quick. Another woman wears a fancy evening gown.

Perhaps a dozen crop-haired Aryan types are clustered near one of the blackjack tables. The most elderly among them wears an old-fashioned brown tweed suit and high-button shoes. He also affects a monocle, and the cheek below is marked by a livid blue scar. They all glance my way and have a private joke at my expense.

Fitted high into the walls are a series of square-meshed grills, each one paired with a prominent sign announcing, THE PREMISES IS MECHANICALLY AIRE-COOLED. But there's Mitchell, sweating over his card and his notepad. Brooks is here, too, bent over the wheel of fortune. From what I can see, Brooks places the identical bet on every spin—one dollar on red.

The gambling hall is patrolled by a scattering of young men in brawny gray business suits—Pinkertons, pacing through the wide-eyed crowd with eagle eyes and puffed chests. There are also armed guards near the tellers' cages.

"The number is . . . Eighteen! Eighteen pays!"

"The dealer stands pat."

"Six is the gentleman's point. Six."

Mitchell won't lift his attention from his calculations, but Brooks finds me. Holding aloft a handful of red chips, he waves me toward him . . . . No, no. My gambling days are done. I've shaved my last point spread and pitched my last penny. I'm not smart enough anymore to predict the future. And I never did believe that my own desperate wishes could influence the rolling of a steel ball or a pair of dice or the whims of the widow of spades. Purely out of curiosity, however, I'll investigate the craps table, arriving just in time to witness a brief fracas.

Apparently, a tuxedoed sharpster has attempted to substitute his own loaded dice for the house brand, and his clumsy hands have incriminated him. *Whoops! Slipsies!* Even so, the dance of the bones never surprises a good croupier, and this one says with barely lifted eyebrows, "Sir, it appears that your point is fifteen." Immediately, the bumbling gambler is apprehended by a brace of Pinkertons and escorted through a rear door marked "Private."

I wander toward the farthest corner of the large room, attracted by a sliding glass door that accesses the swimming pool. Enough of yellow darkness and blue smoke.

The pool is a huge trough of red and white tiles and poured concrete dried gray as sand. The green, captive water resembles melted Jell-O and at poolside, dozens of white-slated wooden lounge chairs are occupied by the casino's guests. Overweight women and chicken-chested men. Oiled slabs of prickly flesh. Gaunt faces and eyes clenched shut, worshiping mankind's most ancient god.

Near the shallow end, several shapely showgirls lie at their leisure in the huge shade of red-and-white-striped sun umbrellas. A few kids frolic in the green water (why aren't they in school?). And a noisy, splashing crowd stands hip-deep in the center of the pool, their eyes focused on a floating crap table. With their chips in hand, the half-wet women wear starkly-colored bathing suits piped in reds and yellows with matching flared skirts. The bare-chested men wear long woolen trunks that nearly reach to their knees. The croupier wears a long-sleeved Gay Nineties bathing suit, an eyeshade, and a black bow tie.

The water-logged bettors cheer every roll and fall of the dice. Snake-eyes. Box-cars. Craps. Ten-the-hard-way.

One especially robust woman bounces high on her toes whenever she casts her luck upon the green velvet, deliberately creating waves to rock the cradle and bless her desperate arithmetic. But then her buoyant enthusiasm overflows, and a single road-mapped melon-shaped breast leaps from her bathing suit and plops onto the table. The droll croupier says, "Madam, I regret to say that I am unable to cover your wager."

I sit on an empty recliner and face the sky, closing my eyes against the light that blinds. I could easily fall asleep here. Then suddenly I hear a voice saying, "Rabbi? Rabbi? Could I have a word with you?"

Opening my eyes, I see a fleshy man in a bathing suit wearing his body hair like a thickly knitted sweater. The effect is enhanced by a white scoop that's neatly barbered around his neck. An expensive straw hat is perched on his head, hiding his face in its brittle shade.

"My name is Nathan Polan," he says with an adenoidal New York accent. "Used to be Polansky. Born and raised in Brooklyn and proud of it. Where you from, rabbi?"

"Excuse me?"

"I'm here on vacation with my wife, Selma. You too, huh? If you ask me, I think rabbis also need time off once in a while. Reading all those crooked little Hebrew letters. Talking to God all the time. It must be quite a strain."

"Excuse me, sir. I'm not—"

"Hey, you can call me Nate. Nate the Grate, that's me. I sell those gratings that they put on the sidewalks over the subway trains? Or sometimes over sewers and stuff? Nate the Grate. Get it? G-R-A-T-E. Not G-R-E-A-T. Get it?"

"I'm not what you think—"

"So anyhoo, I've got a little idea, rabbi. You see, I been coming here for years. It's a great little spot, Las Vegas. G-R-E-A-T. Especially since they started building Boulder Dam. It's something to see, all right. The Eighth Wonder of the World, only twenty miles away. You should see it at night with all the lighted turrets and the strings of light along the top of the dam. Beeyoutiful. And that new Lake Meade with all the boating and fishing and waterskiing. That's what my Selma's crazy about. Me, I can't stand water sports. I want to keep my feet on the ground. Or at least on a grate. Get it?"

"Look, Mr. Polan. I'm not a rabbi."

But he only winks broadly and resumes his monologue. "So I counted them all, and there's nine churches here in this town. And guess what? There ain't even one *shul*! Not one! Look, rabbi. I figure there's only two kinds of Jews that come here. Them that wins money and them that loses. It's only logical. If you win and you're a mensch, then you want to go thank God for your good luck. If you lose, you want to pray like crazy for your luck to change. Am I right? Either way a *shul* could make a fortune here. And I need some sort of safe investment to hide some of my money. Get it? A young rabbi like you, the people could be comfortable with. You don't even smell from pickled herring, you know what I mean? If you ask me, one of them conservative *shuls* could make a fortune. A fortune."

"Ba ha, Mr. Polan. Ba ha."

He glances at his watch and says, "Look, rabbi. I gotta go call my bookie. You're staying here for a few days, right? Yeah? Well, I'm in Room Two-twelve. Call me later and let me buy you dinner. Strictly kosher, I promise. Nice talking to you, rabbi."

"Shalom, Mr. Polan."

"Yeah! That's the ticket. And shalom to you too."

Right over there in the luxuriant shade of a palm tree, Ron is standing and chatting with a burly young man who's bursting the seams of his gray suit. Ron catches my eye and beckons me over. "Aaron," he says. "This is Paul. He's a Pinkerton man. A bouncer. Paul, this is my buddy, Aaron."

"Pleased to meet you, Paul."

"The same here, I'm sure." His hand is shaped like a shovel and he tries to crush my knuckles as we shake, sending a painful shiver through my sore finger.

"Paul here was telling me what goes on around here. All the action nonstop. There's nudie shows every midnight. And plenty of snatch for a guy who knows how to handle himself. Right, Paul?"

"You bet," Paul says with a smug grin.

Ron can barely contain his zeal. "And the bouncers also get to beat up on the drunks. Right? And the crooked gamblers too."

"There's plenty of those," Paul says. "We just caught some short-sleeved dicer inside, and I got to break his face."

"No lie?" Ron says.

"Pow-pow-pow. The ol' one-two-three. I'll bet the asshole won't get outa the hospital until next summer."

"And the cops, they don't do nothing?"

"Whadda ya kidding me?" Paul says, offended. "The mob's already moved in from outa Chicago, so the coppers're all on the payroll."

"Holy shit!" Ron yelps. "That's what I call real action! Pow-pow-pow, huh?"

"You bet."

"Well," I say, "got to go see a bed about a nap. Mitchell wants us to meet in the lobby at six."

"Sure thing," says Ron, turning impatiently back to Paul. "What else? What about the booze? What about the ponies?"

"There's plenty of those."

"Tell me about everything!"

Inside my hotel room, the whitewashed walls have dandruff, the windowpanes are greasy and opaque, the linen is soiled. So what else is new? The thin mattress seems to be stuffed with old newspapers that crinkle whenever I move. There's a slowly rolling ceiling fan above the bed that does nothing to cool the room, but does keep the flies off me as I descend into a restless sleep . . .

To dream of something rolling away from me . . . a satchel of money? A loose ball? Whatever it is, just barely eluding my grasp. I chase it uphill and downcourt, running along railroad tracks and into a dark tunnel, running through sand, through a swamp, through crowded city streets, running down the middle of a highway. What does this all mean? It's a dark shape. No, a bright one. A ball of fire? A ball of ice?

Then I'm startled by a loud, abrupt noise. A gunshot. An explosion. The beating wings of the dark angel at the end of the world. "Aaron! Aaron!" (The voice of Moses. The wrath of God.) "Aaron! Wake up! Are you in there? Aaron! It's time to get going!"

The Knights of Pythias Recreation Hall is at the eastern end of town, another red-brick building with white concrete steps and a slate roof. The organization's logo is inscribed above the front door—an eye wide-open inside a pyramid. No doubt there's a secret handshake, also mystic midnight initiations into gnostic mysteries.

Hey, Amos. Ho, Andy. Let my people go.

Inside, a small gymnasium whose cinderblock walls are decorated with swastikas on banners and hanging flags, with enlarged mounted photographs of der Führer. The bleacher seats have been completely unfolded, anticipating a full house of perhaps two hundred spectators. Alas, the playing surface is made of tile and the baskets are of unequal heights.

We are greeted by a short-haired elderly man wearing an out-of-style brown suit and a new fangled swastika armband. The same *Übermensch* I saw at the casino. As before, his features are sharp as broken stones, his light blue eyes are cold and sere. Look at his button-shoes and his monocle. His cheek furrowed by the long purple scar.

"Velcome," he intones, sneering and grinning. "I am August von Schekle." Bowing stiffly and clicking his heels. "Allow me to conduct you to your quarters."

And we follow him down clanking metal stairs to the dressing room—low benches, dented lockers, one rusty shower stall. *Vot den?* Our guide clears his throat and says, "If zere iz anytink I can do to make you more comfort-able, you vould please to let me know." Then he bows again and pivots sharply toward the door.

"Just a minute," Mitchell says quickly.

"Yes?"

"We'd like our money in advance."

"Yes?"

"Yes."

"It iz zo," Mein Herr says, his teeth clenched in another painful smile. Then he digs into his wallet and counts out a thin sheaf of bills.

"Iz half," he says, regarding us with undisguised contempt. Yet his eyes celebrate the confirmation that a Jew is a Jew is a Jew. "The rest will be later? Yes?"

"Yes."

After von Schmekle bows again and finally takes his leave, Mitchell says darkly, "That Nazi bastard. I don't trust him. We better walk on eggshells, boys, and not give these maniacs an excuse to kill us."

We vaguely mumble in agreement, all of us bitchy and pissed off, feeling sorry for ourselves, too, anxious for the game to start, eager to foul somebody, hard.

"Hey," I say. "What's with the Kaiser's scar face anyway? What do you think? A war wound? A nun's fingernails?"

"*Zweikamef*, or something," says Mitchell. "The Prussian dueling clubs that were all the rage in the late nineteenth and early twentieth centuries. The young noblemen would challenge one another over trifles, and there were elaborate rituals involved. Basically, they would square off with razor-sharp sabers while wearing leather masks that exposed only their cheeks. The object of the whole *mishegoss* was to inflict dueling scars on each other. It's strictly from the old school. A mark of bravery and manhood in the ancient tradition."

Saul honks a short laugh. "Kind of like a Prussian *bris*."

"Did I tell you that Brooks lost five bucks?" Mitchell asks. "Did I tell you that I won thirty-three?"

"Yeah. Only five times already."

As we lace up our battle-boots, I can almost see the steam boiling out of Leo's ears. He's particularly hot under his collar because the raunchy ranch is closed on Sundays, the waving whores were made of wax, and he wound up sightseeing with the rookies. "I don't like the looks of this setup," Leo grouses. "What're we getting each of us?"

"Fifty," says Saul.

"Well, for a measly fifty bucks I don't know if it's worth the risk."

"Nothing's going to happen," I say merrily. "It's not a pogrom. It's not a war. It's only another basketball game."

"We need the money," Mitchell adds. "And what would happen if we walked out and the word got to Los Angeles? That's where the big-stakes game is supposed to be. At least that's what Max says . . . . "

"Los Angeles," Leo grumbles. "What's in Los Angeles anyway? We don't even know for sure what the deal is supposed to be?"

"Big money," says Mitchell.

"The land of milk and honeys," I say.

"The end of one trip," Brooks predicts, "and the beginning of another."

Ron reports that the gym is overflowing with "Nazis and their Fraus." The host team is big and very athletic, but "the guards look like soccer players, and the big guys look like shot-putters. They got quick feet, but they all handle the ball like it's twice as big as it really is." The Rhinelanders wear "shit-brown" jersey with the swastika emblem embroidered on the front. "And what the fuck," Ron wants to know, "is a swastika?"

Saul has the answer: "It's an ancient and almost universal symbol used by the Britains, the Celts, the Etruscans, the Hindus, even used in pre-Columbian America. It's a form of solar wheel. The arms of the One Cause acting upon the universe."

"What's that got to do with Nazis?" Ron asks.

Saul shrugs. "All I know is that their swastika is backward. Counterclockwise. What does it mean to them? God as machine, maybe. Wheels rolling within wheels like the tread of a tank. I really don't know."

"Anyway," Ron says, "just by looking at these guys shoot, I'd guess we're about twenty points better. A ride in the park."

"Not so fast," says Brooks. "What do the refs look like?"

"They weren't there yet."

As we walk onto the court, we are greeted with a wild chorusing of *"You-den! You-den!"* One section of the stands also arises en masse and salutes us with a stiff-armed *"Sieg Heil!"*

"Oh, shit!" Leo says as he misses a practice layup.

The opposing center wears #32—he's a splendid physical specimen who shows gleaming white teeth and a firm handshake as we face off to start the game. "You hoff gut luck!"

"Yeah. Same to you."

And fuck us where we breathe if both referees aren't wearing swastika armbands.

Number 32 is slow off his feet, so I capture the tip-off—and we deploy our weaving offense carefully until Leo springs free on the baseline for a layup. 2–0. "These yucks are too slow to guard me!" Leo crows as he runs downcourt. "We'll score eighty points!"

As promised, the Rhinelanders are strong and bulky. But given time and space enough to align their limbs, they are accurate two-hand set-shooters with remarkable range. The big men rebound more with fervor than technique, and a solid boxing-out nullifies most of their interior offense. They do operate a precise pattern for their shooters, with picks down and across that only provide open shots when we're too lazy to switch. Meanwhile, our patient ball movement and our well-timed bursts of speed find gaping holes in their defense.

Sure, we get bumped on almost every play (with precious few whistles in our favor), but only because the Rhinelanders are slow and stumble with confusion. I don't believe they have any conscious intent to harm us. In fact, they seem to be pleasant fellows, apologizing after they knock us down, then graciously lifting us to our feet.

(Ouch! I do manage to smack my finger against somebody's head during a rebound free-for-all. The damn finger's still stiff-knuckled and sore.)

Our lead is 19–8 early in the second quarter, even though we're not playing with our usual intensity. We're shooting well, and when we care to, we can always find a layup. But the Rhinelanders seem to capture every loose ball, and more and more we're finessing our way around their tough picks.

We carry a precarious 24–18 lead into the dressing room—but Leo has to run his mouth. "Not even the refs can steal this one. These guys play like they got shit in their shoes. I can score whenever I want."

"I don't like it," Mitchell says. "We're playing too soft. Fellas, once we cross the lines, we've got to forget about everything else. We're not concentrating. We're being out-hustled. I'm afraid these guys can wear us down if we don't come out in the third quarter and build a big lead."

"I agree," says Ron, and we all look to Brooks for our latest strategy.

"If you do get captured," Brooks advises, "just give them your name, rank, and serial number."

"What the fuck is wrong with you?" I demand of my best buddy. "Are you quitting on us?"

Brooks squints his eyes. "What exactly the fuck are you talking about?"

"I asked you first."

Ron is disgusted. "Fuck the both of ya," he says.

Funny thing—as we're warming up oncourt, an Italian-looking greasehead slides out of the stands and approaches Leo. The *paisano* evidently asks Leo some kind of question, but Leo keeps shaking his head. "No," I overhear Leo saying. "Never heard of him." Then, as the teams gather for the center-jump, the *paisano* sidles up behind our bench and briefly chats with Saul.

What the fuck?

This jump ball also belongs to me. Then as we set up our offense, several young men descend from the bleachers and station themselves near our basket. From now on, whenever we launch a shot, the men violently shake the base of the basket support so that the rim vibrates and nearly all of our shots kick out. Even one of Saul's drop shots. The referees refuse to comprehend our various whines and protests.

"Hey! They can't do that!"

"Nein sprechen! Nein!"

"Hey, you fuckers! Get away from there!"

And the partisan crowd erupts into a frenzy when their favorites finally assume the lead midway through the third quarter.

"You-den! You-den!"

The Rhinelanders claim to be embarrassed by their overzealous fans. "Sorry," says #32. "We do not mean for this thing to happen." But no attempt is made to shoo the basket shakers back to their lawful seats.

And we simply lose our heart. Our defense is half-assed and our shots are impetuous. (I'm as guilty as everyone else. What do I care if we win this game or not?) Before we know it, we're behind by 10 points and the ball game is lost.

"You-den! You-den!"

Leo is accustomed to rigged games, so he just shrugs. Mitchell continues to rag the refs, but they merely smile and repeat, *"Nein sprechen."* Spitting mad, Mitchell calls for Kevin to replace him. When Brooks sizes up the situation, he also dispatches himself to the bench. Now with Saul already subbed for Brooks, I've got no place to hide. My primary concern is to avoid #32's wildly flailing forearm shivers.

At one point, Ron starts screaming at the toughs under the basket, but they hoot at him. *"You-den!"* Ron's instinct is to plunge recklessly into their midst and punch every laughing face. Then Saul grabs his teammate's arm, saying, "Don't, Ron. It's no use." Ron nods sadly, apparently yielding to Saul's logic. But on the next play, as both teams are running downcourt in a transition sequence, Ron blatantly rams #18 with a chopping thrust of his elbow, bloodying both the man's nose and his upper lip.

With blood let, the fans turn violent. Several of the basket shakers leap onto the court and charge at Ron. Thank goodness their threatened attack is repulsed with angry words from the Rhinelanders. Threats and counterthreats are bellowed in German. Number 32 shoves one of our would-be assailants and topples him to the floor. Order is restored only after the refs banish Ron to the locker room—"You go now!" The fans cheer as Ron leaves, safely escorted offcourt by #36 and #12.

While all this is happening, Brooks and Mitchell are on the sideline cursing at each other like sworn enemies. Now they're making furious and dire threats. Brooks finally clinches the argument by pushing Mitchell in the chest. Still swearing, and with his eyes leaking tears, Mitchell enters the game to replace Ron.

There are no further incidents, and our final deficit is 53–37. When the Rhinelanders line up to shake our hands, #32 says to me, "*Numer Drei* is of the hot head, no? But you are the better team than of us, yes?"

Von Schmekle enters the locker room hot on our heels to shout something in German and throw the rest of our money to the floor. Then he stormtroops out the door, slamming it behind him and loosening upon us a dusting of plaster from the ceiling.

"Fuck you too," Ron snarls after him.

Mitchell scrabbles on the floor, collecting and counting the cash.

"It's okay," he assures us. "The money's all here."

By the time we get back to our car, one of the Stars of David has been painted over with a red-dripping swastika.

"Saul, what did that guy want from you? That Italian."

"He asked me where our next stop was, and I told him Los Angeles."

There is no speed limit in Nevada, and Ron is still cursing as he drives with desperate urgency through the desert night: "That asshole! I should've broken his face! Pow-pow-pow!"

And it seems that my latest nightmare is now chasing all of us, through the mountains and into the sea.

From Mitchell's Log:
Day Fifteen — January 20, 1936 — Sunday

	Today	Total
Mileage	342	4,383
Expenses	$25.00	$335.97
Income	$350.00	($3,535.00)

Net Income - $1,950.00
Average Share - $278.57 (Aaron minus $125.00)
Cash on Hand - $462.76 (A = $5.22, B = $2.54, L = $10.00, K = $20.00, M = $100.00)

Max Has - $1,600.00

Won - 44
Lost - 5

DAY 16

"There it is," says Ron. He steers the car off the highway and onto a bare, stony patch at the roadside overlooking the valley. And we all climb out to consider the view.

"I gotta piss," says Leo.

Brooks's laughter sounds almost like a fit of coughing. "Just make sure," Brooks says, "that you don't piss into the wind."

"Ron," Mitchell says sharply, "don't forget to pull the emergency brake."

"Look," says Kevin (and we do). "It's so beautiful."

And it is . . . With the nightlights still sparkling just before dawn and one powerful spotlight searching the heavens, unobstructed by clouds, the beam disappearing into God's eye, announcing the gala premiere of Ziegfeld's latest follies. Also noticeable below us in the foothills are nine billboard-sized white letters, also spotlighted, spelling H-O-L-L-Y-W-O-O-D. The black shrubbery covering the black hillsides turns gray, then pink, then green as the sunrise catches us.

The Promised Land.

And I recall the ice hermit's prophecy—like the biblical Aaron, like Moses, I will behold the Promised Land but never set foot upon its holy soil. And if mad Jesse is indeed the prophet he pretended to be, then I'm faced with two possibilities: Either Los Angeles is *not* the Promised Land. Or else my doom is imminent.

Everybody is glad to be here at last—where Mitchell can find a way into Palestine, where Brooks can emulate Horowitz and unionize the unwashed, where Leo can stop fastbreaking, where Ron can ride the crest between action and reaction, where Saul can get honestly laid and healed, where Kevin can remember things his father never imagined.

But for me, I'm afraid to face Max and hear his lies and alibis. Even more afraid to face Debra and hear mine.

Shmuck that I am!

For convincing Debra to abandon her home, her loving parents. Even though she was eager to leave. Even though both of us are in love with lust. Both of us searching for that divine shiver to make us forget for a few precious moments exactly who we are.

Call me a shmuck for being old enough to need proof that I'm still young.

And a shmuck with earflaps for trusting Max.

Ron drives down the mountain too recklessly. His sport is to avoid the sharp stones that hazard the road while racing as fast as possible. Forty miles per hour. Forty-five!

"Hey, cowboy!" I shout from the crypt. "Slow down, will you?"

"Just what we need," Mitchell laments beside me. "With the end in sight, as if we don't have enough trouble, to get a flat tire or have a fucking accident."

"Bite your tongue," Saul says with a playful solemnity. "Sufficient unto the day is the evil thereof."

"I heard of that," says Mitchell. "It's a saying from the Bible, right? Who said it? Moses? Job? Jonah in the whale? . . . Hey, Ron! You're going too fucking fast."

"Jesus Christ," says Kevin.

"See?" says Mitchell. "You even got the rookie scared."

"What I mean is that Jesus Christ said that."

"What're you talking about?" Leo asks Kevin. "Jesus Christ said Jesus Christ? Is that what you're saying?"

I can only sigh and shake my head. "We're all lunatics."

"Speak for yourself," says Brooks.

"Meshuggener," Kevin says with his broad red-bearded smile. "Very meshuggener."

Of course I've forgotten the name of the hotel where Max has presumably reserved rooms for us. "It's on Wine Street," I say. "The Tree House, or something. When I see the name, I'll recognize it."

But nobody seems to be disturbed by my lapse of memory as we motor toward the fading brightlights, always aiming westward toward Hollywood's slowly dimming version of the burning bush. Coursing through the valley, still several miles west of where we think we want to be, we come upon a series of black, pitchy bogs surrounded by some flimsy, rusting wire fences. They look like sores on the earth, oozing a black, sulfurous pus.

Kevin forms a tiny cross with his forefingers. "Satan," he says, his voice shaky, "get thee behind me."

Closer to the city, we pass small stucco houses similar to those we saw in Las Vegas—also homes shingled in soft black squares of asphalt. A few garden apartments with oversized picture windows. Also—fields of poppies, lupine, and bright yellow mustard. And orange groves, spread over vast acreage or else planted in small clearings behind sharecroppers' shacks. Farther along the way, there's the Los Angeles version of a hobo jungle—Las Colonias—migrant camps for Mexican and Filipino pickers and packers, huts made of scrap metal, cardboard, and rotted wooden boards, and surrounded by a rough barricade of trashed and rusted cars. We see billboards boasting the merits of Burma Shave, Lucky Strikes. A restaurant shaped like a monstrous derby hat. An ice-cream parlor operating inside an overgrown concrete milk bottle. Various stores and juice stands built and colored like gigantic oranges.

And always cars on the streets—limousines and Model As, buses and delivery trucks—more traffic than I've ever seen in New York. Lights changing, horns bleating, people cursing at us. "Sunday driver!" "Get that piece of shit off the road!" There's an urban *colonia*—some dirt-floored cabins built around a communal water faucet. Mexican kids in rags. And always more cars—fleets of Okies and Arkies, the so-called flivver immigrants. On every other street, a boarded-up bank. CALIFORNIA LOAN & TRUST. Now we're stuck behind a yellow schoolbus with children pointing at us through the windows, laughing, thumbing their noses, sticking out their tongues.

On the sidewalk, a fat lady holds a rose-colored parasol against the sun. An old man limps along, handling a frayed leather leash and following a bloated old beagle dog. There's two little twin girls each dressed like Shirley Temple and being prodded on their way by a fussy woman wearing a blue flapper's dress. Here's a buck-toothed hillbilly driving to town with his Packard pickup truck rear-loaded with bales of hay and two lovely farmer's daughters.

"Maybe they're all actors," Kevin wonders. "Or actresses."

"Maybe," says Mitchell, "Halloween comes late around here."

No one protests when Ron detours toward the ocean, driving along a winding, crunching gravel road that traces the shoreline. In view of gray sands and blue crashing waves, of an elderly couple strolling hand-in-hand along the brownish sand at the water's edge. The strip of beach narrows as we travel south, and there's a black cat chewing on a dead bird while angry gulls screech overhead. A young man runs in the sand wearing brown shorts and a white sailor's hat, barefoot, his hairless chest wet and gleaming. The wind slants in from offshore, smelling of salt, of infinity.

"I'm tired," Leo complains. "Let's find the fucking hotel already."

Ron turns inland and we notice that the spotlight has been extinguished by the sunshine.

"Turn left here."

"No, you dimwit. We'll wind up in the fucking ocean. Turn right."

"Where's the fucking map?"

"Somewhere," says Mitchell, "in Wyoming."

When we stop to gas the car, Mitchell asks directions from the pump-monkey, a freckle-faced redhead with a flat Okie face.

"Y'all must be actors."

"Yeah," says Leo. "I'm Clark Gable in disguise."

"Well, howdy, Mr. Gable. I sure do like yer pitchers."

Leo looks askance and whispers to Ron, "Is this guy for fucking real?" But I can see the redhead laughing at us from behind his eyes.

After another fifteen minutes of earnest driving, after a heated argument between Leo and Mitchell over whether the pump-monkey said to go left or right at the third or fourth intersection, we find Vine Street and the Golden Palms Hotel.

"That's the one," I say.

"See?" Leo trumpets. "I told you it was a right."

A long, curved driveway is shaded by towering palms. The grounds are teeming with colorful profusions of poppies, marigolds, snapdragons, and neat green hedges. There's an orange tree potted in a huge wooden tub. The flat-roofed two-story building is walled in whitewashed stucco and embellished with redwood trim. There's a white canvas awning overshading a white-pebbled footpath leading to the front door. Above us, the sunshine turns all the glass windows to gold. And as soon as Ron cuts the engine, we are swarmed by a squad of smiling young men dressed in red and gold uniforms like the queen's grenadiers.

"Don't touch the car!" Mitchell shouts.

"Lay offa my arm!" says Ron. "I ain't no cripple!"

"You!" Leo snaps. "Get your fucking hands offa the merchandise!"

Through a glass door brightly, the lobby is all golden curves and red velvet rests. The furniture is gilded, the carpeting royal red, the floors marble, and the chandeliers gleaming. Only a rose-tinted glass wall separates the lobby from the dining room, wherein a young man in a fancy ruffled tuxedo plays a grand piano, some kind of sweeping classical riff that I can't identify.

Leo is awestruck. "It's like a fucking castle in here."

And sure enough, good ol' reliable Max has reserved seven rooms for us. "T.H.O.M.A.S." (The House of Moses All-Stars.) But the blue-uniformed desk clerk demands to see our drivers licenses. "Proof of identity," he says with a snooty grin. "I'm sure you understand."

"Sure thing," says Leo, holding two yellow cardboard tickets like a pair of aces. "Pick a license. Any license."

"Your own will be sufficient, sir."

The clerk minutely inspects the proffered identification, finds the matching name on his official list, then dings a desktop bell and activates another toy soldier. "Here, boy. The gentleman, Mr. Sloan, is in Room One-twenty."

"This way, sir," the bellhop says as he grabs for Leo's gym bag.

"Leggo!" Leo yelps. "That's mine! I don't need your help to carry something I've been carrying for three weeks!"

Together, they two-step across the lobby and up the broad red-runnered staircase, shouting at each other and grappling for possession of the bag.

"Please, sir! This is my job! My livelihood!"

"Leggo, dammit!"

The desk clerk makes a clucking noise and shakes his head disapprovingly. Then he resumes his phony smile and asks Mitchell to identify himself.

Mitchell will cooperate up to a point. He displays his driver's license, then says, "Okay, pal. Just give us the keys and we'll find our own way."

As we autograph the guest book, Mitchell grandly hands us twenty dollars each for expenses. "What the hell," he says. "Might as well enjoy it while we can."

Then we're straggling and trudging across the lobby when Brooks taps my shoulder from behind and points into the dining room. "Aaron," he says. "Let me treat you to breakfast."

"Sure. But first I've got to make a pit stop."

"G'head. I'll meet you inside."

My room is furnished with spongy gray carpeting, and a stolid redwood bed with matching dresser and armoire. Fluted glass lamps adorn the gray-fabric-covered walls, and set beside a small chair and table is a huge redwood console radio. The high-arched windows are sealed with gauzy white-lace curtains that dull the incessant sunshine and screen the flying insects.

Only the bed is inviting . . . I can readily imagine me and Debra fucking on a downy-soft mattress. If the spirit were to move her, I could easily drape her body cunt-up over the footboard. Here a fucking, there a fucking . . .

And then what? When the come is all gone?

Meanwhile, the bathroom has a miniature Roman bath with blue-veined marbleized fixtures and polished brass levers and spouts. The toilet seat is unexpectedly cold—and I squat there for too long, beset by cramps and slithery shits.

Then I hustle downstairs to join Brooks.

He's sitting beside a glass-topped table, obscurely stationed nearest the kitchen doors. Even from this most distant section of the room, the pinkish doings in the lobby are easily observed through the thick glass wall. But Brooks seems totally absorbed in reading a newspaper and he doesn't look up to greet me.

Just as I'm sitting down unacknowledged beside him, our waitress appears, dressed like a French maid in a short black skirt, white apron, and a white lacy hat. Her nameplate says GLORINDA. Despite our raggedy garments, Glorinda regards us with practiced joy, since Brooks and I might well be talent scouts, agents, producers, famous actors, eccentric millionaires, spies, G-men . . .

"Good morning, sirs. Excuse me if I seem a bit distracted, but I'm trying to learn my lines for a play I'm going to appear in."

"What kind of pies do you have?" I ask.

There's too much makeup on her raccoonish eyes, and her tits are wide-set like waterwings worn backward. She's finally tabbed us as small-timers, but just in case, she blinks rapidly and flexes her tits as she places the menus on the table. "I always recommend the apple pie," Glorinda says. "Because that's the kind of gal I am. And I'll be right back to take your orders, sirs."

As she slinks away toward another customer at another table (he's a sharp-lapeled wiseguy in sunglasses), we can hear Glorinda enunciating in dramatic tones, "A wet bird *never* flies by night . . . A *wet* bird never flies by night."

Then Brooks rudely tosses his newspaper so that it falls on top of my menu. "Look at this," he commands, pointing to a small story on page four . . . . The headline reads, COMMUNIST AGITATOR SLAIN IN WYOMING. It's Horowitz—"beaten to death with a blunt object" and found lying facedown in a ditch. The Casper police say their investigation has turned up "no clues and no suspects."

Horowitz! The poor bastard.

"It's no use," Brooks says tightly, angrily, from between clenched teeth. "No fucking use." Above the luxuriant growth of his graying beard, his cheeks seem bloodless, his dark eyes seem sunken into his skull. How long has he looked like this?

All I can manage to say is, "Brooks. Brooksie."

Gently, he lays his opened palms atop the newspaper as if he were touching Horowitz's dead face. "This is just one more reason, Aaron."

"A reason for what?"

"Ah, shit!" he says, and he's angry again. Now he clenches his hands as though he were holding a baseball bat. Had he been this angry in the hobo jungle in Cedar Rapids, Brooks would have killed somebody.

The waitress returns ("A wet *bird*...") and Brooks solemnly orders black coffee. I'll have oatmeal, coffee, and apple pie.

"A reason for what?" I persist after she leaves.

"You tell me, Aaron. What use are labor unions anyhow? What do they really accomplish? How many heads are busted for every two-cent raise? How many innocents are murdered? For what, Aaron? For nothing, that's what. If they do get a two-cent raise, then the price of everything gets raised three cents. It's all bullshit, don't you see? The working slob gets fucked forever and ever amen. Because the bastards who run this country, they've got all the weapons. The newspapers, the radio stations, the politicians, the judges, the cops, even the fucking army.... And all we've got is bullshit. All we've got is more of our own blood to be spilled."

My first reflex is to say, "No... No, Brooksie. Don't give up! What about the Party? What about the Revolution?"

"Bullshit and more bullshit. And you know something, Aaron? When you get past the jargon and the slogans, it's all very simple. The whole philosophical concept of communism is based on the belief that mankind is inherently good. Unselfish, loving, trustworthy, willing to sacrifice for others. But if it's the other way around, if mankind is inherently evil... then, even if there is a revolution, everything will eventually turn out to be just as fucked up as it was before. And that's what's really happening in Russia, Aaron. What difference does it make to the peasants or the Jews if they're murdered by the Cossacks or by Uncle Joe's henchmen? It's bullshit, I say. No matter what, they'll be eating pork chops and we'll be eating beans."

"The world isn't so black-and-white, Brooks. People are different. People are complex."

"Different. Complex. That's just talk. Hot air. The real truth is that everybody's full of shit, Aaron. That includes FDR, Stalin, Huey Long, Leo, Mitchell, you, me . . . everybody. And no matter what you do, no matter where you go, you can't ever escape the truth. It's unavoidable. You sacrifice something for somebody and see what happens? They steal the eyes right out of your head."

"Those were desperate people, Brooks. C'mon. You know that. They had to feed their children."

"Don't make such easy excuses for them. Everybody's desperate these days. Everybody's got their own good reason for being full of shit."

"Brooks. I can't believe this. Since when are you so cynical?"

He laughs through his nose. "I'm just tired of being a sucker."

"You're not a—"

"And that's why I'm leaving, Aaron. Tomorrow night, right after the ball game. It's just about all set. I've got to meet one more guy and deliver up the money. We're taking an aeroplane—"

"Whoa, Brooks! Hold on! What guy? What money? Where are you going so fast? Don't be rushing into anything."

He glances away to watch the traffic in the lobby: A bellhop wheels a silver tea cart into the elevator. A matron walks toward the front desk cradling a poodle in her flabby arms.

Finally, he says, "Believe me, Aaron. This is no spur-of-the-moment thing. I've been thinking about doing something like this ever since Sun Dancer spoke to us. Remember? He said that there's only one kind of commitment that really counts."

"What are you talking about, Brooks? Sun Dancer never said that. I don't understand . . . . You're going back to Oklahoma?"

"Not Oklahoma, you dope. Ethiopia. I'm going to Ethiopia to fight against Mussolini's fascists. I'm tired of the bullshit and the lip service. Once and for all, it's time for me to put my ass on the line."

"Ethiopia? There's a real live war going on there, Brooksie, with lots of real dead people! Ethiopia? What're you, fucking crazy?"

"That's me, all right. Crazy Brooks. Listen to me . . . Life or death, Aaron—anything less is bullshit."

"Brooksie! Don't do it, Brooksie! It's not even a war. It's a fucking massacre. You can't . . .!"

"I can, I will, and I am. It's the only war in town . . . . Listen, I don't want to talk about it anymore. I've just got to get the hell out of here, Aaron. This country stinks to high heaven. My life stinks. I can't stand myself, Aaron. I can't stand my own mind."

"For God's sake, Brooks. That doesn't mean you have to go get yourself killed."

His eyes are watering and so are mine. Maybe he really is crazy. Crazier than me.

"Aaron. You've got to swear to me that you won't tell any of this to the guys. I don't want any of them to know where I'm going until I'm already gone. You've got to keep your trap shut, Aaron. Swear it."

"Brooksie!"

"Swear it, Aaron! Swear it!"

"All right! All right! I won't say a fucking word!" Then he rises from his chair and turns away from me. "Brooksie! Where are you going? You said you weren't leaving until tomorrow after the game!"

"I'm just going to the beach, Aaron. Somewhere . . . I want to walk along a beach."

"Let me come with you." Now I'm standing in front of him, positioned to draw a charging foul. "We can talk some more."

"No, Aaron. Like I said, it's past talking. I need to be by myself."

Then, just like that, he's gone into the lobby and out the front door. Will I ever see him again? "Brooksie?"

The waitress brings the food and I eat quietly . . . Stunned. Disbelieving. Mourning. The oatmeal tastes like ashes.

To make matters worse, here comes Mitchell sauntering into the lobby, casting inquisitive looks into the dining room. I try to hide my face behind the newspaper, but I'm too slow. Mitchell makes a beeline for me, then he plops into the seat Brooks just vacated and he says this:

"What's with Brooks? I just saw him walking down the street looking like a fucking mope. And hey, you want to know something Aaron? Even though he's your best pal, the truth is that Brooks is a fucking asshole. Did you see what he did to me yesterday? Did you see him hit me? That's right. Punched me in the chest in front of all those people. What an asshole."

Mitchell orders steak and eggs, toast and coffee. "Any chance you got a prune danish?" he asks the waitress.

"What's that?" she says.

"Forget it."

My inclination is to abandon the remains of my meal and make a quick escape. But where to go? To my room to stare at the ceiling? To spy along behind Brooks and make sure he comes back? And besides, in a mere forty-five minutes I'm obliged to meet Debra and Max at the train station. Debra! And Max! (Maybe they've already met on the train! Maybe they've fallen in love at first sight and got married in Chicago!)

"I'm glad this trip is just about over," Mitchell is saying. "I've had it up to here." He holds his shooting hand level with his eyebrows. "I ask you. When was the last time anybody did the laundry? Or even washed the uniforms? I deliberately said nothing about it, Aaron, and notice what happened. Nothing. That's what happened. See what I mean? If I don't make the arrangements, nothing ever gets done. For three weeks I've been breaking my brains trying to keep things going, and what thanks do I get? A punch in the chest."

"He didn't mean it, Mitchell. It's the pressure, the grind . . . . Brooks's got a lot on his mind."

"Oh, he meant it all right."

The waitress returns with Mitchell's breakfast, still batting her eyes and rehearsing her lines: "A wet bird never *flies* by night . . . "

"Mitchell," I say when she's gone. "We *do* appreciate everything you've done for us. We really do. But the record's scratched, Mitchell, and the needle's stuck. You and me, we've already had this conversation, somewhere in some city that I can't remember. The music goes round and round and we all know that we never would've made it without you, Mitchell. We all know it, but we just don't say it."

"Yeah," he says with a modest smile, always pleased to be flattered. "And you've got to admit, Aaron, that I did a pretty good job of shepherding us through thick and thin. Everything would've been hunky-dory if not for Brooks. Deny it if you can. Even Kevin the goy knows that the biggest mistake we made was going to Wyoming to save the poor working man. Ha! But does anyone ever criticize Brooks? Don't make me laugh. So here we are without a pot to piss in."

As he talks, Mitchell steals frequent glances toward the lobby, obviously expecting somebody.

"Mitchell. I need the car to pick Max up at the train station."

"When's he due?"

"In about a half hour."

"That's okay by me, Aaron. I don't need the car myself, but I already promised it to the rookies. They want to drive over to the movie studios. You know . . . MGM, Warner Brothers? They're supposed to meet me here right about now. But I'm sure they won't mind giving you a lift . . . . Anyway . . . More important than that . . . Tell me true, Aaron. Does Max have our money?"

"How the fuck am I supposed to know? I haven't spoken to Max since he left New York."

"Because I really need my cut of the dough, Aaron. I've already made contact with some men who know a certain Greek sailor that smuggles Jews into Palestine. The important fact is that these guys want my payment in hand before I can step foot on the boat. Five hundred smackers they want. Even with Max's money ... with our money ... I'm still a little bit short. That's another reason why the game tomorrow better be what it's supposed to be ... Hello! There's my guys now ... So, don't lose the keys, Aaron. And I'll see you later. Oh, yeah ... after Max gives you the details about the game, leave a note under my door. Okay? I'm in Room One-twenty. One-two-oh. Don't forget."

Two authentic Hasids have stepped into the lobby. (I can tell they're genuine by the dust in the wrinkles around their red eyes.) And they greet Mitchell with *mazel*s and soft applause. Then they clutch at Mitchell, subjecting him to exaggerated hugs and fishlike kisses on his cheeks. (To Palestine he's going? Mitchell's lucky if he isn't shanghaied and winds up on a slow boat to China.)

"A wet bird," Glorinda says flatly as she refills my coffee cup, "never flies by *night*."

I watch the fancy people eating breakfast: A man wearing high leather boots, bloused riding britches, a beret, and a green-tinted monocle, flicking a small whip against his thighs as he talks to a young, vampish brunette. Two drugstore cowboys in fringed Western shirts laugh loudly and slowly, sneaking anxious glances around the room to see if anybody's noticed them. There's a middle-aged man eating alone, dressed in a white safari suit and wearing a pith helmet.

And here come the rookies ... Gasp! Both of them cleanshaven!

As they sit themselves at my table, Saul merely says, "Hi, Aaron. Seen Mitchell?"

"He just left." I show him the keys and he nods.

Both rookies order steak and eggs with orange juice, toast, and tea. Then I conspicuously stroke my scraggly beard and say, "What gives?"

Saul touches his own cheeks like a blind man fingering the face of his lover. "The hair on my face was symbolic, Aaron. And I deliberately use the past tense. It represented everything that I ran away from in New York. As you know, I've been thinking about a lot of things lately. And I finally realized that never in my entire life have I felt really free as long as I had the beard and the *payess*. But now, Aaron . . . now I can start clean." He blushes rosily.

"Abi gezunt!" I say with a vaudevillian Yiddish accent. "So long as you got your helt." Then I poke my Jewish hook at Kevin. "And you? What's your excuse?"

"Well, I guess my face just itched all the time . . . . No, no, I'm kidding. That's not the real reason. It's . . . Well . . . I don't mean no offense, Aaron, but I don't like being mistook for something I'm not."

I laugh too loudly, too coarsely. "Another anti-Semite we got here."

"No, no," Kevin is quick to say. "I like you guys very much. You're the first Jews I ever was friends with. So don't get me wrong. The whole trip's been a great adventure for me, Aaron. One surprise after another. But I guess it's just like Saul said . . . I never felt comfortable with all that hair on my face. It's like I'm in hiding or something. Like I'm some kind of impostor. I almost forgot what I really look like. Now, don't get me wrong, Aaron. I really appreciate the chance to play ball and to travel with you guys. I only wish I could've played better."

Then I say, "Okay, Saul, so you've run away from the beards and the past tense. Kevin, so you've seen that the Thirty-fourth Precinct isn't the center of the universe. That's only a first step. Now what? You must have talked about some possibilities."

"I don't know," says Kevin, reprising his shrug. "I might stay and see the sights around here for a while. Go to Mexico. Then probably go back home and be a cop. Or maybe not. I really like the weather here. Hey, it's January and you can still go swimming in the ocean. So far as I'm concerned, Los Angeles is the best place I've ever been."

Saul lightly fingers a tiny cut on his chin. "I suppose I'll hang out here for a while until I come up with a better idea. What about you, Aaron?"

(I grab my check from the table and Brooks's too—a total of $4.67. Outrageously expensive. And thanks for the treat, buddy mine.) "I'm in the same leaky boat as you guys. But right now I do have to go pick up my brother, Max . . . and a friend . . . at the train station in about twenty minutes."

Before I can pop the question, Saul says, "Let's get going, then. I can get directions at the front desk. Easy as aces. Me and Kevin're going to see where the movies are made, but we're in no big hurry." He looks to Kevin for corroboration.

"Sure," Kevin says eagerly. "I love trains. I had a big electric train set when I was a kid. My dad would set it up around the Christmas tree."

"I've heard so much about Max," says Saul. "Do you think he has our money?"

The way to the station leads us through residential neighborhoods whose houses are separated by narrow alleyways. Broken glass in the front yards. Rusted tin cans. Children in patched clothing, crying, laughing. We pass more garden apartment complexes, more ritzy houses set uphill at the end of long, forbidding driveways. Past palm trees drowsing in the wind. At a red light, a young colored boy sells oranges out of a paper bag. His sign says, "3 4 2¢." Another man leans against a lamppost with an opened cigar box set on the sidewalk before him while he plays soaring melodies on a clarinet.

We easily find the train station, then park the car and wait at the appropriate track. The train is late and the open-air hippodrome is crowded with people coming and going: shoeshine boys with portable step-boxes. "Shine, mister?" A crosseyed man stands near the arrivals-and-departures board shouting jokes at the top of his voice. His outstretched right hand holds a soiled felt hat upside down to coax a coin or two from the busy travelers. "Why did Jesus cross the road? . . . Because he was nailed to a chicken." People frantically consult their wristwatches. Babies cry. An old man hobbles at double time. Announcements come from the sky in a fuzzy electronic voice: "Leaving at one twenty-three from Track Nine. San Francisco. Seattle. Portland." A cop twirls his nightstick and whistles a tune no one else can hear.

Here comes the train. First the locomotive with steam boiling from every seam. The big wheels scream in metal agonies and a tortured whistle toots. Even before the procession of linked coaches rolls to a dead stop, several colored men in wrinkled black uniforms race forth to place small step stools before every opening doorway.

(And I'm dumbstruck with the reality of Debra's impending appearance! What do I tell her? What do I do? What have I done?)

"I guess he'll find us," Saul says. "Off the court, that's the only advantage—being easy to find in a crowd."

There's Max, fatter than I remember him. With his crumpled double-breasted blue suit and his familiar owlish spectacles. (We have the same high-bridged nose, his unbroken.) Max also has a large frame, just like me, but his shins are disproportionately short, so he waddles through the mob like a lost penguin. He carries a brand-new leather suitcase and a furled black-cloth preacher's umbrella.

He spies me and rushes forward, saying, "*Vos macht du,* little brother!" Then he stands back for a dramatic appraisal: "You look thin, Aaron. You look like shit, you should pardon my French." And we embrace. (Max smells faintly of sweat and of poorly digested garlic.) With a wide, aching smile, I deliver the polite introductions. Everybody's "heard so much" about everybody else. All the while, I'm desperately scanning the platform for Debra—and I'm flashed with another foolishly hopeful thrill: Maybe she's not here! Maybe she changed her mind while en route!

Now Max tips up onto his toes and urgently whispers to me, "I've got to talk to you, Aaron! Right away!"

"Take it easy, Max. The boys here'll drive us back to the hotel and we'll have plenty of time to talk there."

But my casual proposal only stokes my brother's agitation. "Right now!" he whispers, loud enough for the rookies to hear. "It's a matter of life or death!"

Then I spot Debra—she's already moving in our direction, waving madly, carrying three bulky suitcases and a hat box. All at once, I remember her short brown hair and her droopy eyelids. Her moist lips and her puffy smile. Her breasts, small and pointy. The golden down on her thighs. Dumbly, I watch her struggle, coming closer. She wants to embrace me, to stick her tongue down my throat, to reach her hands down my pants—but she takes notice of Saul, Kevin, and Max. So we shake hands (mine are slick and greasy, hers are dry), and I say, "Hi. How are you? Good to see you."

How was your trip? Fine. How was yours? Fine.

Saul makes the first move to unburden Debra of her baggage, and as I conduct the further introductions, Max signals me with a dubious fish eye. Kevin bows as he makes Debra's acquaintance, but he's too shy to speak. Max is suave in a nasty way: "Pleased to meet you, young lady. And I do mean young." When Debra shakes hands with Saul, the rookie's nicked and blood-spotted face splits into a silly grin.

"Gee," she says to Saul. "You're so tall. You're even taller than . . . Mr. Steiner."

By now Max is practically jumping up and down like a little boy about to piss his pants. "Life or death!" he croaks. "Let's get a taxi, for Chrissake!"

"Okay, Max. Just hold your horses for one minute."

Max guesses rightly that I mean to include Debra in our taxi party and he hisses at me, "No, no, Aaron. This is private." Aloud, he says, "Excuse us, everybody. Please. I hate to be so rude, but my brother and I have some very important family business that can't wait . . . . "

"Saul," I say. "Could you give Debra a lift back to the hotel? Debra, I'm really sorry about this."

Squeezing her shoulder, I tell her softly and closely, "We have plenty of time to get reacquainted. What can I do? My brother's having a nervous conniption. Here's my key. I'm in Room One-seventeen. We won't be very long. I promise."

She's obviously disappointed and her good humor sags. Instead of sweeping her off her feet, I'm already ditching her.

Then Max grabs my hand and leads me away. In truth, I'm glad for the quick chance to dodge my fate.

Max instructs the driver that our "ultimate destination" is the Golden Palms Hotel. "But take your time, cabbie. Just drive around town until I give you the word." Then Max slides shut the small partitioned window and we sit side by side, silent and hermetically sealed. Max is clearly nervous, fidgeting with his glasses, cleaning the lenses with a snot-stiffened handkerchief.

"Who's the skirt, Aaron? For Chrissake! Is that who I think it is?"

"She's a friend of mine and she's none of your business. Maybe we'll talk about her later. Maybe. Meanwhile, you're the one with the emergency, Max. So what's the big deal that's got your balls in such an uproar?"

With his glasses still clutched in his hands, he stares at me, his naked brown eyes already begging my forgiveness. "Aaron, I'm in trouble. Deep trouble." Now he uses his handkerchief to wipe his suddenly sweating brow.

"So tell me."

"For starters, I don't have your money."

"Don't kid around, Max. Mitchell said he sent it from—"

"Oh, I received it all right, but there's none of it left."

"What? What are you saying?"

"I blew it all on slow horses and fast women," Max says with a small grin. "But mostly I bet on the wrong side of too many rigged basketball games. LIU, Saint John's, Metro. Everybody with a hot dollar bill in his hands knows they're all doing business. Believe me, to bet on roundball, you've got to be in the know. And a poor *pisher* like me never gets the real inside scoop. One guy says this team is in the bag tonight. Another guy says it's the other team. Then I also got a bum steer on the Rose Bowl. I bet SMU plus three, and they lost by seven. Aaron, it's been one thing after another. I even lent some skirt a hundred bucks that I might as well've thrown out the window. My God, Aaron. If I'd bet on the sun rising in the east, on that very same day, the world would turn upside down. I mean it." Now his head is dumped into his open hands and he's crying softly. "It's such a string of bad luck, I can't see the end of it. Aaron. I didn't mean for this to happen."

"None of it left? All sixteen hundred gone?"

Max nods. "It's even worse than that." He squirms in his seat. "I owe Charlie the Cheat a bundle."

"How much?"

"Five grand."

"Jesus, Max. I thought this gambling was just a hobby with you."

"It started out like that." Now he's wiping his face with his greasy gray cloth. "Bad luck can happen to anybody."

Now he's weeping in gasps and heaves. I put my arm around my brother's shoulders, but I can't think of anything to say. (The driver eyes us in the rearview mirror, then he snaps his attention back to the road as soon as our stares intersect.)

Max looks up at me and bravely smiles. "But there is a way out, Aaron. *Tateleh. Boychik*. I'm your big brother. There's only one way out, and you're the only one who can save me."

"Stop talking crazy, Max. What do you want me to do? Go out and rob a bank?" (Max doesn't know about the robbery, about the gunshots, about the rape, about anything.)

"No," he says. "It's not money I need from you. It's a favor. An enormous favor." His tear-streaked face already shows the smallest glimmer of joy, the junkie on the verge of another eternal fix. "It's tomorrow's ball game, Aaron. You're playing against a team personally recruited by Johnny Boy Manfredi, a big-heeled gambler from Chicago. Believe me, if you were in the business, you'd know who this guy is. Johnny Boy Manfredi from the South Side with two senators and the governor in his pocket. And this guy's got deep pockets, Aaron, so he's brought some players in from New York, some from Chicago, some big-shot AAU players from Wisconsin. Believe it or not, he's even got a guy from out here in Los Angeles that's a legit seven feet tall. I'm here to tell you that Manfredi's dishing out a lot of cash and putting his team up in style at the Beverly Hills Hilton. A hundred-percent swank. In fact, Manfredi's coaching the team himself and they've all been out here since last Thursday, practicing like crazy. Manfredi says they're the best team money can buy."

"So? We've played against plenty of good teams. Don't ever

underestimate us, Max. We're no slouches. Take Saul, for example .... He's improved a lot since you last saw him."

"Aaron. *Boychik*. That's not the point. It's ... it's more complicated than who wins or who loses."

The cabbie has taken us along the shoreline to see the waves driven landward, smashing into white splinters against the rocks. The sun glaring off the sand.

"Here's the deal," Max says, his red eyes feverish with hope and redemption. "The game is pick 'em. Strictly even-Steven. That's because you guys've been playing together for so long. You're battle-scarred and battle-smart. And the pot is winner-take-all."

"For how much?"

"Ten grand."

"Jesus!"

"There's a whole lot of money being bet, Aaron. In Chicago, in New York, from coast to coast. The smart-money boys in Chicago were impressed by how tough we played the Lakers in Oshkosh, and they're backing us to the hilt. I hear that Bugsy Siegel has twenty thousand riding on us."

"Holy shit, Max! I'm impressed. Sounds like we'll make some important friends if we win."

Max shakes his head with sad regret. "If you win, little brother, you'll make even more important enemies."

"How so? I don't understand."

"Before I left New York, Manfredi offered me a deal."

"Oh, shit!"

"Listen. Listen, Aaron. If we lose the game, this is what happens: Number one, each of you still gets five hundred bucks."

"That's not such a good deal, Max. We'll get almost fifteen hundred each if we win. I don't—"

"Listen, will you? Just shut the fuck up and listen for once in your life .... That's only the first part. Number two, if you lose, Manfredi will cover everybody's expenses until next Sunday. That's including the hotel and meals and everything. Think of it. Seven whole days counting today."

"Max!"

"Shut up! ... Number three, Manfredi will also handle my debt with Charlie the Cheat. Wipe it clean."

"That's good for you, Max, but what about—?"

"And number four, Aaron. There's a big number on Leo's ass. A bunch of high-priced goons are here from New York *and* Chicago to settle Leo's hash. What the hell happened in Chicago anyway? I just heard that somebody got shot. But it doesn't matter, Aaron. If you win tomorrow, Leo's a dead man. If you lose, Manfredi cashes in some markers and Leo lives to see another sunrise."

"Jesus!"

"It's up to you, Aaron. And you're the only one I've told about this. Just you, me, and Manfredi know. You can save me or bury me, little brother. You can pull the trigger on Leo. *Pow!*"

"Why not go to Leo and let him save his own ass?"

"You know better than that, Aaron. Leo, he'll turn the ball game into a Coney Island sideshow. Then the cat'll be out of the bag .... No, it's on you, Aaron. Little brother. Just you."

Leaning forward, Max opens the chauffeur's window just long enough to get us moving toward the hotel. Then Max licks his hands and runs them through his thin brown hair.

"So, *boychik*. Talk to me."

"I'm outraged, Max." (I say this calmly and with a rational demeanor. After all, a ball game is only a ball game.) "I'm fucking outraged that you could be so irresponsible. So weak. So fucking stupid .... "

"Ah," he says, forming his hands as though in prayer, already knowing that his prayers will be answered.

"So, Max, you shit-for-brains. Looks like I don't have much choice, do I? But let's be totally realistic here . . . . You know as well as I that I can't control a ball game. I'm just not that kind of player. Leo handles the ball and Mitchell gets most of the shots. My role is too limited for me to turn a game around by myself."

"There's no other way, Aaron."

"What about getting Brooks involved?"

"Crazy Brooks? No, we can't risk it. If the word ever got out, then we're all doing the *kazatski* in cement boots on the bottom of the ocean."

"I don't like it, Max. What am I supposed to tell the guys about our money? What should I say about the game?"

"Tell them I brought a cashier's check for the sixteen hundred because I didn't want to travel with all that cash. But the check won't clear the local bank until tomorrow afternoon. Tell them I'll give them their money after the game. And about the game? It's simple . . . . Five thousand bucks. Winner take all. That's all they need to know. The whole story will be in the newspapers anyway. Eight o'clock at the Pan-Pacific Auditorium. One-dollar general admission to keep the lowlifes away. Tell your guys to expect a big crowd and a tough game."

"I still don't get it, Max . . . . This Manfredi character, he's putting up the whole five grand by himself? Then if there's no fix, that means he takes all the risk? It doesn't figure."

"What about the ante-up money you got in your little old strongbox? Surely you would've bet some of it on yourselves anyway. Just like you did in Oklahoma City. Except that now the stakes are higher. You've got what? Nearly four grand so far?"

(What? Max expected us to bet our hard-earned stake all-or-nothing? What's wrong with him?)

It's time to tell Max about the debacle in Wyoming—and his face has a heart attack! "Jesus H. Christ! Why didn't you tell me?" But he recovers his composure too quickly and there's a slippery smile on his face when he adds, "Now you've *got* to do business, Aaron, or everybody winds up with *bupkes*."

Something's really fishy here. Sounds to me like even if Max matched Manfredi's five-thousand-dollar bet dollar-for-dollar, the deal still wouldn't sound kosher. Max has gone to all of this trouble—booking the tour through Livinski, buying and repairing the hearse, fully equipping seven players—for what? Just for the chance to win five grand? Just to have a game to bet on? His own rigged game to bet on?! Then I get it! Of course! Max was planning on us dumping this game from the get-go!

"Max! You fucker!"

He spreads his hands to show he has no hidden weapons, no more purloined cash. "What? What're you screaming? What'd I do now? Hey, nobody wins all the time."

By now we've reached the hotel, and the same red-uniformed marching band awaits us, to open the cab door, to grab Max's suitcase. Taking it all in style, Max flashes a hefty bankroll and tips the cabby five dollars. "Let me go check in," Max tells me. "I've got to make some telephone calls." Then he hides the far side of his mouth behind his left hand and whispers this: "Me and Mr. Bigtime haven't spoken in three days. I've got to contact him, then I'll come and get you later. All right, *boychik*? We'll have dinner or something."

Max casually snaps a crisp dollar bill at the nearest bellhop, saying loudly, "Hey, Junior. Is there a good steak joint around here?"

I knock gently on the door to my room, but there's no response. Now I have to return to the front desk to get another key. Inside the room, there's absolutely no sign of Debra. No luggage, no drawers full of lingerie, no nothing. I telephone Saul's room, but no one answers. Then I flop down on the soft, feathery bed only to discover that the intricately carved redwood footboard shortens the bed's length to maybe six feet. So I shove the mattress to the floor and surrender to my aching limbs, my weary brain . . . .

(I am tramped inside my own skull. My teeth are shut and grinding. My nose is a cave of winds. I take my nourishment from particles of food lodged in the fleshy folds at the base of my tongue. My source of moisture is a chronic postnasal drip. Sometimes I hear dim voices coming from my brain cavity. Maybe some other poor wretch is trapped inside here too.

Yes. Yes. I've heard all the rumors. There's supposed to be another opening at the very top of my skull, where a flowering lotus blossom grows and reaches into heaven. But every surface is solid and slick with blood.)

The sun has fallen by the time I wake up. And nobody's returned to their rooms. Not Max, not any of my teammates. What gives? How come I'm the only one with no place to go?

So I venture outside and eat a stringy hamburger from a greasy all-night grill down the street (just for the sake of filling my belly). Then I set out walking, aimlessly, down avenues bordered by palm trees, past shop-lined streets that are surprisingly devoid of pedestrians. In the shadow of a doorway, a man stands motionless, interrupted and hostile, until I pass by. Above me, a small rim of sky is barely infused with a pinkish incandescence. And the unlit stars remain a secret between me and God.

My attention is suddenly snagged by a passing vehicle—the Black Lady? No—a bright yellow Packard convertible driven by a pigtailed Chinaman wearing a yellow tuxedo.

At the end of a quiet street, I suddenly realize that someone is following me—a flick of my peripheral vision registering a crew-cut man only three paces behind my left shoulder. I try walking faster, then slower, and the man likewise adjusts his pace. I cut through a gas station onto Wilshire Boulevard and the man follows just as quickly. He makes no attempt to conceal himself, and somehow he seems so harmless that I execute a neat double fake and jump into perfect step at his side.

"Hey, bud," I say with a friendlier smile than I'd intended. "Are you following me?"

He's about five-foot-five. He has a thin face, smoky gray eyes, a pencil-line mustache. He wears an expensive sharkskin suit and costly alligator shoes. "Yes," he says matter-of-factly. "Nice night for a walk, ain't it?"

"Do I know you, little fellow? Do you know me?"

"No, no . . . I don't mean to be a bother. I just like to walk at night. Every night. But I have no friends, see? And I don't like to walk by myself. You don't have to talk to me if you don't want to."

"You mean you walk like this every night?"

"Mostly."

"What else do you do? For a living, I mean."

"I used to be an insurance salesman. Need any insurance? Life? Death? Disability? Floods. Pestilence. I even sold locust insurance, but it was very expensive. Anyway . . . Now I'm out of work. Home Relief pays me sixteen dollars and twenty cents every month. Do you know how much of California's population is currently on Home Relief? Twenty percent. The highest in the union. Anyway, I suffer from chronic insomnia, and sleeping pills don't work on me."

"That's awful. You mean you never get to sleep?"

"Maybe an hour a night. Sometimes two hours if I'm lucky. As fast as you're walking, I'll probably be very tired when I get home. How far are you going?"

"To the Golden Palms Hotel."

"I know the place. It's over on Vine Street in Hollywood. Funny, you know? Before the movies were such a big hit, Hollywood was just a small country village that used to grow vegetables for Los Angeles . . . . Over there . . . We have to make a left at the next corner. You must be rich to stay at the Golden Palms."

"Poor as a churchmouse," I say. "My brother . . . Well, it's a long story. Too long."

We march in perfect syncopation, with him taking three quick strides to equal two of mine. "Wiltshire Boulevard's just three streets over," he says. "It's one of my favorite streets. Did you know it's the busiest motorway in the world? And the first street anywhere with synchronized traffic lights?"

There's a slight twinge in my left knee as I step off a curb and cross the street. (Ouch! There it is again.) On the corner, a group of Mexican hoodlums laugh at us and make loud puckering noises. (Now it's gone.) I turn down a side street, past another orange grove, where a night-watchman clicks the safety on his shotgun as we cross his field of vision. Past more abandoned storefronts, neither of us speaking, until I say, "Hey, buddy, what'll you do when we get to the hotel?"

"Hopefully, I'll be able to latch on to somebody else. I'm like a hitchhiker, see? If there's nobody going out, then I'll lounge around the lobby. Sometimes I can even fall asleep in hotel lobbies."

The sky is now spotted with strange new stars, bigger and closer to my outstretched fingertips than the dim stars dangling over New York. And I'm feeling weary myself as we turn a corner and see the hotel's neon sign blinking at the far end of the block.

"What if you're walking with somebody on a deserted street?

And suddenly he enters a building, or climbs into a car, or hails a taxi? What if there's nobody around when this happens? Then what do you do?"

"I'm usually very careful about who I follow. I've got a sixth sense about it. But there was this one time when I followed some guy out into the sticks and it turned out he lived there in a shack in the hills. I swear I had this guy pegged for a long all-night walk. A round-tripper. Anyway, I curled up under a tree and I slept until the sun woke me up. Actually, I had a great night's sleep. Nearly four hours. But try as I might, I could never find the damn place again."

Outside the hotel, we meet a graybeard walking a fat, wheezing beagle on a long leash. "Good evening," I say to the man. "Nice night for a walk."

"Evenin' to you, young man. To the both of you young men. Surely is a lovely evenin' for a walk."

"Where're you headed, if I may ask?"

"Oh, just shufflin' along until Booley here finds a nice place to move his bowels. Of course, Booley here is a mite constipated in his old age. Come to think of it, so am I. So maybe we'll beat the milkman back home. Then again, maybe we won't either. Care to join us? I'm a talker if you're a listener. Took San Juan Hill with Gen'ral Teddy. Yes-sir-ree-bob."

"Sorry, I'm about to hit the hay. But would you mind giving a lift to a friend of mine?"

"Why, certainly."

Back in the room, there's still no trace of Debra. I put my ear, then my eyeball to the keyhole at the door of Saul's room. Then Kevin's room, Max's, and so on. Either nobody's around or they're all safely abed. It's past midnight, so the hotel switchboard is shut down, and I feel much too foolish to knock.

So I return to my own room and set myself down easily on the floor, feeling the heaviness of my body pushing into the soft mattress, pushing into the soft earth, into the soft darkness, falling . . . .

From Mitchell's Log:
Day Sixteen — January 21, 1936 — Monday

	Today	Total
Mileage	126	4,509
Expenses	$140.00	$475.97
Income	0	($3,535.00)

Net Income - $1,810.00
Average Share - $258.57 (Aaron minus $125.00)
Cash on Hand - $322.76 (A = $5.22, B = $2.54, L = $10, K = $20, M = $100)

Max Has - $1,600.00 (????)

Won - 44
Lost - 5

DAY 17

There comes a sharp-knuckled rapping at the door to wake me, to scatter my vague dreams of sorrow and loss. Dreaming of black shapes sucked into the whirling maw of something blacker.

Oh, yes. I remember—the gauze curtains gently ruffling as the sea breeze reaches inland. I'm not in the crypt. I'm lying balls-up under a clean white sheet, lying on a downy mattress set on a padded floor. Wearing only my boxer shorts. The stiff prick I hold in my shooting hand is aching to piss.

The knocking is reprised—bolder now, more insistent. Maybe it's the hotel's maids come to change the linen. "Go away! Come back later!" My first words of the day rattle with phlegm. My breath is thick and rancid. "Go away!"

Knockity-knock-knock. High up on the door. Too high for any maid to reach. "Aaron! Aaron!" The voice crying out is . . . Saul's.

"Yeah, Saul. I'm awake. Come in. The door's unlocked."(Unlocked to facilitate a quick getaway. Unlocked to allow easy entry for the queen of my heart.)

And there's big Saul, in his gabardine rabbi's trousers. Look, he's wearing a brand-new blue sports shirt, a short-sleeved model blooming with floral designs in red and yellow. The big guy starting "clean." The poor bastard. What he's been through. Saul, wearing his basketball shoes without socks, hunching and stooping through the doorway.

Following close behind is Debra, wearing a wrinkled blue gingham dress. She's obviously been crying—her eyes are moist and puffy.

They enter the room—with me lying there like a lox. With my dick in hand. Quickly, I fold my knees and hide my pisshose inside a white tent. Then I sit up and lock my hands around my shins. Chewing on my breath, trying to swallow, finally coughing, saying, "Good morning."

Debra presses the door closed behind her, and Saul steps boldly to the foot of the mattress, standing there, so far above me. From this lowly angle his head seems to brush the ceiling. As he stands there with his feet at shoulder-width, his knees loose, his legs bouncy, I fairly expect Saul to suddenly crouch and demonstrate a defensive sidestep. Instead, he fidgets with his fingers, then stuffs his big hands into his pants pockets.

"Aaron," he says nervously, shifting weight to establish his pivot foot, momentarily revealing Debra, who peeks at me through the space between Saul's left elbow and his hip. A naughty little girl afraid to face the music. "Aaron," Saul says, even more audacious. "We've got something to tell you."

I nod for him to continue, giving him my permission to proceed, hoping they've already run off and gotten married in Las Vegas. (Is it possible that God could be so merciful to all concerned?)

"Deb and me . . . Well, we wound up spending a lot of time together yesterday and we kind of hit it off . . . . " (Saul shifts his balance again, changing his pivot foot. He doesn't look very comfortable. He never does.) ". . . Anyway. Aaron? Deb even told me about the two of you. And everything? But you know something? I don't care, you know? I mean, she told me how you sent her the money for her to come out here and be with you and all . . . . I mean, I know it's your money, Aaron . . . For you and her. It's almost the same thing now, except it's me and her. Deb and me . . . We really . . . I mean, it just kind of came together that way. You know what I mean?"

Happy as I am to be off the hook, I've still been rejected and double-crossed. So I don't say a word. Not even a cough. Just to bust their chops a little. (Who cares about the money?) Will I pull a gun from between hidden thighs and shoot them both? Or shoot only myself? Will I roll over and go back to sleep? Will I bless them?

Debra remains hidden behind Saul's colossal form. Afraid to look at me. Deb.

"That's terrific, kids. I'm very happy for you both."

Saul reaches a long arm behind him and finds Debra's hand to hold. "Deb and me, we're feeling happy, Aaron. But not completely happy. You know? We also feel bad, like we did something behind your back. Like we cheated you."

"No no," I say quickly. "Not at all." I must press my thighs together to keep from pissing the bed.

"We're sorry if we hurt you, Aaron. But we . . . we love each other. Deb and me. I know it sounds so corny . . . . But I guess I don't really mind my life being corny. You know? . . . Anyway . . . So I don't know what else to say, Aaron. I mean, we didn't mean for this to happen. It just did."

"Mazel tov!" I say, afraid to relinquish my chokehold and reach up to shake his hand. "You two deserve every happiness." (I feel like an *alter kocker* on his deathbed.)

Debra is tucked out of sight—just Saul looming hugely, gushing with relief, and actually saying, "Thanks, Aaron! Thanks a million! When we get our money from Max, I swear I'll pay you back every penny that you sent to Deb. The whole a hundred and twenty-five bucks . . . . Jeez. You're such a sport, Aaron! You're such a great guy!"

I harumph silently, intending some kind of ironic contradiction, which Saul interprets as a signal for them to leave. Debra turns and opens the door, their ordeal over, escaping back into their young lives. In love.

"Wait a minute, you two! Hey, Saul! Not so fast! . . . You gotta tell me what your plans are. Saul? Are you still going to hang around Los Angeles? Or go back to New York? Or what else? I think I have a right to know . . . . Listen to me, will you? I sound just like a nagging father."

Debra has one foot over the threshold when Saul turns to me man-to-man. "They offered me a job," he says, his reddening, accentuating his bleeding youth. "At the MGM studio. We were out there yesterday on one of those guided tours, Deb, me, and Kevin. We were on a pirate-ship stage when some flashy-looking man walked over and started asking me questions. What's my name? How tall am I? Where'm I from? Stuff like that. The man said his name is Jonathan Holmes. He said he's a producer for MGM, a vice president of some department or other. He spoke real fast. Well, one thing led to another. You know? He treated the three of us to lunch and he said that he wants me to work for the studio. He offered me a job."

"What kind of job? Doing what?"

"Being the 'house monster.' That's the exact term he used. He said I could play all the giants and the monsters in all of MGM's movies. Would you believe it? Goliath, he said. They've already got a script. Paul Bunyan. The Cyclops. He said I was the right guy in the right place at the right time. He said they'll teach me how to act. He said I could have a long and prosperous career. He offered to pay me a hundred dollars a week for a whole year. Fifty-two weeks guaranteed. He said, if I want, he would also agree to act as my agent. As if that wasn't enough, he also promised to get Deb a job as a script girl. He said that was 'for starters'."

"And? What'd you say?"

"Well, we haven't decided yet for sure. We're supposed to go back and meet with him again today. To be honest, though, the whole business makes me feel even more like I'm some kind of sideshow freak. You know? And lately? I'm starting to think that maybe the only place where I ever really feel comfortable is on a basketball court. You know?"

"Yes. I know the feeling."

"Now, don't get the wrong idea, Aaron. I don't want to seem conceited or anything. But I'm also starting to think that someday I could maybe become a very good basketball player. Maybe?"

"Not maybe," I say, "definitely. And someday soon." (My knees are stiff and I must piss soon!) "Someday soon, Saul, you'll be a *very* good basketball player. I'm willing to bet on that. All right? Okay, so then what happens? So what good will it do you? How could you ever make a living playing basketball? Join another traveling circus? Talk about being a freak .... Saul ... what kind of life would that be for a young couple?

Yeah, maybe someday there might be another rinky-dink professional league like the old ALPB. Then you could at least get by. But right now? These are hard times, Saul. Any job at all's a good one."

He hunches his shoulders, confused, still resisting my arguments. "I know this movie deal could be a great opportunity," he says. "On the other hand, it's so . . . so public. You know? Look, I know that I've got no regrets about leaving the Hasidic life I left behind me in New York. But still . . . the *tzaddik*'s son in the movies?"

"Nobody will know it's you, Saul. You'll be wearing costumes and makeup. You'll change your name to something *goyische*."

"I've thought of that, Aaron. I don't know. The movies. It seems so trivial. Like I'm selling myself short."

"Ah! Short you'll never be. Listen, Saul. You don't have to do this Hollywood *mishegoss* forever. Work for the year he's offering, then you'll see what you'll see. Sufficient unto the day for you too, junior."

"I suppose you're right," he says, his long face finally flickering with the beginnings of a smile.

Meanwhile, Debra has released Saul's hand and moved furtively into the hallway. He senses her absence, then he leans forward and extends his big right hand down from on high. "Thanks again, Aaron. You're a real friend."

I can't move a muscle. "Wait a minute, Saul. Where's the fire? Before you go, there's still one more thing that's got to be done. I have to speak to Debra. Alone."

He moves to the doorway, pokes his head into the hall, and says, "Deb? Honey? I think maybe you should." She resists with some unseen motion, but he insists. "It's only fair. G'head, honey. I'll wait outside."

So she takes small, begrudging steps into the room while Saul shuts the door behind her. There she is, hugging her own shoulders, looking so alone and so vulnerable. Looking so young.

"Debra. It's okay what you and Saul are doing. If that's what you both want, that's fine with me. Only level with me, Debra. Are you being honest with him?"

"Yes," she says softly, obediently.

"Do you love him?"

"Yes. And Saul loves me too. He really does." Now she's crying. "It was crazy for me to come out here. I'm just a kid, Mr. Steiner, but you're supposed to be an adult. You're a teacher. It was you who should've known better. I just wanted to get out of the house so bad .... I talked myself into something that wasn't real. I guess we both did."

"You're absolutely right, Debra. I never really loved you and you never really loved me. Something similar to this happened to me once before, and I should have learned my lesson then. You're right, it was crazy from the start. And you're a brave girl, Debra. Braver than me."

I want to climb out of my shroud, to stand and look down at her. But I have to pee so badly that my back teeth are floating. So I gaze up at her (from this lowly vantage, the tender protrusions of her bosoms partially obscure her face). "Listen to me, Debra. Look at me." She finally peeps at me, her eyes still frightened, yet also amused by the clear sight of me hunched on the floor. "Saul is a wonderful guy, Debra. And I would be very upset if you ever did anything to hurt him. If you ever broke his heart."

"I swear," she says through her soft little-girl's tears. "I'll love him forever."

"All right," I say, believing her, forgiving her, dismissing her. "Now, get out of here. Go. Begone. I hope you both live happily ever after."

Then she runs pell-mell from the bearded dragon's den, slamming the door in her wake. I hear their muffled laughter from the hallway (now she's giggling like she's being tickled). And finally, I set to stand up and stumble in a mad rush to the bathroom.

Later, I find a telephone directory in the night-table drawer right next to the Gideon Bible, and I call MGM asking for Jonathan Holmes.

"Whom shall I say is calling, sir?"

"Just tell him it's a matter of life or death. His."

After a pause and some clicking noises: "Hello? Holmes here. Who's this?"

"This is Johnny Boy Manfredi, you punk. Ever hear of me?"

"Why, certainly, Mr. Man—"

"Well, get this and get it right the first time . . . . Those kids you spoke to at the studio yesterday? The big boy, Saul Jacobson? And the girl? Debra Goodman? Well, you better not be fucking with them."

"Mr. Manfredi, I assure you—"

"Shut your fucking mouth! You fucking shit-for-brains! You like your legs in one fucking piece? Huh? Then you don't fuck with them. *Capisce?*"

"Mr.—"

"You fucking dead piece of meat! You want someone should pay you a fucking visit? *Capisce?*"

"Yes, I *capisce*."

"Good." Then I hang up the phone.

There's no trace of Max downstairs, and I'm hungry—so I'll eat here in case he comes looking for me. (And, by the way, where the fuck is he?)

Glorinda's on duty in the dining room, activating her hired smile, letting me smell her lavender-scented tits as she leans forward to spread my menu on the table before me. "Good evening, sir. If you know what you want, I can take your order right away." She doesn't wear quite as much makeup as yesterday, and even her very breasts seem deflated. She seems sad—and I'm helplessly attracted to sadness.

As always, I'll have oatmeal, coffee, and a knavish curiosity. "Say there, girlie. What seems to be the trouble? You look like your cat just died."

"Nothing, sir," she says frostily. "There's nothing wrong."

"C'mon, Glorinda. Spit it out. Sometimes just the talking helps."

"Sometimes there's nothing to talk about," she says before turning toward the kitchen. (Maybe I should've left her a bigger tip.)

The lecher with the whip and the riding britches is now romancing a redhead. There's two hard-boiled yeggs squirming and ill at ease in white terry-cloth cabana outfits and eating waffles and ice cream. There's a quartet of stylish tennis players eating blinis. Two drunks in soiled tuxedos drink coffee. A countess feeds her schnauzer milk from a saucer atop the table. And on the chair next to me is a used copy of the *Los Angeles Times.*

New Jersey: Mabel Eaton loses custody of her children because of her Communist-party affiliation.
Texas: Mob of 200 lynches 2 Negroes accused of murder.
Cairo: 2 dead, 88 hurt in anti-British riots.
Ethiopia: Italian planes bomb Adowa.—1,700 die.
London: American oil companies to sell to Italy despite British plea for embargo.
Los Angeles: First annual L.A. Challenge Cup matches unbeaten California Crusaders against undefeated Moses All-Stars from New York. Game time is . . . The jackpot will be .

In the last paragraph, only the home team's roster is listed. I've heard of Richie Dalzell, he's the broad-shouldered #32 who most recently played me like a violin in Oshkosh. The other fourteen names belong to strangers. It also says here that Rennie Brown is an "officially measured seven-footer" from nearby Westwood High School.

Glorinda brings my food and sits uninvited in the opposite chair to face me from across the table. From a pocket in her apron she withdraws a pack of French cigarettes, a gold-plated lighter, and a small plastic ashtray. "I'm on my break," she explains, firing up on her own. "Look. I got you some fresh cream with your oatmeal instead of bottled milk."

"Thanks."

The smoke she wafts upward through her pursed lips looks like reddish dust. Then she picks a wet shred of tobacco from her lower lip, and says, "I didn't mean to snap at you, mister. Anybody ever tell you that you've got sympathetic eyes?"

"No, not really."

"Well, you do." She pats her name tag. "My name's Glorinda, as you can see. And you were right, something is bothering me. What it is is I didn't get the part. It was a spy movie, and the producer . . . he just wanted . . . Well, at least he got what *he* wanted. What did you say your name was?"

"Ummm. Aaron Steiner. Room One-seventeen. Ummm. I mean it's a tough town, huh?"

"Tough town. Tough racket. Tough shit on me because I'm still here. I swear to God. I got here ten years ago and what've I done? Slept my way into nine movies and wound up on the cutting-room floor every time. Here . . . this would have been it—the highlight of my so-called career, my one and only line."

The lady is definitely looking for something. No flowers and no violins. No sob stories and no promises. Just a good-time roll in the sack. Not a bad idea, eh?

All at once, I see Brooks rushing through the lobby on his way out the front door. "Sorry," I say to Glorinda, standing and fishing in my pockets for enough money to cover my bill. "Gotta run. It's an emergency. What time you get off work?"

"Nine o'clock by the book. Then I got to help set up for breakfast. That's an extra hour they don't pay me for. Usually around ten, ten-fifteen."

"Okay. Let's say ten-thirty. Unless the game goes overtime or something."

"What game? Who gets overtime?"

"Bye."

I overtake Brooks just as he's easing himself into the rear seat of a taxicab. He sees me and leaves the door open, permitting me to settle in beside him on plump leather seats with plenty of room to stretch my legs. The driver gears the cab into motion. "Where to, pal?"

To the driver Brooks says, "The nearest, most private stretch of beach." Brooks leaves the chauffeur's window open, saying to me, "Okay. You can come along if you promise not to talk about Ethiopia. Not one single, solitary word."

Fifteen minutes later, Brooks and I are striding slowly along a nameless beach, a narrow stripe of gray sand separating the thundering ocean and the highway. The sky above us clots into thick gray clouds that promise rain. The wind is chilling and we must increase our pace to stay warm. Neither Brooks nor I have spoken since he established the ground rules.

What can I say to him that doesn't invoke the forbidden subject? Should I spill the beans about Max and his plan for tonight's game? Or maybe Max is right and the risk of disclosure is too great. Finally, I say this: "Brooks. Tell me straight up and no U-turns. Why did we shave points at Metro? Yeah, I know we hated Coach Halperin. Yeah, I know everybody was doing it. And yeah, we needed the money. We deserved the money. Yeah, yeah. I was so scared shitless of getting caught with all that cash that I went out and spent it as fast as I could. On clothes that I didn't need. On girls I didn't like. You did the same thing, Brooks. So, when all was said and done, it didn't even seem like the money was real, did it? It was play money. It's been how many years? And the only reason I can come up with is that I did it because you did it."

"That's bullshit. You were a consenting adult. It's too easy to put the blame on me."

"I'm not blaming you, Brooks. I always took full responsibility. I'm just looking for reasons."

"Speaking only for myself," he says with a sly grin, "I'd be lying if I told you that I don't like money. Only suckers want to be poor. I like to spend money fast and furious. I like to live high on the hog. Just like everybody else. And money talks in a loud voice, Aaron—don't bullshit me and don't bullshit yourself."

I nod, silently admitting that I did enjoy having cash in my pockets. That I did enjoy indulging myself.

"But I also tilted those ball games just to cause trouble," he says. "To make the fat cats tremble and further the revolution. To be subversive." He laughs grimly. "That's what I told myself back then. Now it all seems so funny. Going through all that trouble, the lying and the scheming, for some bullshit utopian ideals. Everything comes back to that. I don't know. Maybe everything's even simpler. Maybe you and me, maybe we're just crooks at heart. Ha! And here's a little secret for you, Aaron: I was the main connection. Not Lefty. Not Sidney. Not Marty. Lefty dished out the money, but I was the main line to Benedetto, to that Irish jerkoff from Chelsea, to Charlie the Cheat. To Max. Ha! Fooled you, didn't I? I was also the team's high scorer, remember? The most influential player. That's why I also got paid double what everybody else got."

I can't help laughing. "You capitalist pig! You double agent! You fucking asshole! Max was involved too?"

Brooks's grim lips stretch into a self-indulgent smile. "Yeah," he says. "Well, listen to this: There were more ball games in the bag than you ever knew."

"What? How many? Which ones? Tell me, you fuck. Which ones? When we were seniors . . . against Brooklyn College, right?"

"That's one."

"I knew it! I fucking knew it! What else? What else?"

He doesn't answer, pausing instead to pick up a seashell, holding it to his ear. Then he kicks at a clump of seaweed.

"Come on, Brooks! Tell me!"

He finds a stick to poke at the gelid corpse of a slimy sea-thing. Then he stares at me and says, "It doesn't matter anymore, Aaron. All that matters is that basketball should be a celebration. A communion. A joyful dance. Ten players playing one game, and it doesn't matter who wins or loses. That's what it should be and that's what it was when we were kids. Remember, Aaron? Even the half-court games in the schoolyard. The pickup games at Henry Street. The high school games. The freshman team at Metro. When playing basketball almost sanctified us. Remember? When everybody played his proper role and everybody surrendered to the flow. Remember? When life was a metaphor for basketball."

I nod in silent remembrance. Torn pants. Bloody noses. Joy in my heart.

"Maybe," he says, "doing business was the wrong thing to do for all the right reasons. That's why it never worked for us, Aaron. That's why there'll never be any redemption for us. No matter how many games we play for how much money in how many different cities. Whether we win or lose, Aaron, we've already lost."

"No, Brooks. That can't be right. At the start of every game the score is always nothing-nothing. There's no use playing if we've already lost." (What am I saying? What would Max do if he heard this?)

"Ah, this is all bullshit, Aaron. Winning, losing. What's the fucking difference? Do you think I believe that the Ethiopians can win their war? You want to know something? Maybe I don't even give a fuck about the Ethiopians. Maybe I'm doing what I'm doing only because I hate the fascists so much. Those bastards'll kill us all if we don't kill them first. That doesn't seem like much, Aaron. It's easier to hate than it is to love. But that's all I've got. The only question, Aaron, is will you come with me?"

"Brooks—"

"I don't want to argue with you, Aaron. Yes or no."

"Brooks . . . of course not. No—all right? I'm not crazy . . . . "

Then he walks away to sit on the sand and remove his shoes and socks. Without bothering to roll up his pants, Brooks wades into the surf. For a moment I'm afraid he'll keep walking and never come back. But he stops when he's knee-deep, standing there immobilized and blind like the masthead of a half-sunken ship.

"Brooksie."

"Go away," he says into the wind, the words reaching me from someplace far away. "Just go away."

My left knee is stiff as I slowly stalk the margin of the highway, ignoring the oncoming traffic, oblivious of my destination. Then I see a red and tan bus approaching from the opposite direction—the sign above the front windshield is LOS ANGELES—so I weave through the traffic and wave for the bus to stop.

Through a billowing of black smoke, the door hisses open to reveal the driver in his neat white shirt with a black tie and a black-brimmed blue-pie hat with a badge mounted on the front. His eyes seize the road and he talks to me out of the right side of his mouth. "How far you going, bub?"

"That depends on how close I can get to the Golden Palms Hotel on Vine Street."

Without another word, he pulls a steel lever that closes the passenger door with another pneumatic hiss, sealing me inside this rumbling iron lung on wheels. Only when the bus starts rolling forward does the driver poke the stainless-steel coinbox with his nearest elbow. "We stop seven blocks east of there. That'll cost you four cents, bub." So I deposit my pennies and step to the rear.

There's a seat near the exit door, and I squeeze in beside an old colored man wearing blindman's eyeglasses and holding a metal-tipped cane tightly between his thighs. Most of the other passengers are Mexicans—men in sandals and serapes, overalls or cotton pants. In the backseat, a Mexican woman draped in a black shawl cradles a dead chicken in her lap. Across the aisle, a pair of towheaded farmboys sneak sips from a bottle of red-eye. But nobody talks. We listen instead to the thrumming of the tires and the groaning of the gears.

We pass a road crew of jailbirds in their dirty gray-and-white-striped home uniforms, assigned to digging irrigation ditches. Their labors are overseen by a cop and his shotgun, so the convicts shovel and dig like there's no tomorrow.

Except for the driver and the blindman, everybody on the bus turns to see them. One of the farmboys offers the convicts a silent toast.

Back in the lobby there are no messages awaiting me, and Max still isn't in his room. Could he already be in trouble with Manfredi? Fucking Max, the sneaky bastard, it would only serve him right.

However, I do spot Leo in the dining room—talking a mile a minute over grilled-cheese sandwiches to some tanned, leathery-faced man who's dressed in chino pants and a gray sweatshirt. And there's Glorinda, hustling from table to table with her big, happy tits and her small, sad smile.

Upstairs in the hallway just outside my door, a maid smiles and curtsies as we pass. When she thinks she's safely out of my field of vision, she pinwheels an extended forefinger around her own ear to demonstrate to whatever invisible spirits are present that I'm the one who's crazy. A crazy Jew who sleeps on the floor.

Unlocking the door, I note the mattress unmoved and the sheets changed. Then I step out of my clothes and into the shower stall, where the hot water soon pinks my skin. Too bad the showerhead is built to accommodate midgets, forcing me to stoop and twist just to wet my face and hair. Afterward, after toweling my limbs I forget to duck and I bang my noggin on the low-lying doorjamb. It raises a small lump just below my hairline and produces a drop of blood that drips down my forehead, rolling right between my eyes and down the length of my nose. A single drop that I catch with my tongue—it tastes sweet and warm.

It was only a glancing blow, so the swelling will soon cease and the small wound will seal itself. In the meantime, I'll lie back on the mattress, clasping my hands behind my head, staring at the gold-speckled ceiling. Thinking, after all, that Brooks is wrong just this once. Thinking that the only true commitment is to life.

We meet in the lobby, everybody except me and Brooks happy-faced and talkative.

"Did you guys read the story in the papers?"

"Five thousand bucks!"

"Holy shit!"

"We gotta *win* tonight!"

"Anybody seen Max?"

"Yeah," I say. "He says he'll meet us over at the auditorium."

The directions Mitchell has obtained from the desk clerk are slightly ambiguous. A left, a right, another left? Turn here. Yes. No. Leo and Mitchell are poised for another nasty go-round until Saul points out the front window to the sky.

"Look," Saul says. And lo—it's another spotlight, the beam still hazy in the gathering grayness of evening. "I'll bet that's for us."

And it is. We follow the beacon and soon come to the edge of a huge tarmac parking lot. There's the slowly revolving klieg lights attended by a man wearing coveralls and smoking a cigar. Behind them, looking west toward the sea, is a surprisingly squat concrete building, apparently windowless, resembling some kind of futuristic bomb shelter, like Ming the Merciless' last resort. Indeed, the entry steps lead downward to a thick iron door below the skin of the earth.

Inside, the electric daylight casts no shadows—and there's nobody on hand to greet us. Just numerous vendors in dark gray uniforms unwrapping packages of pinkish frankfurters. Other workers are greasing grills, popping corn, or chipping away at large blocks of ice. On our own we wander farther down another staircase, down to the lowest subterranean level, where we find the basketball court. The floorboards are shiny, the footing a little slick. The baskets themselves are anchored by the traditional stanchions and also secured by long guylines stretching from the upper corners of the backboards to certain attachments high in the whitewashed ceiling. Both sidelines sport permanent grandstands, showing gray rows of plastic folding seats, sitting unused and upright, like nameless tombstones of massacred heroes. And an old colored man in denim overalls slowly pushes a wet gray mop toward the naval of the court, the center-jump circle.

"Sir?" Mitchell calls to him.

The old man looks at us and points to a doorway near the

opposite end of the court. "Thadaway."

"Thanks, gramps," Ron says.

Then we duck our heads through the appointed portal, moving down another long flight of stairs, clanky and dusty as ever, until we come upon a set of black doors marked LOCKERS. The door on the right has been thickly chalked with a cross, the left-handed door shows a Star of David.

Our locker room is immaculately clean, the lockers full length and double width. There's a blackboard attached to one wall, and a small grooved shelf below holds several lengths of virginal chalk and a felt eraser. Several padded folding chairs sit perched before the lockers, and the middle of the room contains a padded trainer's table.

"High-class," says Mitchell. "You could eat a meal off the floor."

Barely a minute after our own arrival, a young man in white pants and a white polo shirt pokes his head in the doorway and says, "Anybody need to be taped?" He's maybe twenty and he has cold red eyes like an attendant in a mental institution.

"Sure," says Mitchell. "You can tape both my ankles and a couple of jammed fingers too. So long as it's free."

It is—so we all volunteer, taking turns on the table, the veterans before the rookies. *Zip, zip, zip.* The trainer tears the cold tape effortlessly with his fingers, rapidly encasing ankles and fingers in wrinkle-free and seamless armor. When it's my turn, I ask the young fellow if he'd kindly inspect my left knee. He gladly obliges, manipulating the joint thoroughly, then he flexes and pokes at the "devil's triangle," arousing an occasional stabbing pain.

"Could be any one of several different problems," he says. "There's definitely a small bulge right here." He gently touches, almost caresses, the apex of the triangle where the cartilage is most vulnerable. "Could be arthritis, or a sprained ligament. Or it could be a meniscus tear. There's no way to tell without opening the area and having a look-see. Personally, I'd advise you to lay off for a while."

"I've got to play. We only have seven players."

"At least let me tape it so maybe it won't get any worse. That's also a nasty-looking finger you've got there. Let me tape that too."

"Nah, that's okay. I once had a sprained knee taped in college and I played the worst game of my life. The tape job was worse than the injury. Ankles, fine. But I don't want any tape where it shows. I don't need any excuses."

He shrugs with monumental indifference. "Suit yourself."

After all of our lumpy, puffy, veiny ankles have been mummified, the trainer solicits our names for the "official" scorebook and the "official" player introductions. Undeterred, Leo identifies himself as "Gregory Dodge."

We're making last-minute adjustments, tightening bootlaces, cinching the belts on our shorts, positioning our hip pads, when Mitchell notices a fresh red bruise on Kevin's left shoulder.

"What the fuck is that?"

Kevin blushes furiously. "I got a job today," he says, "as a stuntman and stand-in at the movie studio. They had me try out by jumping from a moving car and landing on a mattress that was covered with dirt. Well, I guess I almost missed the damn mattress and that's how this thing happened. Still and all, they did offer me a job for ten bucks a day. So I took it!"

"That's great!"

"Good going, Kevin!"

Leo is also bristling with news to tell: "Me too! I got a new job too! I found my old buddy, that guy I told you about who's the athletic director at Orange County University? Well, starting next season, I'm his new varsity basketball coach. Twenty-one hundred a year, with a free car and everything. Shit! I even got me a new name to use: Gregory Dodge. Remember those fake I.D.'s me and Ron got in the city? That's right. Nobody's gonna know me. Nobody's gonna find me. Coach Gregory Dodge, that's me. You guys can call me Greg."

We all cluck with congratulations and smile at one another in secret. Leo a coach? Leo a leader of young men? Preposterous.

"Okay," says Mitchell, "I'm delighted to hear that some of us are so gainfully employed. But where the fuck is Max?"

The door opens on cue, only it's Ron bringing his latest (and last) scouting report: "They've got fifteen guys in uniform, and every one of them's for real. The seven-footer is kind of thin and clumsy. Also looks like he only wants to hook right. But he has long arms and, I swear, he almost makes Saul look normal. And, Aaron? Remember that big blond gorilla that kicked your ass up and down the court in Oshkosh?"

"Yeah. I know he's here. I recognized his name in the paper."

"I didn't recognize any of the other guys," Ron says. "But whoever the guards are, none of them miss too much from the outside. Twelve can shoot from the half-court line. There's a Number Sixteen got a running one-hander. Ten got a running hook shot going either way. Number One's a little runt, maybe five-foot-three, but he shoots the lights out with a real quick release. They also got a bunch of big guys who look like good athletes. Far as I can tell, this is a very excellent team."

"What else?" Mitchell asks. "What's the house like? Did you see the referees?"

"Fuck the referees," says Ron. "No, I didn't see them. I did see the crowd. Maybe two grand already here. Room for another five hundred. It's like a Broadway crowd in the summertime. Plenty of highfalutin tootsies. Plenty of wiseguys wearing snappy duds and smoking Cuban cheroots. No-neck apes everywhere you look. I saw one guy, he—"

Ron is interrupted by Max, bursting through the door, dressed in gray pants, white shirt, a red bow tie, and a blue blazer, smiling like he's just been elected dogcatcher, and waving a thick manila envelope that's been hastily sealed with a strip of adhesive tape. "Howdy, boyos," Max says grandly. "Got your dough right here just like I said I would. Well, I don't want to interfere with your strategy session here. So I'll see you right after the game. Good luck, boyos." Then just as abruptly, Max is gone, and the closing door slowly settles on its hinges.

"What's he got in that envelope?" Mitchell wonders. "His IOUs? His dirty drawers? I didn't see any green dollars. Did any of you?"

"Not me," says Leo.

"Lay off!" I say sharply. "Max isn't going anywhere. And don't we have more pressing business to worry about?"

"Yeah," says Ron. "Five thousand smackeroos!"

"That's right!"

"Let's kick their ass!"

Operating under some unspoken yet instinctive summons, we slowly gather ourselves in a tight semicircle around Brooks's locker. He's still dicking with his jockstrap and he's startled when he looks up and sees us. "Oh," he says. Then Brooks closes his eyes and gently pinches the bridge of his nose, gathering his thoughts, preparing our ultimate strategy.

"We've got to realize," he finally says, "that the odds are very long against us. We're tired. They're rested. We're seriously outnumbered. We've also got to anticipate that this ball game undoubtedly represents the last time that we, the 1936 edition of the House of Moses All-Stars—God forbid there should ever be another edition—that this is the last time we'll ever play together. All of us on the same team. So what we each have to do tonight is to play this game with a certain attitude. We have to play like this is the last time any of us will ever play basketball again." He looks straight at me. "Ever again. In our entire lives." Now he looks around the circle, smiles, and bends forward to fiddle with his shoelaces.

"That's it?" Mitchell asks. "Nothing about slowing the pace? Nothing about playing a zone defense to avoid fouls?"

Brooks laughs silently. "You don't need to be told something you already know. Do you?"

Kevin is confused. Saul is deflated. Ron is merely annoyed. And Leo sniggers into the privacy of his own hands.

"C'mon guys!" Mitchell barks. "Let's get excited! We've got five grand on the lines! C'mon! One more time! Let's go get it!"

"Yeah!" says Saul. "That comes to seven hundred fourteen dollars and twenty-eight cents each!"

"Let's do it!" Mitchell screams in a mild hysteria. "The House of Moses All-Stars rides again! Are we ready to win?"

"Yeah!" Leo shouts. "Five thousand fucking bucks!"

Our arrival on the court prompts a few faint cheers that are quickly overwhelmed by generally polite and harmless boos. (In all our travels, why haven't we ever played in a synagogue? Why haven't we ever been the good guys? Because, instead of gymnasiums, synagogues have libraries.)

The Crusaders wear white uniforms with gold crosses stitched on the front of their jerseys. There's #32 from Oshkosh, Richie Dalzell, spitting into his hands, rubbing them together and laughing at me. There's the seven-footer—ugly as sin, with fiery red blotches on his cheeks, with dim eyes and a protruding jawbone. There's Max perched owlishly behind our bench, but I can't locate Debra.

Sitting between two slack-jawed goons near the end of the Crusaders' bench, that must be Johnny Boy Manfredi. He's short and slim, probably in his early fifties—dressed in a pinstriped suit, with a red tie, a red handkerchief drooping from his breast pocket, and on his shoes, red spats to match. A dapper little tyrant with his hair slicked back. Somebody probably aims his dick for him when he pees. What the fuck does a squirt like him know about coaching a big-time basketball team? Advantage to us.

The two referees in striped shirts are thin, cadaverous men who might easily be related to Manfredi. With much ado, they invite the team captains to meet at centercourt, then they squint at Mitchell with serpents' eyes that never blink.

The teams are introduced to the crowd by a small man, who carefully articulates the names into a handheld microphone. His amplified voice sounds huge and all-knowing. "Starting at center for the Moses All-Stars is Number Six, Aaron Steiner. Number Six." One by one, we jog oncourt to line up at the nearest foul line. Imagine Leo's surprise when he's introduced thusly: "Starting at left guard for the visitors is Number Two, Leo Gilbert. Number Two." Leo runs a furtive zigzag route to join the rest of us, then he shoves in between me and Saul while a U.S. Marine plays the national anthem on a bugle.

"All right," Brooks says in our brief huddle. "Remember what Sun Dancer said: It's a good day to die."

"Jesus," moans Leo. "I don't want to die!"

I shake hands with the lump-jawed seven-footer, gripping hard and sudden to crunch his knuckles. "Hey!" he says, wringing the pain from his shooting hand. "What're you, crazy?"

"You bet I am."

When the ball is tossed, once again I move quickly and surreptitiously, stepping on the big man's toes as I leap for the ball. "Hey!" he repeats, but I capture the game's first possession.

The runt is good enough to start at point guard opposite Leo. The little man soon proves to be a bloodsucker on defense, snipping at Leo's dribble, forcing our best ball handler to quickly unload the ball to Ron. Initiating our three-man weave, Ron passes to Mitchell, who promptly turns and snaps off a sudden set shot from beyond the key that neatly plugs the ring.

The scoreboard blinks twice:

HOME - 0 **VISITORS - 2**

As the Crusaders prepare their attack, I assume a legitimate defensive stance, only to have the seven-footer plow my chest with his elbow. Naturally, I defend myself with a forearm clout, thereby giving one of the zebra brothers the chance to tweet his tweeter and call the game's first foul on me. (Foul trouble! Unjustly dispensed! The perfect way out?)

The Crusaders' antizone offense is an elementary four-man rotation, with the "Footer" nailed to the left side of the low post. Otherwise, they're a tricky bunch: Number 32 is chasing Brooks, and he's as mean as ever, the master of the moving pick. Number 16 can shoot like Sergeant York. And the runt is quick yet careful with every possession.

The game unwinds, I continue leaning on the Footer, forcing him left to the baseline, laboring to box him off the boards. All the while, the big fellow directs a nonstop monologue at the refs: "Watch his elbow! Look! He's holding me! Ref! Call the foul!"

Sure enough, when the Footer attempts a turnaround pivot shot from in close, I'm there to swat the ball right back into his ugly face. The sound of skin-on-leather-on-skin. *Whappity-whap!* Next comes a shrill birdcall, and another foul is pinned on me. "That's right!" the Footer shouts.

We lead, 8–4, even though Leo is tentative with his handle and reluctant to shoot. He's apparently convinced that without the ball in his hands he's less liable to be drilled by the worst shot of all, the one you hear too late. So Leo passes too quickly, too often, and our offense is sporadic. Only Mitchell's artistic shooting keeps us ahead.

HOME • 7 **VISITORS • 12**

Brooks is playing his last game with young, lively legs—he's quicker than #32 and able to launch his step-back one-hander at will. Ron plays savagely as ever, bumping #12 and denying him the ball.

For me, no shots mean no misses. Otherwise, I nail all my designated picks. I rebound with all my might and I battle the Footer. OUCH! A pass from Leo bounces off my sore finger and rolls out of bounds. It's a costly turnover at the time, drawing an angry glance from Ron. So far, I haven't deliberately turned a single play against us. Not yet.

We're up 17–10 and Mitchell's having a hot time in the old town tonight. Even when he gets knocked on his duff, Mitchell gets off the floor laughing and cans the foul shot.

Now our lead stretches to 20–11 into the second quarter, with Mitchell having tallied thirteen of our total score. How long can this last?

"Ref!" the Footer whines. "He's holding me!"

"Shut up, you big baby!" I yell at him. "Just play the fucking game like a man!" Then I shove the big pussy too openly and pick up personal foul number two.

To open the second period, Coach Manfredi has asked the runt to move over and guard Mitchell, a shrewd move that effectively denies Mitchell the ball. The maneuver conversely relaxes the defensive pressure on Leo, who continues shunting the ball to Ron.

"Two fouls!" Mitchell yells at me in passing. "Be careful!" To Leo, Mitchell shouts, "Shoot the fucking ball!"

HOME • 17 **VISITORS • 22**

"Hey! Ref! Get him offa me! Don't let him do that! It's illegal! Ref!"

And I'm disgusted with the kid, the fucking Milquetoast! I know he has no guts, because referees are a necessary evil whose dark powers are never conjured by any self-respecting clutch-shooting ballplayer.

HOME • 21 **VISITORS • 24**

Here I go, foolishly trying to run down a loose ball, arriving at the critical junction about five years too late, having to cut too sharply, my left knee suddenly agonizing even as the ball bounces off my outstretched right hand. "White ball!" says the ref. Thankfully the action takes place near our bench.

"Saul," I say. "Go in for me. You've got the big kid."

It's a high-scoring game—Manfredi is intent on utilizing his entire stable, substituting three and four players at a time. That's why the Crusaders never really develop any continuity at either end. Sure, they make fabulous moves and even better shots. Their field-goal percentage must be close to 50-50, but their turnovers are high. Bang! Number 16 evades Ron's defense and hits another one. At the next whistle, #16 is replaced by #8, who twists gracefully to the basket, only to miss a complicated layup.

HOME • 26 **VISITORS • 27**

Brooks rides a hot streak, and the teams trade baskets. And here's Saul, playing the game of his young life, banking in hooks with either hand and rebounding as if each loose ball contained Debra's heart. The Footer is clearly Goliath, and Saul is suddenly playing without the small hesitations of self-consciousness. One of Saul's drop shots lifts the crowd to its feet.

Kevin is in for Brooks—to snag a running one-hander and then put back a rebound over the top of #32. At the half, we cling to a 34–31 lead.

Someone has snuck into the locker room and drawn a swastika on the blackboard. Kevin has the valuables bag, and we each inspect our lockers to see if anything's missing.

"I'm okay," says Mitchell.

"Same here."

"Yup."

We piss as needed. We blot our faces with our own dry and crusty towels. We sit down or stand up. We sip water from the faucet. But nobody offers a first-half critique nor a second-half strategy. Mitchell splashes his face with water. Brooks lies napping on the trainer's table. Sitting quietly seems like a good idea to me too.

After a while, the old colored man knocks on the door. "They's all ready to go get started up."

We're regrouping on the bench, when Max pulls on my arms from behind and hisses, "Aaron! Look up at the scoreboard! What gives?" But I studiously ignore him.

Before our huddle disperses, Leo says, "Let's try surprising them with a man-to-man. They'll never expect it."

Brooks says nothing, so we agree on defensive assignments. Leo wants to guard the runt.

The Footer easily captures the subsequent tip-off, and the runt quickly blows past Leo for an easy score. We try regrouping in a 1-3-1 zone, but the Crusaders easily shoot us to pieces. Desperate to try something new, Brooks goes to the bench, and I play in tandem with

Saul. The two of us play hard and big in the shadow of the basket. Saul's defense confounds the Footer, and I'm having more success than anticipated controlling #32. Until inevitably, the foe's superior numbers begin to tell. Early in the fourth quarter we're finally caught from behind and passed.

HOME • **45** VISITORS • **44**

Before long, another foolish but inadvertent foul (my fourth) forces me to the bench, where, with a towel draped over my knees like an old man in a wheelchair, I watch Saul miss a hard-angled lefty hook. Behind me, Max hoots softly as #12 finds the range and the Crusaders extend their advantage.

"Good job, boyo," Max whispers in my ear. "You're losing by six with only five minutes left." He pats my back, watching as Saul maneuvers around the Footer for a layup. Watching as Saul executes a give-and-go with Brooks. "Maybe," says Max. "Maybe you should go back in for Saul. What's come over him? He used to be such a stiff!"

(I make believe I can't hear him over the crowd's noise.)

As the game gets shorter, I remain benchbound while Saul continues to play out of his mind: Out-hustling the Footer, and outsizing #32 and everyone else who tries guarding him. The clock hands slowly circle. Three minutes. Two-and-a-half.

HOME • **54** VISITORS • **53**

"Aaron!" Max bleats. "Get in there and do something!"

Down the stretch, Brooks has another spurt, and with barely a minute left, he converts a driving hook to put us ahead 61–59. Now Max is cursing. "Aaron! You fucking *putz*! Get back in the fucking game already!"

And he's right. It's time for me to do something.

We're down to our last precious time-out, so I report to the scorer's table, then crouch near the sideline, waiting for the next dead ball . . . . Meanwhile, the game proceeds.

The runt convinces Leo that a head fake is for real, then calmly steps back and sinks a long, arching set shot to tie the score at 61. Leo is pissed and immediately retaliates, taking Saul's inbounds pass and trying to cut his dribble through a knot of defenders. Too bad the runt calmly reaches into Leo's breadbasket and steals the leather loaf . . . . Here comes the runt furiously dribbling upcourt ahead of the pack . . . . And here comes Leo running for his life, diving and crashing the runt to the floor before the shot is released. *TWEET!* It's Leo's fifth foul, so he's banished to the bench, to sit there with a towel over his head, unseeing and hopefully unseen, while the runt makes the free throw. The Crusaders lead 62–61 with only twenty-one ticks left in the ball game when Brooks calls our last time-out.

"We have to run the staggered pick for me," Mitchell insists.

Brooks hesitates—does he want the last shot for himself? Then he shrugs and says, "Okay. The staggered pick for Mitchell. But give it to me, Mitchell, if you get stuck. I've got the feeling tonight."

"I always have the feeling," says Mitchell.

Just before the huddle breaks, I say, "Saul, I'm in for you."

Several of my teammates are alarmed. "That's not such a good idea," Mitchell suggests.

"I don't think so either," says Brooks.

But my logic is flawless: "Who else is going to set the second pick? Does Saul set a better pick than me? Now is when experience counts."

"I don't know," says Mitchell.

Ron also resists. "Saul's playing his ass off. Leave him in."

"I know what I'm doing," I say. (Should I tell them it's a matter of life or death?)

Then Saul and I catch each other staring. He's puzzled, unsure of propriety, of the correct strategy. At the same time, I'm unswervingly grim and resolute, overpowering him for any number of reasons. Saul looks away, saying, "I'm tired anyhow. There's a cramp in my calf. Go get 'em, Aaron."

The play is designed for Mitchell, with, as always, an emergency option for Brooks. Apparently, the game is already out of my hands. But Mitchell is exhausted and he can't shake the runt's relentless defense. So Ron passes the ball to Brooks along the right baseline, where Brooks head-fakes and initiates his dribble, still faking, believing he can eventually beat his man. Meanwhile, I jump into the same-side pivot and lock the Footer behind me. Brooks still hasn't gained an advantage and he pulls up his dribble with the clock ticking loudly.

"Gimme!" I shout at Brooks. "Gimme! I got him!"

Brooks is on the verge of pulling the trigger anyway, attempting a long and lateral hook shot, sans backboard, the worst possible angle.

"Brooks! Brooksie! Gimme! Gimme the fucking ball!"

Which he does—a tight bounce pass that I catch left-handed. Not a moment too soon, I dribble hard left into the lane, then I reverse pivot on my left foot, hoping to initiate my trusty right-handed hooker. And my knee holds! And suddenly my body is perfectly synced . . . . Here comes the left elbow to protect the ball. Now the left shoulder rotates in good time. Twenty years of practice, tens of thousands of repetitions, and my movements are automatic. I could be defended by the Statue of Liberty and the shot would be true. Max? Leo? Who the fuck are they? My body is older and wiser than my mind. Winning is always better than losing. Winning is next to godliness. How could I stomach being the ultimate reason why that fuck-jawed, pimple-faced, overgrown wimp wins the fucking ball game? Besides, it's too late to miss anyway. The conditioned reflex has been activated and nothing can stop me now. I know that my one and only shot is good before it leaves my hand ...

But ...

But the ball rolls off my tender finger and my hand recoils unawares. Now the spin imparted is slightly horizontal .... Even so, the ball rides around the ring once before falling out of grace just as the buzzer sounds.

"Shit!" I scream, but nobody hears me.

Then, while the Crusaders jump into one another's arms, yelling and celebrating, the House of Moses All-Stars move quickly and unnoticed into our locker room.

We sit slumped in the chairs, no one moving to the showers, no one speaking. Dripping with sweat. Mitchell is crying into his hands. Crying like a baby. And for what? $714.28?

Brooks's mask is impenetrable. Ron curses a blue streak under his breath and aims strange looks in my direction. Leo hides once more under the draped towel. Both rookies stare dumbly at their shoes.

But I'm strangely calm and peaceful: Because I was in the flow. Because there was a certain small communion. Yes, because everybody played their role perfectly. Me, the ritual sacrifice. And God, the Ultimate Fixer. Yes. There's a balance here that soothes me.

Still, it's a somber scene until Max blusters into the room, cursing tightly to mask his glee. "Goddammit! Shit! I swore Aaron's shot was down the chute!" Max stomps around the room, deftly straightening his bow tie as he passes a mirror. Then he's beside me, whispering in my ear, "Masterful! You're a genius! Nobody suspects a thing!"

Mitchell sees the two brothers conspiring against him and he screams in his agony: "Max! You fucking ganef! Where's our fucking money!?"

Max is pleased to pluck a pair of manila envelopes from the inside pocket of his jacket, both envelopes freshly sealed with gray masking tape. "Here it is, boyos. Every penny accounted for. Sixteen hundred smackers."

Mitchell snatches the envelope, wets his fingers, and begins counting the bills.

"And I've also got a little surprise for you boyos," Max beams. "Out of my deep appreciation for your long ordeals these past few weeks. And especially for the dreadful screwing you got in Wyoming. Here's a little bonus for each of you!" He takes a fistful of bills out of the second envelope. "Two hundred bucks each! From me to you! How about them apples? Just my way of saying thank you!"

Max gladhands the envelope to Mitchell without another word.

"My God!" Mitchell yelps. "It's true! Here's the sixteen hundred he owes us! And here's another fourteen hundred! . . . Max! I'm sorry for ever doubting you! Max! I take back every suspicious word I ever—"

"It's okay, Mitchell. Bygones are already bygones."

"Hurray for Max!" says Mitchell.

"Hip! Hip!" we chorus, "Hurray!"

"Jesus H.," says Max. "I'm fucking touched."

Then Ron steps forward to fling his wet arms around Max's pudgy neck, and Mitchell is quick to join the fun.

"Max!"

"Good old Max!"

Ron suddenly turns his attention to Mitchell. "Hey! Why don't you divvy it up! Right now! Get the money in my hand!"

Mitchell nods vigorously. "This is my ticket to Palestine! I'm leaving early in the morning! Next year in Jerusalem!"

Ron is suddenly moved to announce that his next stop will be Las

Vegas. "My buddy Paul is sending a limousine for me in the morning. Action! Money! Dames! I love it!"

The rest of us shower while Mitchell counts the bills out on the trainer's table and does the arithmetic on the blackboard, consulting the log book and various scraps of paper he pulls from his wallet, happily mumbling to himself.

Brooks and I step out of our shower stalls at the same time, and he shows me a lopsided grin as we each dry ourselves. "You fooled me," he says. "I thought for sure you'd make the shot. I'll tell you this, though, believe me or not . . . I wouldn't have missed. Not a fucking chance."

There's Max standing near the trainer's table and shouting to gain our attention. "Hey, you guys! After Mitchell hands out the money, what do you say we all meet back at the hotel for a dinner party? It's my treat!"

Another round of hurrahs!

The chalk dust is flying as Mitchell furiously computes sums on the blackboard. "This stuff is complicated," he says. "Some of you guys kicked in money in Wyoming, and Aaron here owes the kitty some . . . Hold on. Hold on. I'm almost there."

Max wears a proprietary look while the rest of us finish dressing. He even hooks his thumbs into his vest.

Saul and Kevin make formal declarations of their employment at MGM. Then Leo has to get into the act. "Gregory Dodge, that's the new me!" When prodded, Brooks only says he has to meet somebody later tonight before making any "immediate plans."

That leaves me. "As far as I can tell, I'm going to stay in the hotel and sleep for about a week." Everybody laughs.

"Hey!" Max says. "I just thought of something: What about the car? The hearse? I put a lot of good money into that machine. Anybody here care to make me an offer? Brooks? Saul? Any of you? You can have it real cheap."

"No."

"No, thanks."

"I've seen all I want to of that heap."

Then I have a brainstorm. "Max, why don't you keep the car? Sure! When your business is finished here, you could drive it back to New York. Hell, that would be a shit load cheaper than taking the train, no? I'm positive you could get a real good price for it in the city. Easily."

"Drive it back home? By myself?"

"Easy as pie," I say. "Mitchell can give you exact directions. Shouldn't take you more than four or five days. Think about it, Max. You could listen to the radio to help pass the time. Music. News. Comedy. Tragedy. The world at your fingertips. The car handles like a dream, Max. And you could stop and eat wherever you want. You could even make a few minor detours and see some of the sights. The Grand Canyon is magnificent this time of year. Pike's Peak. Anything you want."

"Hmmm," he says, stroking his chin. "I don't know .... It's such a *shlep*."

"Not if you take the southern route," I say. "To avoid bad weather. To drive on the best roads. It's a cinch. Drive through Nevada, then south through Oklahoma. The driving's real easy in Oklahoma, Max. And the cowgirls there absolutely love Jews. Ain't that right, boys?"

"Sure thing."

"They'll love you in Oklahoma, Max."

"Didn't you know?" says Leo. "Cowgirls love to toot on a *Yiddle*'s root?"

"You don't say?"

I've got him now. "It's for sure, big brother. If a Jewish boy can't get laid in Oklahoma ... Hey, just ask Saul here. Saul. Didn't you get laid in Oklahoma?"

"A blond shiksa," Saul says agreeably. "With a snatch to match."

"You know something, boyos? I think I just might do that."

I dress in a hurry, then sidle up to Mitchell, saying, "You've got to do me a favor. Just give me the two hundred bucks from Max. Just the bonus money. Whatever's left from the other money, give my share of that to Saul. All right?"

"Sure. No skin off my ass."

"Thanks, Mitchell. And I hope you find what you're looking for in Palestine."

"Sure," he says. "In Palestine I'll find typhoid and malaria, yellow fever and sunstroke. Hopefully, I'll also find in Palestine the chance to make the desert bloom. Imagine, Aaron. Even the possibility of a country all our own where the Jews won't be victims anymore. And it'll happen, Aaron. Oh, yes. The British don't worry me. The British are always humane when they deal with other white men. It's the war that's coming. There's the trouble. The Jews in Palestine will have to steer a careful course. Until then, Aaron, you *momzer*, you know what my biggest problem will be? Learning how to count in pounds sterling instead of dollars. Someday, Aaron, I'll meet you there. In Jerusalem."

"Someday." And we hug each other tightly.

With Saul, I shake hands man-to-man. "Love conquers all, big guy. Good luck to you both."

"We're gonna see you back at the hotel, right? Max is buying dinner."

"Absolutely," I lie with a straight face. "See you there."

Kevin still needs to console me for missing my last shot. "You make that righty hook ninety-nine times out of a hundred."

"It's the way the ball bounces, Kevin. Take care of yourself. Always land on the mattress. And remember, kid, that the world belongs to you."

"See you later, Aaron."

Leo is brushing and pomading his hair like he's Astor's pet horse. "Hey, Leo. It was fun while it lasted. And you were right all along. Those stupid break-a-leg goons never caught up with you."

He's shaking his head in monstrous disappointment. "I finally found you out, Aaron."

"What're you talking about?"

"You missed the fucking shot. The one shot you had to make. You know what I think, buddy? I think you shit in your pants. Simple as that. You choked, Aaron. You choked like a fucking dog."

"Whatever you say, Coach Gregory. In this whole crazy outfit, you're the one who takes the fucking cake."

He laughs at me, then licks a finger to smooth his eyebrows with. "Gregory Dodge," he says. "Straight as a bolt of lightning."

Ron is usually the first dressed and the first to leave. But tonight he stalls with his gym bag until I approach his locker.

"Ron. Be careful, buddy. Don't do anything I wouldn't do."

"Sure thing." His eyes narrow and he pigeon-heads forward to whisper. "Like dumping a ball game?" Then he laughs, the sonofabitch. And he leaves.

Brooks and I embrace, then stand back and look at each other. "Aaron," he says. "What about you? After you've slept, after you've fucked the waitress, then what?"

"I'm heading north, Brooks. It's complicated. North where the compass points."

"So long, buddy. Good luck."

"Take care of yourself, Brooksie. Come back in one piece."

Max grabs me just as I'm through the locker-room door. "Aaron. I'll give you a hundred bucks if you drive with me back to New York."

"Okay. When do you want to leave?"

"Great!" he enthuses, pumping my hand. "Tomorrow morning early. I want to get the fuck out of this town before Manfredi hears any rumors to the contrary."

"Good idea. Listen, Max. I feel like walking a little just to get the kinks out of my legs."

"You're coming to the party, right?"

"Yeah, Max. Sure."

He puts his hand fondly on the back of my neck. "My little brother. Such a mensch. See you later."

(Goodbye, Max. See you never.)

The rain has held up, but the air smells moist. The traffic whizzes past me, going north and south at breakneck speed. And as I walk along the roadside, I toss my uniform and my yarmulke, then my basketball shoes, my socks, and my jock into the weeds. My knee loosening with every step north, north, because from Glens Falls to Los Angeles, I never did feel comfortable on a basketball court. Not in the church, nor in the fucking cage. Not in the jailhouse, nor on the lone prairie, nor the pit, nor anywhere.

Only on that mountaintop in Casper, Wyoming. Only with the sun and the night to find me. Only among the green things growing and the gray things dying. Only there did my cramped soul open wide. Only there, the bliss of self-forgetfulness.

Too bad I can never return there, to Casper, to that mountain standing vigil high above the rich thieves and the poor, above the murderers of innocence.

That's why I'm bound to follow my thumb to the mountains of Oregon, or Washington, or even Canada. Who knows? Maybe I'll be a logger. Or a forest ranger. Or a husband to a fat widow. I don't care which. How far can two hundred dollars take me?

Because my dreams have always frightened me.

That's why I don't even know what to hope for.

Some someday I haven't yet seen,

Some somewhere I've never been.